998 7 131

D0394139

Hearts, Strings, and Other Breakable Things

Hearts, Strings, and Other Breakable Things

JACQUELINE FIRKINS

HOUGHTON MIFFLIN HARCOURT | BOSTON | NEW YORK

hmhbooks.com

The text was set in Adobe Calson Pro.

Library of Congress Cataloging-in-Publication Data
Names: Firkins, Jacqueline, author.
Title: Hearts, strings, and other breakable things / Jacqueline Firkins.
Description: Boston ; New York : Houghton Mifflin Harcourt, [2019] | Summary: Living
with her aunt's family in Mansfield, Massachusetts, for a few months before
turning eighteen and starting college, Edie is torn between Sebastian,
the boy next door, and playboy Henry.
Identifiers: LCCN 2019001111 (print) | LCCN 2019002954 (ebook) |
ISBN 9780358156710 (ebook) | ISBN 9781328635198 (hardback)
Subjects: | CYAC: Dating (Social customs)—Fiction. | Family
life—Massachusetts—Fiction. | Cousins—Fiction. | Private schools—Fiction. |
Schools—Fiction. | Massachusetts—Fiction.
Classification: LCC PZ7.1.F553 (ebook) | LCC PZ7.1.F553 He 2019 (print) |
DDC [Fic]—dc23
LC record available at https://lccn.loc.gov/2019001111

Printed in the United States of America
DOC 10 9 8 7 6 5 4 3 2 1
4500777540

*For Jane, for Jen, and for girls
who sigh in window seats*

Chapter One

AT FIRST THE CAR RIDE WAS SIMPLY ANNOYING. EDIE slouched in the back seat of the SUV, clutching her mom's sticker-coated guitar case. Her uncle Bert kept his eye on the road, characteristically quiet. Her aunt Norah blithely rattled on from the passenger seat, characteristically not so quiet. She was lost in speculation about the challenges Poor Edith would face now that she'd left foster care and come to live in "a real home." Edie didn't have a stable upbringing, a private education, or any exposure to society. Her wardrobe was atrocious. Her posture was appalling. She had bright orange cheese powder under her ragged fingernails, proving she had no understanding of proper diet or personal care. She was practically poisoning herself.

"And that hair!" Norah exclaimed. "Good lord, what will the neighbors say?"

Edie sank a little lower and tried to finger comb through the worst of her tangles, unsure why the neighbors would care about something as trivial as her hair. The purple dye that clung to the tips had long since faded to a subtle shade of lavender. The rest was a painfully ordinary shade of brown. It was dry and frizzy, and she hadn't cut it for a couple years, but it was just hair.

"Don't worry," Bert assured Norah, drawing her attention away from the back seat. "You'll get Edith up to snuff in no time. Why, look what you've done with me."

"Yes, you're right, of course." Norah sighed while adjusting Bert's shirt collar. "I do have a talent for improving people. The ladies in the club are always remarking on it."

Edie assumed Norah was referring to her Great Hearts, Good Causes club, which she'd been boasting about lately. Since joining last summer, Norah had apparently fundraised for Nigerian schoolchildren, Syrian refugees, and hurricane victims in Puerto Rico. Now she was determined to outdo all her neighbors by displaying her Great Heart on her very own doorstep. After all, anyone could send money to "those other people." Few had the fortitude and generosity to let a poor relation live under the same roof, almost like family.

"We're putting you in the east room," Norah said as Bert turned off the highway.

"The big one in the corner?" Edie blinked away her surprise.

"I *know*," Norah said as if surprised, herself. "Normally we save it for guests, but we're not expecting anyone until summer."

Edie gripped the guitar case a little tighter as she mentally checked off yet another title she wouldn't hold during her stay: *family, guest, anyone*. She shook off her growing irritation by silently reciting the mantra she and her best friend, Shonda, had developed while dealing with bitchy customers back at the Burger Barn in Ithaca. *Think it. Don't say it.* She could imagine a giant swarm of flying piranhas busting through the front windshield and reducing Norah to a small mound of bone dust and a pair of pearl teardrop earrings. She simply had to smile politely while she pictured it.

When Bert drove by the ENTERING MANSFIELD, INC. 1770 sign, Edie recalled the last time she'd visited. It was more than seven years ago, back when her mom's massive blowout with her sister led to a mutual boycott on family visits. Edie had been startled by her mom's ferocity, and a little impressed, too. The two of them made a pinkie pledge that day to never enter Mansfield again. Now Edie was breaking that pledge. A little knot of guilt and grief formed in her gut. It tightened as the familiar landmarks continued to speed past: the ice cream shop, the library, the murky and probably polluted lake that Edie and her mom used to plunge into on hot summer days. Childhood memories flooded her, one after the other, rushing in faster than she could handle. She accidentally let out a sniffle. Then another.

Norah craned around from the front seat.

"Don't sulk, dear," she scolded, gentle but condescending. "Bashful, I can handle. Awkward, we can work on, but I can't abide sulking."

Edie wiped her nose on her sleeve.

"I was just thinking about my mom," she said as the tears continued falling.

Bert flashed her a sympathetic smile through the rearview mirror. Edie gratefully returned it. Norah, true to character, took no notice of either of them.

"I understand a few tears," she said, "but while you're with us, please try to demonstrate a little moderation."

"Moderation?" Edie asked, unsure how such a thing was possible. What was she supposed to do, cry every other tear?

Bert reached over and patted Norah's hand where it rested on her lap.

"It's only been three years," he quietly reminded her. "And a girl only has one mother."

"I only had one sister," Norah countered. "But at some point even Frances would want us to move on."

Edie felt her temper rise, simmering under her skin like shaken soda-pop. She could handle being criticized. She'd prepared herself for endless disapproval, mandatory gratitude, and the uniquely tenacious agony of feeling like she'd never fit in. She'd even expected the ugly jolt of betrayal she felt for violating the pact she'd made with her mom. But she couldn't believe Norah was putting a statute of limitations on missing someone. Then again, limitations had always been one of her specialties.

"I suppose a bit of moodiness is to be expected," Norah continued with a sigh. "Frances was always so temperamental, and you know what they say about the apple."

"It keeps the doctor away?" Bert snuck Edie a wink.

Norah shot him a glare.

"It doesn't fall far from the tree," she said.

Edie bit her tongue, desperate to prove Norah wrong about her temper. The task grew increasingly difficult when Norah failed to cease her censure, soften her put-upon sighs, or get eaten by flying piranhas. By the time Bert pulled the car into the long and winding driveway, Edie was ready to explode. A thousand words pressed at her lips, none of them polite. Her only solution was to bolt before she said something she'd regret.

The second Bert's key turned in the lock at the side of the house, Edie ran past him, her old army duffel in one hand, the guitar case in the other.

"Where do you think you're going, young lady?" Norah challenged.

"Somewhere I can sulk," Edie snapped, the words flying out too fast to stop them. "In moderation."

With that, she fled up the stairs, ran down the hall, and slammed the bedroom door behind her. She stood there for several seconds, battling her instinct to flee all the way back to Ithaca. Too bad that wasn't an option. She'd agreed to move here. Papers had been signed. Legal guardianship had been transferred. For the next five months, until she turned eighteen and left for college, she was stuck in Mansfield.

She set down her belongings and reminded herself that the situation wasn't all bad. Her aunt and uncle were offering her room and board, sending her to private school with her cousins, and making an effort to repair the family rift. Edie also appreciated having her own room, even if it was only on loan until guests arrived. She'd shared her last bedroom with two kids half her age. Her foster mother also snored like a stuttering sea cow, and the creepy building manager always waylaid Edie for small chat while he ogled her boobs. Surely a few months in Mansfield would be an improvement.

Edie crossed the room and flopped down on the enormous sleigh bed, jostling the dozen or so eyelet pillows that'd been carefully arranged to imply they'd been dropped at random. It really was a nice bed. She could get used to that, at least. She surveyed her surroundings as she tried to picture herself settling in. Aside from the excess of white, not much had changed since her grandparents owned the house and she used to visit with her mom. The antique furniture was perfectly matched and polished. The door handles were porcelain. The lamps were cut glass. Everything was either fragile, sterile, or both, leaving Edie terrified she was going to break or stain something. It was a nice house but it didn't feel like home.

To Edie, home was safety, comfort, and a place where she could make mistakes because someone was there to help her laugh at them. A place where her seven-legged, bug-eyed caterpillar drawing stayed on the refrigerator years after the paper yellowed and the pipe cleaner antennas fell off. Where she and her mom read desperately tragic novels together. Where they shared Edie's first cigarette, her first drink, her first post-heartbreak cry. Home was where Edie built memories. Home was where someone loved her. Here in Mansfield, Massachusetts, *home* appeared to have a more formal definition.

Edie took out her phone and opened the web page she ran with her best friend: *Shonda and Edie's Indispensable and Only Occasionally Illogical Lexicon.* She posted a new entry.

Home

noun

1. A temporary refuge potentially preferable to foster care, homelessness, or Taisha Duncan's lumpy pullout sofa bed.

2. A residence containing three marble fireplaces, four unused bedrooms, and two dozen sets of shiny black shutters that don't actually shut.
3. A place where the doors are always open but the arms are not.

Edie stared at the screen, desperate to see a ping of connection with her friend. The comment section remained empty. She was starting to suspect Shonda had shut off her new post notifications, or, even worse, she was ignoring the site completely. With a pang of loneliness and an ache of uncertainty, Edie slipped her phone into her pocket and promised herself to check it only once an hour. Maybe twice.

She retrieved her mom's guitar case and sat down at the dressing table that was wedged between two bay windows. A dressing table, she noted, not a desk. God forbid she do anything but prepare herself to look fabulous for the neighbors. With a sigh of resignation, she opened the case. Two things lay inside: a dog-eared notebook filled with Edie's songs, and a stringless guitar, its surface scratched, its tuning pegs askew. One day, when the thought of playing no longer made Edie well up with tears, she'd buy some new strings and make the guitar sing again. In the meantime, she'd simply keep it close. It stored some of her favorite memories: following her mom around to open mic nights, writing songs together, dozing off to a lullaby about sleeping in a crescent moon.

Edie traced a line down the guitar's neck as she recalled the first time she'd played her mom's favorite song, "Water, Water, Wash Me Slowly." She was only seven, barely able to hit all the notes. Her mom had practically burst from pride, telling everyone her daughter was going to be a huge star. That was a good memory. That was a hold-on-to-it-forever memory.

She was about to shut the case when her eye caught on the napkin that was poking out from her notebook. She slipped it out and smoothed down the wrinkles. It was mangled and stained, but the scribbled words were still legible. *I can't. I'm sorry. Move on.* Edie's dad had stuck the note to the refrigerator door with an inauspicious out-of-season Santa Claus magnet when Edie was still a baby. He disappeared that day, for good, but Edie's mom kept the note, brandishing it whenever Edie mentioned boys.

"Edie," she used to say, "never fall in love. As soon as you give a man your heart, he'll shine his two-sided smile on someone else, trading his promises for your regrets."

Edie had few worries on that front. As an outsider in Mansfield, she'd have a hard enough time just making friends. For the rest of the school year, she intended to bury her head in her books, hoping to keep up her grades and earn a scholarship. Then, in August, she'd walk in her mom's footsteps—exiting the same house in the same town, also shortly after her eighteenth birthday—but Edie would be running off to college, not to a husband. Haunted by a scribbled napkin and a flickering sadness that used to pass through her mom's eyes, Edie wanted an education more than a romance.

Mostly.

Chapter Two

EDIE UNPACKED HER MEAGER BELONGINGS, STASH-
ing her wrinkled clothes where her relatives wouldn't examine them
too closely. She nestled a few personal items on her nightstand: a
book, a mug, a photo of her mother. Just enough to feel a *little* more
at home. As she slipped the guitar case under the bed, footsteps
approached in the hallway, sounding vaguely like rhinoceri. Or rhi-
noceroses. Or girl-eroses. A second later her cousins burst into the
room, a dizzying whirl of navy and green plaid uniforms, auburn hair,
and floral perfume. All knees and elbows, and half a head shorter
than her sister, Julia still looked like a child despite her sixteen years.
Maria, now eighteen, was made of three things: voluptuous curves,
catlike green eyes, and (provided nothing had changed over the
years) the unfailing belief that she was superior to everyone around
her.

"You're finally here!" Julia sped across the room, arms outstretched,
slamming into Edie with an eager embrace. "You look exactly how
I pictured you."

Edie studied her cousin, trying to suss out if she'd just received a compliment or an insult. Julia simply grinned, offering no clear indication of either.

"You must be exhausted." Maria spun Edie her way and gave her a big hug. "Didn't you just have, like, a four-hour bus ride?"

"Something like that." Something more like twelve hours, with all the stops, but Edie didn't correct Maria. Maria had never cared much for being corrected.

"I hate buses," she said with a sneer. "They smell like corn chips and BO."

"Or Cheetos and BO?" Edie flashed her stained fingernails.

"Whatever. I didn't mean you." Maria plucked a few pills off Edie's old golf sweater, demonstrating that she'd inherited her mother's annoying talent for improving people. "We're just glad Dear Mama finally stopped holding her stupid grudge and invited you here."

"'Dear Mama'?" Edie choked back a laugh. "Seriously?"

"She can't stand it when I call her that. I use it whenever I can." Maria continued picking and plucking, immune to the concept of personal space. "She said you were upset about leaving all your friends, and our hearts are shattered for you—like, a-million-tiny-pieces shattered. Being new is the worst, but we'll make sure you're never alone."

"Um, thanks?" Edie shrugged, unsure how to explain that loneliness and aloneness were two completely different things. Since Maria had always been surrounded by friends and admirers, she was unlikely to understand either concept.

"We're not allowed to let you sulk," Julia added while straightening a row of tree pictures that didn't need straightening. "It's bad for the complexion. Whenever I cry I get all red and puffy. Maria says I look like a lobster balloon."

"I do not."

"You do too."

"Then don't cry."

"Then don't be a bitch."

Julia marched over to the bed and plunked herself down, arms folded, lips pursed, indignation personified. Not much had changed since Edie's last visit to Mansfield. Her cousins were merely a little taller, a little older, and a little less likely to fight about who was looking at the other one the wrong way. A little less likely.

Maria stepped back and gave Edie a full eye-scan.

"You're so thin," she said. "Like, vermicelli thin. What diet are you on?"

"The eat-what-you-can diet?" Edie shrank in on herself, uncomfortable with Maria's overt scrutiny.

"God, you're lucky." Maria turned toward the standing mirror in the corner of the room. She sucked in her cheeks and pulled back her neck with both hands. "I've tried them all: fat-free, sugar-free, carb-free, gluten-free, meat-free, everything-free."

"You're not fat, though," Edie said.

"Fat enough." Maria pushed out her belly and drew it in again, pressing it firmly into place with the palm of her hand. "As Dear Mama says, 'There's always another pound to lose.'"

"At least you have boobs." Julia tugged at her blouse. "I'd rather be fat than flat."

Edie shuffled over to the dressing table and glanced self-consciously at her own B cup (B for barely worth bothering with a bra) while her cousins continued disapproving of themselves. She really hoped she wouldn't have to spend the next five months telling Julia she was pretty and convincing Maria she wasn't fat. Reassuring beautiful people that they were actually beautiful felt like such a bizarre waste of energy. Besides, only a few minutes in and Edie was getting caught up in the conversation, assessing her reflection just like her cousins. Insecurity sucked, and it spread faster than Ebola.

Like anyone else, Edie had her own unique catalogue of imperfections. The gods had short-changed her chin but been overzealous in the forehead department. They'd also endowed her with one hundred and seventeen completely pointless freckles, one eye smaller than the other, and more cowlicks than a dairy farm on a salt flat. Her knees were knobby. Her elbows were knobbier. Her nose was vaguely unsatisfying as a centerpiece for her face. She was hardly a model of confidence, but she kept most of her insecurities to herself, or she laughed about them with Shonda.

At that thought, Edie checked her phone again. Her heart sank, weighed down by a growing sense of guilt. Shonda still hadn't replied to her post. Surely she understood by now that what'd happened back in Ithaca was just a stupid mistake, a fleeting moment of poor judgment, nothing more. Their friendship was strong enough to get past it. Shonda knew Edie needed her. She wouldn't leave her best friend alone in Snobville without helping to find the humor in her situation.

Maria's reflection caught Edie's eyes.

"Cheer up," she said, more like an order than a pep talk. "We get to take you shopping this weekend."

"Actually, I hate shopping," Edie said.

"No one hates shopping," Maria argued. "That's, like, totally un-American."

Edie bit back her caustic replies. She was a guest. Her cousins were trying to be helpful. This wasn't the time or place to rant about privilege. *Think it. Don't say it.*

"Dad's giving us his credit card," Julia noted.

Maria strode over to the closet.

"We hear you arrived practically empty-handed." She peered in and shook her head as if appalled. "Don't worry. Julia and I will make a project of you. Project Edie. You'll be like Cinderella, only without the evil stepsisters."

Edie cringed as she swallowed yet another retort.

Julia grabbed a pillow and hugged it to her chest, all wistful and dreamy.

"You're totally Cinderella!" she gushed. "Which means we *have* to find you a Prince Charming."

"No, you don't," Edie said a little too quickly.

Maria spun toward her, eyeing her suspiciously.

"You don't have a boyfriend back in Whatsit Town, do you?" Her lip curled as though the mere idea made her ill.

"Or a girlfriend?" Julia added, more to Maria than to Edie.

"Boy, girl, whatever. Some long-distance angsty baggage you have to let linger for obligation's sake so they don't OD on emo and drown in a pool of their own tears?"

"No," Edie started, "but—"

"Thank god." Maria stepped up behind her and turned her toward the mirror. "Then we can go full fairy godmother on you. After all, you have great bones, amazing skin, and fabulous hair. If you, like, comb it or something."

Edie scowled at her reflection, desperate to be neither Poor Edith nor Project Edie. She hated being compared to Cinderella, not just because her defining characteristic was her relationship with a fireplace. The story was terrible, implying a girl just needed a fancy dress, a pair of painful shoes, and some rodent slave labor. Then—*poof*—true love would fall into her lap. That wasn't romance. Not that Edie wanted a romance, of course, but if she *did* pursue one it wouldn't be some superficial fairytale. It would develop over a shared love of books, music, and cloudy night skies that let the stars keep their secrets. No ballgowns. No pumpkins. No princes.

"We'll make sure you look fabulous for Dear Mama's spring garden party," Maria assured her, completely ignoring Edie's overt lack of enthusiasm.

"A garden party?" Edie glanced out the windows, where the trees were barely sprouting. "In the first week of April?"

"Dear Mama likes to be first at everything. Keeping ahead of the Joneses and all that. She gets a zillion heat lamps. Everyone pretends it's the middle of June."

"Half of Mansfield will be there," Julia added. "We'll treat it like your debut in society the way they do in old movies."

"It'll be perfect," Maria agreed. "We'll drink champagne and flirt with cute boys while the old people stand around talking about mortgages, book clubs, and each other."

Edie slumped down on the bed next to Julia.

"I'm not very good at parties," she admitted, recalling her habit of hiding out wherever the fewest people gathered. "Or flirting, or anything involving strangers."

"They won't all be strangers," Julia encouraged. "Remember Tom and Sebastian from next door?"

"Yeah. Of course." Edie rolled away and buried her face in the pillows. She remembered. More specifically, she remembered reenacting Rodin statues with a certain sandy-haired boy her age. It'd started with an innocuous contest to see who could best mimic *The Thinker* and it ended with a toppling approximation of *The Kiss.* Ever since Edie'd accepted Norah's invite, she'd been wondering if the Summers family still lived next door. She was kind of hoping they didn't, and also kind of hoping they did.

Maria popped open a bright pink tube of lipstick and leaned forward to apply it, eyeing Edie through her reflection.

"Didn't you used to have a major crush on one of them?" she asked.

"I was only ten."

"Oh, please." Maria scoffed. "I crushed on every boy I met at that age."

Julia shot her sister a pert little sneer.

"You still crush on every guy you meet."

"It's not a crush if they like you back."

"Brag much?"

"Jealous much?"

As Maria and Julia continued snapping at each other, Edie got up and edged her way over to one of the big bay windows, placing herself out of the line of fire. She glanced out at the tidy rows of elm trees, perfect lawns, and enormous brick houses. It was all so different from what she was used to. She might as well be in Oz.

She clicked the heels of her sneakers.

Nothing changed.

She was about to turn away when she noticed a guy with sandy blond hair and a faded yellow T-shirt dragging two bulging garbage bags down the next-door neighbor's driveway. A guy who might know a thing or two about sculptures. Despite her resolve to focus on her schoolwork, she couldn't help but be curious. Besides, seeing him now would be easier than at some puffed-up party where her cousins were trying to turn her into someone she wasn't sure she wanted to be. They could simply say hello, catch up, revive their friendship.

"I'm going to get a bit of fresh air." She crossed to the door.

Julia jumped up.

"We'll come with you."

"No. Thanks, though." Edie backed across the threshold.

"No sulking," Maria warned.

"I just need a minute alone." Edie took another step back. "I promise I won't listen to any emo." With that, she bolted.

Chapter Three

EDIE GRIPPED THE WAIST-HIGH PICKET FENCE THAT separated Norah's immaculately groomed garden from the neighbors' driveway. About ten yards away, Sebastian was stuffing a garbage bag from a pile of raked yard waste, his back toward her. He was tall now, with long legs, broad but bony shoulders, and a sharp wedge haircut that was dark with sweat at the back of his neck.

Edie tried to muster a hello as she flashed through memories of the ten-year-old boy who'd loaned her his seven-book Narnia set, raced her up trees, and shared her first kiss. The kiss was awesome for approximately six seconds. Then Edie fell on a sprinkler, making her look like she peed her pants and bruising her backside so she couldn't sit down for three days. She'd hated that he laughed when it happened, but she never thought she'd see him again anyway. Now here he was right in front of her, and he looked good (really, *really* good) and she was a Gordian knot of nerves. Did he even remember that kiss? There was no way he remembered that kiss. But if he *did* remember that kiss . . .

Edie ducked behind a tree, took out her phone, and added

another post to her lexicon, hoping to pique Shonda's curiosity enough to elicit a comment.

Crush

noun

1. Squeeze, compress, force inward.
2. A brand of orange soda-pop that would horrify your aunt if you drank it in her house.
3. A feeling you deny to everyone because you're totally focusing on your education — not your love life — but secretly you've been obsessing about this guy for years and now you're about to talk to him, only your social anxiety has skyrocketed so you think you might just vomit and flee.

Edie shoved her phone into her pocket, stepped out from behind the tree, and opened her mouth to say hello. Then she turned away, embarrassed.

"Dammit!" she muttered as she slammed the fence with both fists.

"Hey! What did that fence ever do to you?" Sebastian called from behind her. His voice was deeper now but his harmless teasing tone was exactly like Edie remembered it.

She turned around, slowly, nervously, and undeniably gut-fluttering-ly. Sebastian was smiling, which meant Edie was blushing. He had the sort of smile that came more from his eyes than his lips, like his joy was being channeled wherever he looked. Since he was looking directly at her, she did, in fact, feel a little surge of joy.

Yep. Crush.

She managed a small wave, frustrated with herself for failing her No Boys plan so soon after making it. Then again, she wasn't *really* failing unless she actively pursued Sebastian, which she had no intention of doing, especially since starting a simple conversation was already making her nauseous and neurotic.

"Hi." Sebastian brushed off his hands as he approached the fence. "Nice shirt."

Edie glanced down, certain she'd spilled something on herself.

"Atlas was a shoplifter," he read. "That's funny. Guess Atlas lifted pretty much everything."

"Right. Yeah," she said with a little gust of relief. "Most people don't get it." She eyed the print on his shirt: a cartoon of a guy in a baseball catcher's uniform, crouching in what she assumed was a rye field. "Yours is funny too."

"Most people do get it." His smile tipped higher, reviving her blush. "So, you're back in town for a few months?"

Edie nodded as she tried to gauge his level of interest in that particular piece of information. Her sleuthing proved inconclusive, despite the vaguely hopeful rise in his voice and his temporarily unattended bag of lawn debris.

"Last time I saw you, you were only about this high." He floated a hand just above the top of the fence. "Do you still climb trees and draw on furniture?"

"Trees, maybe. Furniture, not so much."

"I'll bet people call you Edith now."

"Actually, I still go by Edie. Edith makes me sound like I'm ninety, knitting an endless afghan while surrounded by semiferal cats." She shoved a toe across the gravel path and kicked at the fence. "Too bad my mom was such a massive fan of *The Age of Innocence*."

"She named you after Edith Wharton?"

"Yeah. Wow. Don't tell me you've read the book?"

"Not yet, but I might. Want to give me your best ten-second pitch?"

"Um . . . okay?" Edie picked at a knot in the fence-post, peeling away a small strip of white paint, wondering how to describe a romance to a guy she sort-of-but-not-really-but-okay-yes-totally wanted a romance with. "Long-held secrets, missed opportunities, and one hell of a held hand." Her eyes trailed toward Sebastian's hands. His thumbs were tucked into his jeans pockets and his fingers tapped his thighs.

"Sounds great," he said. "Maybe I'll give it a read. You know, to find out what all that hand-holding is about."

"The book's also good for quotes," Edie added quickly, hoping to divert attention from the heat creeping up her neck. "I'm kind of a collector. Words don't take up much shelf space. Unless I count this thing." She tapped her forehead a split second before realizing it was probably as beet red as her neck.

"Cool. Lay one on me." Sebastian smiled again, forming parenthetical dimples in his cheeks, as though his smile was an aside.

"We'll make a game of it. You show me yours. I'll show you mine. These things, I mean." He tapped his forehead, mimicking her gesture, but without the blush.

"I don't know." Edie squirmed, unsure if he was flirting or just being friendly, and equally unsure what she was supposed to do if he was flirting.

"Go on. Take something off that shelf. Something from the other Edith." He rested his forearms on the fence and leaned forward, expectant.

Edie's mind raced until it landed on the perfect quote. It was a little forward but it fit the moment beautifully. She willed her blush to recede as she risked a look in Sebastian's eyes, the color of robins' eggs, September skies, and Berry Blue jellybeans.

"'Each time you happen to me all over again.'"

His smile slowly stretched wider as the world reduced itself to a garden, a driveway, two people, and the single word *again*.

"Nice," he said, sweetly sincere. "I like it."

"Yeah," she agreed, seriously smitten. "Me too."

The world gradually expanded to include boring things like streets, houses, and those little gnatlike bugs that swarmed around at dusk as if determined to turn a perfectly beautiful evening into a spontaneous swat-fest. Edie ignored them all. The ice had been broken. Her anxiety was gone. She'd blundered her way through their reunion, as awkward and bashful as Norah had accused her of being. To his credit, Sebastian hadn't laughed at her once. Whether or not he was flirting—and whether or not *she* was flirting—she got the feeling Sebastian could turn out to be a truly solid friend. In a place like Mansfield, that was important.

The two of them continued chatting from opposite sides of the fence, catching up on the events and nonevents of the past seven and a half years. The conversation was casual until Edie mentioned her mom's accident and Sebastian asked the one question she wasn't prepared for.

"How are you doing?"

Edie opened her mouth to say she was fine, and to thank him for asking, but she couldn't manage it. Something was stuck in her throat, and it was trying to escape through her eyes. As the air grew heavy with unspoken grief, Sebastian patiently waited, his eyes never leaving her face while she bit her lip and willed her tears to ignore gravity. They fell anyway.

"It's hard sometimes," she finally whispered. "People always say losing someone gets easier with time, and it does, but it hits when I least expect it, like the one time someone actually asks me how I am."

"'Gets easier' doesn't mean 'gets easy,'" Sebastian said. "After ten years I still miss my dad. My stepdad's all right. He's just not the kind of guy who'd hold a kid by the ankles and pretend to mow the lawn with him."

Edie nodded and they shared another silence, one that felt good for the honesty, the un-fine-ness, and the memories that didn't need to be tidied up and packed away. No one pretended potholes didn't exist, or pockets, or spare rooms. So why did the heart's empty spaces always have to be "cheered up"? Why did so many feelings have to be felt "in moderation"?

As Sebastian traced a line from picket to picket with an out-stretched finger, Edie quietly murmured, "'Our dead are never dead to us until we have forgotten them.'"

"Oh for two. Who said that one?"

"George Eliot."

"Wow, you do keep a lot up there." He gestured at her forehead without *quite* touching her.

"I read a lot, and I have what my mom called a 'Velcro memory.' It's great for tests and lost keys, but otherwise kind of annoying."

"I always knew you'd grow up to be one of those smart girls," he teased.

Edie shook her head, annoyed, as a little snort of humorless laughter escaped.

"What's the matter?" he asked.

"Girls who get labeled 'smart' quickly become social outcasts."

"That's ridiculous."

"Ridiculous, but true."

Sebastian stepped back and clapped his hands together.

"Then I have the perfect quote for you, to even up the score a little. A line from a play we did at my school last month. Molière. 'Beauty without intelligence is like a hook without bait.'"

"Good one," Edie said, "but I dare you to prove that theory true."

A grin spread across his face, making his eyes dance.

"I'll take that dare." Before Edie could respond, Maria stepped outside and called her in for dinner, pausing to quirk a suspicious eyebrow before heading back in.

"I should go." Edie backed away from the fence, quietly curious about whether or not their dare was officially on record, because she'd sure like to see Sebastian fulfill it. In her seventeen years and seven months she'd never seen a guy pick brains over beauty. Not that the two were mutually exclusive, but most guys she knew cared more about a girl's cup size than whether or not she could analyze number theory or remember literary quotes. "Thanks for talking, and for not talking. You're really nice."

Sebastian flinched. "You know how you didn't want to be called smart? Well, guys don't like being called nice. It scares away the girls."

"Not the right girls."

"No." He smiled again, his eyes on hers, teasing just a little. "Maybe not the right girls."

Chapter Four

─────────────────────────────── ♥ ───

ON SATURDAY AFTERNOON, THE GIRLS HEADED IN
to Saxon's, the big anchor department store at the local mall. Maria
marched in with the resolve of a military scout on a mission. Julia
skipped after her with the excitement of a treasure hunter. Edie
slogged behind them both with a resignation she normally only felt
toward gym class or lima beans. She'd remained staunch for two
hours of shopping, holding fast to her principles about superficial
makeovers and frivolous spending, but her resistance was faltering.
After all:

1. *She wanted to fit in at the party, at least enough to hide
   in the crowd.*
2. *She wanted to look good the next time she saw Sebastian.*
3. *She knew her relatives were trying to be helpful.*
4. *She'd repeatedly resolved to be polite.*

Besides, even Napoleon surrendered eventually, and he'd never
faced off with the Vernon girls.

"Last store," Maria announced. "And we're not leaving until you let us buy you at least one outfit that's brand new, fits you properly, and makes you look like a girl."

"I do look like a girl." Edie glanced down at her ragged jeans and layered knits. "Just not a girl who wears dresses."

"Please, Edie?" Julia adjusted her hold on half a dozen bags, revealing red lines from the handles etched into her forearms. "One dress."

"And it can't be black," Maria added. "Mourning is so two centuries ago. Then again, this cardigan has been around for, like, ever."

"Or, like, three years," Edie mimicked, at the edge of her patience.

"Same diff." Maria poked her fingers through the holes in Edie's sweater cuff. "This might've been cute once but now it makes you look like a walking public service announcement. I'm getting sad just standing next to you."

"Then stand over there." Edie nodded toward the perfume counter. "You won't even have to smell my sadness."

"Whatever." Maria flicked a hand, making her gold bangles jangle. "You know Dear Mama won't let us back in the house unless we can prove you'll be presentable tonight."

"Fine," Edie conceded, unwilling to face Norah's wrath, Julia's disappointment, or a continued barrage of Maria's thoughtless remarks. "One dress. Your choice. Have at it."

Julia cheered. Maria plunged between the racks. Edie simply realigned her sweater cuff, fully aware that being made to shop didn't officially qualify as torture, though in that moment she wasn't sure why.

While her cousins hunted for the perfect outfit, Edie caught her reflection in a mirrored column. Unsatisfied with what she saw, she added another post to her lexicon.

Frumpy
adjective

1. A cartoon cat who has delightful misadventures with a hapless dog named Grumpleskelter.
2. Starbucks' latest coffee drink, complete with ginger-spiced foam and a delicately drizzled maple syrup clef sign.
3. The way you feel after your cousins spend an entire afternoon convincing you that the last thing you want to look like is yourself.

A swift sweep of the store later, Edie was wedged inside an over-packed fitting room, trying on the dresses her cousins hauled in by the armload. As she put on each outfit and stepped into the central aisle, they critiqued the neckline, hemline, color, fabric, trimmings, fit, and even the label. Edie wasn't crazy about anything she tried on. It was all too new, shiny, and expensive. Nothing had an old story hiding within its threads. New clothes came with a strange pressure, as if they were blank slates Edie had to fill. She had to *be* the story. She wasn't sure she was up to the challenge.

"You look so pretty in dresses," Julia remarked as Edie tugged the top of a magenta strapless mini-dress Maria had already vetoed. "And your complexion can handle bright colors. I always look washed out in bright colors. I stick with pastels mostly, and prints, small ones. Bold prints make my nose look big."

"Your nose looks fine," Edie assured her.

"That's because I'm wearing lemon yellow and the stripes are narrower than the space between my eyebrows."

As Edie stepped into the fitting room, she noticed her phone vibrating from inside her jeans pocket. Finally. She opened her lexicon, anxious to see an LOL, a smiley face, or a few words of encouragement. Instead, Shonda had posted her own definition.

Betrayal
noun
1. when your boyfriend deceives you.
2. when your best friend lies to you.
3. when you find said boyfriend and said best friend making out in the McDonald's parking lot while you ran in to pee.

Tears stung Edie's eyes. She collapsed among the discarded dresses, utterly dejected. So Shonda was still mad. *Really* mad. And she still blamed Edie for what happened. Edie thought she'd explained everything before leaving Ithaca. She hadn't been dishonest. She'd just been stupid. She had no idea what James intended until he was lunging across the car seats and planting one on her. She didn't even like him that way. He drank, he smoked, and he thought deodorant was a marketing hoax rather than a hygienic necessity.

Besides, he was Shonda's boyfriend. That was reason enough to leave him alone. Guys had that terrible saying "Bros before hos." What did girls say? "Chicks before dicks"? Gross.

Edie was desperate to defend herself, but what could she say that she hadn't already said? And what if, somewhere deep down, she'd known James might make a pass at her that night? She couldn't say that without seeming guiltier than she actually was, but she couldn't *not* say it and keep claiming she was being honest.

As Maria called for her to hurry her bony ass up, Edie stopped debating her reply and posted a new entry, one that said the truest things she knew in that moment.

Friend

noun

1. Someone who's sorry she hurt you.
2. Someone who misses you.
3. Someone who needs you to forgive her because she's being held hostage by makeover terrorists and she might not survive without you.

She swallowed the lump in her throat and prayed Shonda would come around. Edie would do her best to fit in to Mansfield, to hide her tears and swallow her temper, to let herself be polished and improved upon, but she needed someone, somewhere to love her as she was: flaws, failures, freckles, frayed jeans, and all.

With a heavy heart, she forced herself to try on one more dress:

an emerald green halter style Julia had picked out. It had an empire waist, twisted fabric details across the bust line, and a full skirt that stopped just below her knobby knees. It was pretty, it felt nice against her skin, and it didn't announce itself in bold letters. It simply said hello, which was something she could use a little help with.

Maria approved of the dress while Julia tipped her head against the wall and sighed.

"You look amazing in emerald," she said. "I can only wear mint or moss. Every other green makes me look jaundiced."

"*You* make you look jaundiced," Maria said.

"Yeah? Well, you make you look like—"

"Shoes?" Edie interrupted as she stepped back into the fitting room. "Unless you'll let me wear these?" She held up a ratty sneaker.

Maria and Julia both reeled as though she were displaying a severed head, but they quickly shifted from biting at each other to debating the merits of pumps over peep-toes. Edie loved her sneakers almost enough to beg out of the shoe shopping she'd so hastily recommended, but even she could see that the green dress required something a little less war-torn. She just hoped her cousins would let her escape the mall with a nice safe pair of flats. Otherwise she'd have to spend the whole party sitting down.

Maria paid for the dress with her dad's credit card while Edie stared at the impulse items and tried not to feel guilty. The dress cost the same amount as two weeks' wages at her old drive-thru job. Spending that kind of money on clothes was hard, weird, and a different way of living, but she knew her relatives would never let her give that money to a pet shelter or a disaster relief fund. In this particular instance, *she* was the charity. That was hard too. If she heard the words *poor relations* come out of Norah's mouth one more time, she was going to paint a few teeth black and sit on the front stoop in overalls, a straw hat, and little else, jangling a cup and begging for coins.

Temperamental? Damned straight.

Purchases in hand, the girls headed to the shoe department, where Julia made a beeline for a sparkly rhinestone sandal.

"This is totally Cinderella!"

"Too obvious," Maria said. "And they look cheap. Like, slutty-bridesmaid cheap."

Julia deflated as she returned the shoe to the shelf.

"We need something sexy and sophisticated." Maria examined a high heel that looked like it would challenge even an experienced runway model.

"Maybe not quite *that* sexy?" Edie eyed the heel in terror.

"Fine, but help us out a little here. Someone's hooking up at this party and it can't be me because I'm already spoken for."

"Maria's practically engaged," Julia explained.

Edie spun toward Maria, gaping with astonishment.

"Only *practically*," Maria clarified. "My parents are making us wait until Rupert graduates from Harvard next year and starts work at his uncle's firm. They don't want me repeating your mom's mistake, Edie. Not that Dear Mama thinks *I'm* about to run after some D-list rock star who'll leave me barefoot and pregnant."

All of Edie's efforts at politeness evaporated in an instant. She grabbed a stiletto and imagined spinning it like a ninja star into Maria's forehead.

"Good thing we're in a shoe department so none of us have to go barefoot," she squeezed out through gritted teeth. "Now we just need some condoms. Then we can run after anyone we want."

Maria waved her off, totally unfazed by Edie's murderous glare.

"I'm not about to elope," she argued, as if that were the key point being debated. "I want a huge wedding. Dear Mama wants it too. Desperately. She already picked out a color scheme."

"Buttercream yellow and navy blue," Julia piped in.

"A.k.a. Nauseatingly Nautical." Maria made an exaggerated gagging motion. "I'll change all the orders when she's not looking. It's *my* wedding."

"Yours and Rupert's," Julia corrected.

"Of course." Maria flashed her sister a sneer.

Edie set her weapon back on the shelf as she talked herself down from murderous to merciful. Maria didn't mean to be cruel. Her offhand comments didn't quite warrant a death sentence. A few hours of community service might be nice, though.

Julia fell back onto a sectional seating unit, her bags strewn around her like shopping roadkill.

"Tell her about your summer house," she suggested to Maria.

"Your *what?*" Edie choked back a laugh.

"You know," Julia said simply. "A house for summer."

While Edie tried to process the concept of seasonal housing, Maria spun in her direction, her expression dreamy, as if she were a Disney princess about to burst into song.

"It has this gorgeous porch that faces the ocean." She framed an imaginary view with her outstretched hands. "We'll set up a pair of Adirondack chairs and there we'll sit, me and my sweet, darling Rupert, drinking mimosas and watching the waves roll in as our prize-winning King Charles spaniels, George and Martha, romp around the yard."

"You already bought a house?" Edie blinked, still struggling to hide her astonishment. "Before you finish high school?"

"Of course not." Maria laughed. "The house isn't even for sale. We're just planning ahead. Don't you plan your future?"

"Not in that much detail."

Edie poked through a nearby display table while trying to accept the fact that Maria was already engaged, or practically engaged. Edie'd never even kissed a guy, not really. Shonda had set her up on a few awkward dates, but the guys Edie liked never seemed to like her back. Sure, she'd kissed Sebastian when she was ten, but they were just playing a game. Then of course, there was James, but that was an accident, or at least sort of an accident. Maybe a makeover wasn't such a terrible idea. She didn't need a ballgown or a pair of glass slippers, but she needed to change something. It'd be a lot easier to start with her hair than with her heart, though both were equally prone to tangles.

"Sebastian will be there too," Julia said.

"What? Where?" Edie asked, snapping to attention mid-conversation.

"At the party." Julia stacked a few stray shoeboxes so they lined up perfectly. "And Tom should be home for the weekend."

"I can't believe he's at UPenn now." Maria rolled her eyes.

"What's wrong with UPenn?" Edie asked.

"Nothing, except it's his third school." Maria considered a silver gladiator sandal that looked like it belonged on a sci-fi sex slave. "He got expelled from both Yale and Columbia, but his stepdad keeps pulling strings. Mr. Hayes is well connected in the Ivies. He belongs to one of those secret societies or alumni cult thingies where they, like, sacrifice chickens to decide who gets into what school."

Edie sank down next to Julia and tried to swallow her envy. She would've given anything to go to Yale. She'd applied last fall, knowing how proud her mom would've been. When she received her acceptance letter, she even thought she'd go. Then she got her financial aid forms and the dream disappeared. All her saved-up babysitting money and drive-thru wages weren't enough to cover room and board, let alone make a dent in tuition. Too bad she didn't know how to sacrifice a chicken.

"Tom's a great guy," Maria said. "He just likes to party."

"You would know," Julia chided.

"Whatever." Maria waved her off as she turned to Edie. "We made out one night a couple summers ago. We were both drunk. It didn't mean anything."

"It never does," Julia said.

"Careful. Envy makes you look jaundiced."

"Well, lust makes you look fat."

"You boobless little—"

"How's this?" Edie held up the nearest shoe. It was black, velvety, and at least semi-stable-looking.

"It'll do." Maria flagged down a saleswoman. Then she plopped herself between Edie and Julia, wrapping an arm around each of them. "Tonight we will all look astonishing. Especially you, Miss Edie Price, for you are about to be introduced to Mansfield society."

Chapter Five

BY SIX P.M., MORE THAN TWO HUNDRED PEOPLE were scattered through Norah's garden, with more arriving every few minutes. A string quartet played on the patio, setting a formal, stand-up-straight-and-don't-talk-too-loudly mood. White folding chairs and tables sat in tidy clusters near the buffet area, where several guests were milling about. White canvas canopies flapped in the breeze. White votive candles lined the paths. Perfect white roses perched on practically every available surface, making up for the lack of blooms on the bushes themselves. As always, Norah exhibited great appreciation for order but little patience for color.

While Julia and Maria chatted with friends under one of the countless heat lamps, and Bert nestled himself into a lawn chair with a Jenga stack of sugar-dusted fruit kabobs, Norah led Edie from neighbor to neighbor, flitting through the growing crowd like a seabird looking for a place to land, introducing her poor relation to the community and collecting compliments for her great act of charity. Edie played along, holding back the knowledge that she'd spent three years in foster care before Norah offered her a home. She kept quiet about the family feud that'd split the family for almost a decade. She didn't even bring up her less-than-urgent position on Norah's Good Causes list (number seventeen, below a recent tree planting initiative but above city signage renovation). There was no point making a scene. Norah meant well, in her way. Her Great Heart just had to serve her own needs before it served others.

Eventually one of the women from Norah's philanthropic club asked if she could do anything to help Edie settle into Mansfield. Edie responded by making the egregious mistake of requesting suggestions about where to find a part-time job.

"A *job?*" Norah chuckled as though the idea was hilarious. "Bert and I don't expect you to work. If you want anything, you only need to ask."

The ladies praised Norah's generosity while Edie tried to imagine five months of having to ask for anything she wanted. She didn't need much and she trusted her aunt and uncle to help her with any real necessities (provided they also considered her requests necessities), but they'd only agreed to pay her living expenses through the spring and summer. She was on her own for college fees and tuition. Apparently charity both started and ended at home. Once Edie left Mansfield, there was no need to parade her around as proof of Norah's recent bent for philanthropy. If she didn't earn a scholarship or get a job, she wouldn't even afford state school. Staying in Mansfield wasn't an option. Edie was starting college in the fall, even if she had to hawk Norah's pearls to do it.

Exhausted from OD-ing on hard-wrought politeness, Edie

eventually excused herself to join Maria and Julia by the catering tent with its cucumber sandwiches, single-serving vanilla cakes, and other dainty finger foods that required no silverware and came with little risk of spilling and staining anything. Maria picked at the garnishes while eyeing the cakes. Julia bemoaned her inability to wear ivory. Edie prodded a blister and pined for her sneakers, and they all shared a champagne toast to "looking astonishing."

Rupert arrived a few minutes later. Edie'd been expecting a dashingly handsome New England stereotype in a turtleneck sweater with a bold maroon H, but Rupert was short, pudgy, and disheveled. The tail of his shirt poked out from beneath his argyle sweater vest. His khaki trousers were too big, bunching up at the back under his belt. His dark hair, gleaming with product, fell over his eyebrows, refusing to be held in place by anything short of shellac. While most Mansfieldians probably disapproved of his lack of polish, Edie liked him instantly for it.

"There's my beautiful girl!" He swept Maria into a big bear hug.

"Get off! You'll wrinkle my dress!" Maria gently pushed him away, smoothed out her pleated skirt, and straightened her skinny little belt. "Don't I look fabulous?" She spun around and struck a pose.

"You look perfect. You always look perfect. She always looks perfect."

"It's all for you, sweetheart." Maria tapped her cheek and allowed Rupert a chaste kiss.

"Isn't she an angel?" Rupert looked back and forth between Julia and Edie.

Neither girl responded.

"How did I get so lucky?" he continued while beaming. "The prettiest girl in the room—not that we're in a room, but the prettiest if we were in a room. Well, really very pretty in or out of a room. You know what I mean."

"Yes, sweetheart. I know what you mean." Maria linked her arm through Rupert's, smiling at him as though he were a child who'd just shown her a bug-eyed caterpillar drawing she was anxious to throw away once she'd given it a smattering of praise. "Should we find you a drink and make our rounds?"

"Gosh. Yes. Thanks." Rupert turned to Edie. "Nice to meet you. Wait. Did I meet you, or did I just imagine I met you? You're the cousin, right?"

"Yeah. I'm 'the cousin.'" She managed a smile, despite her mounting frustration at repeatedly being called the girl, the cousin, the poor relation, or anything other than her name. "I'm Edie, and you must be Rupert."

"You'll have to excuse us." Maria pivoted Rupert away before he could respond. "I promised Dear Mama I'd introduce Rupert to those dreadful bores the Bensons. They only talk about two things: investing for retirement and taking care of your teeth. Total yawn-fest, but they're very generous at weddings." She dragged Rupert away, smiling and waving until they merged into the crowd.

Edie continued tracking them as she shimmied a blistered heel out of her shoe.

"He's not what I was expecting," she said.

"He's rich and he worships her." Julia tipped back her champagne and set the empty glass on the table. "He's everything Maria wants in a boyfriend."

"Like a house by the ocean and a matching set of spaniels?"

"Sure, but don't forget the worship." Julia picked up a new champagne flute and downed half the contents. "Besides, Rupert's not stupid. He knows she likes him for his money, but he likes her for her looks. She's like arm candy and he's like ATM candy."

Over near the patio, Maria tugged Rupert along by the elbow while he stumbled behind her, spilling white wine on the shrubbery and sputtering apologies to everyone and no one. They seemed like such an odd couple, joined by something that didn't look much like love. Then again, Edie's mom had married for love and her marriage hadn't turned out to be the romance of the century. Maybe beauty and money made a fair trade, but what would happen if one or the other ran out? A violent custody battle over the spaniels? Poor George and Martha.

"Wouldn't it be amazing to be adored?" Julia absently ran a finger around the rim of her glass until it made a low humming noise. "Not just liked or admired, but totally, utterly worshiped by someone who can't live without you? Like Romeo and Juliet?"

"Actually, Romeo chased anything that moved," Edie pointed out. "If the two of them had lived, he would've had an affair within the first month."

As Julia lowered her glass, looking like she was about to cry from sheer heartbreak, a familiar voice reached them from just over Edie's shoulder.

"Who's having an affair?"

Edie spun around to see Sebastian standing a few feet away, cleaned up and practically glowing in a white linen shirt and trousers. Edie's cheeks instantly ignited. She tried to cool them by thinking of non-mortifying things like Post-its and banana peels while Julia stepped in front of her and placed a kiss on each of Sebastian's cheeks.

"I thought you'd never get here. Remember my cousin Edie?"

"Of course. How could I forget Cousin Edie?"

"We saw each other yesterday," Edie explained, anxious to keep Julia from making assumptions about crushes and kisses. "He doesn't mean, well, you know."

"Totally." He flashed her a glimmer of a smile. "I wouldn't dream of implying you-know."

Edie's cheeks flared again. So much for banana peels.

"Oh, good. We're all friends already." Julia linked an arm through each of theirs. "We can skip the small chat and get straight to business."

"Business?" Edie and Sebastian swapped a wary look.

"Maria and I promised Edie a spectacular night. It's a Cinderella thing. She's in a gorgeous dress—even if we had to force her into it—and she's at a ball—okay, not a *ball*, but a party with a place to dance, if you like old people's music. Now she just needs a Prince Charming."

Edie froze. For someone raised in polite society, Julia sure hadn't mastered the art of subtlety. And if she was going to force Edie on a

41

guy, why did she have to pick Sebastian? The one person who turned Edie from a sane, articulate, physically coordinated individual into a stuttering, stammering blush factory?

Then Julia made things worse.

"Can you introduce her to some of your friends?"

Edie freed herself from Julia's hold as her mind raced, scrambling for a reason she could flee. Being set up with Sebastian was bad enough, but being set up *by* him? Utter nightmare. Then again, why didn't Julia include Sebastian as a setup option?

"You must know someone single," Julia said, "and smart. He has to be smart to keep up with Edie."

"I don't know about smart, but I know a certain 'nice guy' who'd be happy to share a dance." Sebastian held out a hand. "Shall we?"

After a slight hesitation, Edie took his hand. After all, she did want to dance with him. She also wanted to *not want* to dance with him. Why couldn't emotions line up as neatly as Norah's lawn chairs? Why were they such experts at contradicting each other? Jerks.

Sebastian led Edie over to the patio, where he wrapped his arms around her in a loose, uncertain embrace. She linked her hands behind his neck and they began to turn in slow circles amid half a dozen other couples. The music was vaguely waltz-y, gently merging with the sounds of the murmuring crowd and the crickets that were starting to chirp as the sun set and the candles flickered brighter. It was a perfectly romantic setting (for anyone who cared about such things).

"So, Julia suggests we get straight to business." Sebastian's smile tilted up and dimpled a cheek.

Edie averted her eyes to stave off another blush. It was so unfair. If he insisted on growing up to be nice, funny, and smart, why couldn't he have the decency to be hideously ugly? If she only looked at his shoulder, or that little freckle on his collarbone, maybe she could get through one dance without thoroughly embarrassing herself. Except it was a really nice shoulder. The freckle was pretty cute too.

"Please ignore everything my cousins say about me from now until August," she begged. "Especially regarding my supposed need for a boyfriend."

"Don't worry." Sebastian laughed, a soft, low rumble like a barely tapped kick drum. "I won't introduce you to anyone unless you ask me to, but what happens in August?"

"College. Independence. The beginning of everything."

"Everything?" His brow furrowed briefly. "So, nothing's begun yet?"

"Nothing important."

"Hmm. Good to know." Sebastian went quiet for a moment, leaving Edie with the sinking suspicion she'd just said something wrong. As she searched his face, looking for clues, he glanced toward the central courtyard, where his mom was slipping her arm through the elbow of a square-jawed, stern-faced man in a navy suit. "Guess you and I are both itching to leave home." He shuffled past an elderly couple, pulling Edie toward him to avoid a collision.

"Parent troubles?" Edie shifted closer to Sebastian to avoid nothing at all.

"They're okay, just, you know, high expectations, low tolerance for disappointment." He shrugged and shook his head at the same time, resigned but not. "I'm ready to make my own choices, and to be where I'm not 'Tom's little brother' anymore."

"I don't think of you that way."

"A lot of other people do."

"Maybe not the right people?" Edie ventured.

"No. Maybe not the right people." He smiled down at her, warmly, sweetly, sincerely.

The music from the string quartet swelled as Edie hid another blush by focusing on her feet where her shoes alternated with his. They looked nice, those toes: hers black velvet, his perforated brown leather, gently stepping side to side, unaware of how close they were to each other. For a full minute Edie and Sebastian danced without speaking while his simple closeness made her temporarily stop obsessing about things like blisters, absent friends, college tuition, and the reasons octopuses ate their own appendages. As an elderly couple waltzed past with enviable flourish, Sebastian tightened his hold—not much, but enough for Edie to notice and respond in kind.

"So, where are you heading when you begin all your beginnings?" he asked.

"UMass Boston, probably." Edie's answer came out flat. Despite her early admission and partial scholarship, she was a little embarrassed to be choosing her school based on affordability rather than ambition, especially while she was among people who had trust funds, stock portfolios, and stepdads with an inside scoop on the chicken-sacrifice admissions policy. "Where are you going?"

"NYU. My stepdad expects me to pursue a law degree but I hope to take some writing classes." Sebastian grimaced as he pulled away a little.

Edie held on tight, anxious to prevent his retreat.

"What's wrong?" she asked.

"I can't believe I just said that out loud, especially to someone I . . . someone I don't know that well. I feel like I'm jinxing it by even saying the words."

"I think it's great." Edie risked drawing him a little closer, sliding her fingers to overlap her wrists, in case it made him more comfortable, and in case he almost said what she really, *really* hoped he'd almost said. "You should do what you love."

Sebastian's arms adjusted to her nearness, one hand sliding up toward her shoulder blade, the other circling more of her waist. Definitely more comfortable.

"I don't know if it's great, but I feel like I've got something to say. I just don't know how to say it yet." He leaned back and met her eyes. "Ever have that feeling?"

"All the time."

She drew him closer. He drew her closer. They inched toward each other, circle by circle, until her cheek brushed his shoulder without quite resting there. The almost-ness of it all was better than salted chocolate marshmallows, better than front row seats to Moody Clockwork, better than anything. Edie rapidly edited her No Boys plan. Liking Sebastian wasn't going to prevent her from getting straight-As and earning the rest of her tuition money. She just needed to like him . . . in moderation. Was that possible? That was totally possible, though the fact that he smelled all citrusy and soapy wasn't helping.

She closed her eyes and pictured white linen sheets billowing on a clothesline in a perfect summer breeze. Cotton dander floated in soft light. A hand drew aside the closest sheet as Sebastian chased her, slow motion, through the laundry lines, laughing, teasing, catching her at last in a perfect embrace, and then leaning forward to place a—

"Let me guess." His lips were perilously close to her ear now, a voice not just heard but felt: deep, low, and with the perfect hint of an unseen smile. "You're planning to study art?"

"Art?" Edie blinked up him, confused. "No. Why?"

"I figured with your love of Rodin—"

Edie backed away. Her mouth dropped open but words failed to emerge. She knew she had something to say. She just didn't know how to say it. She simply stood there, mortified, as her brain sped through thoughts of soft lips, gentle hands, and a seriously inconvenient sprinkler head.

"Did you think I'd forgotten?" he teased.

"Yes!" she blubbered through a nervous laugh.

"Forget my first kiss? Never."

Edie began to fidget, unsure why she was so embarrassed. That kiss was years ago. Two kids fumbling around. But the more she thought about it, and the more he might be thinking about it, the more she'd think about other kisses, too. Those thoughts led to blushes and crushes and everything else she was trying to rein in.

"C'mon." Sebastian extended a hand. "Let's finish our dance."

"Only if you pretend it never happened."

"I'd rather not." He took a step toward her, his hand still outstretched, his eyes calm and direct, holding her the way his arms had held her: full of delightful, delicious, dreamy almosts.

Whether he was flirting, teasing, or simply being friendly, Edie fell into the spell of his pale blue eyes and kind heart. She shook off her nerves and slipped her hand into his. Sebastian's fingers wrapped around hers. He smiled. She smiled. And Edie decided this wasn't the time to rein anything in. It wasn't the time for questions and doubts. It was simply the time to dance.

Chapter Six

THE BOOMING BASS OF LOUD HIP-HOP MUSIC
drowned out the string quartet as a flashy red sports car sped into
the Summerses' driveway and squealed to a halt beside the house.

Sebastian dropped his embrace. "Does he *always* have to make
an entrance?"

"Your brother?" Edie asked.

"Yep. C'mon. Let's go say hi."

Sebastian led Edie off the patio as the car door opened and
Tom stepped out, sweeping his long brown bangs off his forehead
with the back of his hand, reminding Edie of the way he used to
fight with his mom whenever Mrs. Summers tried to make him get
a haircut. He wore a fancy printed tux jacket, tight jeans, a tighter
T-shirt, and a pair of plastic flip-flops, as though he didn't give a
damn what kind of party he was going to. He removed his mirrored
sunglasses as he walked around the car with a cool strut so pro-
nounced it almost demanded background music.

He swung open the passenger door and let out a beautiful blond
girl in a bright red mini-dress. Edie suspected that the girl hadn't

required help squeezing into the dress, but she'd have plenty of volunteers if she needed help getting out of it. As she stood, she took Tom's sunglasses, put them on, and planted a long, passionate kiss on him. It not only demanded background music, it suggested the need for a content warning.

"That's quite an entrance, all right." Edie glanced around at the now quieter party, wondering how it would feel to enjoy being the center of attention.

"That's nothing." Sebastian continued leading her through the garden, weaving his way between guests, hedgerows, and tastefully draped cupid statues. "Last time Tom visited, he brought the entire women's volleyball team."

Edie and Sebastian stepped out of the crowd and onto the gravel path that paralleled the Summerses' driveway from the back of the property to the road out front. Only a few yards away, on the other side of the white picket fence, the entangled couple continued searching for something at the back of each other's throats. When they showed no signs of ceasing their exploration, Sebastian coughed.

Tom turned toward the noise, a grin spreading across his face.

"Hey, little brother!" He reached over the fence and gave Sebastian one of those energetic man hugs with lots of back patting. Then his eyes caught Edie's. "Holy shit! Edie Price! I heard you were back. Look at you, all grown up. Wowza!"

Edie started to wave but her arm was soon pressed against her chest as Tom enveloped her in a big, friendly hug. Awkward? Check.

Bashful? Double check. Sulky? Actually, still a little fluttery from her dance with Sebastian.

"Guys, this is Jess." Tom wrapped an arm around her waist, casually possessive. "Jess, this is Edie and my little brother, Sebastian."

"I wouldn't call him little." Jess dabbed at the saliva on her lips.

"Don't let his height fool you." Tom winked, still grinning. "Six foot two but he still climbs trees, reads books about cowboys and aliens, and can't finish an ice cream cone before it melts all over him."

"Oh, I don't know." Jess ran a thumb across her lower lip. "There are worse things than licking sticky fingers."

Sebastian sputtered out a cough while Tom bellowed with laughter and Edie tried to think about anything nonsexual: burnt toast, dust bunnies, arid sand dunes, making out with Sebastian. Dammit.

A cute little orange convertible pulled into the Summerses' driveway and parked behind Tom's car.

"Well, look who's here," Tom said. "Fashionably late, as always."

"She's only a few minutes later than you are," Sebastian pointed out.

"Yeah, but I drove all the way from Philly." Tom squinted toward the car. "Wait, did she bring a date?" He turned to Sebastian. "Is there something you haven't told me?"

"That's not her date," Sebastian explained. "That's her older brother. He's visiting from Boston, helping their parents out with a few financial matters. Apparently he's some kind of stock market whiz. She said he was going stir-crazy so I suggested she bring him along tonight."

While Edie was busily wondering who "she" was, the car doors opened and out stepped a guy and girl who appeared to be around twenty. They looked almost like twins: tall and slender with wavy black hair, tan skin, angular cheekbones, full lips that pulled upward at the corners as if tugged by a wicked secret, and large, dark, disturbingly mischievous eyes. They reminded Edie of demons, vampires, or some other paranormal species that'd evolved to look insanely hot in order to seduce their prey. Since no one else was scrambling for a crucifix, Edie held her ground.

As the guy stepped around from the passenger side, a distinct swagger in his step, the girl slipped her keys into her purse, adjusted her miniskirt, and strode across the driveway, sweeping her long, thick hair over her shoulders and balancing so perfectly in her mile-high heels even Maria might've been impressed.

"Great to see you again, Tom." The girl placed a kiss on his cheek. Without even glancing at Edie, she reached over the fence, linked her fingers through Sebastian's and gave him a quick but approving appraisal.

"Look at you, all in white," she practically purred. "So Gatsby."

"Then you read the book after all?" Sebastian asked.

"Saw the movie. Same thing."

"Right. Okay." Sebastian's eyebrows flickered. "So, um, introductions." He scratched at the back of his neck, oddly shifty, as he pointed everyone out. "This is Edie, that's Tom and Jess, the guy just joining us is Henry, and this is my girlfriend, Claire."

As the word *girlfriend* pushed its way into Edie's brain, her heart plummeted to earth and landed with a violent, nauseating *splat*. Of course he had a girlfriend. Why did she assume he didn't have a girl-friend? And now he wouldn't even meet her eyes. He was probably embarrassed she'd so obviously been crushing on him. Awesome. Mansfield day one: mixed bag. Day two: raging failure.

"You're the cousin?" Claire asked with a welcoming smile, the sort often seen on restaurant hostesses, real estate agents, and, well, nice people.

"Yep." Edie's jaw tightened. "I'm 'the cousin.'"

"Maria mentioned you'd be joining us at Saint Penitent's next week."

"I start Monday." Edie forced herself not to gape. Claire was still in high school? But she was so cool, so confident, so . . . top-heavy.

"Saint Penitentiary's." Tom took his sunglasses from Jess and slipped them on even though the sun had fully set. "School motto: High SAT scores, low fun."

"It's not that bad," Claire assured Edie. "I'll help you settle in. I was new last year so I know exactly how you feel."

Edie manufactured a smile, grateful for Claire's kindness but uncertain a girl with Claire's easy manner and magnetic smile could empathize with all of Edie's feelings, particularly those related to being sulky, bashful, awkward, or prickling with envy. She was prob-ably smart, too, even if she hadn't read *Gatsby*. Otherwise Sebastian wouldn't have tossed out that quote about beauty being unattractive without intelligence. Edie felt so stupid. She'd actually let herself believe he was trying to compliment her mind.

As the group filled in a few blanks on the quick introductions, Edie scanned the party, searching for a plausible excuse to go tend to the sharp-clawed, green-eyed monster that'd so swiftly taken up residence in her chest. Maria and Rupert were playing croquet with two other couples in the center of the open lawn under a canopy of little white lights. Julia was polishing off yet another glass of champagne behind her parents' backs. Bert and Norah were chatting with the charity club ladies while Bert's combover fluttered in the breeze, making him look like a baby bird.

Edie turned back to the group and opened her mouth to say she had to go do something she hadn't figured out yet. As she struggled to assemble her words, she noticed Henry staring at her.

"What?" She patted her face, searching for crumbs or streaked makeup.

"My sister's a liar." A rakish smile dented his cheeks. "This party won't be boring at all."

Claire rolled her eyes. "Edie, watch out. Henry's a terrible flirt."

"Not true. I'm an outstanding flirt." He did a little sleight of hand, producing a tiny white rose, which he held out to Edie. The gesture was showy and well rehearsed, making it seem like he'd offered a hundred roses to a hundred girls.

"No, thanks." Edie waved him off, unimpressed.

"You don't like flowers?"

"I don't like bullshit," she blurted, too steeped in rejection to pre-edit herself. She was about to apologize when she realized everyone was laughing, including Henry.

"Guess you'll have to find another way to entertain yourself while you're in Mansfield, Henry," Claire said.

"Good luck with that." Tom's arm slipped around Jess's waist again. "This town is Dullsville. Nothing to do but golf, gossip, or guzzle. Make sure you tell everyone you're only visiting. Otherwise my stepdad'll be on you to join the Mansfield Men's Golf League."

"I don't golf, and if I'm going to join a sports league, it has to be coed." Henry's eyes crept toward Edie's. "But I suspect I can find more interesting entertainment while I'm in town." He cocked an eyebrow.

Edie folded her arms and shook her head. She was in no mood to "entertain" anyone, especially a guy who oozed arrogance and mistook it for charm.

"Speaking of entertainment, it's time to join the party." Tom climbed over the fence, clumsy but laughing, catching his jeans cuff on a picket, losing a flip-flop, and nearly falling face-first into Norah's garden. Once he righted himself, he swept Jess up in his arms and swung her over the fence as if he were rescuing a damsel in distress.

"My hero." She fell against Tom and they promptly locked lips, cooing and giggling with no care for who might be watching.

Sebastian sheepishly extended a hand to Claire.

"Sorry," he said. "I'm not as heroic as my brother."

"Too bad for me," she teased.

Her tone was light, without bite or sting, but Sebastian still flinched as if wounded. Claire didn't seem to notice. She was busy assessing the fence, testing her grip and nestling a foot on a horizontal framing board. It was a small but weird moment. Edie couldn't help but wonder why Sebastian had deliberately referenced his brother after admitting how much he hated being compared to Tom all the time. And why did Claire take the comment one step further? She had to know it would hurt. Or did she?

Edie pondered the possibilities while Henry stepped forward, allowing Claire to brace herself on his shoulder. She took Sebastian's hand and hoisted herself over the fence, her long legs easily clearing the top of the pickets.

"Wow," Sebastian said. "You're *my* hero."

As they leaned toward each other, Edie bent to tie her shoe, only to remember it was buckled, not laced. Claire and Sebastian might've embraced. They might've kissed. They might've teleported to Budapest and back. Edie didn't look up to find out. She remained crouched, examining her blisters while everyone waited for Henry to stroll casually down the driveway and up the other side of the fence, preserving both his clothes and his dignity.

Once they were all gathered, Tom led the group toward the catering tent on the other side of the mazelike hedges. He wove his way through the milling crowd while nuzzling noses with Jess and barely avoiding a marble birdbath, a cater waiter, and three men in golf shirts who scurried out of his way. Sebastian and Claire followed, his arm around her waist, her fingers toying with his hair. Edie trailed at the back while Henry fell in line beside her as though he was her designated partner, flashing her a you-know-you-want-me smirk every time she made the mistake of glancing his way. He looked like the ultimate player with his perfectly fitted designer clothes, impeccably groomed black hair, and cultivated air of self-assurance. He was *so* not Edie's type, though he was attracting plenty of flustered looks from the middle-aged women they passed. Hopefully one would draw him away soon and request a few private tips on insider trading.

As the motley procession approached the little courtyard where Norah and Bert were chatting with the Great Hearts, Good Causes ladies, Edie considered excusing herself to join her aunt and uncle. They had their backs to her but their voices grew audible as she drew closer.

"I just wish she was a little more grateful for the home we're giving her," Norah was saying with her usual tart superiority. "If I were in her position I'd be bending over backwards to show my gratitude, but then no one ever swept in and offered me everything a girl could possibly want."

"Do you want anything, dear?" Bert asked.

Norah paused as if considering.

"No, thank you," she said. "But one does like to be asked."

Edie changed her mind, hurrying forward with her hand shielding her face. Anything was better than Norah's company, even if it meant watching Claire's hand trail down Sebastian's back and pull his hip against hers. They were so affectionate with each other, all touchy-feely like they were really in love, the way people always looked in perfume ads. They probably rode tandem bicycles, shared fancy milkshakes, and tried on hats together. They probably had amazing sex.

Edie forced herself to look away, furious her brain had gone there. It was the absolute last thing she wanted to think about. Desperate for distraction, she turned to Henry and pasted on a smile.

"So, how long are you in Mansfield?" she asked casually.

"Depends what I find to keep me here," he replied not so casually.

"You don't go to college? Or have a job?"

Claire shot him a playful grin over her shoulder.

"Henry's a 'man of leisure,'" she said.

"Seriously?" Edie asked, astonished such a thing existed.

Henry shrugged, his demon/vampire eyes locking on hers.

"Why work when I can afford to play?"

Edie searched his smug expression, wondering if he ever uttered anything that wasn't dripping with innuendo.

"What *exactly* do you play?" she challenged.

"The stock market, naturally."

"Naturally."

"And poker."

"Right."

"And a little guitar."

"Guitar?" she asked with more interest than she'd intended.

Claire and Sebastian stopped and turned around, still attached at the hip.

"Careful," she warned Edie. "He only learned to play so he could serenade easily infatuated girls. Don't fall for it."

"Don't worry," Edie said firmly. "I won't."

Henry laughed while Sebastian smiled at her in a way she really wished he wouldn't now that his smoking-hot girlfriend was wrapped around him.

"Edie used to always have a guitar in her hands," he explained to the others before turning back her way. "You still play, right?"

"Sort of." She recalled the stringless guitar under her bed, the notebook filled with songs, and the hope that she'd soon be able to play them without tearing up.

"Me too." Sebastian's smile widened. "We should 'sort of' jam sometime."

An image of playing guitar together filled Edie's mind: knee to knee in the shade of the tree they used to climb together, singing, strumming, laughing, happy. It was perfect. His sympathetic company was exactly what she needed to push through her grief. He'd understand if she cried. He'd get why playing was complicated. After three long years, she'd finally make her mom's guitar sing again.

She was about to blubber out a *yes!* when she caught Claire's eyes, watching her as if sizing her up. Edie'd seen that look before, or something like it. Shonda had looked at her that way right before running across the parking lot, leaving Edie and James alone in his car. She must've sensed a tension or attraction. Either that or she'd overheard James promise to give Edie something to remember him by before she left Ithaca.

Edie's stomach sank. She'd forgotten he'd said that, or rather, she'd convinced herself she didn't know what he meant. But as she saw the echo of Shonda's suspicions in Claire's eyes now, she realized she did know. And she'd consciously put herself in a situation she knew she should avoid. She couldn't change it, but she'd make sure she didn't do it again.

"Edie?" Sebastian prompted. "Guitar? Maybe next weekend?"

"Actually, I'm more comfortable playing alone," she said.

To her surprise, Sebastian's smile dropped away completely,

almost as if she'd slapped him. He studied her for a moment, his expression unreadable. Then he turned and walked away with Claire while Edie was left to wonder what she'd done wrong. For god's sake, his girlfriend was *right there*. What was Edie supposed to say? That they should wait till Claire wasn't around so the two of them could make beautiful music together? The situation was impossible. Her crush was practically painted on her skin. He had to know. Besides, Claire seemed great, the sort of girl who could make a big differ-ence in Edie's first few days at her new school. Edie wasn't going to mess that up over petty jealousies. She needed a friend more than anything else right now.

They all caught up with Tom and Jess in front of a table lined with tidy rows of pre-filled wineglasses. Without hesitation, Tom started passing out the drinks. Apparently no one at Norah's party was checking IDs or worried about who was drinking. Edie found this odd. She couldn't keep up. As soon as she thought she had a handle on Norah's rules and regulations, something made her feel like an outsider again, uneducated in the ways of high society. So when Henry handed her a glass, she simply took it. As he let go of the stem, his fingers brushed hers, barely, but enough to snap her nerves into alertness.

"If you change your mind about playing solo," he murmured, low and languid, "I know some spectacular duets."

"Coed duets?" Edie stared him in the eye.

Henry smiled as if amused, which wasn't the reaction she'd been aiming for.

"As Shakespeare says, 'Music is the food of love.'"

"Only if you have an appetite for it."

"Oh, I have an appetite."

"I'm sure you do."

"Everyone does."

"Some more than others."

"Some more *openly* than others, maybe." He took a calculated step toward her. "But we all want things."

Edie glanced at Sebastian where Claire's arm twisted around his like ivy, or tentacles. Unable to deny Henry's assertion but desperately hoping her wants were well hidden, she planted her blistered feet and squared off with him.

"You think you know what I want?" she asked.

"Not necessarily, but I know how to take direction."

"What if that direction is to exit stage left, pursued by a bear?"

He laughed as he set a hand to his chest, reeling like he was wounded.

"Then off I'll go. Nursing my broken heart, waiting, pining, hoping."

Edie rolled her eyes as she turned away, leaving Henry to look elsewhere for entertainment. No doubt he'd find plenty of chances to hand out tiny white roses and charm some other girl into "directing" him, some girl who didn't care if he wore more entitlement than cologne, although he did smell kinda good.

"Why don't we take your brother on a tour of Mansfield tomorrow?" Sebastian suggested to Claire. "See if we can entertain him for a few hours?"

"You mean a few minutes," Tom joked, already on his second glass of wine.

"I think it's a great idea." Claire nestled against Sebastian's chest as he held her the way he'd *almost* held Edie. "Who wouldn't love a private tour with John Gatsby?"

Jay Gatsby, Edie thought, but she kept the correction to herself, certain Sebastian already knew and no one else cared. She caught his eye for a second while his gaze lingered on hers, asking a question she couldn't quite parse. What was going on with him tonight? One second he was all confidence. The next he was a vortex of confusion.

"You should come too," he offered, cautious and hesitant. "We can revisit a few old haunts. Maybe grab some ice cream. They still have that strawberry rhubarb flavor you used to like so much."

Edie skipped a breath as a giddy little tremor ran through her. She couldn't believe Sebastian remembered her favorite ice cream flavor. Maybe she didn't have to totally avoid him. He was only asking her on a friendly afternoon outing, one his girlfriend was going on too. This wasn't like the situation with James. Sebastian would never make a pass at her. He wasn't that kind of guy. Besides, he only thought of her as a friend. She'd learn to only think of him as a friend. That was possible, right?

"So, are you in?" His warm smile brimmed with anticipation while his eyes locked on hers as if her answer really, *really* mattered.

"Yeah," she said, far too fluttery for friendship. "Sounds great."

Chapter Seven

ON SUNDAY AFTERNOON SEBASTIAN TOOK CLAIRE, Henry, and Edie on a tour of Mansfield. Edie gazed out the back window as he drove past the private country club, the even more private country club, and—for anyone who didn't care for full-sized golf—the putt-putt course with the obligatory windmill and gaping-mouthed spooky clown face. With an endearing enthusiasm that made Edie like him even more, Sebastian pointed out all his favorite landmarks, including the old brick library and the big stone church that sat on the main square in the center of town. Then he wrapped up the tour by offering to buy everyone ice cream at Cold Shoulder.

Sebastian headed inside the shop while Claire, Henry, and Edie waited on a bench out front. Edie scratched at an ink stain on her cardigan while trying to ignore the fact that she was wedged between Sebastian's impossibly beautiful girlfriend and said girlfriend's impossibly irritating brother: a.k.a. the tenacious slime machine. A simple *no* last night should've been the easiest thing in the world. How had she gone so spineless in the space of a single smile? Crushes seriously sucked, and they were shockingly potent.

Edie took out her phone and added another post to her lexicon.

Affluence

noun

1. A high level of wealth exemplified by the fact that the cheapest item at the local dollar store costs $9.95.
2. A font that automatically adds extra letters to words like olde and shoppe.
3. The elegant tint of eggshell Mansfield storeowners use to paint everything not made of brick, brass, or glass.

She willed herself to be patient. Shonda would forgive her eventually. A little light humor was the best way to connect right now. Edie shouldn't be too pushy, especially since seven texts, four voice mails, and three emails were probably pushy enough. Self-control had never been Edie's strength. It wasn't Shonda's strength either, which was why she and Edie were so perfect as friends. They both cried at public service ads for pet shelters. They coped with angry customers at the Burger Barn by enacting violent revenge scenes with ketchup-covered french fries. Mostly they laughed.

Edie checked her phone again, just in case.

Nothing.

As Claire finessed her already-perfect eyeliner and Henry chatted up a woman walking a dog in a sweater set (the dog, not the woman), Edie leaned back, closed her eyes, and let the sun warm her cheeks. She tried to focus on the little light speckles that danced across her eyelids. If she stared at them long enough maybe the speckles would drift down, seep into her skin, and fill all the empty spaces she'd been accumulating lately. One for Shonda. Another for her mom and her music. One for Sebastian and the curious chasm of an unfulfilled what-if. One for—

"So, you and Sebastian used to come here together?" Claire asked, jolting Edie from her thoughts.

"Sometimes," Edie said. "When my mom and I were visiting my grandparents."

"Have things changed since you were kids?"

Edie spun around to glance at the gold block letters on the window behind her.

"I think they repainted the sign."

"The sign." Claire chuckled softly. "Right."

Henry stifled a knowing smirk. Edie scowled at him, uncertain what was so entertaining. She didn't have long to consider the possibilities because Sebastian exited the shop with his hands full of ice cream cones. He handed a plain vanilla cone to Claire, a decadent, chocolate-caramel cone to Henry, and a pink, fruity cone to Edie, all while struggling to keep his rainbow-sprinkled bright blue double scoop from toppling.

"See?" he said to Edie. "They still have my favorite too."

She laughed, charmed that he hadn't outgrown his love for Technicolor sweets, or his inability to consume them without making a total mess.

"You always looked like you murdered a Smurf after you ate one of those."

"Only because you bit off the bottom of the cone whenever we swapped tastes." He flashed her an unexpectedly coy little smile, one that would've called up a blush if Edie didn't force herself to look away. He turned to Claire as he flicked sprinkles off his fingers. "Hope you don't mind if my tongue turns blue."

"As long as I can kiss you while you're still nontoxic." Claire scooted forward and wedged her knees around his.

Edie leapt off the bench. Sebastian stepped back to give her space.

"What's wrong?" he asked.

"I need to, I just, you know." She pointed over her shoulder. "Window shopping."

"I love shopping for windows," Henry said. "Mind if I join you?"

Edie opened her mouth to say that yes, she did mind, but as Sebastian nestled himself onto the bench and Claire leaned over to taste his ice cream in a way that implied she'd willingly kiss him no matter how toxic his tongue was, she changed her mind. Henry was annoying, but he was company.

"Sure," she said without enthusiasm. "Why not?"

Edie and Henry wandered down Main Street, circling the central green where the old church stood sentinel over a handful of oak trees and a perfectly mowed grass rectangle. They passed by three hair salons, a wax bar, and a pampered pet shop before pausing in front of one of the many antique stores that dotted the center of town. The window was filled with objects that sparked Edie's imagination:

rusty farming tools that looked like horror movie weapons; a stack of landscape-colored quilts; and a faded American flag with a molting, button-eyed corduroy elephant sitting on a corner.

Edie began mentally composing. *So many old things, no longer bold things, not yet sold, to unfold, all these stories-yet-to-be-told things.*

"Nice window," Henry noted. "Though it depends what you're shopping for. And what's actually for sale." He smiled subtly, in a way that implied he meant more than he said. Then he nodded at Edie's cone. "Still your favorite, or have your tastes changed?"

Edie shrugged and feigned interest in a display of old typewriters, but her eyes kept darting to Claire and Sebastian. They were snuggled together back on the bench, laughing at something only they could hear.

"He's not worth it," Henry said.

Edie felt the words like a slap. She turned to face Henry, her gut knotting. To her surprise, he wasn't grinning like he was full of himself. His expression was softer, kinder.

"There's no point liking someone who doesn't like you back," he said. "It'll never make you happy."

"Oh yeah? What makes you such an expert?"

"I've been around a block or two."

"So I hear. I believe your sister mentioned a 'trail of broken hearts.'"

"Better to break a heart than to have your heart broken." He watched her, unblinking, letting his statement sit between them like an ugly truth.

Lacking sufficient evidence to argue the point one way or another, Edie kicked at the moss growing between the sidewalk cracks, channeling her irritation into the ground.

"So whose heart are you planning to break next?" she asked.

"Obviously not yours."

"Obviously."

As Edie emphasized the point with a sharp glare, Henry peered into the shop window, shielding his eyes and pushing his thick black bangs off his forehead.

"I like your cousin," he said, tossing the words out like an afterthought.

"Stupendous." Edie decimated more moss, smearing green and brown sidewalk guts across the toe of her sneaker. "Which one?"

"Both, actually, but Maria's more interesting than Julia."

"Maria has a boyfriend."

"Maybe that's what makes her interesting."

"Competition?"

"No. The confidence a girl has when she already knows someone likes her."

Edie stopped kicking at the sidewalk as she gritted her teeth. Hard.

"A girl can't be confident without a boyfriend?"

Henry shrugged as he turned away from the shop window.

"I don't know, maybe, but having a boyfriend doesn't hurt." He crossed the sidewalk, leaned against an ornate lamppost, and polished off the last of his cone while Edie watched him, locked in place by a growing conviction that while Henry might not be a demon or a vampire, he was at least a little bit evil. "All I'm saying is that Maria doesn't need me for anything, but it would be fun to figure out what she wants."

Edie's cone snapped in her fist, collapsing to bits inside the wrapper.

"You can't be serious."

"I *can* be serious, though I generally prefer to be otherwise." Henry tossed his paper wrapper into a nearby trash can and brushed off his hands.

"I thought you were only in town for a few days."

"I'm in town as long as I have a reason to be in town."

"A reason like ruining someone's relationship?"

When Henry offered no defense, Edie turned and marched away, pitching the remains of her cone and rethinking her desire for company. She sped past a nail salon, three virtually identical boutiques displaying pastel tailored coordinates, and a portrait studio, all while trying to convince herself that Henry's little scheme didn't stand a chance. Her efforts failed as images from last night's party scrolled through her mind:

1. *Maria meeting Henry (enthusiastic).*
2. *Henry meeting Rupert (calculating).*
3. *Rupert spending the rest of the night conveniently parked with talkative neighbors, and without Maria (painful).*

Henry soon caught up and matched Edie's pace, too close for anything even approximating comfort. She was so preoccupied with trying to put space between them, she stepped out into the street without checking for traffic. Henry grabbed her arm and pulled her onto the sidewalk as a car zoomed past.

"Thanks," she said as she stumbled backwards.

"Anytime." His hand remained on her arm.

She glared at it until he let go.

They waited in silence for the walk signal beside three impeccably groomed businesswomen in their thirties, all of whom eyed Henry like he was something to eat, and Edie like she was something to fumigate. Edie patted down her unruly hair while Henry simply watched the traffic go by, his hands in his pockets, a smile on his face, totally unconcerned about what anyone thought of him. For a moment Edie's mounting animosity was replaced with simple envy. Where did he get his rock-solid confidence? How could she find some for herself? If she asked him, could he teach her a few things, or was all that cool carelessness just a by-product of growing up rich and beautiful?

She pondered that thought while they crossed the street, turned the corner, and headed up Union Street, the park to their right, the shops and salons to their left, the general air of wealth everywhere.

"I don't know why you're so mad at me." Henry jogged a few steps to catch up with Edie's aggressive pace. "You and I both know Maria and Rupert will soon be Splitzville, with or without my intervention. That relationship is a ticking time bomb."

"Not true. They have plans."

"Plans change."

"Not always."

Henry stepped forward and spun around in front of her, walking backwards, bending down to catch her eye. Edie zigzagged across the sidewalk, hoping he'd back into a lamppost, a sandwich board, or a short-tempered pedestrian with a really spiky purse. But he was persistent, and while she fumed, he seemed to think the whole thing was a game — teasing, testing, pushing his boundaries.

"You know I'm right," he said.

"I know you're a jerk."

Henry laughed, impervious to insult in a way that was seriously grating on Edie.

"If Maria's so committed to Rupert," he said, not missing a beat, "then explain why she spent half the night flirting with me."

Edie scoured her brain for a credible answer. Failing utterly, she threw up her hands and beelined her way back to the ice cream shop. The only thing more infuriating than arguing with someone who assumed he was always right was arguing with him if he *was* always right. And if Henry's confidence was as well earned as it seemed, pretty soon Edie wouldn't be the only one in Mansfield nursing a broken heart.

Chapter Eight

BY THE TIME EDIE, MARIA, AND JULIA ARRIVED AT Saint Penitent's, Edie's ponytail was escaping its elastic and her stretched-out knee socks were slouched around her ankles. Norah didn't feel it was necessary to buy Edie her own uniform, not when Julia's spare would do. Too bad it didn't quite fit. The blouse strained across Edie's boobs and the skirt barely zipped over her hips, making the plaid pleats go all wobbly. The outfit even felt ugly. The skirt chafed against her thighs. The shirt collar was too high and tight. The polyester jacket seemed useful for only one thing: high-speed sweat production. Edie hoped the uniform would at least help her blend in with the other girls. If everyone was wearing the same thing, maybe no one would sense that she didn't belong.

She braced herself as she shifted her borrowed messenger bag back onto her shoulder, stumbled up the front steps, and followed her cousins into a bright hallway teeming with girls in uniform.

"Time to learn who's who," Maria announced. "There are only, like, two hundred girls at Saint Pen's, so you can't disappear among the unwashed masses like you're used to."

"Awesome," Edie replied. "Glad I showered."

Maria ignored her sarcasm as she waved at a small cluster of pretty girls in heels, simple jewelry, and uniforms that'd been pinned or tailored to fit perfectly.

"Those are the only people you need to know. My people. I'll introduce you at lunch." She nodded toward a group in sneakers and loafers with loosened ties and rolled-up sleeves. "Jocks. Sweat and ponytail crowd. No offense." She pointed at a group with neatly knotted ties and backpacks that weighed down their shoulders. "Techies and grade chasers. Don't be fooled by the lack of glasses. Just steer clear." She sneered at a trio with printed stockings and colorful dyed hair. "Manga freaks. Steer even clearer."

Edie tugged at her jacket sleeves and gave her skirt hem a quick yank, wishing both were about two inches longer. Apparently blending in with the other girls was a pipe dream. The uniform didn't help at all. She might as well be wearing a nametag that said, *Hello, my name is Charity Case.* Her insecurities deepened when she spotted Claire among the crowd, strutting down the hall like a runway model, her high heels clicking, her full hips swaying, her shampoo commercial hair sweeping her shoulders. It was truly amazing that the same outfit could make Edie look like a 1980s Scottish librarian and make Claire look like a sex goddess.

As Claire swapped friendly greetings with nearly every girl she passed, Edie quickly confirmed what she'd already begun to suspect at the garden party. Claire was *that girl.* There was one at every school. She was the girl who had everything, and because she didn't need anything from anyone, she was powerful. If she liked you, laughed at your jokes, invited you into her inner circle, hell, if she even knew your name, your social status increased. Despite the cliché, the Claires of the world weren't necessarily cruel. They were something far more formidable. They were confident. Edie didn't stand a chance with Sebastian. When *that girl* picked you, you held on.

Edie got her course schedule and paperwork in the main office. Then her cousins walked her to her first class through off-white hallways with old-fashioned architectural details, rows of shiny maroon lockers, and gray marble floors. Despite the atmosphere of tradition and sophistication, the ceiling was lined with the same quivering fluorescent lights that'd illuminated Edie's old school, though these were cleaner, brighter, and devoid of dead bugs.

As the girls turned a corner toward the classrooms, they passed a bulletin board with several catchy signs soliciting votes for prom queen. Edie paused to take a look.

"You guys have a prom here?" she asked. "With just girls?"

"Of course we have a prom." Maria pulled out a compact and finessed her lipstick. "*With* boys. We join forces with Holy Cross, the all-boys school on the other side of town, but you can bring anyone you want, or pine away dateless like poor Julia."

Julia glowered, folding her arms and locking them firmly across her chest.

"I'm only dateless temporarily," she said.

"You don't seriously think you-know-who is going to ask you?" Maria scoffed as she snapped her compact shut. "He's so far out of your league you aren't even in the bleachers. You aren't even, like, the hot dog vendor."

"That's not true." Julia stood up a little straighter. "He thinks I'm beautiful."

"He thinks you're a child."

"He asked for my phone number. And he gave me this." Julia reached into her jacket pocket and pulled out a wad of tissues. She carefully unfolded them, revealing a small, wilted white rose.

Maria sputtered with laughter while Edie covered her face with both hands, peeking through her fingers as though trying not to see what was desperately apparent.

"Don't tell me you're hoping Henry Crawford asks you out," Edie said.

"Maybe." Julia darted a defiant look at her sister.

Maria egged her on by wiping away fake tears.

"Steer clear of that guy," Edie pleaded.

"Why?" Julia asked. "Because you like him?"

"God, no." Edie grimaced. "He's slime on rice. He'll use you to feed his ego and then spit you out again. Hold out for someone who'll treat you better."

"Julia likes bad boys," Maria teased. "She'll date anyone with a motorcycle, a skull tattoo, or a pierced nipple."

"Well, you'll date anyone at all," Julia spat.

"At least I have options."

"Bet Rupert's glad to hear that."

Edie halted the bickering by reminding her cousins they needed to get to class. She prayed Julia's crush was just a brief flutter of flattery and that Henry wasn't actually serious about his heartbreaking agenda. Maria could probably handle herself but Edie wasn't so sure about Julia, especially if he pursued both girls at once. God forbid.

Edie struggled through her first few classes, disoriented and displaced, though her biggest challenge wasn't following a lecture on a book she hadn't read, recalling how to find derivatives, or conjugating irregular verbs she'd never seen. It was being around Claire for three hours. Trying not to hate someone was exhausting, especially when that hatred was totally irrational. Claire didn't do anything to earn Edie's animosity. On the contrary, she informed Edie about how to get on the good side of each teacher, offered to share her notes, and otherwise fulfilled her promise to help Edie settle in. Still, did she have to be *so* gorgeous? Couldn't she have one tiny flaw, just to make the people who sat in her shadow feel less like mutants in comparison? A mole, a wart, or an embarrassing unicorn tattoo hastily inked after too many wine spritzers?

When the French teacher played a short film about a family picnicking in Marseilles, Claire spun around from the seat in front of Edie.

"My brother likes you," she whispered conspiratorially.

"Your brother likes a lot of girls," Edie whispered back, recalling the dozen or so roses she'd seen him pass out at Norah's party, as well as the blushes he'd incited and the phone numbers he'd collected.

"He wants to know what kind of guitar you play."

"One without strings." Edie pursed her lips, hoping to end the conversation there.

"Interesting. That's his favorite kind. Of guitar, I mean." Claire bit down a sly smile as she turned toward the front of the room, lazily twisting her hair up into a big, open-jawed clip, leaving a few black wisps tickling her slender neck.

Edie tensed. She wasn't sure what was annoying her more: Henry's repeated appearance in the day's conversations or Claire's flagrant display of freckle-free skin. Deciding on the latter, Edie snuck her phone onto her lap and added a post.

Impulse
noun
1. A mischievous heart rate.
2. A dive bar on Hillview that isn't particular about IDs.
3. An inexplicable urge to draw googly eyes on your arch nemesis's flawless skin.

For the next few minutes, Edie forced herself to focus on the French family's vocabulary-infused feast as she pined for the simple pleasures of bread and cheese after a weekend of Norah's organic vegan cooking. When her phone vibrated in her lap, she frantically opened the lexicon.

James Miller
noun
1. My boyfriend.
2. My boyfriend.
3. Oh, and also, my boyfriend.

Edie stared at the screen, guilt-ridden, until she realized the film had stopped and the lights were back on. She hated that Shonda was still so mad, but at least she'd written back. It was something. It was more than something. It was enough to give Edie hope that she'd find a way to break through.

At lunch Maria introduced Edie to four of her friends: Phoebe, Taylor, Katie-with-a-K, and Catie-with-a-C. Phoebe was the student activities chair (but totally not a nerd), tall, slim, and blond, with a heart-shaped face that matched her heart-shaped jewelry. Taylor was short and curvy, with a burst of corkscrew curls that was barely restrained by a velvet headband. She was an aspiring actress (but totally not a drama geek) who was aching to play all the Tennessee Williams roles that kept being given to white girls. Catie and Katie were athletes on the school's lacrosse team (but totally not jocks), with bobbed brown hair, rosy skin, and sloped noses. They were distinguishable primarily by the unique arches of their carefully plucked eyebrows. Where Catie's bent like boomerangs, Katie's curved like wind-filled paragliders.

Shortly after introductions were made, talk turned to prom.

"Julia wants me to help get Edie a date," Maria informed the girls over the top of her diet shake, sipping at a lipstick-stained straw. "Too bad Miss Picky over here turns up her nose at every guy she meets."

"Not every guy," Edie muttered to her carrots.

"Whatever. So you once made out with some emo nerd at his crappy garage band practice back in Yawn-burbia. I'm sure it was life-changing and he'll write a painfully earnest song about it."

Edie pushed a carrot through a beige puddle of tasteless dressing, wondering how the carrot would look if she "painfully earnestly" jammed it up Maria's nose.

Maria went on to explain with great exasperation about how she'd introduced Edie to several of Rupert's Harvard friends at the garden party but Edie barely spoke a word to any of them, preferring to hide among the hedges and sulk about something.

"I warned you I wasn't good with strangers or parties," Edie said when she couldn't stand the diatribe anymore. "Which is why I don't need to go to prom."

The girls practically leapt on top of her, a rapid-fire chorus of indignation.

"You can't *not* go to prom," Catie said.

"Everyone goes," Katie said.

"It's prom," Taylor pressed. "You know, *prom!* Big deal? High school ritual? Best night of our lives?"

"It's, like, the only reason to go to school." Phoebe slammed down her fork for emphasis.

"Okay, okay!" Edie waved the girls off. "I'll go to prom, but I don't need a date."

As another round of outrage ensued, Edie stopped torturing her carrots, letting them lie beside the dressing as though they were sunning themselves poolside. In truth, she did want to go to prom, but not if the event came with a load of pressure to be some perfect, romantic night. She wasn't Cinderella, Juliet, or the heroine from a sweeping love story. She was just Edie Price: standard-issue introvert, temporarily stunted musician, and best friend betrayer.

"My brother's single," Taylor offered as she scrolled through her phone.

"Great." Edie forced a smile. "What's he like?"

"He's tall, dark, and handsome." Taylor showed Edie his photo. Then her expression clouded. "He also laughs at his own farts, he plays a lot of video games—a *lot* of video games—and he wears too much aftershave. Never mind. Sorry I mentioned it."

"What about Jacob Carver?" Phoebe asked.

"Ew. Bacne." Catie made a face.

"Levi Chu?"

"Taken."

"Ashton Hanson?"

"Gay."

Edie slithered down in her chair as the girls continued to solve the problem she didn't know she had, showing each other photos and comparing assessments on various potential prom dates. She ignored the screens as they flashed past her but when Katie uttered the word *escort,* Edie bolted upright and slapped both palms on the table.

"You know what I need more than a prom date?" she said. "A job."

Maria let out a snort of laughter.

"There's no way Dear Mama will let you work. The neighbors

would stop fawning on her for being, like, humanitarian of the year."

"But I need the money."

"For what? Iron-on patches for those things you call jeans?"

All five girls stared at Edie. They awaited her response while she shifted in her chair, hating the attention she'd hastily drawn to herself.

"Fall tuition," she said quietly.

As everyone went uncomfortably silent, Claire shimmied her way between Maria and Taylor. She set down her lunch tray and pulled up a chair directly opposite Edie.

"Sorry I'm late," she said. "What did I miss?"

"We were talking about prom," Maria said, "till Edie tried to bore us to death by talking about money."

Edie's jaw clenched. Naturally, money was boring to anyone who had it.

"Oh, prom." Claire waved a dismissive hand. "I don't think I'll bother this year. You've seen one, you've seen them all."

The girls all leapt in again.

"Totally."

"Exactly."

"Who needs another stupid dance?"

"I bet the band won't even be good."

Edie gaped, stunned by the girls' instant one-eighty. Maybe she should move to another table. Despite Maria's attempt to open up her social circle, Edie didn't speak Popular Girl. She might learn the language in time, but she doubted full immersion was the optimal route toward fluency.

"Doesn't Sebastian want to go?" Maria asked. "It's his prom too."

Claire shrugged as she picked up her apple and rubbed a spot with a napkin.

"Dancing's not really his thing," she said.

"So what?" Maria asked. "He can still pin a rose on your boob and look hot in a tux for one night. That's, like, boyfriend basics. Even Rupert'll get that part right."

Claire's eyes flickered to Edie's and then settled on her apple again, where her buffing efforts were growing more vigorous.

"I'll ask him about it next weekend." She flashed everyone a smile that looked oddly forced. "If everyone else is going to prom, we should at least make an appearance."

The girls cheered and carried on talking about boys while Edie wondered why Sebastian had asked her to dance at Saturday's party if dancing "wasn't his thing." And why was Claire still scrubbing away at her apple? Surely it was clean by now.

Edie was still trying to analyze the subtext of the conversation when Phoebe elbowed her from the chair to her right.

"Pass me your phone," she whispered.

Edie handed off her cell. Phoebe typed something in and handed it back. Edie expected to see a phone number, a guy's photo, or a dating site. Instead, she was looking at a page with the school's banner at the top and a bulleted list of links.

"What's this?" she asked.

"Scholarships," Phoebe said quietly. "The school counselor assembled a list. We're not all rich, you know, even if some of us don't advertise that fact."

"Wow, thanks." Edie smiled. Maybe she had a place with the popular girls after all.

Chapter Nine

DURING THE TWO WEEKS FOLLOWING HER START AT
Saint Penitent's, Edie researched every scholarship on Phoebe's list.
While still in foster care, she would've qualified for dozens of opportunities. Her grades and test scores were excellent, she had a clear
sense of direction (a music degree with an English minor), and she'd
participated in just enough extracurricular activities to round out her
application materials. Ironically, now that her legal guardians could
afford to send her anywhere (if they chose to, which they didn't), she
was forced to concentrate her efforts on only a few scholarships that
were completely independent of financial need. The most promising
one was worth $3,200, enough to make a solid dent in her remaining
tuition costs for the upcoming year at UMB. She had almost eight
weeks to complete the application and the requirements seemed
simple enough. All she had to do was write fifteen hundred words
on who she'd be if she could be anyone.

On Friday after school, Edie finally found some quiet time to get
started. Bert was at work, Norah was meeting with her philanthropic
society, Maria was shopping, and Julia was getting milkshakes with

Henry (an activity Edie prayed wasn't a euphemism for something that didn't actually involve ice cream). Edie settled herself on one of the curved stone benches that surrounded the fountain in Norah's garden, determined to use the afternoon productively. She opened her notes and made an extensive roster of her favorite writers and musicians. She groaned as she assessed it. Her approach to the essay was so clichéd, she didn't even want to give herself money. Desperate for a more unique subject, Edie looked up some lesser-known female firsts.

> *Elena Lucrezia Cornaro Piscopia (first woman to get a doctorate degree)*
> *Victoria Woodhull (first woman to run for U.S. president)*
> *Junko Tabei (first woman to climb Mount Everest)*
> *My mom (first woman to raise a completely incompetent essay writer)*

She followed these with a few female scientists and social activists, wondering if smart girls had always hated being called smart. Maybe Amelia Earhart was over the moon about it, or at least over the Atlantic Ocean, until of course she wasn't over anything. As Edie continued to expand the list she came to only one concrete conclusion: figuring who she wanted to be was a lot harder than she'd anticipated.

Eventually she gave up on the essay and started writing a song instead, humming a mellow tune as she filled a few pages of her well-worn notebook with lyrics, scribbling away about empty spaces, unconquerable distances, and unbridgeable almosts. Her songs often cycled back to similar images, like variations on a theme, or variations on a girl. Within about an hour, she had a solid draft of a little love song she called "Secondhand Heart." Writing songs was so much easier than writing essays. Edie didn't have to figure out what everything meant before she put words on a page. She didn't have to develop a thesis statement or write in complete sentences. She didn't even have to tell the guy she wrote the song about that he kept slipping into her music.

And speaking of people who entered her thoughts uninvited . . .

Edie reached into her messenger bag and took out the little box Claire had given her at school last week, a "tiny token of affection" from her brother. It was still wrapped in brown paper, unopened. Edie examined it for the hundredth time, wondering why she'd kept it and why she was keeping it now. She figured as long as she didn't open it she hadn't really accepted it, but her curiosity was growing stronger by the day. The box probably held another stupid rose. It might be even empty, just a test of her fortitude. It could also contain jewelry. It was the right sized box. God, she hoped it wasn't jewelry.

Edie was about to slip a fingernail under the tape when Maria's car pulled in to the driveway. Like a guilty child, Edie stashed the box in her bag, vowing to throw it away before she broke down and opened it. She would *not* give Henry another reason to gloat. He had enough of those already. She watched her bag for a few seconds, ensuring the box wasn't burning a hole through the canvas like some sort of satanic talisman. Then she banished all thoughts of Henry (mostly) and jogged over to help Maria unload what appeared to be a very full trunk.

"Is all this for one night?" Edie asked as Maria handed her several shopping bags.

"Unlike you, I require options. And there'll be other parties."

"You can't wear the same thing to two parties?"

"Seriously?" Maria scoffed. "That'd be like bringing Jell-O to a potluck."

"What's wrong with Jell-O?"

"Hello? Like, artificial everything? And everyone knows you only spent a buck on the ingredients. God, Edie, sometimes I forget you grew up in Sticksville."

"You mean Ithaca?" Edie challenged.

"Whatever. I meant it as a compliment."

Edie might've argued the finer points of flattery, but as Maria plunked the last of the bags into her already laden arms, she caught a glimpse of her sneakers peeking out from below her ragged jeans cuffs. She hadn't thought about what she'd wear to Rupert's party tomorrow night. No one had expected fancy dresses or high heels at the parties she and Shonda used to attend in Ithaca. But Edie was in Mansfield now. The expectations were different, and fitting in had proven challenging so far. It would be easier if she put a little more effort into her appearance. Besides, Claire was bringing her boyfriend to the party. It was the world's worst reason to want to look attractive, but Edie couldn't help herself. Was it wrong to want to be wanted? Not necessarily. For her looks instead of her brain? Possibly. By someone else's boyfriend? Definitely. No doubt Henry would have a few smug words to say on the topic, though hopefully there'd be enough pretty girls at the party to occupy his attention elsewhere.

Edie peered into one of the bags.

"Anything in here that might fit me?" she asked.

Maria went still, gaping like a baby bird waiting to be fed.

"Seriously?" She flicked a hand at Edie's outfit. "You're, like, over the homeless tomboy thing?"

Edie nodded. Maria didn't ask twice.

The girls parked themselves on the benches by the fountain, where they unpacked several pairs of fancy shoes, spilling an excess of glittery tissue paper onto the cobbled path like princess guts. Fortunately Maria and Edie were almost the same shoe size. Unfortunately Maria thought anything even remotely stable should be considered a dog's chew toy. Edie soon settled on a pale gray satin pump with three-inch heels and six tiny, labor-intensive buckles on each shoe. It took so long to get out of them she decided she might as well wear them in for a bit. That way she could at least make a blister prevention plan and avoid the dermal grotesquerie of the last party.

"Help!" Edie teetered as she stood. "I need a hand."

"What you *need* is to take off the training wheels." Maria took a step away.

Edie wobbled over to the nearest cupid statue. While she desperately attempted to hold herself upright, Maria pulled a paperback out of Edie's bag.

"Put this on your head. It'll help you stand up straight." She handed off the book and sleeved her forearms in shopping bag handles. "Don't break anything while I'm gone."

"What do you mean, 'gone'?" Edie lost her balance, windmilled her arms, and gripped the cupid by the neck. "You're leaving me alone out here?"

"*Runway Road Kill* is on. I'd much rather watch beautiful people stab each other in the back than watch you stumble around like a baby giraffe. So painful." Maria shot a look of disdain at Edie's unsteady feet. "Work on the shoes. We'll do dresses after dinner." She snatched the last bit of tissue off the rim of the fountain. Then she turned and marched away.

Alone and uncertain about her attempt to assimilate with the natives, Edie made an unsteady circuit around the fountain. She quickly lost patience. Her balance was terrible. She needed a cane or a walker. Lacking either, she at least needed someone to help laugh away her frustration.

She propped herself against the bench and added a post.

Belly flop
noun
1. A percussive failure similar to the jingly dud.
2. An abdominal agitation experienced by overweight twerkers.
3. A poorly executed dive into a body of water or onto a garden path, as demonstrated by yours truly in approximately six seconds.

She waited, staring at the screen, as hopeful as ever. When no reply came, she pocketed her phone, resolving to make the best of both her shoes and her friendlessness. Placing her book on her head, she let go of the bench. She managed six whole steps before the book flew into the bushes.

"Dammit!" She dug through the branches, waist-deep in foliage. "Dammit, dammit, dammit!" She leaned forward, pigeon-toed, elbows out, ass in the air. And this, of course, was when she heard Sebastian's voice.

"Are you beating up that poor fence again?" he called from his driveway.

Edie fluttered a wave, doubtful she could credibly feign deafness or effectively impersonate a cherub statue.

"This time I'm annihilating the azaleas. Next step: pummeling the petunias." She finally dislodged the book. As she turned toward Sebastian, she brushed greenery from her clothes and glared at the cupids in the corners of the courtyard, marveling at their inept guidance of her love life. Why had they let her shoe-practice near his side of the garden, where all that divided her from Sebastian was a hedgerow, a gravel path, a picket fence, and a lexicon's worth of unspoken feelings?

"What are you doing?" he asked with a good-humored chuckle.

"Girl-ifying. It's a trial and error thing. Mostly error." She placed the book on her head and baby-giraffed her way toward him. "Maria swears I'll get used to wearing heels, but I don't know, and Charlotte Brontë would be horrified at how I'm using her work."

"*Jane Eyre?*"

"*Villette.*"

"What's it about?"

"It's about six ounces."

Sebastian laughed in earnest, making the pesky butterflies in Edie's stomach flutter as she stumbled toward the fence and edged her way past the hedgerows. She caught a toe on a flagstone, nearly belly-flopping onto the gravel path, as anticipated.

"Seven point eight from the American judge." He mimed holding up a placard.

"What do I have to do to get the full ten?"

"Backflip?"

"You first."

"Sorry. I'm a ground-under-my-feet kinda guy." Sebastian ran a hand through his hair as a little nervous laughter escaped. "If Tom were here he'd try it. He's always been the fun one."

Edie parked herself by the fence and waited while his expression settled.

"Why do you always do that?" she asked.

"Do what?"

"Compare yourself to someone you're not."

He shifted. He shuffled. He shrugged.

"I don't know," he said at last. "Doesn't everyone?"

Edie glanced at her feet. She felt ashamed of herself. Then she felt ashamed for being ashamed. They were just shoes. She wasn't trying to be Claire any more than Sebastian was trying to be Tom. Yet there they stood, the two of them, both struggling to escape someone else's shadow and taking the least effective means possible.

Edie was about to apologize when Sebastian patted the top of the fence.

"Want to climb over?" He tipped his chin toward his driveway. "Pavement has to be easier than all those rocky garden paths. And you can lean on my shoulder."

Edie hesitated. She was pretty sure she couldn't lean on his shoulder without touching him, and she was dead certain touching him would make her want to do a lot of other things that were totally off-limits. She'd only seen him for a few neighbor-to-neighbor chats over the past couple weeks, but he'd played a key role in some seriously steamy dreams that were still tattooed on her brain.

"What's the matter?" he teased. "Something wrong with my shoulder?"

"Not exactly." She carefully assessed his shoulder through his thin, gray T-shirt. He wasn't all buffed up like athletes or underwear models. He was a bit gangly, as though he hadn't been hinged perfectly so his joints were too loose, leaving his arms and legs to swing more freely than most. He wasn't clumsy or awkward. He was just . . . beautiful.

"Fine," he said. "Have it your way."

Next thing Edie knew, Sebastian was hauling himself over the fence and leaping down by her side. As she laughed at his less-than-graceful dismount, he steadied himself and held out an elbow. Edie eyed it like forbidden fruit.

"Shall we?" he asked, the same way he'd asked her to dance, calling up memories she'd been trying not to obsess about, wondering if he'd felt anything at all when he held her close as the music swelled and the stars came out.

That was just a dance, she told herself. *This is just a walk.*

"Okay," she said. "But I'm not sure who's supporting whom."

"Interesting." He gave her a little nudge. "I like the sound of that."

Edie took Sebastian's arm and the two of them set off down the gravel path. Every few seconds, Edie wobbled. Just as often, Sebastian fake-wobbled, sending them both into little fits of laughter. His cheerful company was exactly what Edie'd been craving when she strapped on the shoes. As they reached the benches near the fountain, Edie set her book by her bag. She didn't need it, not when she had Sebastian's arm to rely on.

Her eye caught on the little box where it was peeking out from her bag. Maria must've jostled it while she was extracting the book. Either that or Henry's demonic powers were deliberately invading her perfectly wonderful stroll with Sebastian, forcing her to think about the last person in the world she wanted on her mind in that moment.

"So, what's that really about?" Sebastian asked.

Edie prickled with anxiety as her mind raced for an explanation that wasn't there. Then she realized Sebastian meant the book, not the box. She shut Henry out of her thoughts yet again and locked her eyes on the novel. A light breeze fanned the dog-eared pages, many of them marked with blue ink where Edie'd underlined her favorite phrases and sentences, words she swore Charlotte Brontë had written just for her.

"A woman finding her voice," Edie said. "And unrequited love."

"She doesn't get the guy?"

"He's in love with someone else." Edie forced a lighthearted tone as they set off toward the fence again, leaving both book and box behind. "Someone prettier and more confident." She stumbled, gripping Sebastian's arm more tightly. When he pulled his arm against his side, she considered stumbling again. "The story's not totally tragic, though. There's a second guy, one who loves her back."

"So it has a happy ending?"

"It has a surprise ending. I don't want to spoil it for you."

Sebastian nodded, Edie teetered, and they shared one of those comfortable silences they were so good at. As they turned onto the path that paralleled the fence, Edie began to wonder how anyone wore heels in gravel without something solid to hold on to. In fact, how did anyone do anything without something to hold on to? Or someone? Without Shonda, Edie wasn't part of an *us* anymore. She was only a *me*. The feeling was wearing on her, even though Maria's friends were nice and Julia was fun to be around sometimes. No one in Mansfield shared Edie's interests, her goals, her anxieties. No one except—

"Got a quote for me?" Sebastian asked. "Something from your friend Charlotte? The latest addition to your collection?"

Edie adjusted her hold on his arm as she thought through all the beautiful words she'd read and reread, elegant and gloriously relatable phrases about hope, desire, and the endless struggle to reconcile oneself with the unfairness of the world.

"'If life be a war, it seemed my destiny to conduct it single-handed.'"

"Damn." He shook his head, incredulous. "That's impressive."

"Not weird?"

"A little weird, but still impressive." Sebastian smiled. His hint of flattery painted another blush on her cheeks. He cupped a hand over hers where it wrapped his elbow. His gesture was simple but it felt surprisingly intimate, especially when it dusted his cheeks with pink as well. The pair walked on, each sneaking glances at the other, but Sebastian's attention was soon drawn to something over her shoulder. "Hey, look at that." He stopped and peeled back a thin strip of white paint near the top of a picket, revealing a flash of bright yellow.

Edie's lingering bout of loneliness fell away, replaced by a little surge of joy.

"Our yellow brick road." She released Sebastian's arm. As she backed up to scan the fence, she pictured two seven-year-old kids covered in paint splatters, chalk dust, and marker stains, proudly finishing a yellow line that snaked all the way from the back of the property to the edge of the garden, passing Munchkin Country, the Scarecrow's cornfield, the Tin Man's orchard, the poppies.

"My dad thought our Oz was a masterpiece," Sebastian said.

"My mom laughed her ass off at our flying monkeys." Edie's throat tightened. "But she loved our Emerald City."

"I couldn't believe the way you remembered all the details from the book." He peeled away another white sliver, creating a yellow spot the size of his thumb. "I thought you were the smartest girl in the whole world."

Edie braced herself against the hedge, unsure how to respond.

Sebastian might've admired her at age seven, and even at ten, but what did he think of her now?

"How many coats did your grandma make us paint over everything?" he asked.

"Three, I think. Four wherever she could still see the glitter."

Sebastian shoved his hands into his pockets and studied the fence. His face twitched the way it always did when he was deep in thought.

"I miss hanging out and making up worlds with you," he said, "back when my dad would hand us paintbrushes and say, 'Have at it.' When no one read off postgraduate employment statistics over dinner or emailed me comparative salary charts." His jaw tensed as his shoulders inched higher. "Sometimes I worry I'll spend my whole life doing what other people expect me to do, not what I want to do. You ever feel that way?"

Edie squinted at him. Was he still talking about his parents or was he asking about other "other people"? He was close enough for her to see the gray speckles in his pale blue eyes, but she couldn't for the life of her make out what lay behind them.

"I think it's usually worth making your own choices," she said. As his shoulders relaxed and his expression softened, she flashed back to the moment when a car door slammed and Shonda ran across the parking lot. Alone. "As long as they don't hurt anyone," she added quickly.

He backed against a nearby elm tree, suddenly solemn, slipping his hands out of his pockets and jamming them in again, as if whatever indecision he was wrestling with had trickled to his fingertips.

"And if there's no way to avoid hurting someone?" he asked.

"I don't know." Edie considered the matter, unsure why he was treating her like some sort of expert. "Hide in your room, watch funny cat videos, and hope things sort themselves out?" She searched for his smile. She didn't find it. "Sorry. Bad plan. I know from experience." She joined him by the tree, steadying herself on the fence, wondering why he was using a tree and she was using a picket if they were supposed to be supporting each other. "Honestly? I guess you just weigh the options and do the best you can. If you mess things up, you try to mess them up a little less the next time."

"There you go, being all smart again," he said as his smile finally emerged.

"It's only fair while you're being all nice."

"Am I nice?" he asked. "Sometimes I wonder."

They shared another silence, this one a little less comfortable. The tree cast shifting shadows and sunlight across Sebastian's dimpled cheeks as if it were toying with his features and teasing out his smile. A breeze ruffled his hair the way Edie's fingers might if she reached forward and drew him toward her. His lips would meet hers. His hands would slide up her shirt, molding to her shoulder blades while he held her against him. She'd press herself even closer. The collar of her shirt would slip off her shoulder, peeled away by gentle fingers as Sebastian's cheek brushed hers and his lips tickled her skin in that little spot where her pulse was pounding, pushing, hammering away and— Wait, was that a hickey on his neck?

Edie's gathering butterflies instantly grounded themselves. Right. Sebastian had a girlfriend. No matter how sweetly he smiled, how eagerly he leapt over fences, how often he shared emotional truths with the sort of intimacy Edie rarely felt with anyone, or how quickly her mind wandered to places it shouldn't whenever he was close by, he only thought of her as a friend. She should only be thinking of him as a friend.

"I think I'm good with the shoes," she blurted.

"You sure?" Sebastian stepped forward. "We could do one more lap."

Edie staggered backwards.

"Can't." She pointed over her shoulder, floundering for an excuse to bolt. "There's a . . . thing . . . in the thing, that I need to do the"—she circled a hand—"with."

"Sounds urgent," he teased through a chuckle. "See you at Rupert's party?"

Edie nodded and edged toward the fountain, narrowly avoiding a collision with the nearest hedgerow. Sebastian clambered over the fence, narrowly avoiding a full face-plant onto his driveway. They both scrambled to regain their composure. Poorly.

"Leave some space in that collection of yours," he called as he jogged away. "I'll bring you a quote to add to it tomorrow. I have some catching up to do."

"Sebastian, I—"

"Gotta go! There's a thing in the thing."

Edie trailed his departure, pressing a hand against her gut where a single butterfly of anticipation flapped its stubborn little wings, determined to fly.

Chapter Ten

RUPERT'S PARENTS' HOUSE QUICKLY FILLED WITH girls in tight dresses and guys in tight jeans. The electronic dance music began to throb from the basement. The air grew thick with the smell of cold pizza and spilled beer, even though caviar and Cabernet might've fit better with the formal décor. Maria proudly played hostess, a mirror image of her mother two weeks earlier. Julia followed Henry around while trying ineffectively to be subtle about it. Claire barnacled herself to Sebastian and chatted cheerfully with virtually everyone, displaying an enviable ability to charm a room. Henry flirted with too many girls to count, exchanging a few carefully selected Shakespeare lines for a blush, a sigh, and eventually a phone number. Through it all, Edie parked herself against walls, quietly observing everyone despite Maria's emphatic instructions to have fun, or at least pretend to have fun. It was always hard to tell at a party who was doing which.

Two hours after arriving, Edie scrounged together a vodka-cranberry and settled herself in the doorway between the kitchen and living room, where she was within view of the tall blond guy who'd promised her a quote but hadn't yet delivered one. As she tried to catch his eye across the crowded room, a group of Rupert's friends pushed past her on their way into the kitchen, jostling her drink, stepping on her toes, and making her wish she'd worn a suit of armor instead of three-inch heels and a flimsy chiffon dress Maria had loaned her. She felt even more underdressed when Henry passed through from the kitchen and ran his eyes over the length of her body.

"Damn, you look good in blue." He sipped something that smelled like barbecue-flavored nail polish remover.

"And you'd look spectacular in vodka-cranberry." She raised her cup and tilted it toward him. "We could coin a new cocktail: the pink bastard."

While Henry laughed, Edie's eyes crept toward Sebastian again. His arm circled Claire's waist. Her head rested on his shoulder. Her hand lay against his chest. Envy rippled across Edie's skin like a thousand tiny pinpricks, followed swiftly by the dull ache of shame. She shouldn't have gotten all dolled up tonight. What had she been thinking? She could ride in on a star-spangled elephant, juggling live toads, and belting out the annoying jingle from the Burger Barn ads. Sebastian's attention would stay glued to his girlfriend, and rightly so. Considering how often Edie'd been described as smart, she was making some really dumb choices lately.

"It'll never make you happy," Henry reminded her.

"No one asked you."

"Doesn't mean it's not true."

Edie shot him a look of pure loathing, but he didn't take the hint. Instead he leaned against the nearby bookshelves and lazily swirled his drink.

"Did you like my present?" he asked as if already certain of her answer.

"I didn't open it. I threw it away."

He studied her for a moment, slyly smirking.

"No, you didn't."

"How do you know?"

"I play a lot of poker. I know a bluff when I see it." He continued watching her with his trademark air of arrogance and amusement.

Edie tried not to squirm, frustrated she couldn't manage even the simplest lie. The box was in her bedside table, unopened but not yet discarded. It was her private battle with temptation, one she was determined to win. Eventually.

"I'm really not interested," she reiterated for the umpteenth time.

"Doesn't mean you're not curious." Henry reached behind her ear, produced a tiny white rose, and held it out.

"Doesn't mean I'm anything other than not interested." Edie took the rose and dropped it into his drink. Then she turned to depart for a less Crawford-infested locale.

She'd barely stepped forward when Julia emerged from the throng in the kitchen. Her eyes were glassy. Her breath reeked of fruity wine spritzers. An empty plastic cup dangled from her fingers.

"Edie! Henry! Hi!" she sputtered as she stumbled into the living room.

Henry leapt forward to prevent her fall. Julia let her cup drop as she melted against his chest. He shrugged as if pretty girls fell into his arms all the time and there was nothing he could do about it.

"I love you," Julia said. "And I need to pee."

"Dare you to find the Shakespeare quote to fit that one," Edie challenged.

"Think I'll just help her to the bathroom." In one swift movement, Henry swept the gangly girl into his arms, tucking her knees over his elbow as she draped her arms around his neck.

Edie glowered, suspecting Henry had more than help on his mind.

"Don't worry," he assured her. "I'm strictly transportation."

"I find that hard to believe. Unless you have a broad definition of transportation."

"Transportation, maybe, but I have a very clear definition of consent." Henry leaned close to Edie and lowered his voice. "Besides, there's a ticking time bomb I need to help detonate." He nodded toward Maria and Rupert where they stood halfway across the living room, him babbling cheerfully, her keeping a close eye on Henry. "Oh, wait. I forgot. 'They have plans.'"

"You're malignant." Edie stepped away.

"You're wonderful." Julia burrowed into his neck.

With a broad grin and a mischievous wink at Edie, Henry set off toward the bathroom with Julia still wrapped around him. Not trusting him with either cousin, Edie scoured the party until she found one of Julia's friends to play chaperone. She planted the girl outside the bathroom with strict instructions to be on the lookout for a hot guy with tight clothes and loose morals. Then she confirmed that Maria was safely parked next to Rupert. They were showing photos of their prospective summer house to some friends, not a time bomb in sight. Meanwhile, Henry had been swept into a group of college girls who were practically leaping on top of each other for a chance to entertain him.

Crises at least temporarily averted, Edie attempted to approach Sebastian and Claire for the hundredth time that night. Things didn't have to be weird between the three of them. They were all friends. Edie'd simply merge in with whatever discussion they were having. No big deal. She was halfway across the living room when Sebastian leaned down to nuzzle Claire's nose. Edie stopped short. Okay. Things were weird. She instantly initiated plan B: escape from the party. She'd spent enough time watching Sebastian give his smile to someone else and Henry give his smile to everyone else. Julia was drunk. Maria was occupied. The rest of the Saint Pen's girls were scattered through the house with their classmates and dates. If Edie was going to be lonely, she'd rather be alone.

She pushed her way through the crowd and stepped onto the back patio, filling her lungs with warm night air. A few of Rupert's friends were smoking in the corner and a couple was making out on the steps that led down to the yard, but a circle of empty chairs beckoned at the far end of the lawn. She followed a winding brick path toward what turned out to be an empty fire pit. There she folded herself into a wicker rocking chair and added a post to her lexicon.

Vanish

verb

1. Recede from view, become nothing.
2. Like car-ish, but bigger.
3. Act of disappearance you crave whenever you don't fit in, but you're not sure how to reconcile the idea of wanting to become nothing with the reality of wanting to become something. Or someone.

Edie stared at the screen, willing it to light up with a reply.

Her screen faded to black, as unresponsive as always.

She leaned back and watched the stars for several minutes. They were clear here, twenty miles from the center of Mansfield. She located the Big Dipper, Orion, the Seven Sisters, and a few constellations she invented herself, pictures and stories made of speckled light: a bird, a hand, a series of music notes, maybe even the face of her mom.

Who would you be if you could be anyone? she thought as she searched the sky for inspiration. *Cassiopeia? No, too vain. Andromeda? Too helpless. A nameless girl made entirely of stars and sky? Possibly.*

Edie smiled. She'd felt so small in Norah's house, so clumsily large at school, and so insignificant in Rupert's, but out here in all this space, for the first time since she'd reached Mansfield, she felt exactly the right size.

Chapter Eleven

♥

EDIE SNAPPED AWAKE IN THE WICKER CHAIR. HER
head was canted back at an awkward angle, her back was arched,
and her hands were pressed between her thighs. She glanced around,
frantic, jerking her head like a meerkat scanning the tundra. She was
sitting alone in Rupert's backyard while the party continued inside
and around the house, too far away for witnesses. Thank god.

Her dream had unfolded slowly, gently, almost like a ritual.
Sebastian held her and kissed her neck, her back, her stomach . . .
lower than her stomach. His hands ran down the sides of her body,
tracing her rib cage the way he'd traced the top of the picket fence,
his fingers exploring every little ridge and ripple, lingering like he
was committing her entire body to memory. His touch didn't quite
tickle but it did make her twitch, unexpected and electric. More
important, he looked at her in a way she'd always wanted to be
looked at: like he really saw her and he was happy with what he
saw. The whole experience was breathlessly beautiful, except that
it happened at Disneyland for some reason, probably because her
cousins' Cinderella obsession had recently resurfaced, thanks to a
pair of shiny shoes.

As the warm night air blew across the sweat on Edie's neck and shoulders, sending a not entirely unpleasant shiver down her spine, she came to three conclusions:

1. *Liking a guy was way more complicated at seventeen than when she was ten and expressed her interest by leaving little presents in the tree branches.*
2. *If she didn't at least kiss someone by graduation she might overheat in her sleep and burn down her bedroom.*
3. *Nothing ruined a perfectly good sex scene like the arrival of a creepy theme park mascot, unless you were into that kind of thing.*

The vividness of Edie's dream soon receded as she glazed over at the night sky and tried to reclaim the just-the-right-size feeling she'd had before falling asleep.

"'Oh, bright star,'" she recited absently. "'Would I were as steadfast as thou art.'"

"Keats," said a low but gentle voice. "Even I know that one."

Edie spun toward the voice. Sebastian stood beside her, his smile mirroring the crescent moon, his head haloed by starlight, his loose linen clothes rippling in the breeze.

"I didn't mean to sneak up on you." He pulled out a chair and sat down. "I have a bad habit of doing that."

Edie scanned the yard, searching for Claire, but Sebastian was alone. She was glad they'd finally have a chance to talk, but she wasn't sure an intimate conversation was the best idea while she still felt the imprint of his hands on her skin. Could he tell? He could totally tell. Was there such a thing as post-sex-dream face? Oh, god, of course there was. It probably even had an emoji and a hashtag.

"How are the shoes?" he asked.

"They're having a blast. They love a good party."

He smiled, which meant she blushed, grateful for the darkness.

"I mean, how are *you* doing in the shoes?"

"Actually, I'm getting used to them, which I feel kinda weird about." She rotated an ankle, sending a ripple of moonlight across the buckles. "Today: cozy in heels. Tomorrow: mani-pedis with the Ladies Who Lunch Club."

He leaned back, kicked out his long legs, and balanced one foot atop the other.

"Don't worry," he said. "You're still you, even in the fancy shoes."

"Stop being nice."

"Stop being smart."

He smiled again but Edie couldn't quite smile back. His teasing tone hadn't changed since they were kids, but the implications behind it were different now. She turned toward the house where silhouettes of people chatting, dancing, and making out filled each illuminated window, casting their shifting shadows onto the lawn like a page from a comic book. Edie was reluctant to return to the throng but she knew she shouldn't sit there alone with Sebastian, amassing more almosts, feeding her crush. She started to stand while still forming a departure excuse that didn't involve the word *thing*.

"I brought you a quote," Sebastian said. "As promised."

Edie sat back down, her resolve yanked out from under her in an instant. She seriously had to work on that.

"It took me a while to find something you might not have in your collection, and to memorize it." Sebastian tipped his head back and gazed up at the sky. His words came out softly, sweetly, the way his kisses always felt in Edie's dreams. "A quote about quotes. 'I envy my words once spoken, for they're closer to your ear, closer to your heart than I am. They live, inked in your memory, when I'm absent. They tiptoe through your dreams when you sleep, and if you speak my words, they'll lie more softly still upon your lips, where I have yet to dwell. My words go where I cannot and I'll never forgive them their trespasses.'"

Edie's last shred of willpower completely vanished as images of trespassing lips swam across her brain.

"Two for three," she said, full of wants that had no words at all. "Who said that?"

"I'm not telling. I'm simply going to enjoy the fact that I gave you something you didn't find on your own." A triumphant smile crept across his face, still turned to the sky.

"It should be a song," Edie said, already hearing a tune form. "It sounds like lyrics, but so do most things. To me, anyway. Do other people think in lyrics or do most people think in prose?"

"It probably depends on your medium." He rolled his head toward her. "Maybe mathematicians think in numbers and artists think in colors. Maybe Picasso spent an entire day thinking, *Blue, pink, brown, eyeball, ochre, ear.*"

Edie laughed as her eyes trailed to the spot where Sebastian's hand gently gripped his armrest, inches from hers, not unlike the "hell of a held hand" she'd mentioned from *The Age of Innocence.* Two sets of fingers that slowly laced together, finding what connection they could in the limited time available, a moment so painfully brief but so ecstatically electric, bursting through all the off-limits things. A quickening of breath, an exploration of skin. Fingers, palms, wrists. That was it, but that was everything.

"What do writers think in?" she asked.

"I don't know yet. Coffee shops, apparently."

As they exchanged a smile, she inched her hand closer to his, convinced he wouldn't have shared a quote about dwelling on lips unless he'd at least thought about kissing her. Okay, so he had a girlfriend, and, yes, Edie really wanted to prove she'd learned something from what she did to Shonda, but this was different. She had real feelings for Sebastian and he obviously felt *something* for her. Besides, his hand was *right there.* She could simply brush his pinky with hers. If he flinched away she could say it was an accident and never touch him again, ever, but if he didn't flinch away—

A shadow fell over their hands, one that smelled like expensive perfume and cheap buzzkill.

"Hey, handsome." Claire stepped up behind his chair. "Oh, Edie! I didn't see you there. You're so quiet sometimes, it's easy to overlook you. I'll try not to do that again."

"I'll try to be less overlook-able," Edie muttered. "Save you the trouble."

Claire's eyes narrowed, barely, but enough to make Edie acutely aware that her impulsive response might've turned an already strained friendship into an actual rivalry, one she had no chance of winning. She felt ashamed of herself. What was she doing out here, talking about dwelling on lips and thinking about holding hands? Claire and Sebastian were happy together. Edie needed to leave him alone before she ruined not just one friendship but two.

While she tried to decide if bolting would make her private convo with Sebastian seem unnecessarily suspicious, Claire leaned against his chair and draped an arm around his shoulders, looking all sexy with her Wonder Woman hair, her sparkly little mini-dress, and her impossibly long legs, crossed at the ankle above a pair of heels Edie could only imagine wearing while lying down.

"What were you two talking about?" Claire asked. "Out here? All alone? Under the stars?"

Edie said, "Coffee shops," as Sebastian said, "Picasso."

"Interesting." Claire smoothed a wrinkle in his shirt. "Did I miss anything especially illuminating?"

"Not especially." Sebastian linked his hand through hers and smiled up at her sweetly, but his expression twitched as if part of his brain was working through complex equations or conjugating irregular verbs.

"Actually, we were just looking at the stars," Edie offered.

Claire chuckled softly.

"Don't tell Henry you're a stargazer. He'll start rattling off poetry about velvet nights and spangled skies."

"Your brother likes poetry?" Sebastian darted a glance at Edie.

"My brother likes anything he can use on girls. Why else would anyone read all those stuffy old writers, except to pass AP English?"

Sebastian shifted his focus to his armrest, where his fingers drummed away, agitated. Edie tried to catch his eye but he wouldn't look up. Why wasn't he saying anything? He loved all those "stuffy old writers." When the silence went on too long to bear, she leapt in.

"Sebastian's going to be a—"

"Lawyer." He shut her down with a look.

"And a damned good one." Claire blinked down at him, confused. "But what does that have to do with anything?"

"It doesn't." Sebastian drew Claire into his lap and quickly diverted the topic by pointing out patterns in the sky, playing into Edie's suggestion that they'd simply been stargazing.

Edie almost fell out of her chair as the truth smacked her sideways. Yesterday when Sebastian said he was worried about fulfilling everyone else's expectations instead of his own, he wasn't just talking about his parents. He was talking about Claire, too. Holy crap. Maybe Claire and Sebastian weren't that happy. For two people who always had their hands all over each other, they clearly had some issues. Edie had no idea how much Sebastian hid from Claire, or what motivated him to hide anything at all, but she knew one thing for certain: she needed to let them sort it out for themselves.

"I should go check on Julia," she announced as she stood. "She over-spritzered herself tonight."

"No kidding." Claire chuckled again. "Last time I saw her she was practically molesting Henry."

"I'm sure Henry can take care of himself."

"Yes, but he'd be much happier if you took care of him." Claire smiled archly.

Edie bit back a diatribe on all the ways she'd really like to take care of Henry, most of them involving sharp objects, toxic substances, or one-way tickets out of Mansfield. She was searching for a way to condense all that into what she hoped would come out as a brilliantly cutting retort when she noticed Sebastian eyeing her intently, as if he was hanging on her response. He really needed to stop doing that. She could almost interpret his interest as, well, interest.

"You need a ride later?" he asked.

Edie hesitated, still drawn in by any hint that he wanted to be near her. She quickly shook off the thought. He lived next door. He was only being polite. He was cradling his girlfriend in his lap, for god's sake. One hand was on her bare thigh. The other was tucked under her shoulder strap. She was rotating her body toward him with a bent knee creeping up his chest. They were seconds away from stripping each other naked and going at it, right there in the goddamn chair.

"I'll, um, get one of Maria's friends to drive me," Edie stammered as she stepped away. Her heel slipped off the side of the brick path, making her wobble and undercutting her attempt to make a smooth getaway. "You guys have fun."

"Don't worry. We will." Claire leaned toward Sebastian with a hand on either side of his face.

Just before their lips met, Edie turned and fled.

Chapter Twelve

♥

EDIE CROUCHED AT THE SIDE OF RUPERT'S HOUSE, her back pressed against the rough wood siding, her shoes full of bark bits. She deep-breathed through her frustration while pep-talking herself into returning to the party. She hated that she was so upset—or in Norah's words, "being temperamental"—but she had to feel what she had to feel. There was no way around it. Thinking Sebastian was dating the perfect girl had been hard enough. Knowing he chose to be with someone he had to hide his goals and interests from? Way worse. Edie should've steered clear of him from the moment she found out he was in a relationship. Better yet, she should've followed her mom's advice about never falling in love in the first place. But was that possible? What if love wasn't always a choice? What if it just happened? Like chickenpox, mildew, or Wednesday?

Edie was still cycling through a thousand questions when Henry, Maria, and Rupert exited the house onto the back patio a few yards to Edie's right. Edie edged her way behind a rhododendron, anxious to avoid Maria's scolding about how she was hiding from the party instead of joining in on all the fun everyone kept talking about but didn't always seem to be having.

Through a network of leaves, Edie watched as Maria perched sidesaddle on the balustrade while Henry and Rupert settled themselves on either side of her.

"I told you you could see a million stars out here," Maria said.

"And I'm not disappointed in the view." Henry locked his eyes on Maria.

"The view's better farther from the city," Rupert babbled cheerfully, "not that we're in the city but we could be farther, or not as far, but you know what I mean."

"Yes, sweetheart," Maria cooed. "We know what you mean."

"The city lights block the stars, which are also lights, I guess, though not like the lights on the houses, or like the streetlights, but maybe brighter, but—"

"I'm a bit chilly." Maria rubbed her bare arms. "Rupert, will you please fetch my coat? It's in the pile on the bed."

"You bet. Can't have my girl getting goose bumps." He turned to go. Then he turned back again. "What does it look like? Your coat, of course. I know what a goose bump is."

"It's black. With a zipper. You can't miss it."

"I'm on it. Back in a jiff." He gave her a quick peck on the lips and headed inside.

Edie remembered the mountain of outerwear. Black? With a zipper? That description fit at least twenty coats. Poor Rupert would be digging half the night trying to figure out which one was Maria's.

Unwilling to play witness to what might happen in Rupert's absence, Edie started to climb out from the bushes. Her skirt tangled around a branch and stuck her in place. As she wrestled with it, the scene to her right continued.

"Let's take a closer look at those goose bumps," Henry said.

"We're supposed to be stargazing," Maria admonished.

"Do you always do what you're supposed to?"

"Seldom, if ever."

"Then can I map the stars on your skin?"

"You can and you should."

"Here's that bright one at the end of the Big Dipper."

"Ooh, I like that star."

"See that strain of Seven Sisters? One."

"Mmm."

"Two and three."

A giggle.

"Four."

A sigh.

"Five."

"Yes."

"Six."

"Hello, six."

"And seven, heavenly seven."

Muffled moaning, eventually broken by Maria's throaty voice.

"Let's go find out where number eight is."

They ran off the patio and into the night as Edie finally yanked her dress free, teetering in her heels and leaving a chunk of fairy-like blue chiffon in the claws of the evil rhododendron beast. God-damned dress, goddamned shoes, and goddamned shrubbery! Next weekend she was going to lounge around in her jeans and sneakers while feeding her funny cat video addiction all day, alone, no matter how much her cousins tried to persuade her to attend another stupid party.

She trudged up the half-dozen steps to the patio, picking at the pulled threads in her skirt and praying she didn't look like she'd just wrestled with a bush and lost. As she ducked under a low string of lanterns, Julia appeared in the doorway, panting, frazzled, and dangling a shoe from each hand.

"Edie! Hi! Did you see where Henry went?"

Edie froze, failing as always to conjure a credible lie under duress.

"That way, I think." She gestured out into the yard. The whole yard.

"Was he alone?"

"Well . . ."

Julia's face went as red and puffy as a lobster balloon.

"I hate you, Maria Vernon!" She flung a shoe into the yard. "I hate you, Henry Crawford!" Her other shoe went flying, tumbling across the brick path, pinging against a lantern, and rolling into a bed of tulips. "Maria already has a boyfriend. It's not fair."

"I know," Edie said, at a loss for more comforting words.

"Why does he like her more than me?"

"Henry likes attention. Maria's giving it to him. That's all."

"I give him attention too." Julia slumped onto the steps and began to sputter.

Edie sat down beside her and drew her into an embrace, offering warmth and affection where words were useless. Crushes couldn't be talked away. Julia's infatuation would have to run its course, as would her own. Until then, at least the girls had each other, which felt pretty good, actually.

They were still sitting there when Rupert exited the house carrying an armload of black coats. Sleeves and hoods poked out all directions. Belts and drawstrings dangled toward his toes, causing him to stumble.

"I couldn't tell which one was yours, so I brought anything that . . ." He trailed off. He glanced around. His posture drooped. His expression melted into something like heartbreak. "They're not here, are they?"

"No," Edie confessed. "They're not."

Rupert dropped the coats, letting them scatter on the porch. He plopped down next to Edie, propped his elbows on his thighs, and dropped his head into his hands, the picture of dejection.

"I won't bother going after them. Not if they want to be alone." He brushed cigarette ash off the step with the side of his shoe. "I knew she was too good for me."

"No one's too good for anyone," Edie said. "Sometimes we just like people who don't like us the same way."

"'We?'" He blinked at her. "You mean you, too?"

Edie flicked at her torn skirt, notably silent.

"She's in love with Sebastian," Julia interjected.

Edie started, shocked to hear the words aloud, and from Julia.

"We're just friends," she said.

"Right. And I can wear purple."

"You *can* wear purple."

"No, I can't. I'm not a winter." Julia held up a fistful of her auburn hair as if it proved her point. "Anyway, I've seen the way you look at him."

Edie cringed. She didn't think anyone had noticed. Anyone except Henry, of course, and, okay, probably everyone but Sebastian. Lacking further rebuttal and knowing she was in good company, she turned to Rupert and mustered a sympathetic smile.

"Yeah," she conceded. "Me too."

"Me three." Julia blew her nose into her cardigan.

"We're quite a trio," Rupert noted, markedly stutter-free. "Sitting here with all these coats and all these stars but feeling like we've been left in the cold and in the dark."

Julia sniffled. Rupert sighed. Edie tried to stop thinking about Sebastian's eyes, Sebastian's hands, and Sebastian's quote. *I envy my words once spoken.*

"I do love her," Rupert said.

"I know," Edie assured him.

Another sniffle. Another sigh.

For they're closer to your ear, closer to your heart than I am.

"I wish the Crawfords would move out of Mansfield," Julia said. "Things would be so much better without them."

"There," Edie said, "I completely agree with you."

Chapter Thirteen

EDIE SAT CROSS-LEGGED ON HER BED, BAREFOOT
and dressed in her comfiest clothes. She scribbled lyrics into her
notebook while reeling from the events of the party and wondering if everyone had gone home yet. Julia was nestled in her own
bed, hopefully sound asleep, but when they'd left Rupert's about an
hour ago, Maria and Henry were still exploring the links between
astronomy and anatomy while Claire and Sebastian were off doing
their own version of stargazing, which probably involved very few
stars and very little gazing.

Edie kept trying to get the image of the two of them out of her
head, but it refused to vanish. It sat there like granite, cold, heavy,
and hard, a monument to her stupidity. She thought back to her old
coping strategy. *Think it. Don't say it.* It seemed like such a simple,
straightforward philosophy, and it'd saved her from some impulsive
outbursts with both Norah and Maria, but she was starting to wonder if sometimes her thoughts were just as problematic as her words.
After all, thoughts led to actions, such as trying to attract the attention of someone who wasn't available, and accepting that attention
when it was offered, even if it would ruin a friendship.

Still uncertain how to fully explain her choices to herself, let alone to Shonda, Edie turned her attention back to her songbook, hearing a melody form as she wrote.

> *I dwell in Blue. Deep, dark, almost indiscernible blue.*
> *The kind of blue that hides in a shadow, the way I hide.*
> *The center of the sea as it swallows a storm,*
> *The way I am sometimes swallowed.*
> *The underside of a thundercloud waiting to burst,*
> *The way I wait.*
> *The way, one day, I too will burst.*
> *If I stay here too long in Blue.*

With a heavy sigh, Edie opened the drawer in her nightstand and slipped her notebook inside. Her eye caught on Henry's box, sitting there in its brown paper packaging, daring her to resist it. After what she witnessed tonight, resistance was no longer an issue. She didn't want anything from Henry. His moral compass was set on the South Pole. His ego was the size of the *Titanic*. He was more presumptuous than . . . something really presumptuous she couldn't think of in that moment.

Edie snatched up the box, marched over to the dressing table, and pitched it into the nearby bin. She sat on the bed. She returned to the waste bin. She sat on the bed again. She looked to her mom's photo, silently seeking advice. What was worse: pining after a guy who preferred someone else or accepting the attention of a guy who was kind of an asshole? Or doing both?

Edie's mom simply smiled, leaving Edie to make her own choices, alone.

Tired of torturing herself, Edie clambered up and retrieved the box. She tore open the packaging and looked inside. She sank against the dressing table. Henry hadn't given her jewelry. He'd given her guitar strings. The gift was thoughtful, personal, and sort of perfect, actually. Crap.

As she carried the box over to the bed, she heard a soft knock on her door.

"Edie?" Maria whispered through the door. "Can I come in?"

Edie froze. If she was really quiet, maybe Maria would go away. It was late, Edie's brain was spinning, and the last thing she wanted was a play-by-play of Maria's tête-à-tête.

"I can see your light on," Maria insisted.

Edie rolled her eyes at her mom's portrait. Her mom smiled back, as encouraging as ever. *Family's family*, she could hear her mom saying. *You have to love them, but you don't have to like them.* Resigned to the inevitable, Edie slipped Henry's gift into the drawer and opened her bedroom door.

"Thank god you're awake." Maria swept past Edie. "I need to talk."

"Can't it wait till morning?" Edie begged.

Maria plopped herself down on the edge of the bed.

"It *is* morning. Besides, you're up anyway. Better to talk to me than to spend all night reading *The Miserables*." She held up Edie's book and slapped it down on the nightstand. "Yawn-fest. How are you not asleep after, like, two pages?"

Too tired to argue about a book Maria would probably never read, let alone pronounce correctly, Edie shut the door and climbed onto the bed near the mountain of pillows. She tucked her knees inside her XXL WORLD'S BEST GRANDPA T-shirt, settling in for the conversation she was too polite to refuse. Oblivious as always to her intrusion, Maria fell backwards and sprawled out like a pinup girl: face to the ceiling, arms spread wide, one leg bent, the other dangling toward the floor.

"Well?" Edie prompted. "Go ahead."

"Okay, so, did you ever, like, make a decision, and that decision felt really right? It wasn't even a decision. It was just something you did, like putting on deodorant or picking olives out of your mom's disgusting vegan lasagna. But after you fell into this decision, another option came along and you started to question everything?"

"An option named Henry Crawford?"

Maria scooted onto her elbows.

"How did you know?"

"I'm not blind, Maria. Neither is Rupert and neither is Julia."

"I know, I know." Maria smoothed out the air bubbles in the duvet. "But I told Rupert everything and he forgives me. And Julia has to forgive me because she's my sister, so stop staring at me like I'm a horrible person. God! We just kissed a little."

"A little?"

"Okay, we kissed a lot, but that's all we did. I love Rupert. I do, but ..."

"But?"

Maria's eyes lit up as she fell back against the pillows.

"But kissing Henry was *amazing!* I know you think he's slimy or something, but seriously, I've never been kissed like that, and believe me, I *have* been kissed. This was just"—Maria let out an emphatic groan—"you know?"

"Um, okay?" Edie grimaced, struggling to conjure any sympathy while she pictured poor Rupert slumped in a pile of coats, wrestling with rejection, and Julia blubbering over the loss of her Prince Romeo. Edie'd made some questionable choices herself recently, but still . . .

"Seriously, Edie, have you ever *really* been kissed?" Maria's eyes widened. Her cheeks flushed. Her body shifted about, restless and ecstatic. "Like, toes curling, knees buckling, and just, oh my god? Where all you know are his hands and his lips? Where you can't breathe but, like, who cares because you're about to spontaneously combust anyway?"

Edie tucked the hem of her T-shirt around her toes as she wrestled with the acute awareness that her only kisses had been awkward, bashful, and kind of mushy. Her latest kiss had lasted only a few seconds and its only real impact was the demolition of a friendship. Sure, Edie'd imagined the kind of kisses Maria described, ones that looked and felt like Rodin sculptures of entwined lovers. She couldn't deny that she wanted to be kissed like that, but what if she simply wasn't that kissable? Especially to the guys she wanted to kiss? That sounded awful but maybe it wasn't such a bad thing, at least until she got to college. After all, she was focusing on her education.

Mostly.

Maria rolled over, leaning forward until she caught her reflection in the mirror. She combed a hand through her hair, erasing the evidence of her writhing.

"Compared to Henry," she said, "Rupert's too . . . dependable."

"Dependable's bad?"

"It's boring. Every kiss is the same. It's like working through a to-do list. You lean this way. I'll lean that way. Your hand goes here. Mine goes there. Step one, step two, step three." She counted them off on her fingers. "Henry's different. He's exciting, he's mysterious, and he's sooo sexy. I mean, wow, he can do this thing with—"

"Stop!" Edie frantically waved her hands. "I don't want to know what Henry can do with his anything."

Maria sighed as she toyed with the lace duvet, mirroring one of Julia's most frequent fidgets. Maybe the habit ran in the family. Maybe Norah kept lace in the guest room for a reason.

"I'm only eighteen," Maria said. "I don't know what else is out there yet."

"So?"

"So tell me what to do!"

Edie blew a sigh toward her forehead, making her cowlicks flutter.

"You really want my advice?" she asked.

"Yes."

"You're sure?"

"Yes!"

"Then make a choice and be honest about it."

"I don't want *that* advice." Maria got up and walked over to the standing mirror, where she adjusted her boobs and pushed in her stomach.

Edie swiveled to face her.

"If you want to kiss Henry, kiss Henry. God knows he doesn't care if you're dating someone else. Just don't do it behind Rupert's back."

"But Rupert would break up with me if I kept kissing Henry."

"Probably."

"And I don't think Henry wants a relationship."

"Unlikely. No."

"So I'd be alone?" Maria sank in on herself, wilting like time-lapse cut flowers, no longer the prettiest girl in the room, or a sexy siren, or a practically engaged future owner of a summer house in Maine and a prize-winning pair of spaniels. Just a lost girl, desperate to be somewhere someone other than she was. Desperate to be loved.

Edie turned toward her mom's photo, uncertain what to feel now that her anger and annoyance had been yanked away by a pair of sad eyes and slumped shoulders. Eight years hadn't dimmed the memory of the day her mom stormed out of this house, Edie in tow, after Norah's lecture to the girls on how to avoid ending up a single mother like Frances: unloved and poor, trying to follow some ridiculous pipe dream about being a musician instead of growing up, anchoring to someone, and accepting her responsibilities. The words *single, alone,* and *unloved* had been thrown like daggers, working their way through even the toughest skin.

Yes, Maria was selfish and thoughtless, but maybe she was doing the best she could with what she knew. Maybe she was living in her own Blue, as ready to burst as Edie was. And maybe it was high time Edie took her own advice.

She scooted to the edge of the bed, took Maria's hand, and gave it a squeeze.

"You're clever, you're beautiful, and you exude a kind of confidence that makes people want to be around you. You wouldn't be single for long. Besides, you have friends and family. You're not alone."

Maria straightened up, her face full of hope.

"You think?"

"I do, but whatever you decide, please talk to Julia. She's worth a thousand Henrys. Even if kissing's off the table there."

"Okay. Thanks." Maria gave Edie a big hug. Then she spun on her stiletto and strutted to the door. "You know, you're pretty smart."

"I've been told that. One of these days I hope it feels more like a compliment."

Maria blew her a kiss and slipped out into the hall.

Edie let the conversation settle as she pushed her toes through the carpet and thought through everything that'd happened since her first day in Mansfield, and in the week before she left Ithaca. She considered the choices she'd witnessed and the ones she'd made. Then she got out her phone and typed an email.

Shonda,

Here it is. Full disclosure. No more excuses. No more evasions. No more blaming James. Just the truth. You're right. I

knew, even though I told myself I didn't know. I couldn't bear to
think of myself that way. No one had ever wanted to kiss me
before. I guess I wanted to be wanted so badly, I didn't care who
wanted me. And I didn't stop to think about what that meant for
all of us. It was all so abstract until it actually happened. But it
did happen. I know that now.

I stayed behind on purpose. I sat there in silence while
James tossed out a couple cheesy lines I was too keyed up to
hear, but I got the gist. I watched him lean over the gearshift
without discouraging him. I waited till his lips met mine and I
didn't tell him to stop. I just sat there like a horrible, horrible
person, making no choice except to not make a choice.

I did betray you. I betrayed myself, too. I've never
regretted anything more in my life, and that includes the great
marshmallow/microwave experiment back in fifth grade. And
that time I freed the school hamster too close to the bus stop.
And moving to Mansfield. I know I don't deserve to be forgiven,
but I'll never stop trying. It was my fault. I'm so, so sorry.

Miss you like bacon
Love you like you
Edie

She hit send before she could start obsessing about every word,
looking for ways to backtrack or capitulate. Her message felt raw but
right, even if it didn't earn Shonda's forgiveness.

Before settling back into bed, Edie decided to complete one

more task, something to make her look forward instead of back. She took out her mom's stringless guitar and the pliers she kept in the case. She found Henry's little box in the bedside table. She removed the package of strings that lay inside, nestled in a bit of tissue paper. Uncertain how gratitude and loathing could coexist, along with a hundred other emotions Edie couldn't yet identify, she began, at last, to string her mom's guitar.

Chapter Fourteen

♥

WITH MAY CAME WARMER DAYS AND BRIGHTER sunshine. After school on a Friday, when the temperature spiked to an unseasonable high, Maria (still practically engaged), Julia (still waiting to be adored), and Edie (still playing referee between the two) compiled a playlist of peppy pop tunes and laid towels on the lawn in the garden, ready to soak up the sun. Julia stretched out in a gray polka-dot bikini and scrolled through the latest entries of her favorite beauty blog, *A Better You.* Maria—elegantly clad in a striped linen halter dress that would coordinate nicely with a summer house in Maine—meticulously buffed her toenails. Edie—comfortably dressed in cutoffs and a 1970s tank-top with a glittery roller-skating centaur on it—rotated between three equally frustrating tasks.

Failure

noun

1. A state of unemployment that occurs when most jobs require transportation you don't have and

local references your relatives claim you don't need.

2. An accumulation of over two dozen useless essay drafts due to your persistent uncertainty about who you want to be.

3. A continued compulsion for writing love songs about the boy next door despite staunchly declining all his invites to play guitar, go swimming, watch a movie, or do anything else that might make you want to dive-bomb his face.

Edie deleted the entry before she posted it. Shonda was unlikely to find the humor in anything involving someone else's boyfriend. Aside from an accidental butt dial and an occasional snarky entry about deceit or duplicity, Shonda still hadn't replied to Edie's email. Edie persevered anyway, adding posts, sending texts, and forwarding the scholarship list with a heartfelt plea to join her at UMB next year. She knew the chances were slim, but even a glimmer of hope was better than no hope at all.

She set aside her phone and opened her notebook, willing herself to write a few lyrics that weren't about starlit smiles or an almost held hand.

> Don't go racing rainbows for gold that isn't there.
> Don't go chasing sunbeams for a handful of hot air.
> Don't follow the fireflies when their moments are so few.

Don't dash after daydreams because all you'll ever find is you.

As she started working out a refrain, Julia rolled onto her belly, letting her sparkly flip-flops dangle from her toes.

"Ooh! Quiz!" she exclaimed. *"Naughty or nice: Are you bad enough to get him into bed?"*

Edie groaned. "Why do you read that stuff?"

"Why do you read *that* stuff?" Maria nodded at Edie's messenger bag, where a thick, dog-eared copy of *Bleak House* poked out.

Edie shot her a withering glare. Maria completely ignored her.

"Actually, this blog has taught me a lot," Julia said. "Like how to stop being too picky, how to be sexier without being sluttier, and how my body language was sending boys the wrong messages."

"You have no body language," Maria said. "You barely even have a cup size."

"At least I'm not a thirty-six fat."

"Better than a thirty-two flat."

As her cousins continued to snap at each other like coked-up turtles, Edie tried to forget what they were really fighting about: Henry Crawford. Despite his love of magic tricks, he hadn't managed to perform a vanishing act yet. Instead, he'd worked his way into the hearts of both Vernon girls, giving Julia just enough PG-rated attention to keep her hanging on, and secretly meeting Maria well after dark for what presumably fell into the NC-17 category. Edie didn't ask for details. She didn't want to know. The whole situation confused her. She couldn't understand why two sisters would fight so hard over a guy, especially one who didn't care much about either of them. Then again, he had an uncanny knack for knowing precisely how to incite a girl's interest.

"Well, go on." Maria flicked the end of her nail file against Julia's bare heel. "Let's find out how bad you are."

Julia shifted her feet away and scrolled through her phone.

"*Question one,*" she read. "*Your boyfriend dumps you for another girl. You a) move on, b) key his car, c) key her car.*"

"C." Maria unscrewed the lid of her dark maroon nail polish. "If some slut moves in on my man, she'll pay for it."

"What if he just gets swept away by a few starlit kisses while you're busy looking for his coat?" Julia practically spat.

"She still gets her wheels punctured."

Julia shot her sister a sneer. Maria carried on with her pedicure, unfazed. Edie continued working on her song, not that she was making much progress with it.

"I'll go with B." Julia jabbed at her screen. "*Question two. At a party you a) clean up everyone else's mess, b) drink too much, c) kiss at least two guys.*"

The girls pinballed a round of loaded glances.

"Right. B. *Question three. How often do people call you a bitch? a) never, b) regularly, but only my besties, or c) who's counting?*"

Unable to concentrate, Edie lay back, set her open notebook over her face, and attempted to ignore the rest of Julia's quiz. She knew the blog existed to sell products, not to preach truth, but she wasn't immune to the hype, especially after spending time with girls like Claire and Maria. Claire was so confident and comfortable around other people. Maria was so assertive and unapologetic. They both had friends who looked up to them and boyfriends who'd do practically anything for them. Edie didn't want to be like those girls, exactly. She didn't want to be "bad" either. But she wasn't sure yet how to get a guy's attention by simply being herself.

"Here's me," Julia said once she'd entered all her answers. *"You're so bad, I'll bet you think this song is about you. You keep your bad self in check but you know how to embrace your inner bitch."*

"God knows I've seen your inner bitch," Maria said.

"Thanks a lot," Julia muttered.

"What? I thought you wanted to be bad."

"Yeah, but when you say it, it sounds like an insult."

"It *is* an insult!" Edie threw down her notebook and sat upright. "Julia, do me a favor. Turn that thing off for an afternoon."

"No, I need it." Julia clutched her phone against her chest. "Besides, the quiz isn't supposed to be taken literally."

"Well, a little bit literally," Maria hinted.

"What does *that* mean?" Edie scowled, uncertain she wanted to hear the answer.

"No one wants to date some sweet and innocent type who's only ever locked lips with a tube of Chapstick. Then again"—Maria assessed Edie's outfit, arching an eyebrow and curling a lip—"no one wants to date Ghetto Roller Girl."

Edie prickled as Maria's words hit home.

"Sorry I didn't dress to impress your mom's begonias," she said.

"Whatever." Maria slipped a pair of oversized sunglasses from her pocket. "I'm not saying you have to actually *be* bad, but you could hint at it a little." She put on her sunglasses and peered over the rims, Lolita-style, waiting for a reply.

"No thanks," Edie said. "I'd never pull it off."

Maria tipped her chin toward the neighbors' house.

"Even if it'd make you-know-who ditch his you-know-what so you can have his little blond babies?"

Edie felt her whole body flush as her fist tightened on her notebook. She scrambled for an argument but she suspected any denial would be painfully unconvincing if her face was the color of ripe strawberries.

"How did you know?" she asked.

"Hello? This is obvious calling. No one works that hard to avoid a guy unless she really likes him." Maria flicked a ladybug off her knee, sending it spinning into the grass. "Oh, and Julia told me."

Edie spun toward Julia.

"Sorry." Julia cringed. "It just slipped out. I thought she already knew."

As Edie's gut churned, knowing her crush was in Maria's less-than-discreet hands, Sebastian's boxy little blue car pulled into the driveway next door. Edie started packing up her belongings, ready to make a quick getaway.

"Point made," Maria said to Julia.

Edie went still. Maria was right. She was being ridiculous. No one was going to dive-bomb anyone, or even think about kissing, hand-holding, or naked time at Disneyland. She wasn't *that* low on willpower.

"Please don't tell him," she begged.

"Why not?" Maria asked, as if the answer wasn't patently obvious.

"Because there's no point. He has a girlfriend."

The girls all sat up a little taller, craning their necks to peer past the picket fence to where Sebastian was bent over with his car door open, awkwardly rooting around for something in the back seat.

"Look," Maria said pointedly, "I like Claire and I like Sebastian, and they obviously like each other, but do you seriously see them lasting past high school?"

"I don't know." Edie flashed through memories of the couple sharing ice cream, working parties, and braiding their bodies together on a lawn chair. "Maybe?"

"Oh, please." Maria pushed her sunglasses up her nose and reclined onto her elbows. "The moment Claire gets to New York, she'll find some sexy city boy she doesn't have to beg to show up at a dance. She'll be partying uptown at Columbia while Sebastian's down in the Village crushing on a ponytailed librarian who texts him in iambic pentameter. They'll never make it."

"Maybe not," Edie conceded, "but by then I'll be elsewhere too."

Maria scoffed, exasperated.

"So tell him he's dreamy," she said. "Buy a decent bra. Recite entire chapters from moldy old novels for all I care. Just get off your bony ass and *do* something already. God!"

"I *am* doing something." Edie jammed her notebook into her bag. "I'm detoxing. I'm getting him completely out of my system. I've spent nineteen days sober. And counting."

"Interesting." Maria smiled wryly. "How's that working out for you?"

While Edie flailed, searching for a cogent rebuttal, Sebastian shut his car door and glanced their way. She tried to duck out of sight but Maria waved him over.

"Come say hi!" she called. Then she lowered her voice, nudging Edie with a newly pedicured toe. "I can picture them already, all your socially maladjusted little towheads, reading Russian novels by age six, holding up walls at parties by age sixteen."

Edie scooted away. "I kind of hate you right now."

"You'll get over it. Julia always does."

Edie took out her phone, preparing to look really interested in whatever was on the screen by the time Sebastian met them in the yard. In an effort to save herself the trouble of pretending, she opened her favorite montage of funny cat videos. Beneath a shot of an adorably clumsy tabby sliding down a curtain onto the face of a Labrador retriever, a pair of buckskin shoes stepped up to the base of her towel.

The cat, Edie told herself. *Focus on the cat. Only the cat.*

"You guys busy tonight?" Sebastian asked. "Tom's on his way from Philly. He wants to host a little barbecue while my mom and stepdad are in Belize."

Maria and Julia both enthusiastically agreed to head over later but Edie remained silent, hoping no one would notice she hadn't replied.

"Edie?" Sebastian prompted. "You coming?"

"Can't." She watched six little kittens pile out of a watering can. "I need to do a, finish a, there's a"—*don't say* thing, *don't say* thing—"deadline coming up."

When no one responded, she finally looked up from her screen. There he stood, looming before her, thumbing a dog-eared paperback, his smile warm and sincere, his eyes the color of the sky. Dammit. Three weeks of detoxing ruined in an instant.

"You sure it can't wait for one night?" he asked. "I know Tom would like to see you. And it'd be nice to catch up." He gave her the look that always wore down her resolve, the one that said her answer *really* mattered. Then he added the kicker. "I finally finished that book you recommended." He held it up to reveal the cover of *Villette*. "I've been dying to talk about the ending with you. And the second guy she falls for."

A hundred yeses fluttered up inside Edie, ready to fly out of her mouth. She was desperate to discuss books with Sebastian but she was also desperate to prove she wasn't as spineless as she felt. She looked to her cousins for support. Maria was peering over the rims of her sunglasses, barely smothering a smirk. Julia was nervously biting her lip as if all of Edie's future happiness depended on what she did in this moment.

Edie's patience vanished in an instant, as it always did when she was floundering in front of an audience. She was sick of Maria's patronizing prodding, Julia's unrealistic Prince Charming fantasies, and Sebastian's oblivious hey-come-hang-out-while-I-get-all-meaningful-and-then-grope-my-girlfriend-in-front-of-you invites. With a burst of temper, she spat out the only excuse she thought would shut everything down.

"Actually, I have a date."

Julia's jaw dropped but Maria simply quirked a skeptical eyebrow.

"That's, um, great." Sebastian scratched his neck. "Bring him along. The more the merrier." He stumbled backwards. "Don't forget your suits. The pool's ready to go."

Edie flashed him a polite smile. Then she returned her attention to her phone, anxious to avoid logging too many clues about the effect of her impulsive little lie. In less than two seconds she'd already registered the flattening of Sebastian's smile, the tightening of his posture, and the sudden obsession with the back of his hairline, a gesture she'd come to think of as his tell for feeling awkward, bashful, and maybe even a little bit sulky. She hated to admit it, but it felt good, way better than simply avoiding him for weeks on end. Maybe Maria was right. She could be a *little* bit bad.

"Cool," she tossed out like an afterthought. "See you later then. If we can make it."

Despite a niggle of guilt for lying, Edie felt a strange surge of pride. In the space of only a few words, she'd stopped being Poor Edith, sitting around pining for a guy who didn't like her back, subject to Julia's pity, Maria's mockery, and Henry's self-satisfied lectures. She wasn't comparing herself to Claire. She wasn't hanging on

Sebastian's attention, watching for him through her bedroom windows, or storing up quotes to share. Sebastian wasn't *the* guy. He was *a* guy. Nothing more.

Her eye caught on her dad's rumpled napkin note, where it was poking out from the front cover of her notebook. *I can't. I'm sorry. Move on.* In that moment, Edie turned her mom's greatest heartache into her own personal rallying cry.

No more pining. No more waiting and hoping. It was time to move on.

Chapter Fifteen

Bad
adjective
1. Unpleasant, unacceptable, or a little bit naughty.
2. An appropriately uninteresting chord progression.
3. A bizarre combination of fierce and fearful you feel when your cousin offers you an array of swimsuits to choose from, and you forgo the one-pieces for a seriously sexy black bikini.

Norah was briskly chopping kale when the girls passed through the kitchen on their way out. Bert was sitting at the table, doing a crossword and dabbing dribbled hummus off his potbelly.

"No hot dogs," Norah instructed the girls, brandishing a knife that looked more like a murder weapon than a tool for dicing wilted greenery. "And don't forget to moisturize if you go in the pool. Chlorine's brutal on the complexion. Home by two."

"A curfew? Seriously?" Maria locked her arms across her chest. "We're only going next door."

"As long as you live in my house, you'll follow my rules, right, Bert?"

"Of course, dear," he replied while dipping a napkin in his water glass.

"Don't condescend," Norah scolded. "No one likes condescension."

Maria rolled her eyes and headed out the front door. She marched straight through the nearest flower bed, deliberately trampling a few tulips. Edie and Julia skirted the landscaping and caught up near the street.

"What are you going to do if Sebastian asks where your date is?" Julia asked Edie as they headed up the Summerses' driveway toward the backyard.

"I'll just say he canceled."

"Emergency at Nerd Con?" Maria asked.

Edie bit her tongue and kept walking, wishing to god someone had taught her how to lie properly. The moment Sebastian left the Vernons' yard, Julia had showered Edie with questions she couldn't answer. Who was the guy? Where did she meet him? What did he drive? Maria simply waited in knowing silence until Edie caved and admitted she didn't actually have a date. Fortunately her cousins agreed to keep up the pretense for the evening, buzzing with the excitement of collusion. Edie was far less enthusiastic. Conspiring with her cousins was a shaky proposition. If Julia drank too much, she'd say anything to anyone, and Maria would only keep a secret if it served her own interests. Nonetheless, Edie was on a mission. She might not arrive at the party with a date, but with a concerted effort to overcome her shyness, she hoped to leave with one.

Tom and Sebastian's "little barbecue" turned out to involve well over a hundred people. Since Tom never did anything halfway, the scale of the party wasn't a complete surprise. Edie's social anxiety skyrocketed anyway, making her especially self-conscious about what she was wearing under her tank-top and cutoffs. Thankfully Maria restrained herself when she'd helped Edie blow out her hair and put on a little makeup. Edie still suspected she'd overdone it. She was attending a pool party, after all. Everything would wash out the moment she got wet, though as Maria had assured her, swimsuits weren't necessarily for swimming.

The girls quickly spotted Tom, dressed in a KISS THE COOK apron and loud pair of printed trunks. He was working the barbecue and passing out beers from a cooler on the deck. Lounging beside him was a gorgeous girl in hot pants and a halter top. She was petite, with a cheerful face and a sleek black braid draped over her shoulder. In other words, not the curvy blonde he'd brought to Norah's party a month earlier. A short, muscular guy was setting up speakers at a nearby table. Tattoos covered his arms and neck, peeking out the edges of his snug black T-shirt. He had dark buzz-cut hair and a silver stud poking through his soul patch.

Maria nudged Julia. "Think he has a skull in all those tats?"

"Shut up."

"Pierced nipple?"

The girls joined Tom at his chef station, where energetic hugs were exchanged and drinks were handed out. Then he introduced his friends as Linh and W.B., both of whom had driven up with him from Philly.

"What does W.B. stand for?" Maria asked.

"Washboard." He lifted his T-shirt and displayed his sculpted abs, rippling under snakes, crosses, and tribal symbols as he flexed.

"Seriously," Maria whispered to Julia. "Go be your bad self."

"Stop it!" Julia gritted her teeth as her fists balled up.

"Ignore this punk," Tom joked through a hearty laugh. "He just likes showing off his six-pack, and his ink."

"Can't blame him," Linh said. "I don't mind looking at that."

Tom made a great show of being jealous, falling to the deck with his hand on his heart. This led to some flirty but impressively athletic wrestling with Linh while the rest of the group did their best to carry on nearby.

W.B. dropped his shirt down as he flashed the girls a row of perfect white teeth.

"Actually, I picked my nickname up in my freshman English class," he explained. "My last name's Yates. Apparently W.B. Yeats was some famous poet."

Not just some poet, Edie thought as she silently recited one of her favorite quotes. *"But I, being poor, have only my dreams. I have spread my dreams under your feet. Tread softly because you tread on my dreams."* She wished, despite herself, that Sebastian were there to share the moment. She scanned the crowd until she saw him at the far end of the pool, perched on the edge of Claire's chaise, where they were sharing a plate of nachos.

Edie's fight-or-flight instinct instantly kicked in, tipping far closer to flight than fight. Apparently "moving on" took more than a quick pep talk and a few layers of waterproof mascara. She glanced longingly toward the Vernons' house, where a pair of dormers led to a quiet room with no bikinis, no boys, and no burning questions about what kept two people together beyond their genetic good fortune and their impressive inseam measurements.

As she turned back toward the party, Maria caught her eye.

"You're not seriously going to run away already?" she asked.

"No, I just—"

"Thank god—then let's find you some man candy before you waste that makeup job by impersonating a floor lamp again." She linked her arm through Edie's and dragged her away while Julia remained behind, inundating W.B. with questions about his tattoos.

The girls sat down by the deep end of the pool. Maria reclined as if posing for a fashion spread while Edie removed her sneakers and dangled her legs in the water. It was cool and refreshing, lapping at her skin where stress-induced sweat had collected behind her knees. She and Maria surveyed the crowd, casually assessing the various dancers, divers, and drinkers to decide who Edie should approach for a conversation, or in Maria's words, who she should show off her boobs to.

Edie was drawn to a shaggy-haired guy sitting on the patio near the house, watching something on his phone. He looked shy and unintimidating. He also seemed to be alone, though that theory went to hell once he starting kissing another guy who'd just arrived. Maria encouraged her to hit on an athletic alpha-type who was aggressively swatting an inflatable ball around in the shallow end with some friends.

"How much do you think he'd charge to pretend he likes you?" she asked.

Edie bit back her annoyance, accustomed to Maria's offhand derision by now.

"I'm hoping to do better than pretend," she said.

"You're the one who claimed you were bringing a date," Maria argued. "So see it through. Take off your shirt and let's go hire Mister Muscles to drool all over you."

As Edie began explaining that neither drool nor bribery were on the night's agenda, the guy in question pounded the ball into another guy's head. The two started swearing at each other with such unnecessary aggression, the girls promptly directed their attention elsewhere.

They were speculating about a wiry guy wearing glasses and an old Holy Cross Fencing Team T-shirt when they spotted Henry leaning against the cabana door and holding a white rosebud out to a pretty girl in a sundress. All tanned, toned, and in his little red swim shorts, he looked like a lifeguard from a TV beach scene.

Edie squinted at him, wondering where the rose had come from. As she concluded that there was only one place he could've kept it, she quickly stopped pondering the matter. Beside her, Maria showed no signs of agitation. She simply shifted the neckline of her dress to best display her cleavage. Edie was astonished. Considering the Great Cousin Wars, she would've expected Maria to storm over and yank the rose from the other girl's hand.

"Watching him flirt with someone else doesn't bother you?" Edie asked.

"Why should it?" Maria replied with a dismissive flick of the wrist.

"Because you're still seeing him?"

Maria opened her mouth as if she was about to spout out a denial, but Edie held her gaze, unflinching, ready to refute any claims at innocence. Maria's expression clouded for a moment. Then she swept her hair off her shoulders and pasted on a smile.

"Whatever," she said. "It doesn't mean anything."

Edie flashed back to her first day in Mansfield, when Maria made the same comment about kissing Tom. Edie knew Maria didn't really think kisses were meaningless. She was just putting up a good front, hiding her vulnerabilities like everyone else. Edie considered calling her bluff but decided against it. Maria's little act could prove useful. If they could all get through one evening without any bickering over Henry, Edie'd count the party a raging success, no matter what happened with her own impulsive little lie, her attempt to talk toward strangers, or the bikini bottoms that kept creeping to places they didn't belong.

As she glanced at Henry again, her mind wandered to the guitar strings, releasing a slew of contradictory feelings she'd been trying to ignore for the past couple weeks. Fortunately Maria's phone soon buzzed, interrupting her thoughts. Rupert had just pulled in next door, an hour earlier than expected. Maria hypothesized that traffic from Boston was unusually light, but Edie suspected Rupert's efficiency was driven by more personal reasons, ones that were strutting around the pool in a pair of red shorts. The thought allowed her to revive her acrimony. One sincerely beautiful gesture didn't make up for all of Henry's carelessness and callousness. She could still hate him.

Mostly.

Maria excused herself to go meet Rupert, leaving Edie to sort out her dating needs on her own. She sat quietly for a minute, finishing her beer and steeling her nerves. Then she got up, found an empty chair, and shimmied out of her tank-top and shorts. She could do this. She could walk up to a guy and introduce herself. Once they'd covered the basics—name, hometown, number of siblings, history of criminal activity—she could ask him out. Simple. Straightforward. No big deal. She wasn't looking for anything long-term, profound, or approaching perfection. She just needed to set up one date with someone who was available, able to hold a relatively engaging conversation, and potentially interested in kissing her. Ideally, he'd also have decent oral hygiene.

As she adjusted the ties around her neck and assessed her astonishingly well-padded boobs, she heard a low, husky voice behind her.

"Change your mind yet?"

Edie spun around to see Henry flashing her a broad smile. His thick black bangs dipped down over one eyebrow and his skin glistened with something that smelled like tropical islands and narcissism.

"Change your everything?" she said.

"I'm not so bad once you get to know me."

"I have no reason to test that theory." Edie tucked her clothes under the chair, careful to position herself so she wasn't flashing

Henry a panoramic view of her butt. Sure, she'd wanted to look sexy tonight, but not for Henry. Taking part in his little love games would only amplify her struggle to prove she had a will of her own. She wanted to be kissed, not played.

Assuming their conversation was over, Edie turned and took off toward the deep end, heading toward Tom's corner of the deck where she could swap her empty bottle for another beer. If she was going to walk around half-naked, talking to strangers, she needed a little more help bolstering her nerves. She was passing the diving board when she realized Henry was still by her side.

"So where's the guy?" he asked.

"What guy?" she said without thinking.

Henry laughed. His tone was hearty and good-humored but Edie stopped short anyway, mortified at how quickly she'd slipped.

"God, you're a terrible liar," he said, still chuckling.

"Sorry I don't live up to your standards."

"When have you seen me lie?"

Edie opened her mouth, ready to rattle off a dozen examples. To her surprise, she couldn't name a single one. As far as she knew, he'd never promised to replace the security and adoration Maria found with Rupert. He'd never told Julia he wanted to be her boyfriend. He'd been almost too honest with Edie, telling her flat out what he thought about her, her cousins, and anything else that crossed his mind.

Stuck without an argument, Edie apologized for her accusation. Henry gracefully accepted. Next thing she knew, she was explaining how her lie had slipped out, and now it was sitting there like a springboard for whatever she did next. She couldn't believe she was opening up to Henry of all people. Maybe it was the beer. Maybe it was the guitar strings. Maybe it was the way that he always seemed to figure things out before she said them. There was a strange sort of comfort in that.

"Maria suggests I find a guy to play along," she said as they neared the barbecue.

"Shouldn't be difficult. Not in that suit."

Edie tugged at the top, willing it to cover a little more skin. Where did the manufacturers hide all the padding, anyway? There wasn't any fabric to pad.

"I'm not good with boys," she said. "I get all tense and end up blushing, blubbering, and bolting."

"You have no problem talking to me."

"Yeah, because I don't like you."

Henry let out a sharp bark of laughter.

"Fair enough," he said. "But if you run out of options, I'm up for the job."

This time it was Edie's turn to laugh.

"He'd never believe it. *I'd* never believe it."

"I'm a pretty good actor."

"I'm not."

As Edie got another beer out of the cooler, Julia spotted Henry. She skipped away from W.B. and threw her arms around Henry's neck. He did his best to stem her enthusiasm, carefully settling her an arm's length away. They exchanged a few words but when Julia finally realized he was far less excited to see her than she was to see him, she marched over to the side of the pool and plunked herself down in a huff.

"Nice work," Edie said.

"Guess I should go make a few repairs."

"You don't strike me as much of a handyman."

"I'm handier than you think."

"I'm not talking about that kind of 'handy.'"

Henry laughed and strolled over to console Julia. Edie kept a watchful eye on the proceedings while chatting with Tom and his friends, clinging tightly to the only other people present who weren't total strangers even though she was supposed to be flirting her way into a date. As Tom started reminiscing about the time he almost lit his parents' house on fire, Edie noticed Sebastian heading toward her, alone, his loping stride displaying the not-quite-hinged-right quality she found so adorable. He was wearing a pair of baggy blue swim trunks and a soft linen shirt that was unbuttoned, flapping openly over his bare chest and the cutest little belly. For a guy who didn't play a lot of sports, he was surprisingly fit, which meant Edie was unsurprisingly blushing.

She started to panic. She wasn't ready. She didn't have a plan, just a half-assed lie and no ability to credibly sustain it. He was going to ask about her date. She'd stammer out a faulty excuse. He'd see right through her. She'd end up confessing everything, just like she did with her cousins and with Henry. Humiliation would ensue.

Like a passenger on a plummeting plane, Edie assessed her routes of egress: driveway, fence, back door, deep end. Then she reminded herself she did have a plan. Just before Sebastian reached her, she spun on her heel, marched over to the boy in the fencing shirt, and held out her hand.

"Hi," she said. "My name's Edie. What's yours?"

Chapter Sixteen

FENCING GUY WASN'T INTERESTED. NEITHER WERE
Water Polo Boy, Econ Major Dude, the ginger with the funny accent,
nor anyone else Edie had introduced herself to. She'd tried her best.
Her best had failed. Now she was standing in front of the mirror in
the Summerses' bathroom, tugging at her skimpy bikini bottoms
and trying to convince herself to return to the party, as dateless as
ever. God, she sucked at talking to strangers. Girls like Claire made
it look so simple, with her warm smiles and light banter. Then there
was Maria, bulldozing into conversations with no fears about what
anyone thought of her. Even Julia had a way with other people. Her
open exuberance and natural curiosity had completely charmed W.B.
Meanwhile, Edie was contemplating hibernating in her room until
August, dedicating all her time to books, music, and funny cat videos.
It sounded pretty good, actually. Except, of course, for the loneliness.

When someone knocked on the door, anxious to use the toilet,
Edie gave up her sanctuary. She stepped into the den and poked
around, clinging to a few more minutes away from the crowd. The
room was large, about half the span of the house. The walls were

dotted with legal certificates. The shelves were lined with golf trophies and tidy rows of decoy ducks. Everything was spotless, formal, and carefully arranged in right angles. She tried to picture the room the way it used to be, full of books and games, with well-worn furniture scattered about and family photos on the walls.

"Doesn't look the same, does it?" asked a voice behind her.

Edie spun around to see Sebastian entering from the stairwell, a box of garbage bags in one hand, a roll of paper towels in the other, and a spray bottle of cleaning fluid tucked under his arm. She considered bolting but she knew she'd look ridiculous. She could hardly claim there was a poolside emergency when she'd been wandering the den like a rapt museum patron. She might as well try to have a simple conversation.

"I barely recognize the place." She examined a decoy duck. "Does it bother you? Seeing your home change around you?"

"Every single day." He crossed the room and paused by a shelf of leather-bound books. "Tom doesn't get it. He likes change. Where he doesn't find it, he creates it."

Edie set down the duck, carefully lining it up in its militant ranks despite a powerful urge to stack them all into a pyramid. She wanted to tell Sebastian she admired his ability to hold on to things. She shared his appreciation for consistency, reliability, and big books that took weeks to read. Only she couldn't figure out how to say all that without weighing it with eight layers of meaning. Besides, there was one thing she did want him to change, even though she was trying *really* hard to change herself instead.

Sebastian piled the cleaning products on the corner of the leather sectional. He leaned against the back, settling in with his ankles locked. Edie remained on the other side of the room, uncertain what to say next. She should probably apologize for avoiding him for weeks on end. It's what a friend would do. They were friends, right? Or at least they could be? She braced herself to be brave, or at least to be honest, though the two were starting to feel a lot like one in the same.

"So, can I finally apologize?" he asked, beating her to the punch.

"For what?"

"For what I did at Rupert's party." He spoke as though his answer was self-evident, but it wasn't.

Edie studied him, searching for clues about what he was referring to. His expression was inscrutable, as always, so she simply took her best stab.

"You mean lying to Claire?"

"That, among other things." His shoulders inched up, his gaze trailed toward his feet, and his face twitched as though he was chewing on the inside of his cheek.

Edie took a moment to mentally eject the phrase *among other things* so she wouldn't revisit it later, picking it apart until she found at least one way he could be implying he liked her, even if it was followed by several others that proved he didn't. Then she edged a little closer, parking herself at the opposite end of the sectional.

"Why doesn't Claire know you want to be a writer?"

"I brought it up once. She thought I was kidding. I was too embarrassed to correct her." Sebastian traced the sectional stitching the same way he'd so often traced the top of the pickets. "She has this idea of who we are together. It's a nice idea. It's just hard to live up to sometimes. I don't like disappointing her." He shifted his attention from the furniture to the hem of his shorts, straightening the fabric where it cupped his knee. "When the subject of my writing came up again, it'd already become a joke so it was even harder to tell the truth."

Edie nodded, pondering the notion of little white lies and their swiftness to snowball. Was her own already on its way downhill or was it still teetering at the summit, ready to roll in whatever direction she pushed it?

"And your parents?" she asked.

"I stopped trying to explain things to them years ago. They mean well. They just don't understand why would anyone give up all this"—Sebastian spread his arms wide to take in the entire room—"for something most people think of as a hobby."

"Most people?"

"Most people I know, anyway."

Edie wanted to contradict him, but she remembered visiting her grandparents when she was little, and how critical they'd been about her mom's music. Norah still hadn't stopped rattling on about Frances's lack of responsible choices: her love life, her finances, her career. Sebastian had probably faced something similar. Maybe Claire and Henry had, too, but they'd naturally gravitated to less artistic pursuits. Edie felt incredibly lucky. Sure, her mom had never earned enough money to buy a big house in the suburbs or a condo in New York City. Sometimes she had a hard time scraping together bus fare or rent, but she'd always followed her dreams, and encouraged Edie to do the same.

With a swell of sympathy, Edie walked over and sat down beside Sebastian. They were quite a pair, both pretending to be someone they weren't, and to the people they were closest to. Sebastian might have some hidden career goals, but Edie was faking at least a dozen things that night. She had a date somewhere at the party. She was the sort of girl who felt comfortable in a string bikini. She'd be content to kiss a guy she barely knew rather than fall deeply in love with someone who took the time to know her and love her back, mistakes and all. She hadn't taken a *really* close look at Sebastian's knee while he was tugging at his shorts. She wasn't desperate for a friend.

"My turn to apologize," she said. "Sorry I ghosted you. Things have been ... challenging lately. I took the coward's way out and vanished. I'd like to do less of that. Maybe we can get together and chat about *Villette* sometime, like you suggested?"

Sebastian nodded as a smile dimpled his cheeks.

"I'd like that," he said. "I'd like it a lot."

Edie returned his smile, proud of herself for taking one step toward him instead of ten steps away. With a little practice, she could get used to this friendship idea. She could still talk with Sebastian about books, music, family, and school. The conversations just needed to end with a quick hug instead of a steamy make-out session.

"Friends?" Edie asked.

"Always." Sebastian's smile widened.

She nudged him with her elbow.

He returned her gesture, a glint of mischief in his eyes.

"I used to like this game," he said. "Especially since I always won."

"Yeah, because you cheated and used your hands."

"Cheat? Me? Impossible!"

Before Edie knew what was happening, he scooched toward her and used his shoulder to knock her backwards onto the sectional. They toppled together into a tangle of arms and legs. Edie laughed as she wriggled out from under him, only to find him rolling over her again. It was all silly and chaotic, like they were kids again, shouting taunts and trying to overpower each other without using their hands, but when Edie felt her stomach rub against his, then her knees, her thighs, her chest, her everything, the game started to feel a lot less like two kids wrestling and a lot more like one of her dreams.

Her laughter trickled off. Her movement slowed. Her breath caught.

Oh, god. This wasn't good. This was *so* not a kids' game, not for her, anyway.

"So when do I get to meet your date?" Sebastian threw a leg over hers, rolling her onto her back with a swift shove of his hip.

Edie shimmied backwards, holding up her briefs with both hands.

"He, um, couldn't make it. He had to"—*work, study, fly to Paris, save the whales, fend off zombie hordes, exist*—"he just couldn't make it."

"Let me guess." Sebastian leaned over her, his hands locked behind his back, a knee between her thighs. "There was a thing in the thing?"

Edie went dead still. Did he know? Could he tell? Had he seen through all of her painfully thin evasions? Did he sense that every stuttered lie was just a clumsy way of saying *kiss me, want me, love me back*? In that moment, none of it seemed out of reach. He definitely wanted something. *She* definitely wanted something. Energy pulsed between them, almost electric, and the look in his eyes mirrored the way she felt: like she was standing on a precipice, staring out at a beautiful but dangerous chasm, dying to leap off and freefall into the unknown. Was she imagining that look? Did it matter? Did anything matter but the easily erasable space between them?

As his expression lost its mirth and his face inched closer, maybe by accident, maybe by intent, Edie flashed to a memory of James, leaning toward her in a car, his lips parted, his eyes closing. Another image followed: an almost-held hand that slipped its way into another's. A third image came right on its heels: a napkin with the words *Move on*. She quickly blinked herself out of her spell. She was *not* doing this again, sitting by—or in this case lying by—craving the affection of someone who hadn't chosen her.

Edie grabbed Sebastian by both arms and swung him off her.

"Hey, you cheated." He rolled over on the sectional.

"Actually, this time I didn't." She shuffled her way to standing and adjusted her bikini, yanking her hair free where it'd tangled with the ties on the bra.

Sebastian clambered up and drew his rumpled shirt onto his shoulders.

Claire stood in the doorway, looking thoroughly pissed.

Chapter Seventeen

Drunk
adjective
1. A doctor of
2. A sound made when
3. The inability to finish a thought after you

Edie blinked at her phone, trying to make the little letters line up before she hit Post. The pool party was dwindling to an end. Only about two dozen people remained. Sebastian had smoothed things over with Claire, emphatically assuring her that he and Edie were just friends, a phrase that bit into Edie's skin a little deeper each time he said it. If it was so true, he shouldn't have to say it so often, even if Claire had a right to be suspicious. Edie'd supported Sebastian's claims. What else could she do? There was no point making a muddle of things, not if he still preferred his girlfriend.

Now Edie was curled up in a chaise, cataloging the night's failures and wondering why the Vernons' house seemed so far away. As she tried to picture a zip line appearing and carrying her to her bedroom, Sebastian walked by with an armload of empty bottles. He dropped them into a recycle bin while Tom shut down the barbecue a few yards to Edie's left.

"Our parents are going to kill us." Sebastian assessed the damage from the party: garbage everywhere, towels and random pieces of clothing strewn about, toppled furniture, a busted patio umbrella, an inner tube in the trees, another on the roof.

"Lighten up, little brother." Tom gave him a hearty clap on the back. "We'll deal with it in the morning. Go have some fun." He handed Sebastian what looked like either a condom packet or an unusually shiny piece of ravioli.

Sebastian tucked it into his shirt pocket while looking over at Edie, his expression apologetic. She tried to meet his gaze but she couldn't focus, or maybe she didn't want to. She closed her eyes, willing the world to steady itself. When she finally thought she could manage it, she swung her legs off the chaise and planted her feet on what appeared to be the ground. She wobbled as she stood, which was a strangely familiar sensation even though she was wearing her sneakers. Cinderella probably never drank. She also didn't lie, lust after Prince Charming's knee, wrestle half naked in front of his girlfriend, or do anything else that was bad. God, she was boring, except for that whole singing-to-mice thing. That was kinda cool.

Edie took a step forward. The action turned into something like a backbend. As she surrendered to gravity, a firm hand appeared out of nowhere and steadied her, spread flat against her back. Edie turned to see Henry standing next to her. His hair was wet, making it even blacker than usual. His damp, half-buttoned dress shirt clung to his sculpted chest and arms while his muscular legs extended from his little red shorts. He looked like a high-end cologne model, if Lucifer endorsed cologne.

"Where did you come from?" Edie slurred as he helped her sit down.

"Over there." He nodded toward the cabana where the pretty girl he'd been flirting with earlier was yanking her sundress down and glaring at Edie.

Edie squinted at the girl, and then at Henry.

"Didn't she have her legs wrapped around you a second ago?" she asked.

"You were watching?"

"You weren't?"

He shrugged as his trademark smirk appeared.

"I had better things to look at."

Edie tried to make sense of his implication but in her muddled state, his words slipped away almost instantly, leaving her blinking brainlessly in his general direction. Damn, he was pretty. Did she know that already or was it new information? Why did she hate him again? Something about her cousins?

"How many girls did you kiss tonight?" she asked.

Henry considered for a moment.

"Only two. Three if you count the woman who delivered the pizza, but we have a regular thing going." His smile tipped higher. "Delivery in ten minutes or the next one's on us."

"Unbelievable." Edie shook her head, a gesture she swiftly regretted. She wedged a cheek against her palm and clumsily propped her elbow on the arm of the chaise. "Know how many guys I kissed?" She rolled her fingers against her thumb to make an 0.

"I'd offer to change that but I'm not as much of a jackass as you think."

"Are you just the jack or just the ass?"

Henry busted into a laugh.

"That's not bad for someone in your condition."

"My cognition?"

"Close enough." He held out a hand. "C'mon. Let's get you home."

Ignoring his hand, Edie hauled herself off the chaise. She stood up too quickly. The yard spun. Her vision blurred. She swayed, stumbled, and fell backwards into the chaise, banging her head on the metal frame. As she righted herself, her stomach lurched.

"I think I'm going to . . ." She put a hand over her mouth and bent forward.

With lightning-fast reflexes, Henry grabbed a nearby chip bowl and held it under her chin. The bowl arrived not a moment too soon. Up came a burning surge of warm beer and contraband hot dogs. While Edie sputtered and hacked away, Henry knelt beside her, gently rubbing her back until she finally went still.

"That it?" he asked.

Edie waited a minute before nodding. Then she dropped her head onto her knees, closed her eyes, and prodded the sore spot on the back of her head, cursing her lack of restraint for turning an embarrassing night into an epic humiliation. If she was going to puke her guts out she could've at least hidden behind a shrub. Why did she drink so much, anyway? She was supposed to be kissing someone by now, not pining for a breath mint while the only kissable guy around collected her barf. God, this sucked.

"Stay there a minute," Henry instructed her. "I'm going to go take care of this."

He left with the evidence of her shame but he soon returned and sat patiently by Edie's side without speaking or touching her. This surprised her, having previously assumed Henry wasn't capable of sitting next to a girl for ten whole seconds without trying to get into her pants. Maybe she'd underestimated him. Or maybe she was totally wasted and this wasn't the best time to make judgment calls.

"I got the strings," she admitted.

"I know," he replied simply.

Edie rolled her cheek onto her knee so she could see him, leaving the rest of her body bent double with her arms dangling, ape-like, on either side of her hollow legs. Henry watched her with a hint of amusement in his eyes. She considered declaring she wasn't going to fall for him or insisting she could've bought her own strings. Instead, she just said, "Thank you."

"You're welcome."

When the worst of Edie's dizziness dissipated, she sat upright and got her bearings. Tom and Linh were tangled together in the pool, chatting, laughing, and giving each other sweet little caresses.

Maria and Rupert were side by side on the diving board, hands linked and heads tipped together. Julia was nestled against W.B.'s shoulder, swaying to the music with a smile on her face, despite the tattooed dagger on his neck that was aimed at her forehead. Claire and Sebastian were heading inside to do who knew what, or, okay, everyone knew what. A few other couples were cuddling by the pool or out past the trees on the lawn. Everyone was in someone else's arms.

A wave of loneliness washed over Edie, a profound emptiness she couldn't shake off despite her mom's warnings about steering clear of romance. Here she was, still just a me, wishing she were part of an us. The us didn't have to be complicated or permanent, but for a moment, for *that* moment, she simply wanted to be held.

"Let me know when you're ready and I'll walk you home," Henry offered.

Edie squinted at him sideways.

"You know I only live next door, right?"

"I'm still going to make sure you get there."

Edie inched away. Yes, she wanted to be held, but not badly enough to fall into Henry's arms, strings or no strings.

"Don't worry." He held up his hands, laughing. "I'm only going to linger nearby in case I need to grab an elbow. Or a bucket."

Henry did that thing Edie'd seen him do once before. He dropped the smugness and smiled, not like slime on rice but like a guy who actually gave a shit. In that moment, woozy, wobbly, and surrounded by people who'd found a connection that night, Edie decided that sharing a walk down the driveway wasn't such a bad idea after all, even if it was with a demon/vampire.

"Okay." She prodded his chest with a rubbery index finger. "But there's a crucifix in the hall and I'm not inviting you over the threshold."

Chapter Eighteen

SUNDAY MORNING EDIE AWOKE WITH HER SHEETS twisted, her skin on fire, and everything between her knees and elbows throbbing. For a few luxurious seconds, her mind swam with images of wet skin and long fingers that lingered as they traced the inside of her thighs and peeled away her bikini bottoms. Then she blinked herself into alertness, guiltily scanning her bedroom for witnesses. Finding none, she curled up in a ball, buried her aching head in her hands, and waited to die. She wasn't sure which felt worse: her increasing sexual frustration or her raging hangover.

She was going to blush the color of Red Hots the next time she saw either Sebastian (thank you, pornographic dream) or Henry (thank you, regurgitated pork products). At least Edie didn't dream about Henry. The instant she woke up from that dream, she was starting an intensive course of NoDoz. Admittedly, she did wonder what kissing him would be like when he'd dropped her off last night, a fleeting thought she ascribed to excessive alcohol, a profound state of rejection, and Maria's emphatic speech about how amazing he was. He was also pretty great about all that barf. Even Shonda had never held Edie's hair up.

Edie groped around for her phone so she could check the time. She was startled to notice she had a text message from a local tutoring center she'd contacted earlier in the week. They were interviewing Monday afternoon if she was still interested in a job. As she replied to confirm a time, someone knocked on the door, making her jump. Maria peeked into the room a second later, uninvited.

"Oh, good. You're up." She marched in with Julia in tow. She carried a mug of black coffee and a bottle of aspirin. She plunked them down on Edie's bedside table and settled herself next to Julia on the edge of the bed.

Edie gratefully threw back a pair of painkillers. Then she wedged herself against a mountain of pillows with the bitter but bolstering coffee nestled between both hands. She waited for someone to say something, but her cousins simply stared at her.

"What?" Edie asked when she couldn't stand the scrutiny any longer.

"Hello?" Maria let out an indignant little huff. "Spill, please."

"Spill what?"

"You didn't"—Julia bit her lip—"you know, I mean, did you? With Henry?"

"No!" Edie sputtered with laughter. "God, no!"

Julia melted against the footboard, exhaling with relief.

"I told you she wasn't that drunk."

"You mean *he* wasn't that drunk," Maria corrected.

Edie gripped her mug more tightly while imagining the army of bed pillows coming to life and pummeling Maria from all sides.

Julia picked at the lace on her PJs, giving the duvet a rest for once.

"I thought you might be giving Sebastian a taste of his own medicine," she said.

"I wasn't giving anyone a taste of anything." Edie took another sip of coffee, blinking away the shock of bitterness.

Maria examined the items on the nightstand: a stack of paperbacks, a few guitar picks, the photo of Edie's mom.

"It wouldn't be the worst plan." She popped open a cocktail umbrella set it on the books. "Not for real, of course, but Henry would probably be up for a few well-timed embraces, for the right price."

"Awesome," Edie said. "I'll see if he'll work on a sliding scale."

"Whatever." Maria held up a chipped I ♥ MANATEES mug, sneered, and clunked it back down. "For what it's worth, I'm totally over him."

"Glad to hear it," Edie said, only half listening and less than half convinced.

"I realized last night how perfect Rupert and I are together. He forgives me when I flirt with another guy. I forgive him for letting me flirt."

Edie and Julia swapped a look. Maria ignored them both. With nothing left to disapprove of on Edie's nightstand, she wandered over to the standing mirror to assess her reflection. While she finger-combed her bedhead and Edie slowly sipped her coffee, Julia cleared her throat.

"I have news," she said.

"You bought your first tampon?" Maria taunted.

Julia sat up a little straighter, ignoring her sister's derision.

"W.B.'s going to prom with me," she announced.

Edie and Maria both gaped at her, shocked, curious, and a little impressed.

"Does that mean you played his washboard last night?" Maria asked.

"No." Julia pursed her lips, facing off with her sister. When Maria failed to needle her further, Julia let her story spill out in a rush. "We were joking about how we were both triangles and we both liked a band named the Triangles and he was being really nice, so I asked if he had a girlfriend and he laughed and said no and then I blurted out the question about prom and he said, 'Sure, why not?'" She paused and took a breath. "So, yeah, I have a prom date," she finished, more resigned than excited.

"Congratulations!" Maria said, more excited than resigned.

"That's great," Edie said, unsure how to feel, except a little sad that Julia sounded so disappointed to have a prom date after weeks of sighing for a storybook romance.

"Make sure W.B. wears a turtleneck when he picks you up on prom night, or Dear Mama's going to choke on her pearls," Maria said.

"I think his tattoos are beautiful." Julia laid a hand against her neck.

"Of course you do." Maria rolled her eyes. "It's such a cliché: the princess and the punk. Does he drive a motorcycle?"

"I don't know. Maybe."

"So you finally hooked yourself a bad boy!" Maria pinched her thigh and frowned at her reflection. "You guys'll make the cutest little skull-tatted babies. And they'll be so short you can use them as footstools till they head to college."

"Shut up!"

"Just don't take the family to Disneyland. No one will let you on the rides."

"At least we'd fit under the safety bar!"

"Not if they don't let you past the height restriction."

Edie set down her coffee, buried her head in the pillows, and let the sounds of squabbling muffle. She had bigger things to worry about. Once she removed all signs of last night's egregious pork product consumption, inadequate skin care, and illegal binge drinking, she needed to talk to Bert and Norah. Bringing up work again wasn't going to be easy. Her only hope was that Norah had long since finished torturing the organic greens and put away the kitchen knives.

The following afternoon Edie sat outside the tutoring center, elated that her interview had gone well and she'd finally be starting a job, taking her one step closer to college, independence, and the beginning of everything. In the meantime she had to wait for Maria to return from the mall to drive her home. Maria had been appalled at the idea of waiting during Edie's interview, but she had no problem making anyone else wait for her. Good thing Edie would have alternate transportation once she started her job. Bert had offered to dust up one of the bicycles from the garage. More importantly, he'd helped convince Norah that becoming a tutor would demonstrate their niece's diligence, intelligence, and compassion for others, all things he admired in Norah. Edie'd always assumed Norah had the upper hand in her aunt and uncle's marriage, but yesterday afternoon she realized the sides were surprisingly well matched. Bert just picked his battles carefully, taking Norah's kale and condescension in stride and saving his energy for when it mattered most.

Uncertain how much time she had to kill, Edie took out her phone and opened up Facebook. She skimmed through her feed, flashing past Julia's beauty blog links and an annoyingly happy selfie of Claire and Sebastian together at the pool party. Then she typed Henry's name into the search bar and opened up the text box, intending to send him a thank-you message. Composing it proved challenging. Everything she typed sounded like an opening for flirtation. Two days ago that wouldn't have mattered. Edie would've shut him down with a barbed retort or by simply ignoring him, like usual, but now there was another problem. She was no longer certain she wanted to ignore him.

As Edie's brain chewed on that unnerving thought, she typed *Thank you* and hit enter. Simple. Effective. Utterly free of innuendo.

Her phone pinged almost instantly with a response.

Henry: How was the hangover?

Edie: Not as bad as it could've been

Henry: You could say the same about me

Edie laughed. Sure didn't take him long.

Edie: Anyway. I owe you one

Henry: One what?

Edie: Don't know. Favor?

Henry: I think they call that an offer you can't refuse

Edie: I don't mean sexual favor

Henry: Neither do I. What're you up to?

Edie lowered her phone, considering her response. Telling Henry she was waiting for a ride after a job interview sounded so boring, which was why it was precisely the right thing to say, but Edie was tired of being boring. Her ability to turn an introductory conversation into a stilted interview had destroyed her chances of landing a date on Saturday. Henry was the only guy there besides Sebastian she could just be herself with.

Hmm . . .

Maybe he could help Edie get over her crush, not as a date but as a distraction. Granted, he was a self-proclaimed seduction artist who mass-distributed roses, spoke only in Foreplay, scavenged Shakespeare plays for pickup lines, spent more money on hair gel than Norah spent on carpet cleaner, and turned a pizza delivery slogan into an invite for sexual deviance. But he was interesting.

Edie: Thinking about testing those strings

Henry: Need help?

Edie: I know what I'm doing

Henry: So do I

Edie: So I hear

Henry: Glad I come highly recommended

Edie: Not touching that one

Henry: I'm still hoping to change your mind on that philosophy

Edie laughed again. Damn, he was relentless. If he dared to send her a dick pic she was deleting it immediately and blocking him forever.

Edie: You're unbearable

Henry: Bear me anyway?

Edie: I think they call that an offer you CAN refuse

Henry: I'm just asking for a conversation

Edie: I've seen you converse. It didn't involve much talking

Henry: Depends who I'm conversing with

Edie: Bullshit

Henry: One hour. Six strings. A few tunes. That's all

Edie stared at her screen. Behind the little message box, Henry's profile page displayed a panoramic photo of him staring out from a white stone balcony with a hand shielding his eyes and a peach sunset highlighting his features. It looked like a shot from a magazine. Everything was elegant, exotic, and beautiful. Her own banner image showed her and Shonda, laughing hysterically, covered in icing and cake batter after turning Shonda's eighteenth birthday party prep into a massive food fight. What was *that* girl doing messaging *this* guy? And why was he messaging back? It made no sense.

Edie: I'll be home in an hour. You know where I live

Chapter Nineteen

AS SOON AS EDIE GOT HOME FROM HER INTERVIEW, she changed out of her school uniform into her favorite pair of jeans, a thrift-shopped T-shirt from the Koslovski family's 1986 reunion, and the ratty but beloved vintage cardigan Maria kept threatening to throw away when no one was looking. Edie assessed her reflection, wondering if she should make a little effort. She could at least attempt to sort out the bedraggled Rapunzel look she seemed to be sporting, or she could cover up the worst of her freckles. She waved off the thought as quickly as it'd come on. She was about to see Henry. Getting his attention was hardly a problem, which felt kinda good, actually.

Edie twisted her hair into a loose knot so it wouldn't get in her way. Then she poked around in the dressing table drawer until she found her little brass locket buried in an assortment of knickknacks. It was a simple heart with a bird etched on the lid. She smiled, quietly humming the love song she'd written last month. *I'm not myself to myself, let alone to you. Let alone, yet alone, I am missing a part of my incomplete secondhand heart.* It was sappy and sentimental, but then so was Edie. She cut down her mom's photo, carefully nestled it into the locket, and slipped it over her head. If Edie was finally going to start playing guitar again, her mom didn't need to watch from the bedside. She should have the best seat in the house.

Twenty minutes and one painfully awkward cousin convo later, Edie and Henry were sitting on one of the benches that faced the fountain in Norah's garden. Edie'd selected the location due to the four-foot-high hedges that sheltered it from the house, though she wouldn't have been surprised to find Maria and Julia crouched nearby with pith helmets and binoculars. She'd assured them both that this wasn't a date (paid for or otherwise) but she knew she was in for a full interrogation the moment Henry left.

As Edie tuned her guitar and practiced her fingering, she and Henry settled into a surprisingly easy conversation. She related a few Burger Barn misadventures with Shonda and described the love song she'd played for Chad Whipple in the fifth grade talent show, after which he'd priggishly informed her that her freckles were early-onset acne. In between her stories, Henry talked about a trip he'd taken to Kathmandu as a kid, his stage debut as Hamlet during his sophomore year of high school, and the day he got kicked out of a cooking class for accidentally setting the teacher's apron on fire.

"But she forgave you?" Edie asked.

"Yeah." His smile crept upward. "She forgave me."

"Good god," Edie choked out through a laugh. "Do you ever shut off?"

"Want to find out?" He inched closer.

"No!" Edie shoved him away with the end of her guitar, still laughing. She found Henry exasperating, but he was also growing on her, like fungus, maybe, but growing. Beneath the endless innuendoes, he was kind of nice, funny, and down to earth. He didn't take himself too seriously. He went after what he wanted, and he always seemed to get it. Which led to a question . . .

"Henry? What's your endgame here?"

"My endgame?"

"Why did you want to come over?" Edie lowered her guitar and waited, unsure what she wanted to hear.

He kicked out his feet and draped an arm over the back of the bench, at ease in any setting, from palace to poolside.

"Because I like you," he said simply.

Edie frowned. She'd waited so long to hear those words from a guy, but she'd always expected them to mean something. They meant something whenever she said them, even if the boys she said them to got all shifty, abruptly changed the subject, and/or ran away. When Henry said them, they sounded so ordinary, like he was explaining why he bought french fries or watched some stupid sitcom.

"You like all girls," she pointed out.

"But you're different."

"Because I don't drop my pants when you toss me a bit of Shakespeare?"

He laughed, making his dark eyes dance in a way that *almost* incited a blush.

"Maybe," he said. "I don't know. I do enjoy the challenge."

Edie shifted backwards, disgusted.

"Of trying to make me drop my pants?"

"Of trying to make you smile," he assured her. "I don't usually have to work this hard."

"I'm well aware." Edie glanced toward the house, checking the upper-story windows for cousins with spy gear. Despite Maria's repeated assertions that she was over Henry, and despite Julia's prom plans with W.B., neither cousin had effectively feigned indifference to Edie's announcement about her impending company. When Henry made his mark on a girl's heart, he used some seriously indelible ink.

While Edie tried to figure what mark he intended to make on her own heart, and what mark she wanted him to make, she finished reintroducing herself to her mom's guitar, testing the way the strings responded so willingly to every flicker and flutter, as if they were aching to sing, shout, and cry the music they held inside. After three years of leaving her mom's guitar stringless, she'd expected this moment to feel sad, reminding her of her mom's death. Instead, it reminded her of her mom's life. Suddenly Frances was a little less gone and Edie was a little less alone.

"Ready for a song?" she asked once she was certain her tears were at bay.

Henry settled in to listen while Edie strummed a few chords. She fumbled from lack of practice but she soon found her way into a familiar series of notes. Realizing she'd inadvertently begun one of her many love songs, she shifted gears and played Henry a quirky, upbeat little tune called "Thirteen Women Named Frances" about all the nametags her mom had collected from part-time jobs. She'd pushed brooms, run registers, waited tables, done anything that would pay the bills until she could afford to try another tour. Then she'd return home and start again, dauntless. Edie's voice quavered when she neared the final chorus, quoting her mom's words, *Be brave and be kind. Everything else is just a job*, but she held herself together through the final notes, eliciting a warm round of praise from Henry.

As the song settled around them, the newly whetted memories gradually softened, leaving room for the ones that were being made in the moment. Edie was about to start another tune when Henry gestured for her to hand him the guitar.

"My turn," he said.

Edie stiffened as Claire's words echoed through her brain. *Henry only learned to play so he could serenade easily infatuated girls.* Despite how much Edie was enjoying his company, and how glad she was to not hate him anymore, she wasn't about to become the next girl on his hit list.

"Please?" Henry nodded at the guitar.

Edie eyed him dubiously but she went ahead and handed him the guitar, curious what he'd choose to play her. Henry strummed a few frenetic chords as if he was about to break into a hard rock song. Then, to Edie's surprise, he picked out a lyrical, old-fashioned folk ballad. His hands slid quickly across the strings, producing an intricate pattern of notes. His voice was low and gravelly. His words were almost spoken.

"Farewell! You are too dear for my possessing,
And I suspect you know your beauty's worth.
The smile behind your eyes leaves me but guessing;
One look lends to my lover's hope rebirth.
But I hold you not till parted lips say 'yes,'
And greatest riches can't make me deserve
One fluttering kiss upon those lips to press,
One solace for my fragile fettered nerve.
But if for one moment you did acquiesce,
And kiss for kiss did deep desire beget,
And sourest 'no' turned sweetest simple 'yes,'
When morning comes, she'd bring with her regret.
Thus have I had you, as a dream demands:
In sleep a king, but waking with a pauper's hands."

As the song faded out, Edie closed her eyes and became one with the bench. Her arms lay limp at her sides. Her face turned upward to the sky. Her heart was full. Her mom's guitar was singing again, something sweet, sad, and sincere. Edie didn't want the song to stop. She wanted to stay in that magical place where things like absent parents, ruined friendships, and persistent crushes didn't exist; that place where nothing died; that limitless, wordless place where music distilled the entire world into a series of notes and a surge of indefinable emotion.

Silence gradually took over and then rescinded its hold to the noises the song had kept at bay: birds in the branches, cars out on the road, a kid calling for his dog.

"Thank you," Edie said softly, as though she was afraid to break the spell she was under. She turned toward Henry and gave him the smile he'd been seeking. Once given it felt like a pretty cheap payment for the joy in her heart.

"Edie, I . . ." Henry took her hand. She flinched but she left her hand where it lay, wrapped in his too-warm fingers, pressed against his too-soft skin. It wasn't *The Age of Innocence*, but it was the age of something. "Say you'll go out with me."

She shook her head, unbalanced by his unexpected earnestness.

"Give me a chance," he begged. "Please?" He leaned down to meet her eyes the way he had back on that horrendous Mansfield tour day, the day that—if Edie was totally honest with herself—had been a little less lonely thanks to his company.

She searched his dark eyes for something deeper than vanity, teasing, or playing games. She recalled his thoughtful gift, his timely hand against her back, and the way he'd said good night over a threshold she wouldn't have reached without him. Despite Henry's smugness, he had a heart and a pretty good one at that. And yet . . .

Edie withdrew her hand and tucked it close beside her.

"I don't think that's a good idea." While she liked the thought of spending more time with Henry, she didn't want to date him. He was obviously trying to make her fall for him. She was determined *not* to fall for him. She lived with two people who already *had* fallen for him. They couldn't just pass him to the next girl in line. They were a camera away from becoming a reality TV show.

Henry glanced over his shoulder toward the Summerses' house.

"In other words, you're still hoping that other guy comes around?"

Edie sighed. The moment had passed. The music had ended. The glorious, languid, just-the-right-size feeling she'd been wallowing in vanished, erased by the intrusion of annoying realities.

"I'm over it," she said. "Mostly." She got up and took the guitar from Henry. It was time to head inside. Henry had been the perfect diversion from everything that was stressing her out, but the conversation had soured, turning to the absolute last topic she wanted to discuss. Why couldn't they just end their afternoon with a song and a smile?

Henry casually reclined as if he was in no hurry to leave.

"If it's any help," he said, "they've been fighting like crazy lately."

A little flutter of hope tickled Edie's belly, followed quickly by a rush of self-loathing for hanging so pathetically on anything that fed her fantasy.

"I don't need to know that," she said.

"I could do some reconnaissance for you."

At the suggestion, something snapped inside Edie. She planted herself in front of Henry, scowling hard enough to wilt the roses.

"What are you doing?" she demanded.

"What do you mean?" He blinked up at her, all innocence and confusion.

"One minute you're singing me this amazing song and asking me to break my heart over you. The next, you're offering to help me get another guy, one you've repeatedly told me not to hold out for."

"Maybe I just want to see you happy."

Edie opened her mouth, ready to spout a whole slew of denials. Henry wasn't an altruist. He only wanted to make *himself* happy. He was collecting conquests, scheming to win her over by any means possible so he could add one more broken heart to his growing list. Then again, what if, just this once, he wasn't tossing out another sweet but hollow phrase, presuming it was what she wanted to hear? What if he really meant it?

"Henry? Have you ever been friends with a girl?"

He considered for a moment, running a thumb along the back of the bench.

"I guess not."

"Well, there's a first for everything."

Chapter Twenty

IN THE DAYS THAT FOLLOWED THE COMMENCE-
ment of Edie's unlikely friendship with Henry, she started her job
and caught up on her homework. She also wrote three more discard-
able essays: one about Catherine the Great, one about Catherine de'
Medici, and one about a woman named Catherine who busked by
the Burger Barn back in Ithaca. Meanwhile, Julia was glum. Maria
was aloof. Claire was polite but terse. She avoided Edie in the halls.
She switched seats in any classes where she was previously only a
desk away. She used the lunch hour to gloat about Sebastian: their
amazing night last Saturday, the romantic getaway they planned
after graduation, and the condo she was going to help him furnish in
New York, where they'd be all cozy together on weekends. The girls
cooed and sighed, goading her on, but Edie suspected Claire's stories weren't just an attempt to share her joy or entertain her friends.
She was staking her claim.

Without kissing anyone, Edie had managed to upset three girls.
This might've given her good reason to steer clear of both Sebastian
and Henry for a while, but it had the opposite effect. Edie felt even

more isolated and therefore even more desperate for a friend. At that particular juncture, only two people were volunteering for the position.

Thus Edie found herself on Friday afternoon in Sebastian's bedroom, scanning his shelves for books to borrow while he sat cross-legged on his bed in a loose pair of linen shorts and a Yale T-shirt Tom had given him before getting expelled. The room was large but bland, with simple, modern furniture and an almost oppressive amount of navy blue. Neatly organized bookshelves lined one wall while a trio of sailboat photos hung above the bed on the other side of the room. When asked, Sebastian confessed that his mom hung the photos about five years ago. She thought he was into sailing because he had a toy boat as a kid. He didn't want to disappoint her so he left the pictures up. Sensing a theme in his life, Edie dropped the subject there.

They continued to chat while Edie picked out a few books. Sebastian noted that he and his parents had been looking at condos near Washington Square. Edie talked about how much she enjoyed her new job. She pulled out an old hardback copy of *Adam Bede* and stared at the cover, wondering why the title was jarring her. Then she remembered it was the George Eliot novel she'd quoted on her first day back in Mansfield. As she removed it from the shelf, ready to ask Sebastian about it, a chunk of papers slipped out with the book, folded in half and stapled together. She unfolded it and read the front page: *The Safety of Boxes, by Sebastian Summers*. In the top corner was a handwritten note that said, *Submit this,* followed by a few lines of illegible scribbles and an A+.

"What's this?" Edie returned the book and held up the paper.

Sebastian pressed his long legs against his chest, crossing and uncrossing his ankles as if he didn't quite know how to make all his pieces fit together.

"A short story I wrote for class," he admitted. "I guess my teacher liked it. She thinks I should submit it to a literary magazine, but I don't know. My parents would be really hurt if they knew other people were reading about our family."

"What's it about?" She forced herself not to peek past the cover page.

Sebastian ran his full gamut of tics and twitches, scratching his neck, tugging at his collar, smoothing his hair. Edie was about to apologize for prying when he spoke up.

"It's about that day in June. When we hid in my dad's old wardrobe."

Edie closed her eyes as the memories swept in: two kids cramped in a cabinet, knees to noses, drawing lampposts and lions on old wood, their wool scarves wrapped around their necks in the middle of summer, certain that if they waited long enough, Mr. Tumnus would take them to a land of endless winter. Playing Narnia had been one of their favorite games, a way to escape into their combined imaginations. Then, one day, when the house was filled with people in black suits and black dresses, whispering their *sorry*s and sympathies as if saying the words any louder would shatter the listeners, the wardrobe became more than a game. It turned into a refuge where an eight-year-old boy could hide his tears while a seven-year-old girl wrapped her gangly arms around his bobbing shoulders and they shared one of their first silences.

"I remember that day." A lump rose in Edie's throat, making her breath jagged.

"I begged my mom to keep the wardrobe but she said there was no point holding on to broken things."

Edie wrapped a hand around her locket, brushing the loose hinge with the side of her thumb.

"I kinda like broken things," she said.

"Yeah. Me too." Sebastian rubbed at a worn corner on his bed-side table, his eyes downcast and his expression unsettled. After a long moment, he looked up and met Edie's eyes. "I don't know how I would've pulled through that summer without you. How did you always know exactly what I needed when I needed it?"

"Did I?" Edie's voice cracked, as though her body were expanding to make more room for all her emotions.

"You were the best friend a boy could ask for."

They shared a smile as they added another complicated silence to their expanding repertoire, full of mutual awareness that life was sometimes difficult, often unfair, always imperfect, and best when shared with someone who loved you. As all the things that didn't need to be said gradually settled, Edie glanced at Sebastian's story, saddened to think his teacher might be the only one to ever read it.

"Will you ever let me read some of your writing?" she asked.

"I guess so. If you let me hear one of your songs."

Edie lit up at the idea. Now that she was playing again, she had so many songs she wanted to share with him, not the love songs but the ones about empty spaces, unexpected losses, and unspoken good-byes, the sort of songs Sebastian would understand. He wouldn't tell her she was being melodramatic, sentimental, or temperamental. He knew how it felt to redefine words like *home*, *family*, and *us*.

"Promise?" she asked.

"Yeah, just, um, maybe not today? And maybe not that story?" Sebastian tipped his chin toward the papers, biting back what Edie finally realized might be tears.

She wedged the story in with the books.

"Okay," she said. "Whenever you have something you want to share."

Edie and Sebastian settled into an easy camaraderie for the rest of the afternoon, thanks largely to Edie's proposal that they escape their deep thoughts by busying themselves with an activity. Sebastian suggested swimming or shooting hoops while Edie tossed out a few ideas that didn't involve bare skin or the risk of physical contact. After an increasingly silly brainstorming session, they decided to try baking. Neither of them had much experience, but at least the task got them out of the bedroom.

Over the next couple hours they burned three batches of choco-late chip cookies while they lost themselves in an animated discussion about the courses they wanted to take next year, the bands they were each listening to, and the ending to *Villette*, which had left them both reeling. The only topic they completely avoided was their love lives. Edie of course had lied about hers and hoped she'd never have to admit it. She wasn't sure about Sebastian's motives for avoiding the topic, but she didn't question them for long. Less Claire was all good.

As Edie scrubbed the encrusted cookie pan and Sebastian threw away the evidence of their mutual distraction, she smiled to herself. She might not be as "over" her crush as she'd claimed to Henry last weekend, but she'd made some strides in building a friendship. Not just any friendship. One that really mattered. Maybe Edie'd finally learned her lesson about unavailable guys. Maybe an afternoon with Henry had provided the diversion she needed. Maybe the repeated blare of the smoke alarm prohibited a romantic mood. However the change had transpired, things were finally good between her and Sebastian, culinary catastrophe notwithstanding.

When Edie was ready to head home for dinner, Sebastian walked her to the door. He paused in the foyer while she stepped onto the front stoop, carefully balancing a small stack of borrowed books. The two of them faced each other, both shifting awkwardly as per habit, but without the tension that'd plagued so many of their interactions. He no longer seemed racked by an internal dilemma. She no longer felt preoccupied with what she couldn't have. There was no fence between them.

"Got a quote before you go?" he asked. "Something from our pal C. S. Lewis?"

"I read those books a long time ago."

"C'mon. Show off that Velcro memory."

Edie took a moment to consider Sebastian's unread story, his secret longing to be more like the kid he once was, and his incongruity within a house filled with too few broken things. Then she thought through all her favorite phrases about frigates, forests, fawns, and fantasy, seeking a quote that might resonate not to a child, but to a guy who hadn't yet realized that his imagination was something to use, not something to hide.

"'One day,'" she said, "'you will be old enough to start reading fairytales again.'"

A smile spread across Sebastian's face, slowly, sweetly, sadly.

"You're amazing."

"I'm a freak of nature."

"Guess the score's four to two now."

Seizing the moment to prompt a little honesty, Edie took a bracing breath and forced herself to meet Sebastian's beautiful, blue, nice-guy eyes, nestled perfectly above softly slanted cheekbones and a pair of almost-dimples.

"We don't need to keep score anymore," she said. "Especially when you can quote yourself."

He leaned against the door frame and combed a hand through his hair, maybe because it was messy and maybe just because.

"I had a feeling you'd figure it out," he said.

"I Googled it. When I typed *I envy my words once spoken*, all I got was a bunch of definitions for 'envy.'" She adjusted her armload of books but she kept her eyes on his. "I liked what you said."

"Really?" he asked as if astonished.

"Of course," she said as if astonished he was astonished.

His dimples lost their almost-ness as his eyes began to sparkle. Edie felt a little surge of joy, knowing she helped put that sparkle there. God, she was glad she wasn't trying to avoid him anymore. They were good as friends. They spoke the same language. They could cheer each other on among a sea of people who didn't understand them.

Sebastian set his hand on the doorknob. Edie took his gesture as her cue to leave, grateful she didn't need to stammer out an excuse about things in things. As she said goodbye and headed down the front steps, he called after her.

"We should do this again sometime."

She spun around, eyeing him uncertainly.

"The Toll House gods would argue otherwise."

"Not the baking," he clarified through a laugh. "Just, you know, hanging out."

"Sure. Great. Anytime."

"Tomorrow evening?" He watched her in that way he had, as if his questions were bigger than they sounded and her answers held weight.

Edie mentally ran through her Saturday agenda: write her umpteenth useless scholarship essay, study for her calculus test, start reading another dense novel, watch a few cat videos. None of it sounded half as nice as spending more time with Sebastian. Was it weird to hang out two days in a row? Did it matter?

"Okay," she said.

He beamed at her so brightly he *almost* fluttered a butterfly in her belly. Then his smile dropped away, replaced by an embarrassed grimace.

"Sorry. I forgot." He knotted a fist in his hair. "I promised Claire . . ."

Edie forced a stiff smile, thankful for his ambiguity. The less she knew about his relationship with Claire, the better. Her crush had diminished that week, but envy was a wily opponent, prone to stealth attacks. She was about to assure Sebastian they could hang out another time, but he spoke up first.

"Claire and I talked about doing a game night. You up for that?"

"Um, maybe?" Edie wasn't sure she was ready to hang out with both Sebastian *and* Claire, especially after Claire had been so prickly at school. Should she fake a flu or invent a prior commitment? Or was being around Sebastian's girlfriend the next step in cementing their friendship?

"We'd need a fourth." His gaze drifted upward while he drummed his fingers against his lips. "Know anyone who likes to play games?"

Edie almost laughed. Despite all the unanswerable questions swimming through her brain lately, this last one was easy.

"Yeah," she said. "I know someone who *loves* to play games."

Chapter Twenty-One

EDIE OPENED THE FRONT DOOR TO FIND HENRY leaning against the nearest column of the portico. While she'd thrown on her cutoffs and a thrifted tee that declared, CECI N'EST PAS UNE T-SHIRT, he wore a sleek black dress shirt and a pair of dark jeans that sat low on his hips. His arms were folded. His posture was relaxed but confident. His familiar smirk was already in place.

"Thanks for coming over," she said.

"Are you kidding? Eat Your Heart Out is one of my favorites."

Edie shot him a glare.

"Poker only," she reminded him. They'd covered this via text when she reached out to see if he was free tonight. Apparently they hadn't covered it enough.

"We can't play a *little* dirty?" he begged. "You'll lean your head on my shoulder and gaze at me adoringly. I'll whisper nonsense into your ear. Summers will seethe with jealousy." Henry's smirk deepened.

So did Edie's glare.

"Henry—" she started.

"Okay. Okay." He held up his palms in surrender. "But we can at least kick their asses at poker, right?"

"As long as you don't cheat."

"Cheating's not my style. I prefer to earn my victory." He gave her a cheeky look that indicated he meant more than he said. Then he held out his elbow.

Edie ignored both the look and the elbow as she set off toward the Summerses' house with Henry sauntering along by her side. Claire and Sebastian were setting up a card table on the back patio. Claire was holding up a corner, looking perfect as always in a cute eyelet mini-dress and with a thick black braid draped over one shoulder. Sebastian was in his usual slightly rumpled linens, crouched down and extending a table leg. He paused as he spotted Edie and Henry.

"Oh, hey, Henry." He scratched his forehead, twitching and befuddled. "Right. You meant . . . huh. Okay."

"I'm so glad we're doing this," Claire eagerly put in as if to compensate for Sebastian's mangled greeting. "I haven't played poker in ages. Though if I know Henry, competition will be stiff." Despite her iciness all week at school, Claire was back to her usual cheerful, chatty, and charming self. If she had any lingering resentments, she was masking them well. "I hear you two have been playing guitar together."

Sebastian's eyes darted to Edie's. Guilt rippled through her as she recalled his request to play together and her abrupt dismissal of the idea.

"We played a little," she hedged. "To test my new strings."

"Right. The strings." Claire smirked at her brother. "That was sweet of him, wasn't it?"

In the next second, all eyes were on Edie. Claire's were amused. Sebastian's were curious. Henry's didn't even hint at modesty. He simply stood by, waiting for his due praise. Edie forced back an eyeroll as she evaded the question by inquiring about refreshments. Her opinion of Henry's "sweetness" was none of Claire's business, or Sebastian's, or even Henry's. Frankly, she hadn't figured it out for herself yet.

While Sebastian headed inside to forage for food and drinks, Edie gathered chairs, Henry distributed chips, and Claire shuffled the cards. Conversation between the two girls might've quickly grown tense, but Henry provided the perfect buffer, gently teasing his sister or directing the conversation to stay on innocuous topics like the new Jupiter's Grind album they'd all been listening to. Edie had to hand it to him. Whether or not he was sweet, he was remarkable at reading a room—or a backyard—and adjusting his behavior accordingly.

Sebastian soon returned with a stack of tumblers, a couple ice trays, a two-liter bottle of ginger ale, and a bag of pretzels.

"The snack selection's limited," he said as he started filling glasses. "Too bad we burned all those cookies yesterday."

Claire stiffened.

"We?" she asked.

Sebastian paused, mid-pour.

"Edie came over to borrow books yesterday," he explained.

"Borrow books or bake cookies?" Claire smiled, impeccably polite, but the challenge in her tone was impossible to miss, as was the flicker of insecurity in her eyes.

Sebastian stammered out yet another iteration of his earnest but flimsy Just Friends Defense, shuffling in a way that did little to help his case. Claire listened, dead still. Edie watched in silence. She hated seeing Claire hurt and Sebastian guilt-ridden, but she suspected anything she said would only make matters worse. Turning small messes into big messes seemed to be her specialty lately. She should've known Claire would get upset by her afternoon with Sebastian, especially if he failed to mention it for just long enough to look like he was hiding something.

Edie looked to Henry, silently willing him to help. He nodded almost imperceptibly.

"Aww, you baked for me?" He laced his fingers through hers and nestled the knot on the table. "Now who's the sweet one?"

Edie barely had time to process his insinuation when Sebastian fumbled with the soda bottle, knocking over a glass and sending a wave of ginger ale her direction. It splashed down her chest and soaked her shirt. He blurted out a string of embarrassed apologies, but Edie waved him off.

"It's just a T-shirt," she said.

"Lucky you." Claire backed away from the dripping table. "The rest of us would've required dry cleaning."

Edie bristled at the underlying insult, but she let it lie as she excused herself to assess the damage. A minute later, she stood in the bathroom, scowling at her reflection while rubbing her chest with a monogrammed hand towel. The situation was classic. They hadn't even dealt the first hand and Claire was already on the offensive, Sebastian was on the defensive, and Edie was coated in corn syrup. She'd obviously pushed this friendship idea too far, too fast. She shouldn't have expected everything to change overnight. Relationships were complicated, especially when they affected more than two people.

As Edie wondered if she could use the spilled soda as an excuse to abandon the game entirely, Henry stepped into the doorway.

"You all right?" he asked.

"It's just a T-shirt," she repeated.

"I wasn't asking about your clothes."

Edie shrugged as she dampened the towel and wiped off her collarbone. Henry was smart enough to sense how she felt. She didn't have to explain it. While he leaned against the door frame, she took a good look at the Rorschach blot on her chest.

"This is useless." She tossed the towel onto the counter. "I should go change."

"Take one of mine." Henry pulled his dress shirt over his head, catching a black undershirt and removing both at once. "Your choice." He extracted one shirt from the other and held them out. "My vote's for the A-line, but you can make your own call."

Edie didn't reach for either shirt. She stood stock-still, uncomfortably aware that Henry was standing half naked before her.

Despite his professed aversion to sports, especially anything that wasn't coed, he'd obviously found a gym nearby. His arms were strong. His stomach was ripped. His skin was smooth, clear, and a shade too dark for the traditional vampire, though demon was still up for grabs. Edie hated that she noticed his body. She hated even more that he clearly noticed her noticing.

His smile inched up as he waved his shirts at her.

"I'm not putting one on until you do," he goaded.

"And if I refuse?"

"I'll start proposing ways to keep warm."

Edie glanced out the little window behind her. Bright sunshine. Clear skies.

"It's seventy degrees outside," she said.

"Ask me if I care." Henry stepped toward her, all abs and ego.

"All right! Okay!" Edie let out a nervous laugh as she grabbed the dress shirt. She motioned for Henry to turn around. She confirmed he wasn't peeking. Then she removed her wet tee and put on his shirt. It was cozy and soft. She took her time rolling up the sleeves, adjusting the shoulders, and running her hands down the smooth, crisp cotton. It still held his heat and his smell, like juniper and cedar. Either Henry had hugged a tree recently or Lucifer endorsed cologne after all.

Edie thanked him for the shirt. He turned to face her, nodding in approval. She pretended not to notice his body again as he slipped his undershirt over his head and tugged it down to his waist. He pretended not to notice her pretending.

"Better?" He tipped his chin at her shirt while smoothing his own, leaving her to interpret his question at will.

"Um ... yeah." She felt a blush creep up her neck. She quickly distracted herself by balling up her T-shirt, the one that so fortuitously required no dry cleaning. Damn Claire, anyway. And damn Sebastian, too. This mess wasn't all Edie's fault. Things were going just fine until those stupid cookies came up. "I get why your sister doesn't like me," she told Henry. "But I'm not trying to steal her boyfriend."

"So prove it."

"How?"

"Show her you're into someone else."

"But I'm not."

"Then fake it."

Edie went still again. Was he kidding? He had to be kidding.

"We talked about this at the pool party," she reminded him. "I suck at lying."

While she recalled her mortifying string of rejections and her total inability to fake so much as a handshake, he leaned against the marble countertop and picked through a dish of designer soap balls, completely at ease.

"You don't have to lie. Not really. And I'll do most of the heavy lifting." He tossed a soap ball from hand to hand. "Besides, the groundwork's already laid. They know we played guitar together. You apparently made me some truly terrible cookies. Now you're wearing my shirt. We'll plant a few more hints. Claire and Sebastian can make their own assumptions."

Edie folded her arms, astonished at how conversation kept returning to the idea of faking a relationship with Henry, whether Maria was prodding her about making Sebastian jealous or Henry was eager to play more than poker.

"Give me one good reason why I should pretend I like you," she challenged.

"Give me one good reason you shouldn't," he countered.

And there it was, a truth so obvious she couldn't deny it. Pretending to like Henry as more than a friend might not deflect all the tension in the air, but it wasn't likely to make matters worse. Sebastian's Just Friends arguments might hold more weight. Claire might be less inclined to lash out. She was awfully chipper when she was teasing Edie about the guitar strings. Besides, now that Edie'd taken a good look at Henry's shoulders, she didn't totally hate the idea of leaning her head on one of them. The plan kinda made sense, as long as she didn't get stuck lying to her cousins or her classmates later. A single evening should be manageable. A sustained relationship was out of the question.

"Okay," she conceded. "One date. Then we're back to being friends again."

"I can work with that."

They shook on it. Then Henry watched while Edie double-checked her fly, her shoelaces, and her ponytail elastic, anything to stall for a minute. When he started to chuckle, she realized she was being ridiculous. They were just going to hold hands and fake a little flirting. It was hardly cause for high anxiety.

"All right," she said at last. "Let's do this."

She stepped forward but Henry held out a hand and halted her momentum.

"Hold on a second. This setup's too good to waste. Let's at least make an entrance." Henry let down her ponytail and mussed her hair. "Now bite your lips."

"Excuse me?"

"Just chew on them for a couple seconds."

Edie did as instructed. Before she could collect herself, he took her hand and ran into the den. They circled the sectional a few times, clambering over the top, making chaos of the throw pillows, and careening around corners until they were both winded and laughing.

"You look good." He eyed her appreciatively as they paused by the back door. "If you ever want to recreate that flushed, out-of-breath look, I know a few other ways to achieve it."

"Only a few? That's not what I heard."

Henry grinned as they stepped into the backyard. Sebastian and Claire were seated next to each other at the table, hands linked and chatting amicably. The glasses were filled, the chips stacked, the cards dealt. Everything was in place.

Claire raised an eyebrow as Edie and Henry approached the table.

"I can guess what you two have been doing," she said.

"Just stacking the soaps and lining up towels." Henry tossed an arm over Edie's shoulder. "Sorry if we jostled a few things. That bathroom's a tight fit for two."

Sebastian sputtered out a cough.

Edie blushed a deep shade of scarlet.

Claire and Henry swapped an unsettlingly similar wicked smile.

And the game was on.

Chapter Twenty-Two

HENRY SWIFTLY JUSTIFIED HIS BOAST ABOUT BEING good at poker. His moves were unpredictable, his face was unreadable, and he almost always guessed what everyone else was holding. He also played his role as Edie's date with Oscar-worthy thoroughness. He gave her strategic pointers while leaning over her shoulder and touching her neck where his fingers could find bare skin. He liberally doled out compliments. He suggestively alluded to time they'd spent together without ever telling a full-out lie. All the while, his chips stacked up.

Sebastian was a terrible player. He made hasty choices. He kept forgetting the amount of the bets or the number of cards he intended to draw. He laughed at his lack of strategy, readily admitting he'd never learned to bluff or pay attention to what others might have in their hands. All the while, his chips went down.

Edie was as poor a player as Sebastian. Her heart wasn't in the game. She didn't know where it was exactly, but wherever it'd perched itself, it wasn't helping her decide whether to aim for a flush or hold on to a pair she'd been dealt. She only managed to stay afloat because Henry snuck her little clues about whether to call, raise, or fold. She hadn't planned to cheat, but then she hadn't planned to lie, either. For all her lofty moralizing with Henry, maybe her ethics were just as questionable.

Unsurprisingly, Claire was the boldest player with the highest bets. She played poker the way she ran the social scene at school, with the sort of effortlessness that implied nothing was really at risk. If she lost one hand, she'd win another. She didn't have to struggle or strategize. She simply had to play. Victory was inevitable.

After several hands, when Henry and Sebastian had already folded, Claire and Edie faced off on opposite sides of the table. Despite the general sociability of the game so far, Edie was reminded of their school lunches all week: similar positions, different stakes. When playing for social status, Edie instantly resigned herself to defeat. When playing for chips, she could at least engage in the game. If they were playing for anything else, she chose to ignore it. She stared at her two pairs, doubtful they were high enough to win the pot. Her doubts increased as Claire pushed a tall stack of chips into the center of the table, her eyes brimming with challenge.

"I bet it all," she said. "You know what they say. Go big or go home."

"I can't go big." Edie nodded at her dozen or so scattered chips.

Claire shrugged as if already tasting her triumph.

"Then I guess there's only one option," she said.

Edie tensed, sensing that Claire was hinting at more than the game. The bite in her voice was subtle enough to dismiss if anyone remarked on it, but Edie knew it well. Claire had been using it all week as she flaunted her social currency and found clever ways to remind Edie she didn't belong. So much for engaging in the game.

"I'll loan you the chips," Henry offered, already counting them out.

"That's okay." Edie set down her cards. "I fold."

"Why?" Henry asked. "Claire's got nothing."

"How do you know?" she demanded as she scooped up her winnings.

"You have a tell."

"Oh?" Claire waited, blithely curious.

Henry leaned forward, his grin slowly building.

"You smile when you're happy and you frown when you're sad."

Claire narrowed her eyes, unamused by her brother's teasing. Sebastian cooed reassurances and caressed away her irritation as quickly as it'd come on. While Edie tried to ignore their little love bubble, Henry scribbled an IOU and slid a stack of chips toward her. She was about to politely decline when Claire *tsked*.

"You shouldn't be helping her," she said. "It gives Edie an unfair advantage."

"I disagree." Henry settled back in his chair. "It evens things out a bit. Edie's new at the game."

"Then it's a good thing she brought such an experienced player." Claire matched her brother's lighthearted tone, but where Henry's movement was languid, hers was brusquely punctuated, lending her jibes more of an edge.

"So you've played a lot of poker?" Sebastian asked Henry.

"Henry's played a lot of *everything*," Claire answered for him. "He's not very particular about what he plays or who he plays it with."

Edie began to fidget, unable to ignore Claire's implications. Henry must've sensed her growing discomfort, because he rested his hand near hers and flickered her fingers as if taunting her to lace them through his. The gesture was funny and cute. It made her smile, not in a fake way.

"I shouldn't take your chips," she said quietly.

"Sure you should." He linked his pinkie finger around hers. "Hold out a few more rounds. Claire's winning streaks never last. She has no long-term strategy."

As Edie cringed at his double meaning, Claire carefully realigned her chip tower.

"At least I don't get bored after only one hand," she chided.

Henry met her gaze, surprisingly serious, meting out his words.

"My engagement level depends entirely on my opponent, and you've seen me be patient, persistent, and dedicated." After a heavy pause, he turned toward Sebastian, his composure unwavering. "Did you want to keep playing? Apparently Claire still has a few chips to spend."

Claire shot Henry a bitter glance. Edie kicked him under the table. Sebastian didn't appear to register either the glance or the kick. He simply let out a nervous laugh.

"I'm out." He held up his last three chips. "You guys are too good for me."

"Take some of mine," Claire offered as she gathered up the cards. "Edie shouldn't be the only one to accept handouts."

Edie's jaw clenched as her temper threatened to burst. Sebastian caught her eye, his expression apologetic as he smoothed the already smooth wedge cut at the back of his neck. His silent apology was kind but useless. Henry's little scheme had done wonders for about an hour, but it couldn't erase all the underlying rivalries and resentments. Of course it couldn't. Once again, Edie'd walked herself into an impossible situation, naively assuming everything would be fine as long as her intentions were good. What was that old saying? Something about good intentions paving the road to hell? No wonder things were heating up.

While Edie started plotting her exit strategy, Henry brushed aside her hair and started gently massaging the growing knot at the base of her hairline.

"You okay?" he murmured under his breath.

She nodded, grateful for his support and, strangely, his touch. His hand was warm and strong. She concentrated on the slow, spiraling motion of his thumb, trying to relax despite Claire's sharply percussive shuffling on the other side of the table.

"What are your cousins up to this evening?" she asked Edie, all sugar and honey with just a hint of razorblades. "Should we invite them to join us?"

The knot in Edie's neck tightened despite Henry's persistent efforts to untangle it.

"I think my cousins are busy," she lied. In truth, Julia and Maria were probably spying through an upper-story window. Still, better they were up there than sitting at the poker table, vying for Henry's attention and making the game even more awkward.

"It must be wonderful to have such a close family," Claire said. "Tell me, do the three of you share absolutely *everything?*"

Edie grabbed her chips, ready to fling them at Claire, but Henry wrapped his hand around hers.

"She only wins if you let her," he whispered, his lips unnervingly close to her ear, his breath tickling, his deep voice traveling all the way to her toes.

Edie released her chips as Henry continued massaging her neck. Despite her growing desire to draw the charade to a close, she was surprised to realize she was honestly happy to be there with Henry. No pretense. No game. Sure, he was only acting his part, but goddamn, the way his thumb worked away that knot and his fingertips stroked the tendons near her collarbone? That was nothing to complain about.

"So, how's the condo hunt going?" Henry asked Sebastian, shifting closer to use both hands on Edie's neck. "Find anything you like near the NYU campus yet?"

Claire quickly perked up.

"I hope you get that one with the view of the park," she said. "I told everyone at Saint Pen's about it. I can't wait for our first weekend together. I'll show you all the best places to hang out nearby."

"Actually"—Sebastian's glance scurried across the faces around him—"there's been a change of plans."

Claire stopped shuffling cards. Everyone went still. Even the birds and the breezes seemed to go on high alert. Edie got the unnerving sense she was about to witness firsthand why Sebastian didn't always tell his girlfriend the full truth about his goals, and why Claire might be less than thrilled with her boyfriend's lack of candor.

"My friends are renting a brownstone in Bushwick." He gripped the arms of his chair, released them, and gripped them again. "They offered me a room for next year."

Claire's expression hardened.

"You're kidding," she said.

"It's a cool place." He wrapped both hands around his glass and wiped away condensation with his thumbs. "It has big bay windows, a working fireplace, and enough bedrooms to fit five of us."

"Five of you?!" Claire blinked rapidly.

Sebastian sank a little lower in his chair.

Sensing both of their agony, Edie jumped in to fill the silence.

"My mom played a few open mic nights in that area. It's pretty great, actually. Old buildings, awesome graffiti, endless fire escapes. There was an antique shop on—"

"Edie, please." Claire flashed her a palm. "This has nothing to do with you."

Edie clamped her jaw shut and seethed. Henry gave her shoulders a reassuring squeeze. Sebastian started to protest but Claire quickly cut him off.

"You're seriously going to live in a glorified frat house in Brooklyn?" she asked through a strained smile. "Why?"

"I'm tired of owing my stepdad so much, of feeling like I have to do what he wants. I'd rather get a place I can afford on my own."

Edie felt a surge of pride that Sebastian was finally standing up for himself and making his own choices, though she wasn't sure he'd chosen the best time to reveal them, especially now that Claire's knuckles were whitening against the deck of cards.

"What's so awful about being comfortable?" Claire asked.

"What's so awful about being independent?" Sebastian countered.

"People should only slum it they have no choice. No offense, Edie."

Edie leapt up, ready to snap, but Henry stood with her.

"That's our cue to depart," he said.

"I didn't mean—" Claire started.

"You never do," Henry said, his tone surprisingly clipped, "but I promised Edie we'd have some alone time."

As Edie pushed back her chair, grateful to get the hell out of there, Henry bent down and swept her up, flinging her legs over his elbow so she was cradled in his arms. She grabbed his neck and held on tight as he carried her across the patio, pausing at the top of the steps and turning back toward the others.

"You kids have a swell evening," he said. "I hope it's real 'comfortable.' No offense, Claire."

Chapter Twenty-Three

"SORRY ABOUT MY SISTER." HENRY SET EDIE DOWN near the front corner of the Vernons' house. "No one deserves to be talked to like that."

"Thanks. For real." Edie straightened her shirt, or rather his shirt, still scented with foresty, Henry-ish smells. "And that was quite an exit."

"Call that an exit?" Henry glanced past her shoulder toward the Summerses' backyard, where Claire and Sebastian were still sitting at the card table, arguing out of earshot. "They're watching. They're acting like they're not, but neither of them can bluff to save their lives. I had to blow a few hands just to keep the game going." He chuckled softly, but as he turned toward Edie, his expression shifted to a slow, suggestive smolder. "Should we give them a grand finale?"

Edie met his gaze, equal parts anxious and intrigued. As heat crept up her neck, she fixed her attention on a shirt button that didn't need any attention.

"I think I'm done," she said. "That stopped being fun about half an hour ago." Though she had to admit, she'd enjoyed the way

Henry took her side, ready to bite back against Claire in a way no one else either would or could. Edie was insulted, she was angry, and she didn't want to play any more games, but she found herself surprisingly reluctant to say goodbye to Henry, or was that his shirt talking?

"Ten more minutes," he suggested.

"Five."

"Seven and a half."

"Six and a quarter."

"Agreed."

They shook on it. Then Henry set his hands on her waist, backed her up against the side of the house, and tipped his forehead against hers. The action took her totally off-guard, like zooming in from panoramic to close-up in two seconds flat. Really close up. Amber speckles in umber irises close-up.

"I'm not going to kiss you," she said, a little breathless despite her best effort to appear as calm and collected as he did.

"And I'm not going to kiss you, but I'd appreciate it if you took your hands off your hips. Otherwise this'll look like the world's worst make-out session and I have a reputation to uphold."

She set her hands on his shoulders, letting them flop there, limp-wristed, fingers dangling, in a move she silently dubbed Dead Bunny Paws.

"How did I let you talk me into this?" she asked.

"Let's get one thing clear." He laid a hand against her cheek, gentle but unmoving, a touch that was merely for show. "This non-make-out session is a non-coerced, non-forced activity. If anything doesn't feel like a non-coerced, non-forced activity, you'll say so and said activity—or non-activity—will immediately cease."

Edie nodded.

"Good." His hand shifted against her cheek. Barely. "Now that the official business is out of the way, go left."

She mechanically tilted her head to the left. He stifled a laugh.

"Not very convincing," he said.

"I've never really"—her shoulders inched up—"you know, with a guy."

"You've never *not* made out with a guy before? I'm shocked!" Henry's eyes danced.

Edie forced her shoulders to relax. He was having fun with this. Why couldn't she?

"You know what I mean," she said. "And I've seen you, with other girls . . ."

"Only when the interest is mutual." His hand slid from her waist to her hip where his thumb laced through her belt loop and inched her closer, just for show. Maybe. "Is the interest mutual?"

"No!" She laughed, unsure if anything was funny or if her nerves were trying to escape through their only possible outlet.

"But you do want to fake it?" He lowered his head so his eyes were level with hers.

She exhaled, bracing for an extensive internal debate about lies, longing, and a hundred uncertainties around how Henry fit into all that. But there he was, standing so close with his flirty smile and his beautiful body and his warm hands, and wouldn't it be kinda great to just enjoy all that for a few minutes?

"Yes," she said. "I do."

"Then let's try to make it look a *little* more believable."

"Right. Okay." She blew out another breath as the hands that'd been resting so innocently on his shoulders began to explore nearby territory. Damn, those were brazen hands, and damn, those were nice shoulders. "You're not going to suggest I moan or anything are you?"

"You can if you want to." His hand wove through her hair, slow, calming, but not.

She leaned into his caress. It seemed like the believable thing to do.

"I don't want to," she said.

"Then don't. Go right."

She tilted her head to the right, slightly less mechanically this time. His knee slid past hers, brushing the outside of her thigh as his body drew closer.

"Moaning wouldn't have much impact," he said. "They can't hear us from over there."

"So I can say anything?"

"Anything."

"Man walks into a bar. Ouch." She ran her hands along his arms, finding the hollows where one muscle ended and another started. Damn, they were nice arms, too.

He smiled, a little bit demon/vampire, a little bit slime on rice, and a little bit just plain gorgeous.

"Giraffe walks into a bar," he said. "Orders a longneck." His fingers wrapped the edge of her waistband, barely grazing her skin.

She shivered. Seventy-degrees-in-the-sun shivered. Dreams-that-twisted-sheets shivered. No-way-to-hide-that-one shivered.

"Photographer walks into a bar. Orders a round of shots." She traced the edges of his biceps, feeling him tense under her touch. There was strength in those arms, and something clenched, held back, waiting to burst.

"Go left." His cheek swept hers as they swapped sides. His breath tickled her ear. His fingers continued pitter-patting a slow, irregular beat at the edge of her jeans. His thumb stroked her hip bone, probably not for show. "Wheel rolls into a bar. It'd fallen off the wagon."

Her hands crept down his back and slipped under the hem of his shirt.

"Lumberjack walks"—she drew a line along his spine—"into a bar"—collecting the little beads of sweat that trickled downward. "Orders a logger."

He tipped his forehead against hers again, his dark eyes inches away. He was breathing faster now. They both were. Her mind swam, unable to lock on a single clear thought. *Eyes. Skin. Heat. Hands. We all want things,* he'd said to her once, and she did want things. The tension she'd built up over the poker game was gone now, replaced by an inexplicable but intense desire to melt against Henry's body, to stop holding things in, to stop questioning and defining things. A desire to just be.

"Should I go right?" She held still as Maria's words rang in her ears. *Kissing Henry was amazing. Amazing. Amazing.*

He shook his head.

"Stay where you are. For ten." His hand wrapped the back of her neck, cupping her head and tilting it toward his. "Nine."

She drew him closer with both palms pressed against his back, one sliding up and the other sliding down.

"Eight."

She gripped his belt. He gripped her hair. Her breath caught in her throat.

"Seven." His hips met hers, barely, but enough to make one thing abundantly clear. "Six." His gaze never faltered. "Five."

The tip of her nose brushed his. And stayed there.

"Four."

Was that her pulse or was someone driving by with really loud bass music?

"Three."

Was spontaneous combustion a real thing?

"Two."

Those eyes, those demon/vampire, seduce-their-prey eyes. Good god, why were they still staring like that and why did his hands feel so strong and his skin feel so warm and his breath, his heat, his smell, and she leaned forward to close the distance and set her lips against—

"One."

He let go and stepped away, bending in half with his hands on his knees. While he caught his breath, she remained pressed against the house, unsure what would happen if she attempted to self-support. They stayed like that for a full minute, neither of them speaking, neither of them moving. Eventually Henry straightened up. He rolled his neck, shuffled his shoulders, and adjusted his jeans.

"I think they bought it." He nodded toward the Summerses' house.

Edie shrugged, unable to form words. What just happened?

"All that acting experience is good for something," he said.

She stared, blank, addled, stunned into silence.

"Let me know how you want to play the breakup."

Hands. Heat. Sweat. Skin.

"I'll go along with whatever."

Fingers against her waist. Breath on her lips. Eyes probing, wanting, resisting.

"See you around sometime?" he asked.

"I guess so," she managed.

He took a step backwards.

Touch. Tense. Shiver. Melt.

"Henry?"

"Yeah?"

Breathe. Think. Locate your brain.

"Thanks for . . . well, just thanks."

"Don't mention it." He took another step back, digging in his pocket and pulling out his car keys. As he continued retreating, they swapped a wave. Then he turned away and headed toward the road. He passed the paving stones that led toward the front door. He passed the white marble birdbath. He passed the perfectly pruned pear trees.

"Henry?!"

He spun around.

"Want to hang out next Friday? Just the two of us?"

A smile spread across his face, one that was simply happy.

"Fuck, yes."

Chapter Twenty-Four

MONDAY SUCKED. TUESDAY WAS WORSE. BY Wednesday, Edie was researching bus fare to California, where she planned to busk for taco money until August. On Thursday she wrote her most original "Who I'd Be if I Could Be Anybody" essay, which was a list of famous women who shared one distinguishing and enviable trait: they were dead. Despite Edie's amicable aspirations over the weekend, the poker game resulted in three decidedly unfriendly consequences:

1. *Henry made an appearance in her latest sex dream, which for some reason also involved a rowboat, a snowman, and a lot of really weird jazz music.*
2. *Sebastian went radio silent. No texts. No waves over the fence. Nothing.*
3. *Claire's antagonism escalated from veiled to vengeful.*

Edie wasn't sure why Claire was so mad at her. Henry was the one prodding her during the game. Edie'd barely said a word, and

Sebastian hadn't paid her any noticeable attention. Maybe Claire blamed her for corrupting the Great Manhattan Love Nest Project. Or maybe the Crawfords followed some mysterious sibling code, forcing Edie to take the blows Claire wouldn't aim at her own brother. Then again, maybe Edie had done to Claire exactly what she'd done to Shonda: deliberately sought attention that belonged to someone else. No matter how hard she tried to treat Sebastian like a friend now, the damage was already done. She couldn't fix it in one weekend, especially if Claire still sensed an underlying rivalry. Her posh boyfriend was already "slumming it" by renting a room in a Brooklyn brownstone. His chummy relationship with the neighbors' charity case was simply too much to bear.

Claire was clever in her assault. She wasn't overtly mean in front of the other girls. She simply made it clear that Edie's presence at Saint Pen's was tolerated, not welcomed. She cut Edie out of conversations by turning the topics to designer clothes, exotic vacations, and other subjects Edie couldn't engage in. She launched subtly mocking comment threads on social media. She deliberately initiated activities when Edie was working. Then she posted extensively about the fun everyone was having without her. To top it all off, a rumor "somehow" circulated that Edie hadn't been in a foster home before she moved to Mansfield. She'd been in juvenile hall.

By Friday afternoon, Edie was eating her lunch on the back stairs by the fire exit, alone. She couldn't bear to sit at the table with the other girls, knowing they didn't want her there. She was also tired of the sly looks she'd been receiving all week as the other students speculated about whether she'd robbed a gas station, sold drugs, or Edie's personal favorite: started a fistfight with a shopping mall Easter Bunny. She was attempting to choke down a bean sprout and tofu paste sandwich on the world's driest spelt bread when Maria stepped out and sat down on the landing. She popped open two cans of diet soda, plunked a straw into one, and held the other out.

"I thought you might need this," she said. "Dear Mama's sandwiches are basically hairy sawdust on moldy cardboard. And that's the nice way of putting it."

Edie took the soda and set the sandwich aside, grateful for both the beverage and the unexpected company. The girls sat quietly for a minute, sipping their sodas and looking out at the empty soccer field. A lanky man in coveralls was repainting the white lines with what looked like an old lawnmower. As he started down the centerline, Edie turned toward Maria, watching the breeze play with her thick red hair.

"So, you're not mad anymore?" she asked.

"Was I mad?"

"Um, yeah. I think? About Henry?"

"Whatever." Maria flicked her hair over her shoulders, plucking a stray strand off her jacket and sending it off with the wind. "I know he's just helping you out."

"Right." Edie turned toward the field again, vaguely uneasy about hiding the full truth but uncertain anything would be gained by trying to explain a relationship she didn't understand herself. She hadn't spent much time with Henry and most of it did relate to her attempts to put her crush behind her, but a lot could happen in a few days, or even in six and a quarter minutes.

"You going to hide out here till graduation?" Maria asked.

"Depends when Claire retracts her claws."

Maria nodded while chewing on her lipstick-stained straw.

"I didn't think she'd go all *Mean Girls* about a little competition, especially from an ex-con who sold meth to the Easter Bunny." She let out a snort of laughter.

Edie slumped sideways against the iron handrail, utterly humorless.

"I should've stuck to my Avoid the Boy Next Door plan," she said. "That was working just fine."

"Except that it was boring us all to death."

Without responding, Edie peeled open her sandwich. She glared at the wilted sprouts as if they were responsible for all her problems, lying there, half-embedded in tasteless beige mush that pretended to be something it wasn't.

"Look on the bright side," Maria encouraged. "Claire wouldn't be playing Social Survivor unless she was threatened. Sebastian must like you more than you think."

"No, he doesn't. He won't even return my texts."

"Maybe he's confused."

"Or maybe his girlfriend told him I'd sexually assaulted Santa Claus."

As Edie shoved an errant sprout into place, Maria grabbed the sandwich, marched over to a nearby garbage can, and pitched it, sneering as if deeply put out by both the sulking and the sprouts. She brushed off her hands as she returned to the stoop, planting herself at the base and tapping a toe until she had Edie's full attention.

"Just so you know, Claire and Sebastian have been having issues for weeks. I mean, when they first met they were totally into each other. She loved that he wasn't like the macho assholes she was used to dating. He was blown away that this fun, popular girl liked him instead of fawning on Tom like anyone else he'd been into. They're obviously still hot for each other, but let's face it, she's bored and he's exhausted. Now I think he's mostly trying to prove something."

"To Claire?"

"To himself." Maria rummaged through her pockets and pulled out a sleek gold lipstick tube. "I mean, seriously, his brother hasn't committed to a girl for more than, like, the time it takes to burn microwave popcorn. And his mom started dating less than a year after his dad died. He was really pissed about all that."

While Maria applied a fresh coat of lipstick, Edie recalled the hours spent sitting in trees with Sebastian when they were kids, discussing his great confusion about how everyone and everything around him seemed so replaceable. He wasn't just angry. He was afraid he'd be next.

"You think he needs to prove he can make a relationship last?" Edie asked.

"I don't know. Maybe."

"Even if it's the wrong relationship?"

"So tell him what the right one is." Maria nudged Edie with a toe.

Despite a prickle of irritation, Edie felt a smile tug at her lips.

She might never fully escape Maria's patronizing prodding, but it felt less annoying now. Maria didn't have to spend her lunch break detailing Sebastian's relationship history and coaching her cousin back from despair. She could be inside making snarky remarks with her friends. She'd never turned down the opportunity before, especially where her poor relation was concerned. She was only outside with Edie for one reason: because she cared.

"I'll deal with the rumors." Maria pocketed her lipstick. "Except for the Easter Bunny one. I kinda love thinking you KO'd a creepy perv in a fur onesie. Some of those guys deserve a punch in the nose."

Edie laughed as she tossed the rest of her lunch and prepared to head inside.

"Why are you helping me?" she asked. "Claire's your friend."

"Yeah." Maria scoffed. "But *you* are family."

With a swell of something Edie could only call love, she threw her arms around Maria and gave her the biggest, most painfully earnest hug she could manage. Edie might've lost a place at a table that week, but in exchange, she'd gained a family. As spoils of war went, she couldn't ask for more.

Chapter Twenty-Five

MARIA PROVED TRUE TO HER WORD. WITHOUT directly confronting Claire and escalating matters further, she deftly shut down the gossip mill and ushered her cousin back into the fold. Edie didn't understand how Maria had accomplished everything, especially within a matter of hours, but she was profoundly grateful. She promised herself that if she was ever in a position to do something nice for Maria, she wouldn't hesitate, no matter the circumstances.

When Friday's classes finally slogged their way to an end, Claire slipped away to a dance lesson, Catie and Katie headed to lacrosse practice, and Edie walked out the front doors of Saint Penitent's with Maria, Taylor, and Phoebe. Phoebe was reminding everyone to vote for prom queen when Julia burst through the doors and begged Maria for a ride. They'd barely begun to squabble when Edie stopped short.

Thirty yards away, at the base of the school steps, a fancy white sports car was parked in the drive that circled the flagpole. The car looked like it belonged in a sci-fi movie. It was long, low, and spotlessly shiny, with headlights like narrowed eyes. Leaning against the car was an impossibly gorgeous demon/vampire wearing a sharp black suit and tie. Even more disconcerting, he was holding a piece of paper with MISS EDIE PRICE written on it.

"Holy shit." Taylor gripped Edie's shoulder as the chatter dropped off.

"Isn't that Claire's brother?" Phoebe asked.

"Yep." Edie glanced at her cousins, worried they were about to throttle her.

Julia slumped against the wall and pouted in silence while Maria pulled out a compact and finessed her mascara, a gesture that would've proven a better ruse at masking her curiosity if her mirror wasn't facing directly at Henry.

"Hot date?" Taylor asked.

"Just a friend," Edie said.

"*That* doesn't look like friend material." Phoebe canted an eyebrow.

"Friend with benefits, maybe." Taylor fanned her face.

Edie squirmed, uncertain what she'd gotten herself into. She was pretty sure she and Henry were just friends, but they hadn't discussed faking a breakup yet. They hadn't actually discussed anything about what happened last weekend. Since Edie'd been ousted from the social circle all week, she wasn't even sure what Claire might've mentioned to the other girls. Little to nothing, probably, since Claire would consider Edie beneath Henry's notice for anything but a few heated minutes in a bathroom.

While Edie stewed, Maria extended her lashes with an almost surgical focus.

"I can't believe you got him to pull a rom-com for you," she chided.

"I didn't 'get him' to do anything," Edie argued.

"Whatever. I don't need to see the invoice. Go have fun with your new 'friend,' Edie, unless you're waiting for him to show up with a boombox or on a lawnmower." With an exaggerated eyeroll for Taylor and Phoebe's benefit, Maria returned her attention to her eyelashes, which were proving remarkably difficult to perfect unless her mirror was at *just* the right angle.

Edie decided to embrace Maria's pretense of indifference, even if she was just putting up a good front for her friends. Julia was another matter. Edie glanced her way, silently asking questions she was afraid to voice aloud.

Julia shrugged, her whole body drooping.

"If I were you, I'd be in that car by now."

"If you were her, you'd be in his lap by now," Maria said.

Julia spun on Maria, her bony fists clenched at her sides.

"At least I didn't stick my hands down his pants."

"You wouldn't know what you were looking for if you did."

"Did you really?" Taylor asked.

"Maybe." Maria looked up from her mirror. "I mean, I'm totally committed to Rupert now, but I figured I should know what I was turning down."

"And?" Phoebe prompted.

Maria smiled appreciatively, her catlike green eyes narrowing.

"Let's just say if Edie enrolls in extended benefits, she'll have a very good time."

Everyone laughed while Edie did her best to hide both her embarrassment and her judgment. Her best wasn't very good. She kept picturing poor Rupert slouched on his patio while his joy did a nosedive into a big black pool of forgotten. Meanwhile, here was Henry, utterly unscathed. He was the epitome of confidence, leaning on his gleaming car as his lips, his hands, his everything reminded Edie of six and a quarter minutes she wouldn't mind repeating, minus the Dead Bunny Paws. It didn't seem right. It didn't seem fair. So why did she want to get in that car so badly? And not get out again until every last window was thoroughly steamed over?

"Go on," Julia said.

"You sure it's not weird?" Edie asked.

"Oh, it's weird. Just don't tell me any details."

Edie finally conceded and headed down the school steps, keenly aware that at least four pairs of eyes were trained on her back. She stopped a few feet away from Henry and folded her arms, trying to manifest control despite how swiftly she was distracted by his mischievous smile and his woodsy scent.

"What are you doing here?" she asked.

"I thought we were going to hang out."

"I meant later."

"Patience isn't my greatest virtue."

"Neither is subtlety."

Henry tossed his sign into the back seat. Then he walked around to the other side of the car and opened the passenger door.

"At least let me give you a ride home," he offered.

"No games? No bargaining? No wicked little schemes?"

"Just a ride home." He waited there, posed like a chauffeur, until Edie overcame her last iota of resistance and climbed in.

"What's with the suit?" she asked as they settled into the deep bucket seats.

"I was helping my mom at her office today." Henry cinched his tie in the rearview mirror. "I also thought it made me look trustworthy."

"Not with those eyes."

He bent lower to assess his reflection.

"What's wrong with these eyes?"

"I know where they've been."

"They've reformed."

"Doubtful." As Edie swung her messenger bag onto her lap, it banged the dashboard and popped open the glove compartment. Inside was a stack of papers, a tin of mints, a pack of cards, and about a dozen condoms. "Good god." She gaped openly. "How much sex do you have in this car?"

Henry leaned back and lazily rolled his head toward her, his black hair cow-licking over the corners of his forehead, his dark eyes dancing.

"You really want to know?" he asked.

"No. Sorry." Edie slammed the compartment shut. "Forget I asked."

Henry started the ignition while Edie pretended seatbelts and airbags were the only forms of protection at hand. As he put the car in gear, he gave her a quick appraisal.

"Love the uniform," he said.

Edie grimaced, tugging her skirt to cover a bit more leg.

"One more comment like that and I'm exiting the car, even if it's in motion."

"Fair enough." He flashed her a grin, his white teeth glowing brightly against lips that had no right to look so kissable. "Don't forget I'm new at this whole friendship idea. Give me some time to figure it out."

"You have fifteen minutes. Let's see if you can make it to the Vernons' without another revolting line."

"Only fifteen minutes?"

"You do remember where I live?"

"Sure, but the route's a little longer if we go my way."

Two hours after leaving Saint Penitent's, Henry pulled up in front of the Vernons' house. He put the car in park and rested his forearms on the steering wheel. He watched Edie gather her belongings, which now included two additional items: an antique table runner Edie'd purchased for herself and an old hardback copy of *Twelfth Night* Henry had purchased for her. Edie knew the gift was a calculated maneuver, but she was impressed that he remembered their first conversation, back when she'd chided him for quoting "music is the food of love." Henry noticed things. Edie liked that about him. She also liked that she didn't have to fight for his attention, wonder what he was thinking, or censor what she said around him.

"Well?" he prompted as his fingers drummed the steering wheel.

Edie tensed. Was he asking if he could kiss her? Did he think this was a date? She'd only asked him to hang out. *Without* Claire and Sebastian. Didn't she? Or did she inadvertently imply something else?

"Well what?" she asked.

"When can I see you again?"

With a strange mix of relief and disappointment about the kissing issue, Edie thought through her schedule. Now that she had a job, she didn't have much free time. She planned to fill most of it with homework, fruitless essay generation, and a few online guitar lessons she'd set up to bring in some extra money.

"I don't know," she said. "I'll text you?"

Henry narrowed his eyes.

"Are you playing hard to get?"

"I'm playing hard to pay for college."

"Ah." He nodded knowingly, though as a "man of leisure" he probably never had to worry about money. "Can I help by buying you dinner this weekend?"

"That sounds a lot like a date."

"Does it? Damn. Guess I really am terrible at subtlety."

Edie laughed and promised she'd find another time for them to hang out next week, just so he could get a little more practice being friends with a girl. In turn, he promised to pay close attention to any instruction she was willing to impart.

While he drove away, she added a post to her lexicon.

Friendship

noun

1. A mutually affectionate relationship, exclusive of family or sexual relations.
2. The association you're trying to form with a guy who's way more interested in sexual relations than a bond of mutual affection. Or is that you?
3. A word you keep trying to apply to other people even though you still associate it most with the person you hope will eventually read this and find a way to forgive you.

Edie stared at the screen, praying for a response. After five weeks in Mansfield, she still hadn't received a single kind word from Shonda, despite uncountable texts, emails, phone messages, and lexicon posts. Edie might've claimed to Sebastian that she liked broken things, but friendships were best kept whole. Once damaged, they were far too hard to mend.

She was putting away her phone when the front door swung open. Maria stood inside the foyer, her arms folded, her toe tapping.

"Have a nice time?" she asked with faux civility.

"Yep." Edie started to edge her way into the house, hoping to avoid Maria's usual round of Twenty Questions I Won't Quite Ask About Henry. She was halted by a dull *thunk* and a metallic rattle from the Summerses' driveway. She craned her neck toward the noise but she couldn't see anything past the corner of the Vernons' house.

"He's been out there for, like, ever," Maria said. "I thought he was shooting hoops, but it looks more like he's trying to torpedo a hole through his parents' garage."

Edie and Maria crept over to the edge of the portico where they had a full view of the Summerses' driveway. Sebastian was backing away from his garage while dribbling a basketball. He was barefoot, shirtless, and drenched in sweat. Edie felt her skin flush as her eyes lingered on his shifting back muscles, reminding her of the Rodin sculpture that'd inspired their fumbling kiss all those years ago.

"Hot, huh?" Maria whispered. "I mean, he's a total nerd, so don't get him talking too long or anything, but I see why you want to play naked Twister with him."

Edie's blush deepened. She hadn't previously considered naked Twister, but the idea had its appeal.

Sebastian hauled back and flung the ball, full force, not into the hoop that hung just below the peaked roof, but straight at the garage door, where several gray smudges marred the off-white panels. As the girls crept backwards, he collected the ball and hurled it at the door again, grunting with the effort. Edie was stunned. She'd never seen Sebastian get angry before. He'd always been so kind and soft-spoken, far more likely to escape into a book or a wardrobe than to lash out physically.

"Did he and Claire have another fight?" Edie asked.

"How should I know?" Maria swatted away a fly, glaring as though it'd flown past deliberately to annoy her. "Why don't you ask her brother now that you two are such good 'friends'?" She enunciated the final word, punctuating her question like a challenge.

Sebastian rattled the drainpipe with an ill-aimed throw, startling both girls and saving Edie from answering Maria's question directly.

"They must've practically come to blows," she said. "Maybe you were right about their relationship."

"Maybe." Maria let out one of her trademark scoffs. "Then again, the harder the fighting, the hotter the makeup sex."

Edie groaned as she wilted against the corner of the house.

"I didn't need to hear that."

While Sebastian continued torturing his garage, Edie peeked around the corner and Maria leaned a shoulder against the nearest column, her eyes trailing Sebastian.

"Actually I think Claire's still at the dance studio. So this bizarre display of man-rage might be because you were out with Henry all afternoon."

Edie nearly dropped her bag, unsure which part of Maria's statement startled her most: the idea that Sebastian knew she'd been with Henry, or the notion that it might've upset him so badly.

"How did he know I was with Henry?" she asked.

"Because I told him." Maria gave Edie the same glare she'd given the fly a minute earlier. "That was the point of Henry's little limo service, right? It's not going to make Sebastian jealous if he doesn't even know. God, you suck at subterfuge!"

Edie couldn't quite tell if Maria was goading her to make a confession or if she really did think Henry was on hire. Edie was about to set things straight but she didn't know what to say. How many times could she argue that she and Henry were just hanging out as friends? The more she said it, the more she sounded like she was only trying to convince herself.

As if sensing Edie's quandary, Maria wrapped an arm around her shoulders and gave her an affectionate little squeeze.

"Forget about boys," she said. "Let's go find some comfort food."

"You eat comfort food?"

"Totally, but only on Fridays, full moons, and even-month holidays."

Edie laughed as she leaned into Maria's embrace, grateful one relationship wasn't making her head spin.

"C'mon." Maria steered Edie toward the front door. "We've got about ten minutes to raid my dad's secret snack drawer before Dear Mama gets home."

"Does he still keep mango gummy squares in there?"

"I'm pretty sure he orders them special, just for us."

Chapter Twenty-Six

SUNDAY AFTERNOON, AFTER NORAH SENT HER outside for "making a racket," Edie sat in the garden, strumming her guitar and trying to form words out of feelings, which was like trying to make pudding out of astronomy. Softly, quietly, to the birds, the trees, and the cupids that were kind enough not to laugh, she sang.

> *"What would you say if I told you okay?*
> *Would you dress up my yeses in velvet and gold?*
> *What would you think if we went to the brink?*
> *Would you leave me uneasy with no hand to hold?*
> *How would you feel if your dream became real?*
> *Though people in deep will still wake up alone?*
> *What would you do if I broke my heart over you?"*

When a car door slammed to Edie's right, she crept through the hedges and peeked toward the Summerses' driveway. Claire was pulling away in her cute little convertible, tailpipe smoking, tires screeching. Sebastian stood beside his house and watched her leave, his hands jammed into his pockets, shaking his head. After a long and painful pause, when Claire's car was well out of sight, he picked up a rock and weighed it in his hand. Then he flung it toward the street, cursing as the rock arced its way down the driveway and rolled to a stop near the mailbox.

Edie stepped backwards, not wanting to intrude on a private moment. A branch caught her guitar string, announcing her presence with a sharp *twang*. Sebastian spun toward her. She waved, barely, as the heat flooded her cheeks. She was mortified to be caught spying. She hadn't meant to spy but she could hardly claim she was doing anything else while she was basically hugging the shrubbery.

Sebastian approached the fence, pointing over his shoulder.

"I, um, we just, that was—"

"Doesn't matter." Edie sidled out from behind the hedges. She set her guitar on a bench and stepped onto the gravel path. "You guys'll work it out."

"I don't know. Maybe." He stared off toward the road as his face ran a gamut of indecipherable but joyless expressions. "Sometimes I feel like I'd do anything for her. Other times I wonder, if we don't make each other happy, is it all worth it?"

Edie shrugged, offering him the most noncommittal response she could muster since *Hell, no, run screaming, she's sucking your soul* seemed hyperbolic, inflammatory, and less than helpful for Sebastian's current state of confusion.

"Sorry I went AWOL." His gaze traveled from the street to his toes, avoiding Edie entirely. "Things have been weird since the pool party. I probably shouldn't have mentioned the cookies. Or set up the poker game. Claire thinks, I mean, she got the impression"—he traced a groove in the driveway with his toe—"she just worries about things she shouldn't. I didn't want to make the situation worse."

Edie cringed as she silently rescinded her ungenerous thoughts. Claire wasn't sucking anyone's soul. She might've put undue pressure on Sebastian and done her utmost to make Edie's life miserable lately, but she had her own problems, not the least of which was a boyfriend who wasn't totally honest with her, or with himself.

As Sebastian continued redrawing lines and as Edie scrambled for words that wouldn't come, a silence stretched out that was far too complicated to be comfortable. It was finally broken when a group of kids rode their bikes down the street, daring each other to take their hands off the handlebars. They laughed and shouted, gloriously oblivious to anything more complicated than the need to be home before dark.

"I used to do that," Sebastian said. "I used to be fun."

"You're still—"

"No, I'm not." He shook his head as his shoulders crept upward. "Not like I want to be."

Edie studied him, frustrated that he was beating himself up again. She knew better than to argue his point, but she wondered if she could show him he was fun, in his own way. She pointed to the giant sycamore in the back corner of Norah's garden.

"Remember our tree?" she asked.

"Of course." He peered past her shoulder, shading his eyes with a hand. "You used to tie Pixy Stix to the branches."

"Only the green ones."

"Because you knew they were my favorite?"

"Because they made you look like you licked a frog." And because they were his favorite.

Sebastian smiled just enough to make Edie feel like she'd *finally* said the right thing.

"I haven't climbed a tree in years," he said.

Edie backed away from the fence, edging toward the tree.

"Maybe it's time to renew old habits," she hinted.

"Right now?"

"Why not?" She continued backing up. "Carpe diem. Or carpe tree-um."

His smile widened but he made no move to follow her.

"You're serious?" he asked.

"Serious enough to get there first!" She spun on her heel and took off.

Behind her, Sebastian leapt the fence and chased her through the garden. They hurdled over flower beds and careened around hedges, laughing like they were ten again.

"That tree is mine, Price!"

"In your dreams, Summers!"

She peeked over her shoulder. He skidded on the paving stones near a leaking sprinkler. His stumble bought her just enough time to sprint across the open green and beat him to the tree. She began to climb, bracing a sneaker against the trunk and hauling herself onto the lowest branch. The bark was rough against her palms but easy to grip as she shimmied to her armpits and onto her stomach. Seconds later, with a grin wider than Montana, Sebastian flung a leg over the bottom limb and pulled himself to her side.

"You cheated!" he teased.

"I had to cheat. Your legs are twice as long as mine now."

Shoulder to shoulder and elbow to elbow, they climbed their way upward until they were twenty feet off the ground. As Edie straddled a thick, Y-shaped branch and caught her breath, she was thrilled to see that a few remnants of their childhood treasure trove remained: a pair of carved initials, a rusty compass dangling from a nail, a shredded loop of magic string that was supposed to give the tree a human voice, and three plastic guitar picks wedged firmly into the bark.

Sebastian perched in front of her and extended a hand.

"I declare this race a draw."

"Agreed."

They shook on it. As his fingers wrapped hers and as hers wrapped his, Edie felt the same thrill of connection that'd coursed through her the last time he held her hand. Only this time it wasn't *The Age of Innocence*. It was the Age of Confused. Her crush was still palpable—her inexorable pull toward him, the flutter of joy she felt whenever he smiled at her—but something else was distracting her, drawing her in another direction.

Sebastian's hand slipped away and rested on the limb between them, leaving Edie's hand empty, but strangely . . . not.

"You haven't changed," he said.

"Yes, I have."

"Okay, you probably don't hide Lego pirates in trees anymore."

"No. I don't hide those."

As Edie ran her fingers through some ratty strands of Mylar ribbon that were still tacked to the branch, a bird chirped at the end of a nearby limb, a motorcycle rumbled by out on the road, and a trickle of laughter echoed from half a block away. This wasn't a moment for silence. All of Mansfield seemed to sense it, conspiring to fill the quiet, making the moment simply a moment.

Edie and Sebastian settled in back to back, legs straddling the branch, feet dangling. They looked nice, those feet, hers in torn gray canvas, his in gently worn brown leather, softly swaying to and fro, unaware of how close they were to each other. For almost two hours, Edie and Sebastian sat in their tree. They talked about books, music, and cloudy night skies that let the stars keep their secrets. They vented about their families. They laughed about their dumbest mistakes. They shared their hopes for change once they got to college, for the promise of blank slates and blank pages. They also mourned the absence of the parents who wouldn't get to see who their children became.

As the sun began to set, Edie had grown so at ease with their conversation she found herself telling Sebastian about Shonda—but not about their antics at the Burger Barn, or their early band practices, or any of the other humorous stories she'd shared with Maria, Julia, or Henry. Instead, she confessed to kissing her best friend's boyfriend, describing the profound regret and the gaping void left by Shonda's retreat. After holding everything inside for weeks, it felt good to say the words aloud, as painful as they were. A weight lifted off Edie's chest, reminding her how badly she needed a friend more than anything else, a real friend, one she could share the ugliest parts of herself with.

"I assume you've tried apologizing?" Sebastian asked when she'd finished.

"Many times, many ways."

"If you guys were so close, surely she'll forgive you."

"Not necessarily." Edie adjusted her posture so her shoulders nestled more naturally against Sebastian's. "That's the hardest thing about loving someone. You only get to choose how you love them, not how they love you back. The apology was mine to offer. The forgiveness is up to her."

Sebastian tipped his head against Edie's. They sat quietly for a minute while the breeze rustled the leaves and fluttered the Mylar ribbon. It cast dancing spots of light on the trunk, like fairies or fireflies.

"Don't give up," Sebastian said. "If your friend is as important as you say she is, you'll push through this. You just have to find the right way to reconnect."

"'All human wisdom is contained in these two words—Wait and Hope.'"

"Who said that?" He twisted to the left, making his hair brush the top of her ear.

"Alexandre Dumas." She shifted again, bracing herself near the spot where his hands wrapped the limb, wedged in the space between her hips and his. "It's from *The Count of Monte Cristo*. I'm reading it for class."

"Five to one."

"You're not counting your quote?"

"I'm not really a—"

"Yes, you are." She nestled the back of her head against his neck, hoping her words found an equally cozy spot in which to settle. "Want to make it five to three?"

"I don't keep as much on my shelves as you do."

"Not even your own words?"

Sebastian drew in a breath, let it out, ran a hand through his hair, inhaled again, coughed, and pulled a knee against his chest. He repeated the routine with only slight variations until he ran out of tics and twitches and finally went still.

"A few thoughts about words," he murmured to the leaves that were glowing orange in the sunset. "When I write, I spill. I strew. I make messes. I remind myself how little I know. But when I read, the words march on their black-booted feet, parading from the page to attack my ignorance. The *i*'s wield their dots, the *t*'s their crosses, the *q*'s and *p*'s their tongue-tipped tails, strutting, well armed, into my defenseless soul."

Then and there, in measured breath sensed through shifting shoulders, in a connection that felt so natural it didn't demand a definition, and in the kind of silence Edie only shared with Sebastian, the world, for a moment, was perfect.

"So," he said after a long but beautiful pause, "you and Henry, huh?"

And then the world was not so perfect.

Right, Edie thought. *That other guy.*

With the mood shattered, Edie edged away from Sebastian and assessed her means of climbing down. Despite all she'd shared that evening, three subjects remained on her Do Not Discuss list: her crush, his girlfriend, and her . . . friend.

While she swung a leg off the branch, he spun to face her.

"I thought you didn't like him," he said.

"I didn't."

"What changed?"

Edie didn't answer. The question was far too complicated. What *had* changed? And yet, what hadn't? She needed weeks to figure all that out. Maybe more. She lowered herself onto the next branch, frustrated she'd stuck herself in a spot without a safety exit. As someone prone to bolting, she was usually smarter about that. Next time she climbed a tree with Sebastian, she'd bring rappelling gear.

"What did I say?" he asked.

"Nothing. I forgot I promised Norah I'd . . . make something white whiter."

She continued her descent with Sebastian following. As she wrapped her arms around a thick limb and found her footing on the bottom branch, her locket caught on a curl of peeling bark. Sebastian stepped on it and Edie pulled away, splitting the chain, busting the hinges, and sending the locket flying to the ground.

She jumped down and gathered the pieces, feeling the fragility of the broken locket echo through her bones, as though she too were about to shatter. In that moment it was all too much to take. Her mom smiled up from the photo, reduced to a memory. Sebastian crouched nearby, committed to someone else. The house and gardens sprawled out to her right, a far cry from home. Edie'd trapped herself in a lie about a relationship with Henry, one that was confusing the hell out of her. She'd ruined her closest friendship. She wasn't being completely honest with her cousins. She didn't fit in at school. She was sick to death of biting her tongue, playing her music where no one could hear, and eating food she despised. She couldn't even write a stupid essay, a task that'd seemed so simple when she started it. Nothing was as it should be.

Sebastian handed her the heart-shaped lid and a bit of chain, cupping his hands around hers.

"I'm so sorry." He leaned down and tried to meet her eyes. "I'll fix it. I swear."

Edie shook her head and turned away, fighting back tears.

"It's not just the necklace." Her voice strained past the heavy lump in her throat.

"I don't understand."

"I know you don't."

"Then talk to me." He brushed her hair off her face and tucked it behind her shoulder. It fell forward again, as tangled and uncontrollable as the rest of her.

"It's nothing. Forget it." She leapt up and hurried toward

the house, desperate to be alone before she had a complete melt-
down.

"Edie!" Sebastian called after her. "What can I do?"

She spun around as the tears began to flow.

"Wait and hope, Sebastian. Wait and hope. It's what I do."

Chapter Twenty-Seven

♥

EDIE SAT AT THE KITCHEN TABLE, IGNORING THE
rancid kale chips she'd made the mistake of trying. She stared at
her laptop and attempted to figure out who she'd be if she could be
anyone. She was running out of time to complete the task. She was
running out of ideas, too. She was randomly alternating between
Mary Shelley and Mary Poppins when Maria stormed in.

"eBay? Seriously?" She dropped a large package next to Edie's
laptop. "Please tell me this isn't what you meant when you said you
bought yourself a prom dress."

While Edie pushed back her chair and stood up to examine the
box, Julia scampered in from the hallway, slipping on the tiles in her
stocking feet.

"Oh, my god!" she exclaimed. "Is that your ballgown?"

"Looks like it."

"Let me see!" Julia clasped her hands and bit down a smile.

"If I get one whiff of mothballs or BO, I'm shredding that thing."
Maria let out a huff. "I'll never understand why you like wearing
other people's sweat."

As Julia danced around and Maria poured herself a glass of juice, Edie found the kitchen shears and carefully opened the box. She pulled out a 1950s ivory cocktail dress with a strapless, drop-waist satin bodice and a massive tulle skirt that expanded as it escaped its confines. The dress was horribly wrinkled and it did smell a little musty, but to Edie it was beautiful. It held a story in its threads. Another girl might've had her first kiss in this dress. She might've danced under moonlight. She might've run barefoot along a beach while sand caught in the hem and then, decades later, made the journey from Charleston all the way to Mansfield, along with a fair share of cat hair.

Julia ran her hands along the satin bodice, smoothing out the worst of the wrinkles where the fabric puckered over the corsetlike understructure.

"It's totally Cinderella," she said.

"You mean Cinder-smell-a," Maria amended.

"I'll get it dry-cleaned," Edie assured her.

"You'll get it fumigated."

Edie cut Maria a look. Then she reached into the box and pocketed the receipt without glancing at the cost. Wearing what she wanted to prom was worth chipping into her savings, especially if she was going to walk in alone and face a sea of couples.

"Good thing you didn't ask Henry to prom," Maria said. "He'd have to strap you to the roof of his car so he could reach the hotel without passing out."

"I'm sure he's grateful I've spared him the trouble." Edie kept her voice clipped, hoping to end the topic there. She'd considered asking Henry to prom but she knew if they went on an actual date, all the lines she was struggling to maintain between sex, love, and friendship would be erased, and they weren't the sort of lines a guy in coveralls could paint back on. She'd had fun with him over the past couple weeks but once she kissed him, there was no going back, even if she found out afterward that he'd only been playing her. She'd watched her mom wrestle with feeling disposable for years. Edie didn't want to risk it. Even though she also kind of did.

As she collapsed the box, Maria rubbed at the lipstick on her glass. Hard.

"What do you guys do together, anyway?" she asked.

"Play guitar, poke around in shops, eat nonorganic food. Mostly we talk."

"Oh, please." Maria scoffed. "Talking with Henry is like ordering a banana split and only eating the banana."

"Maybe I only want the banana."

"Whatever. Wrong analogy, because I know you want 'the banana.'"

Edie jammed the box into the recycle bin, shoving it down with more force than necessary. She was getting really sick of Maria's prodding about Henry. She'd done her best to be discreet, but it wasn't easy when Maria brought him up every chance she got.

"Can we *please* stop talking about him?" Edie begged.

Maria leaned against the counter, the picture of nonchalance.

"I'm just curious," she said.

Julia snorted from her seat at the table where she was plucking out cat hair.

"You mean you're just jealous," she corrected.

Maria settled her chin at a haughty angle.

"I don't want anything from Henry Crawford," she said.

"Then why do you keep calling him?" Julia prodded.

Maria tensed as her eyes shot to her sister's.

"I don't."

"You do." Julia's lips pursed into a triumphant little pout. "I saw your recents on your phone yesterday. Does he still let you put your hands down his pants?"

"I'll show you where I want to put my hands." Maria sped across the kitchen, her hands outstretched.

Edie leapt between her cousins and put a halt to the bickering before it escalated. She had her suspicions about Maria's continued involvement with Henry. He made no secret about the fact that he was seeing other girls. He had every right to date whoever he wanted. Edie understood that in the abstract, but the idea would be harder to accept if it became concrete, especially if either of her cousins was involved.

As the tension in the room settled, Maria slapped on a condescending smile.

"I have Rupert. Julia has W.B. You can have Henry, with or without his banana." She flicked a hand at the white dress. "Now get that disgusting zombie costume out of here before Dear Mama gets home and makes us eat dinner in hazmat suits."

With a sigh of resignation, Edie gathered up the dress. She

grabbed her laptop and marched upstairs. Once inside the quiet, cousin-free sanctuary of her bedroom she laid the dress on her bed, smoothing out the wadded tulle so it looked less like an ivory tumbleweed. She dug around in her drawers until she found the table runner she'd purchased last week. It was a beautiful cobalt blue, about three inches wide and six feet long. Half a dozen little yellow flowers had been hand-embroidered at each end where the fabric was mitered into points and tipped with silky tassels. Edie wrapped the runner around the dress like a belt, looping the ends so they hung down the length of the skirt. It was perfect. Her dream dress. Now, how badly did she want the date to go with it?

She glanced out the window at the Summerses' house. She flipped through *Twelfth Night*. She read her dad's napkin note. She took out her phone.

Edie: You free for dinner tonight?

Henry: Pick you up in an hour

Edie and Henry lounged on a big flannel blanket in the park. He leaned against a tree trunk and plucked her guitar while she lay on her back, reading *The Count of Monte Cristo* and debating whether or not to ask Henry to prom. A picnic basket sat open with a half-finished bottle of sparkling lemonade and some remnants of bread, cheese, and fruit. The sun shone through dappled shadows. The birds twittered. The trees whispered sweet nothings in the warm spring breeze. It was a perfectly romantic setting (for anyone who cared about such things).

Edie'd barely made it through two pages in ten minutes. Concentration was proving elusive while Henry strummed away next to her, his fingers deftly navigating the strings the way they'd once begun to navigate her skin, his legs outstretched so close to hers, his dead-sexy smile always a second away. Maybe she should ask him to prom. They'd dance. They'd laugh. He'd draw her into an impassioned embrace. His breath would mist her lips and his eyes would stare into hers, brimming over with desire until she fell against him, toppling every last almost. It could be wonderful.

As she turned her page, the ad she'd been using as a bookmark fluttered out.

"What's this?" Henry examined the notice and handed it back.

Edie gave it a quick glance before slipping it into her book. It was a listing for a weekly open mic night at the Brockton Arms, an unassuming little pub about a twenty-minute drive from Mansfield. Edie's mom used to play there, back when Edie would sit at the front table, sipping a root beer (because she was in a pub so she *had* to have a beer) while her mom sang her heart out to a small but rapt audience.

"I'm thinking of playing one night," she said. "I have some new songs to try out."

"Awesome. Let me know when. I'll drive you."

"Thanks." She smiled, flattered by the offer. "But only if you're not busy."

"Why would I be busy?"

Edie let out a soft laugh.

"I've seen the inside of your glove box. *You* might not be occupied, but your car could have other plans for the night."

Henry joined her laughter, letting her sarcasm wash right over him, as usual.

"She does get around." He glanced past Edie to where his sexy little sports car was parked by the side of the road.

Edie felt a sudden urge to ask Henry how much *he* got around but she kept the question to herself. The moment he gave her a concrete number, she wouldn't be able to get it out of her head. Maybe she shouldn't ask him to prom. No matter how amazing his kisses might be, she didn't want to be one of many. She wanted to just be one.

She lay back and found her place in the novel but Henry soon piped in.

"How's the book?" he asked.

"Good. It's about a guy who becomes a great con artist. You'd like it."

Henry laughed but something not entirely cheerful dulled his eyes.

"You really don't think much of me, do you?" he asked.

"I'm here, aren't I?"

"Part of you, yes. The rest of you is with that other guy." He nodded at her book. "The Frenchman with the sword and the cape. I should've bought some spurs, grown a mustache, learned how to swashbuckle."

Edie set down her book, ready to explain why she couldn't

neglect her homework. As she caught the subtle challenge in Henry's expression, she realized he wasn't talking about a fictitious Frenchman. He was talking about that *other* other guy.

"Your only competition is the guy showing up on my English test." She was pleased to realize she meant what she said. She might feel differently in a week, a day, or even in the next minute, but at that particular moment, she understood that waiting and hoping was useless. Her energy was better spent elsewhere.

"Good to know." Henry's smile slowly built. "About the book, I mean."

With that, Edie gave up on the Count, opting to eschew all other swashbucklers so she could enjoy her present company. Noting her shifted attention, Henry eased his way into a song. It was gentle and old-fashioned, like the one he'd played in Norah's garden. The song might've been sung a hundred years ago, in another patch of grass, while another wind placed whispered kisses onto someone else's skin.

> *"I love your eyes, but they my soul assail;*
> *Aloof, unyielding, frozen with disdain.*
> *Close your lids, each lash a mourning veil;*
> *Look not so coldly on my poor heart's pain.*
> *Let lashes veil with blackest thickest shroud*
> *The disregard, which stabs me in my lover's breast.*
> *Conceal your stony stare, your glance so proud,*
> *Your fairest eye, which teaches me unrest.*

It fairly judges my unworthy heart,
But I cannot accept my well-earned fate,
So veil your eyes, take on a mourner's part,
And keep them in that grieving keening state.
Your eyes say 'no,' admitting no uncertain guess,
So close them up. Let me imagine 'yes.'"

Edie closed her eyes as commanded, letting Henry imagine her yeses, which were getting perilously close to her lips as the music melted away her doubts and concerns.

"That's beautiful," she said.

"You're beauti— Sorry, almost slipped out."

Edie lay still, only vaguely aware of Henry's shuffling next to her. She was lost in the rippling aftereffects of his song. The notes stayed with her, humming in her blood, sweeping her up in a euphoric crescendo and then laying her softly on a flannel blanket, swimming in silent yeses. When she finally opened her eyes, Henry was lying inches away. His hands were laced behind his head. His face was turned to the sky as he peered up through the branches at kaleidoscopic patches of blue. He really was beautiful. His perfect Cupid's bow lips tweaked up at the corners with imminent laughter as his deep, dark eyes dared the world to impress or amuse him.

"Henry? What did you mean when you told Claire she'd seen you be patient, persistent, and dedicated?"

He rolled toward her, bringing his eyes, his lips closer.

"You heard that, huh?"

"I did, and it made me curious."

He tucked a fluttering strand of hair behind her ear. The gesture was simple, utilitarian, but as his fingers brushed her skin, curving slowly toward her earlobe, he left an imprint that was far more than friendly.

"When I was a sophomore in high school, I fell for a girl in the drama club. I spent three years trying to get her to go out with me. I begged. I pleaded. I wrote her truly terrible poetry." He swept a crumb off Edie's collarbone. Maybe. "When we got cast as Romeo and Juliet in our senior year, she finally said yes. I spent a few weeks in utter bliss, convinced that perseverance was the key to love. Then I discovered my Juliet fooling around with Friar Lawrence. And Lord Capulet."

Edie winced as if struck.

"Yeah," he said. "It hurt, all right, but I learned my lesson."

"'Better to break a heart than to have your heart broken'?"

Henry let out a half-laugh/half-sigh as something new crept into his expression, something that looked—of all things—a little bit lonely.

"Sure," he said flatly. "Something like that."

As his eyes skipped across her face, Edie felt her neck flush, then her cheeks, then the tips of her ears. She forced herself not to glance at Henry's lips. She was *not* thinking about kissing him. She wasn't remembering his thumb drumming her hip bone or his back muscles shifting when she ran her fingertips down his spine. She definitely wasn't imagining that the breeze blowing against her neck now was his breath as he pressed his cheek against hers while their bodies inched closer.

"Is that your real endgame here?" she asked. "Are you hoping to break my heart?"

Henry brushed her fluttering hair off her face again, letting the back of his knuckles graze her cheekbone.

"Actually, I was hoping to put it back together."

Edie's breath caught. He was too good, too smooth, saying just the right thing at the right time. His words had to be calculated but he made no move toward her, and she made no move to bridge the distance between them. The two of them simply lay there, reading each other's eyes, searching for the unspoken desires that hid beneath the surface.

"Circle walks into a bar," he said. "Orders another round."

The sun dialed itself up a notch as six and a quarter minutes replayed themselves in Edie's mind. *Skin. Sweat. Eyes. Lips. Breath. Hands. Arms. Tense. Hips. Want. Burst.*

"Barn painter walks into a bar," she said. "Orders the house red."

He reached toward her but he paused and retracted his hand. She took it in her own, lacing her fingers through his. He closed his eyes and took the kind of deep breath people normally saved for fresh baked goods and fabric softener commercials.

"Carpenter walks into a bar." Henry opened his eyes, so dark, so deep, so close. "Orders six screwdrivers. Says he plans to get hammered."

Edie laughed, making Henry's smile stretch across his face. It was the smile she liked best: not smug or full of mischief, just happy.

"Girl walks into a bar," Edie said. "Asks, 'Will you go to prom with me?'"

Henry's smile somehow stretched even wider.

"I thought you'd never ask."

Chapter Twenty-Eight

AS A WAY OF PROVING SHE HAD NO HARD FEELINGS about Henry, Maria offered to give Edie a comprehensive makeover on prom day. Ready at last to fully commit to her cousin's prodigious artistry, Edie accepted. After an hour of pore evacuation and three more hours of tweezing, taming, buffing, and waxing, Maria dragged Edie into the garden. While the sun shone, the tiered fountain trickled away, and the cherubic archers engaged in their eternal standoff, Maria filed Edie's "atrocious" fingernails and Julia stretched out on a nearby bench, reading from an article on ten things not to do if you liked a guy.

"*Number ten: Don't make the first move. Let him be the hunter.*"

"That's ridiculous," Edie said. "When was that thing written, 1950?"

"Don't mock my gospel." Julia flashed her a palm. "*Number nine: Don't refuse his help. Let him pay for dinner, open your door, or replace your light bulb.*"

"Or let him buy you a necklace." Maria prodded Edie's cuticle a *little* bit harder than seemed absolutely necessary.

Edie forced herself to leave her hand where it was.

"I told you," she insisted. "I tried to give it back. He wouldn't take it."

"Weren't you listening?" Maria's scarlet lips twisted into a smirk. "You're supposed to 'Let him be helpful.' Then tonight you can 'Let him be the hunter.'"

"Yeah, and then I'll make sure my poodle skirt only shows six inches of leg." Edie scowled, and not just because of the article. While Julia and Maria had both professed support for her prom date, Henry's gift had reignited tensions. He'd given her the necklace yesterday when he picked her up after school. It was truly extraordinary, like something that belonged on a Russian czarina or a fairytale queen. It had a dozen delicate constellations of clear stones with a single blue faceted heart dangling from the center, all nestled in a black velvet box with a card that read, *When a heart gets broken.* When Henry decided to mend a heart, he took the job seriously.

Apparently Maria had told him about the broken locket. Always the showman, he'd seized the opportunity to sweep in with an extravagant replacement. Edie was flattered but uneasy. Friends bought each other burgers or bus fare, not expensive jewelry. After an extensive discussion, Henry assured her that a) accepting it would only mean she liked the necklace, nothing more, b) he wouldn't make a single "unfriendly" move without invitation, and c) he kept the receipt and could return the necklace after prom if she decided she didn't want to keep it. Convinced that it came with no expectations, she agreed to wear it. Now she was having second thoughts.

"*Number eight,*" Julia read. "*Don't complain about the trivial events of your day. Save your grumbling for your girlfriends.*"

Edie groaned. "I'm not sure I can take the art of sexist seduction today."

"But this is good advice," Julia argued.

"It's painful advice."

Maria scoffed and poked at another cuticle. Hard.

"So says the girl who only knows how to be friends with a guy."

Edie snatched her hand out of Maria's vise grip. She marched over to the fountain and tucked her hands into the sanctuary of her armpits.

"I *know how* to be more than friends," she said.

"I'm not talking about locking braces under the bleachers with some beatnik band geek." Maria shook her head with even more exasperation than usual. "You do realize the hottest guy in Mansfield has somehow agreed to be your date tonight?"

A dozen retorts flashed through Edie's head while she wondered what a nail file would look like embedded in Maria's forehead. She was still composing a less vehement response when Sebastian waved from his driveway.

"Hey there!" he called. "Putting on the finishing touches?"

"More like holding an intervention." Maria sauntered over to the fountain, where she brushed Edie's hair off her shoulders, fussing like a beautician assessing a client. "I'm trying to prevent Edie from looking like one of the Miserables tonight."

"Can the intervention pause?" Sebastian asked. "I have something for you, Edie."

With a nervous glance at her cousins, Edie trudged toward Sebastian, cautious but curious. Maria and Julia followed, probably just curious. The moment they all reached the fence, Sebastian's eyes locked on Edie's face.

"You look . . . different," he said.

Heat flooded Edie's cheeks. He was looking at her the way she'd always wanted him to: as though he really saw her and he liked what he saw, as though he didn't want to look away. She had mixed feelings about the fact that hours of primping had been required, but maybe he wasn't just seeing what'd changed on the outside. Maybe he was seeing what'd changed on the inside, too: less fear, more decisiveness, and a genuine excitement about the night ahead of her.

"This is nothing," Maria boasted. "I just weed-whacked Edie's eyebrows and introduced her to an exciting new invention called a comb. Wait till tonight."

"I, um, yeah. Okay." Sebastian ran a hand through his hair and continued to stare.

Julia nudged Edie while biting down an irrepressible smile. Edie glanced at her sideways and shook her head, hoping to stave off any Prince Charming insinuations.

"You said you had something for me?" she asked Sebastian.

"Right. Of course. Sorry." He dug through his pockets and handed her a tiny manila envelope.

Edie opened it and poured the contents into her palm. It took her a second to realize she was holding her locket. The hinges were complete, the lid was in place, and the chain had been replaced. She looked up, stunned.

"You fixed it."

"I said I would."

"Yeah, but—"

"Maria gave me the pieces."

Edie scowled at Maria.

"Did you alert all of Mansfield?" she asked.

"What?" Maria waved a dismissive hand. "I couldn't take the sobbing."

"Or obey the Keep Out sign on my drawer?"

"I don't believe everything I read."

Edie bit back her acrimony as she slipped the locket over her head. She hated that Maria had invaded her privacy on multiple levels, but in this particular case maybe the ends justified the means.

"Your mom's photo is still in there," Sebastian pointed out. "I got a stronger chain, though, in case some clumsy oaf steps on it again."

"It's perfect. Thank you." She pressed the locket to her chest, grateful he'd known how important the little token was, that wearing it helped her feel like her mom was still present, offering Edie much needed guidance, encouragement, and reassurance.

"I made sure the jeweler repaired it right away." Sebastian nervously drummed his fingers on a fence post. "In case you wanted to wear it tonight."

"Aww." Julia clutched her hands to her heart. "That's so sweet."

"Edie has a necklace to wear tonight," Maria announced. "You should see what Henry gave her. Diamonds and sapphires and—"

"*Fake* diamonds and sapphires," Edie interjected.

"I doubt that." Maria began to file one of her own nails. "Henry doesn't do imitations."

Edie set a hand to her gut, praying Maria was wrong. Even the suggestion nauseated her. It was too much. Way, *way* too much. Henry might've offered the gift without expectations, but others might feel differently, herself included.

Sebastian shoved his hands into his pockets, awash with disappointment.

"I didn't realize," he said. "I guess there was no rush on the locket then."

Edie's gut churned harder, not like the tentative butterflies she usually felt around Sebastian, but like a fog that refused to dissipate, choosing instead to extend its clammy fingers and wrap them around her neck. She wanted to reassure Sebastian that the locket meant far more than diamonds. It was humble and thoughtful, not lavish and overdone. It was what she wanted, not what he wanted her to have. It was everything Edie thought of Sebastian. And yet, it wasn't what she'd wear to prom.

"Save a dance for me, okay?" he asked.

"Claire won't mind?"

"She brought it up, actually."

"She did?" Edie eyed him suspiciously. Was Claire plotting something? Was this like that scene in the movies where the prom queen sets the school dork up for some sort of public humiliation? Or had Claire finally let her jealousies go?

"She's cool with it." Sebastian scratched the back of his neck, glanced at his garage, and shook his head. "She, um, she knows we're just friends."

Edie gripped the fence, wondering if Henry felt the same sharp jab every time she called him "just a friend." She should seriously rethink how often she used that phrase. She should at least stop using it as a shield for all the other things she felt.

Sebastian waved goodbye and shuffled toward his back door. The girls stood side by side, trailing his retreat. Edie's hand rose to her locket, turning her mind to hearts, strings, and other broken things. She hadn't lied when she told Henry he had no real rival. Waiting for Sebastian to pick her over Claire was a lost cause. She knew that in every molecule of her body. Yet every time she tried to let him go, he found a way to reignite a tenacious little spark of hope. It was like that line from *Jane Eyre,* where the heroine feels like she has a string under her ribs, tightly knotted to a similar string in Mr. Rochester. Some people were simply tied to each other. Some knots never came unraveled. Some strings never broke.

As the girls finally headed inside to continue their pre-prom preparations, Edie forced herself to extinguish all thoughts of Sebastian. Tonight wasn't about him. It was about her. She had a beautiful dress to wear, two contentious but beloved cousins to celebrate with, and the company of a guy she really liked, no matter what words she used to describe him. None of them were quite right anyway: friend, date, demon/vampire, slime on rice, Narcissus in tight jeans. Only one word seemed to fit: Henry.

With that thought, her hand slipped from her necklace and she began to smile.

Chapter Twenty-Nine

Transformation

noun

1. A dramatic change in form or appearance.
2. A cheerleading squad made up of gender fluid members.
3. The effect of eight hours (or two months, really) of smoothing, stripping, straightening, painting, plucking, pinning, pushing, pulling, powdering, primping, shining, and refining every possible flaw until your cousin announces she's FINALLY not embarrassed to be seen in public with you.

The girls stood in the bathroom before a wall-to-wall mirror and a white marble countertop that was completely obscured by beauty products. Maria adjusted her cleavage and checked the slit on the side of her dark red sheath dress, ensuring that it hit her thigh *just so.* Julia twirled, testing the flutter-ability of eight rows of peach chiffon ruffles. Edie stared at her reflection, still trying to recognize herself. Her hair was piled high on her head in an elegant series of twists. Her dramatic makeup plumped up her lips and made her lop-sided eyes look sultry and symmetrical (except when her fake eye-lashes stuck together). Her dress, now dry-cleaned, lacked all traces of zombie, cat hair, or sweat. The strapless bodice revealed a pair of bare but surprisingly confident shoulders, between which sat a seri-ously spectacular necklace. The blue sash dangled from a little knot at her waist. A pair of only slightly teeter-y rhinestone-coated shoes sparkled down below several fluffy layers of white tulle that stopped just below her knees.

Edie patted the necklace to make sure it was really there. She couldn't deny that it was stunning, glamorous without being gaudy, the perfect match for her dress. Too bad she felt like she was wearing a hundred carats of guilt around her neck.

"God, he has good taste," Maria said.

Julia stopped twirling and slumped against the glass shower stall.

"I wish I could wear sapphires," she said. "My eyes look muddy in blue jewels."

"I'm terrified I'm going to lose it or damage it." Edie cringed at her reflection. "Maybe I shouldn't wear it after all."

Maria paused, mid-boob-lift.

"You've got to be kidding."

"If anything happens to it, I'd never be able to pay him back."

"Hello? It's called a present. He's not expecting you to pay him back." Maria examined her profile, pulling at her neck and sucking in her cheeks. "If Rupert gave me diamonds, I'd sure as hell wear them."

"You have a very different relationship with Rupert than I have with Henry."

"Edie, seriously." Maria spun away from the mirror and planted her hands on her hips. "Ditch those annoying principles already. They're, like, more tedious than nature documentaries."

"I like nature documentaries."

"Of course you do. You also think extra credit is a dare." Maria shot an exasperated look at her sister. "Just be normal for one night!"

Edie assessed her glamorous reflection again, feeling anything but normal.

"If you don't wear the necklace, can I wear it?" Julia asked.

"Won't it muddy your eyes?" Maria challenged.

"Yeah, but come on. That necklace has more right to go to prom than I do."

Edie started to laugh, followed soon thereafter by both Maria and Julia.

"We all look perfect." Maria corralled Julia and Edie in her outstretched arms, just like when she'd bought Edie's first pair of heels. "Julia, your boobs look great, no matter how many tissues you jammed into your bra. Edie, you look like a supermodel. I can't believe I pulled it off. You can thank me later." She gave them each a kiss. Then she adjusted her neckline one last time and strutted to the door, demonstrating enviable equilibrium in her patent leather heels. "We should get moving. Dear Mama's been perched on the edge of the ottoman for hours with her camera ready and waiting."

"You guys go ahead," Edie said. "I'll be down in a minute."

Julia and Maria headed downstairs while Edie darted into her bedroom. She wasn't leaving for prom without sharing a moment with the two people she desperately wanted by her side. First she took a mirror selfie and sent it to Shonda along with a simple text that said, *I miss you. I love you. I'll never stop hoping.* Then she opened the dressing table drawer. She took out her locket and popped the lid. Her mom smiled up at her, eternally locked in a moment of joy.

As Edie stared at the photo, she recalled a night when she was ten years old, sitting in the Denny's in Ithaca, across from her mom. An almost-finished milkshake with two straws perched between them. Half a dozen cherry stems lay at the base of the glass near a barely legible bill. Edie's mom counted out a handful of change: nickels, pennies, dimes, anything someone had dropped into her case while she'd been busking that evening. She sighed as she set her last quarter on the table.

"For the cherries," she said.

"But the bus—" Edie started.

"But the cherries," her mom replied firmly.

Edie glared at the mound of change. She appreciated her mom's generosity and maybe the cherries did warrant an extra tip, but she wasn't convinced they'd be worth the long walk home. Her mom took Edie's hands and held them, palms upward.

"Anything you keep in these is temporary." She laid a hand on Edie's cheek and gently tapped her temple. "This is where you keep the good stuff." She set a hand on Edie's heart. "This thing's fickle, but check in with it once in a while. Just bring that thing with you."

She tapped Edie's temple again. "The two together can take you places no bus will ever go, and if anyone tells you otherwise, tell them to fuck right off."

A lump rose in Edie's throat as she pictured her mom standing behind her now, relaying another unique pep talk, gushing with compliments, and trying not to happy-cry. Norah would've called the well of emotion temperamental, but it was exactly what Edie craved in that moment. She might look perfectly polished on the outside. Inside she was a bundle of nerves. She was about to walk into a room full of people and she doubted she'd be able to disappear into a corner, not while dressed in a giant white ballgown and with Henry by her side. She wasn't even sure she wanted to disappear but she didn't know what to do with that thought. It wasn't one she was familiar with.

When Edie couldn't force herself to return the locket to the drawer, she found a safety pin and fastened the little heart to the inside of her bra, tucking the chain around it. Tonight she'd wear two hearts: one visible, one hidden. She laid a hand against each of them and took a final look in the mirror.

I may let my heart drive tonight, she thought, *but I promise to copilot with my brain.* Aloud and full of conviction she added, "This one's for the cherries."

By the time Edie entered the living room, Rupert and Maria were posing for pictures by the fireplace. Norah kindly let them pause so Edie could give Rupert a hug.

"Wow, you look great," he said. "You all look great, not that you've ever not looked great, Maria, but you look even greater tonight, or is it more great? Greater-est?"

"We've always been proud of our girls." Norah tucked a stray curl behind Julia's ear, making thoughtful use of her talent for improving people.

"Always," Bert murmured as he beamed from the corner of the sofa.

"Speak up, dear," Norah barked. "No one likes a mumbler."

"Tonight I'm proud of *all four* of my girls." He darted each of them a sweetly loving look. "I have an overabundance of riches."

"Speaking of riches," Rupert said. "That's quite a necklace, Edie."

"Henry gave it to her," Julia noted.

"Henry?" Rupert's eyes shot to Maria's. "Not the same Henry who—?"

"Yes, Rupert." Maria linked her arm through his and patted his hand.

"The guy you—?"

"Yes, Rupert," Julia said.

"But I thought—"

"It's all good, sweetheart," Maria said.

Rupert scratched his head, accidentally releasing a heavily pomaded cowlick.

"I don't know how he does it."

"I didn't know who else to ask," Edie explained. "It's not serious."

"If you say so, but that set of rocks sure looks serious. He must really like you."

"Look at the time." Maria practically leapt away from Rupert. She kissed her parents on their cheeks and told Julia and Edie she'd see them after dinner. With a strained smile, she yanked Rupert out the front door and slammed it behind her.

"She grew up too fast," Bert lamented, his eyes still on the door.

"Don't be maudlin, dear." Norah slyly dabbed the corner of her eye. Twice. "She grew up at the same rate everyone else does."

"Exactly," he said. "Which is too fast."

W.B. arrived a few minutes later. He clumsily pinned a corsage to Julia's dress. The couple posed for photos while Norah squinted at his neck where the edges of his tattoos peeked out above his collar. When she offered him a tissue to wipe off the "bit of dirt" at the base of his jawline, he graciously took it. Then he ushered Julia out to his motorcycle, which she'd instructed him to park a block away.

Edie sat fidgeting with her dress, her nails, and the tassels on her sash while Norah rattled on about how lucky Edie was to enjoy "a real prom" at "a real school." The conversation/monologue was virtually unbearable until Bert snuck Edie a wink behind Norah's back. The gesture didn't erase two months of exclusion and forced gratitude, but for a moment, it helped dull the sharp sting of her mom's absence.

When the doorbell finally rang, announcing Henry's arrival, Edie jumped up and answered the door. There he stood, the demon/ vampire with the laughing eyes, the upturned lips, and the . . . holy shit, he looked good in a tux.

He opened his mouth as if to say something but he stopped

before words emerged. Something was wrong. Was Edie's dress slipping down? Was her false eyelash creeping across her forehead like a lopsided caterpillar? Oh, god, was the necklace missing?! She set her hand against it, trying not to panic.

"What's the matter?" she asked.

Henry laid his hand on his heart and staggered back a step.

"Breathless, Edie Price. Breathless."

He smiled his most honest-looking smile to date. As his lips curled upward and his eyes went glassy, a few dormant butterflies tickled Edie's belly, feeling less like their usual confusion and more like joy because these butterflies were allowed to fly.

Chapter Thirty

♥

THE HOTEL BALLROOM WAS PACKED BY THE TIME
Edie and Henry arrived after dinner. Blue and green streamers hung
down from a ceiling of balloons, Mylar confetti scattered every surface, and a quartet of disco balls shot dizzying dots of light around
the room. Two hundred people bobbed up and down on the dance
floor while others sat at a ring of tables, shouting over the music,
taking selfies, and poorly pretending they were sober.

Edie and Henry wove their way across the room and joined the
Saint Pen's girls at a table near the corner of the dance floor. Maria's
friends were all present, except for Claire and her boyfriend. The
missing pair was either out on the dance floor, still at dinner, or
attending a more . . . private function. Edie dismissed that thought as
she introduced Henry to anyone who didn't already know him. The
girls all flashed signs of approval while Maria cocked a questioning
eyebrow at Henry. He simply smiled and returned his attention to
Edie. As she set her purse on the table, he pulled out two folding
chairs and settled in beside her, knee-almost-to-knee, though his
precise distance was hard to gauge under a billowing mass of tulle.

"I like your necklace," he said.

"Thanks." She set a hand against the stones. "My personal stylist picked it out."

"Tell me about this stylist." He leaned in, his dark eyes dancing the way they always did when he was teasing out hidden truths as though he already knew them.

Edie pretended to consider the matter.

"Well, he's vain," she mused. "He's also shallow and insincere. But I suspect he has a few hidden talents up his sleeve."

Henry shook out his arm and tugged on his shirt cuff. Edie suppressed a laugh.

"Don't you dare pull a rose out of there," she warned.

Henry laughed outright.

"Didn't I already try that once?" he asked.

"Twice, actually."

"Tonight I'll try to be less predictable, especially if I have to compete with some devious designer." He picked up the end of her sash and studied the embroidery, slowly tracing it with his thumb, much like he'd once traced the curve of Edie's hip bone, and with much the same effect. "That conceited jerk better not show up here tonight."

"I hope you practiced your swashbuckling," she teased, dizzily distracted.

"Oh, I buckled my swashes. I buckled *all* my swashes."

Henry scooted closer, all steady confidence and smoldering eye contact. For a brief but breath-catching moment, Edie imagined him tugging the sash, pulling her forward, and pressing his lips to hers as she willingly yielded to the desire that swam through his eyes. She waited, perfectly still. He watched her, relishing the moment. Seconds passed, uncountable and unknowable, until he let the sash fall to her lap, breaking the tension between them.

Right, Edie thought, snapping into awareness. *Prom. Balloons, streamers, disco balls, bad music, cheap cookies, other people.*

Henry soon engaged Rupert in a discussion about the drive between Mansfield and Boston. Rupert proved himself a good sport by responding with mild enthusiasm, despite his clear discomfort to be sitting next to his rival. While they man-chatted, Taylor announced that she'd been cast as Blanche in a summer production of *A Streetcar Named Desire*. After a thorough round of congratulations, Phoebe asked Edie how her scholarship application was going. Edie admitted she was still floundering but she hoped divine intervention would endow her with a jolt of brilliance before the impending deadline. Through it all—much to Edie's relief—Maria kept her eyes and hands glued to Rupert, letting neither wander unnecessarily to Henry.

When a slow song began, Henry led Edie onto the dance floor. With a practiced smoothness, he drew her against him in a formal dance embrace. She held his hand and wrapped an arm around his shoulder, not one jot of Dead Bunny Paws.

"So, I know we're only here as friends," he said. "But can I tell you how beautiful you look tonight?"

"Flattery will get you nowhere."

"Where will honesty get me?"

"I'll let you know when I see it."

Henry laughed and drew her closer, inching his hand across her back, not that she could easily feel his touch under her heavily boned bodice and the long-line push-up bra Maria had insisted she wear. Was that what was making her so breathless tonight?

"You know I've never lied to you," he said.

"Actually," she said, considering, "yeah, I do."

He did a quick rotation, pivoting her around him. She leaned into the motion, letting the centrifugal force pull at her body until he drew her against him again, slipping his arm further around her waist until he erased the space between his body and hers.

"I don't know why," he said in a register deep enough to reach her toes, his cheek brushing hers, his lips dangerously close to her ear, "but I have an intense urge to tell man-walks-into-a-bar jokes right now."

Edie smiled as she rested her head on his shoulder. It really was a nice shoulder, broad, strong, and the perfect height to pillow a forehead. How did he always manage to smell so good, too? Like wintry spices, cedar shavings, and something utterly unrecognizable, a heady mix of the cozy and the exotic.

"Plumber walks into a bar," she said. "Asks what's on tap."

"Architect walks into a . . . never mind." He laid his chin against her forehead. "I'm just going to enjoy this for a few minutes."

They nestled against each other as the space Edie thought didn't exist got even less exist-y. She closed her eyes and settled in to the gentle swaying motion, the solidity of Henry's body, and the lilt of an earnest love song. Despite Henry's careless games, heart-breaking schemes, and calculated flirtations, Edie allowed herself to trust that on *this* date, for *this* night, she could simply enjoy being held, free of confusion, free of fear.

Like all good things, the song eventually ended. A drumbeat kicked in, lights flashed, and the world leapt into motion. Edie suggested returning to the table. Glass slippers were pretty but they were probably meant for girls who sat down a lot. Henry escorted her across the dance floor with an arm around her waist. As they neared the perimeter, they passed Julia and W.B., bouncing, spinning, and flinging their arms with wild abandon. W.B. paused his gymnastics to say hi while Julia slowed to a standstill. Edie forced a smile, even though Henry's hand suddenly felt like it was burning an imprint onto her waist. She was still trying to figure out what to say when Henry cleverly averted any awkwardness by suggesting that he and W.B. find some drinks while the girls had a moment alone. Fortunately Julia didn't break down in tears as she so often had about Henry. She simply tipped her head against a pillar and watched the crowd swallow him, her expression wistful but resigned.

"'Nothing serious,' huh?" she asked.

"I'm sorry." Edie shifted, her position as uncertain as it was indefensible. "I didn't mean for anything to happen. Not that anything's happened exactly, but, well . . ." She trailed off, lost once again about how to make words out of feelings.

Julia blew a sigh into her already disarrayed bangs.

"It's okay. I'm not going to lie. I totally wish Henry was here with me tonight but he isn't. And W.B. might not know any Shakespeare or look like a movie star, but it's nice to be with someone who texts me back, who doesn't make me compete for his attention, and who makes a little effort, you know?"

"Yeah." Edie laid a hand on her heart. "I sure do."

Somewhere around ten p.m., Claire and Sebastian finally made an appearance. They arrived just in time for Claire to win her tiara and share a dance with the square-jawed prom king from Holy Cross. Edie applauded along with everyone else, setting aside past resentments while Claire enjoyed her moment in the spotlight. Then she snuck away to use the restroom.

She was attempting to tame an errant eyelash when the door swung open and Claire entered with Taylor and Phoebe. Taylor wore a bandage dress. Phoebe went Grecian. Claire rocked a simple sheath made of beaded fringe, with bangles and sandals to match. She didn't need to wear a tiara. She *was* a tiara. She paused as she spotted Edie. Then she strutted across the room, craning around as if she was searching for something.

"I want to make sure there are no boys," she told the girls. "Edie likes making out in bathrooms. It's probably the mirrors but that could be Henry's influence."

The girls laughed as Edie stopped fussing with her eyelashes. Taylor and Phoebe seemed to take the remarks in good fun but Claire narrowed her eyes just enough to lend her words an edge. Edie tried to ignore it but she prickled with defensiveness.

"We didn't actually—" She halted there, trapped between truth and fiction.

Claire arched an eyebrow while flashing Edie the barest hint of a knowing smile.

"You didn't what?" she challenged.

"Nothing. Never mind." Edie jammed her compact into her purse. This was exactly why she shouldn't lie. She always bumbled her way into the truth eventually, and usually at the worst possible times.

As the other girls stepped up to the mirror and began fixing their makeup, Edie swept her purse off the counter, ready to bolt. In her haste, she spilled the contents. She swiftly knelt to gather her things, though swiftness was relative in a massive ballgown and a precarious pair of heels. Phoebe helped her out while Taylor and Claire chatted about an afterparty they were both planning to attend.

"Sebastian's being a mope," Claire said. "But he'll go if I ask him to. He knows it's important to me. I'll make it up to him later."

"I'm sure you will," Taylor teased.

"It's my big night," Claire boasted while adjusting her tiara. "And you know what they say about selfishness. It must be forgiven because there's no hope for a cure."

Edie hid her annoyance while grabbing her keys from under a sink. Sure, selfishness was forgivable, but what about manipulation?

Phoebe handed off Edie's phone, the last of her scattered goods.

"Are you and Henry going to the party?" she asked as they clambered up.

"I don't think so." No one had invited Edie to an afterparty. The omission stung but it was also kind of a relief. Prom provided her plenty of time around crowds for one night, especially when Claire was among the throng.

"Edie and Henry have other plans," Claire said through a trickle of laughter. "Unless you're still holding out on him?"

Edie snapped her purse shut as her face burned. She could handle a bit of teasing about a supposed bathroom fetish. She could get past Claire's gloating about Sebastian. But was Claire seriously pressuring her to have sex with Henry?

"My love life is none of your business," Edie said.

Claire laughed as though she'd just heard the most amusing thing ever.

"Oh, Edie. I think we both know that's not entirely true."

Chapter Thirty-One ♥

EDIE DID HER BEST TO LET CLAIRE'S INSINUATION go as everyone crowded around their table. Her best wasn't perfect, but Henry was spectacular at distracting her with his flirty banter and steady attention. On the opposite side of the table, Claire regaled the group with cheerful chatter but Sebastian soon settled into a contemplative silence. While everyone else shared school memories and discussed post-graduation plans, he folded a paper napkin into a tiny square, only to unfold it and fold it again. He readily engaged in the conversation when someone addressed him directly, and he seemed perfectly content out on the dance floor where Claire draped herself on him like Spanish moss, but his eyes kept wandering to the corners of the room, betraying his discontent.

When the night started to wind down and a slow song came on, Claire whispered something to Sebastian. He tensed as his eyes skipped over the faces around him. He whispered something back, his expression stern, but Claire peppered him with kisses until she coaxed a smile out of him. Edie left them to it, desperate to focus her attention elsewhere, but a moment later, she looked up to find Sebastian standing beside her.

"Can I steal a dance?" he asked.

Edie glanced across the table, expecting Claire to throw down a subtle challenge, lure Sebastian away, or otherwise prove she had him wrapped around her little finger. Instead, Claire simply fluttered a little wave. Considering their conversation in the bathroom, Edie wasn't sure why Claire suddenly felt like sharing her boyfriend. However, she doubted Sebastian would risk a dance unless he was certain it wouldn't affect his relationship. If he wasn't concerned, maybe she shouldn't be either.

"Do you mind?" she asked Henry.

"Me? No. Of course not." He smiled but his shifting eyes gave away his bluff.

"You said you didn't lie."

"As you so wisely put it to me once, there's a first for everything." He stood and patted down his pockets. "Well, I didn't bring a sword, I failed to grow a mustache, and I don't actually know what swashbuckling is, so I'll just leave you guys to it while I take my jealousy out for a little fresh air."

He turned to leave but Edie slipped her hand around his, holding him in place.

"Come back soon, okay?"

This time when he smiled, his eyes remained steadfast.

"You're damned straight I will."

He headed outside while Sebastian and Edie found a little

pocket of space on the edge of the crowded dance floor. Unlike the last time they'd shared a dance, Sebastian's posture was stiff. His arms were rigid. His hands barely brushed her waist. While Edie knew he'd always relegated her to the friend zone, she wondered if he'd demoted her to the distant acquaintance district.

"What's wrong?" she asked. "I feel like I'm dancing with the Tin Man."

Sebastian's eyes skated across the crowd while his shoulders twitched and tensed.

"Claire and I had a massive fight tonight," he confessed. "We talked it out but I didn't want to come. I hate pretending to be cheerful."

"You're a lousy pretender."

"Which is why I avoid situations where I'm expected to be fun no matter what."

Edie smiled to herself, recalling her first day back in Mansfield, when she'd met Sebastian by the fence, her ears ringing with endless urgings to cheer up. He hadn't added another. He'd let her be awkward, bashful, sulky, and temperamental. He accepted her as she was, and she felt the same about him.

"You don't have to pretend anything with me," she assured him. "Be whatever you want to be, or whatever you need to be. Enough fun people are here tonight. This party can accommodate two people who are . . . undefinable."

"Thanks, Edie. You're the best."

Second best, she thought, but she kept the words to herself.

Sebastian relaxed his hold as his shoulders finally settled and his expression softened. Edie tried to inch closer but he maintained his distance. They skirted a couple that'd stopped dancing in order to make out, and another that probably hadn't even started dancing. They passed a dreamy-looking Julia, who was resting her head on W.B.'s shoulder, her eyes closed, softly smiling. As they found a bit of elbow room at the center of the dance floor, Sebastian began to fidget, inhaling like he was about to say something and then exhaling as though he'd changed his mind.

"So," he finally managed, his voice straining above the music, "about Henry."

Edie tensed as something prickled the back of her neck, something besides the chain from her necklace.

"What *about* Henry?"

"Claire asked me to talk to you about him." Sebastian's arm jerked as though he was dying to raise his hand to his head but he was forcing it to stay on her waist. "She thought I could reassure you that he's a good guy. A great guy, actually, so maybe you should stop holding back and just go for it."

Edie dropped her embrace and backed away, though space was scarce amid a crowd of couples who were only paying attention to each other. Sebastian tried to shove his hands into his pants pockets but his tux jacket was in the way. He let his arms rest by his sides while his fingers curled and flexed as if they didn't know what to do without a line to trace or a place to hide. Edie simply gaped.

"Let me get this straight." She parceled her words out slowly, taking her time so she could understand them, herself. "Claire asked you to convince me to . . . what? Fall for Henry? Sleep with him? Fly to Vegas for a weekend wedding?"

Sebastian cringed. All his not-quite-hinged-right joints came unpinned as his body collapsed in on itself and his six-foot-two frame suddenly looked about six inches shorter.

"I'm sorry," he said. "I shouldn't have said anything."

"No shit." Edie glanced toward their table but Claire wasn't there. Apparently she was so sure of her agenda she didn't need to bother watching it play out. No wonder she didn't care if Sebastian asked Edie to dance. He wasn't giving undue attention to another girl. He was moving in on an unsuspecting target, ready to sting like a spring-loaded trap. "God, she's good. I'll bet she's laughing her perfect ass off right now."

As Edie turned back to Sebastian, the music changed to strident techno and the dance floor erupted with movement.

"What are you talking about?" he shouted as a heavy-lidded girl stumbled into him and staggered back to her friends. "What would she be laughing at?"

"It's a setup, Sebastian. Claire's making fools of us both. She's proving you'll do anything she asks you to. She's forcing me to take dating advice from the last guy I want to hear it from. And she *knows* I'm not going to fall for Henry because I'm in love with"—Edie stopped herself, barely—"someone else." She stood stock-still, stunned by what she'd just said. She shouldn't have said it. He shouldn't have heard it. It shouldn't be true, not after she'd tried so hard to let him go, to convince herself Henry was a better choice, or better yet, to convince herself she didn't want anything from either of them.

Sebastian studied her, his lips parted, his forehead rippling in confusion.

"So, your date for the pool party . . . ?" he started.

Edie struggled to hold her stance, jostled among the crowd. She felt a powerful urge to extend her lie but she was sick of pretending, of holding her feelings inside, of sorting them out in her head rather than flinging them into the world and seeing how they landed. She'd come this far. He might as well know everything.

"I made him up," she admitted.

"And the poker game? With Henry?"

"Total bullshit."

Sebastian's hand finally made its way to his head where his fingers tangled in his hair, pinching straw-colored tufts between his knuckles and raking toward the back of his neck. While he stood there, furrowing and fidgeting as though too baffled to do more, a twerking guy knocked Edie sideways. Her glass slipper bit into the side of her foot. She winced as she lost her balance. Sebastian reached out and took her arm. She met his eyes, startled by his sudden closeness. As he stared back, mute and unmoving despite all she'd laid bare to him, the clarity of her situation smacked her broadside. Sebastian wasn't by her side to support her, to love her back, or even to be her friend. He was just following the orders of his goddamned girlfriend, the one he was *never* going to leave.

Something splintered inside Edie, something she'd grown tired of keeping whole.

"Thanks for the advice about Henry." She yanked her arm free. "Consider it taken." With that, she turned and stormed away.

"Edie, wait!" Sebastian called as he jogged after her.

Edie didn't wait. She was done waiting. She sped up, elbowing her way through the crowd and running across the lobby until she burst out the front doors of the hotel. Desperate to ensure Sebastian didn't extend their agonizing conversation for another second, she ducked into a nearby alcove with a stone bench that was probably meant for people awaiting a ride. She hid in the shadows until the sounds of Sebastian's pursuit faded. Then she leaned back, feeling the rough brick against her bare shoulders and the warm spring air on her face, hoping simple, knowable things would help calm her down.

The entire night replayed in Edie's head as her questions mounted. She'd been having a perfectly wonderful time with a perfectly wonderful guy. How had it come unraveled so quickly? Why did she say all that to Sebastian? She thought she'd moved on. She had moved on. Sort of. How could she have such intense feelings for two guys at once? And which feelings? All those little words looked so similar — *like, love, lust* — as if some long-ago lexicographer was deliberately trying to confuse people. What did any of them really mean? How was a girl supposed to know which was which? What was she supposed to do if she didn't know? She couldn't hide in an alcove forever.

As Edie tried to exhale her confusion one deep breath at a time, Claire and Henry walked past a few yards away.

"You're kidding, right?" Claire chuckled, light and lilting.

"No, I'm not," Henry replied, uncharacteristically serious.

"I thought you planned to make her fall for you, not the other way around."

"I was such a jerk when I said that, but I didn't know her then."

"So you're really in love with her?"

"Head over heels."

As their voices faded and they entered the hotel, Edie sank onto the bench. Her hands trembled. Her pulse pounded. Her mind reeled as her thoughts and emotions stacked themselves one upon the other, too much to sort out in one night. So the guitar strings, the text-flirting, the romantic serenades, the afternoon outings, and the extravagant necklace were all part of a plot, a thorough deception cleverly calculated to break another heart. Of course they were. Nothing excited Henry more than a good challenge. Girls were something to woo, win, and toss aside. Edie should've known he planned to do the same with her. She felt stupid and naive, just another girl drawn in by a hot guy who knew how to make her feel wanted, liked, special.

But that other thing Henry said . . . if he meant it . . . but surely . . . or not so surely . . . Goddammit! Wasn't everything muddled enough already? Or was it all one big game she wasn't sophisticated enough to understand, full of bluffs and schemes wherein everyone had to "go big or go home"?

Edie stayed in the alcove for several minutes, trying to make sense out of things that failed to fall into tidy definitions or even meter. Unable to un-mess the situation, she eventually concluded that her only option was to stop trying to clean everything up. She marched into the ballroom, heading straight for the table with the Saint Pen's girls and her no-longer-maybe-date. She sped past Maria and Rupert as they took a selfie. She ignored Julia's wide-eyed gaping. She continued, undeterred, as she passed Claire and Sebastian arguing heatedly by a streamered column. She focused solely on Henry, whose eyes tracked her across the room. She stopped in front of him and held out her hand.

"Dance with me," she said.

He clasped her hand and followed her to the dance floor. He wrapped his arms around her. She wrapped her arms around him. As they started swaying to the beat, he laid a finger under her chin and tilted her face toward his. His eyes were serious, with no hint of their usual mischief.

"I know I'm not supposed to say this, but I'm tired of pretending I think of you as a friend. I've tried. I failed. I love you."

"No, you don't."

"But—"

"It doesn't matter. Kiss me anyway."

Slowly, gently, Henry placed his hands on either side of Edie's face. He met her eyes. She held his gaze, unflinching, unblushing.

There in the middle of the dance floor, Edie had her first skin-tingling, breath-stealing, knee-weakening, heart-pounding, lip-burning, tongue-tangling, bone-decimating, chest-exploding, hair-gripping, brain-erasing, blood-bursting, where-am-I-who-cares-good-god-make-this-last-forever kiss.

Chapter Thirty-Two

♥

EDIE OPENED HER EYES. HENRY WAS SMILING AT her, his face inches away, his cheeks flushed, his lips swollen, his eyes sparkling.

"Are you okay?" he asked.

"Yeah. Wow." Edie touched her lips to make sure they were still there. Lips? Yep, present and accounted for. Necklace? Check. But what about the rest of her? Who'd replaced her bones with Jell-O, put this hammering thing inside her chest, and turned her blood into gushing lava?

As she stumbled back a step, Henry caught her and pulled her close, one arm around her waist, the other cradling her head against his shoulder.

"You have no idea how badly I wanted to do that," he said.

Edie melted against him, bewildered by what she'd just done but deliriously happy about how good it felt. What on earth had she been waiting for all these weeks? Was she really protecting her cousins? What cousins? And who cared if Henry had been playing her? Crush not only crushed, but banished to the furthest outskirts of oblivion.

As Edie's lips stopped tingling, she blinked herself into awareness. She and Henry stood in a small clearing, surrounded by gyrating dancers, many of whom were looking her way. Her skin prickled as she sensed people watching her, judging her, zeroing in on her flaws. The strange claustrophobia of being alone among many.

"People are staring," she whispered.

"Actually, people are trying not to stare," Henry corrected.

"Then let's go where there are no people at all."

"Nothing would make me happier."

Henry kept his arm firmly wrapped around Edie's waist as they swept past their table. They grabbed her purse and said a swift, eye-contact-avoiding good night to the remaining couples. Then they slipped out the doors before anyone could ask questions, rate their performance, or pepper them with commentary.

As they got into Henry's car, he asked, "Where to?"

Edie considered asking Henry to drive her home. She'd confessed her love for one guy and kissed another — all in a very public setting. For a girl who'd made it almost all the way to graduation without going on a date, it was enough for one night. More than enough. And yet, as the memory of Henry's kiss swam through her brain and rippled across her skin, she decided the night didn't need to end just yet. In fact, she kind of hoped the sun wouldn't rise for a long, long time.

"Surprise me," she suggested.

Henry tapped his fingers on the steering wheel, considering.

"I have an idea." He started the ignition. "I think you'll like it."

As he pulled out of the parking lot, he nodded at the glove compartment. "There's something in there you might like, too."

Edie tensed as she eyed him sideways.

"I know exactly what you keep in the glove compartment."

Henry laughed, thoroughly amused, as he turned onto the main road.

"Don't worry. I cleaned it out. I didn't want you getting the wrong idea."

Edie popped open the glove compartment, half expecting a slew of condoms to fall onto her lap, but the cubby contained only a small stack of papers and an elegant silver flask. She took out the flask and ran a thumb over the bold, block-print HC.

"I filled it with vodka-cranberry," Henry explained. "In case you wanted to make a pink bastard."

Edie smiled at the memory of Rupert's horrible party, back when she'd known a different Henry, and when she'd been a different Edie. Sitting next to him now, with her lips tingling and her whole body on fire with anticipation, she had no intention of pouring a cocktail over his head. Instead, she took a few judicious sips, just enough to still her nerves without risking a reprise of the Great Pork Product Projectile Incident. Meanwhile, Henry drove a mile or two to the center of Mansfield. Once there he led Edie to the gray stone church that sat in the middle of the town green.

"Church?" she said with a laugh. "I didn't know you were so devout."

"Still think I'm a vampire?"

"Honestly? I'm a bit lost about what you are."

He took her hand, locking his fingers with hers, knuckle to knuckle.

"I'm just a guy out with a beautiful girl on a beautiful night, hoping to share as much of it as possible with her." He kissed her hand and held it to his chest.

She let her eyes linger on their little knot of fingers. It wasn't the hell of a held hand from *The Age of Innocence*. It wasn't the uncertain and fleeting connection from the Age of Confused. Maybe, just maybe, it was the onset of the Age of Yes.

Hand in hand, Henry and Edie climbed the steps to the front doors. There, he tugged on the big brass handles while she folded her arms and watched him struggle.

"What? No midnight service?" she teased.

"Oh, there'll be a midnight service, but we may need to slip in the back way."

"You can't be serious."

"I'm perfectly serious, as you perfectly know." He held out a hand.

Edie hesitated, gauging the up-to-no-good-ness in Henry's eyes. He might not care about silly things like rules and laws, but Edie suspected getting caught breaking and entering would do little to help her strained relationship with Norah, her summer employability, or her scholarship application. Henry flapped his hand, waiting, hoping, and smiling with un-kissed kisses hidden in his lips. Really. Amazing. Kisses.

Edie took his hand.

Together they skirted the church and stopped beneath a stained-glass window at the back. It was chest high, about two feet wide, and four feet high, depicting a saint with a halo of light and an outstretched hand. Henry slipped his fingers through a narrow gap at the edge of the window. He pulled until the window creaked open.

"Do I want to know how you discovered 'the back way'?" Edie asked.

He shot her a wry look over his shoulder.

"Let's just say I get bored easily."

"That I knew."

"And I accidentally left something behind when my family came for mass."

"Like a long list of sins to atone for?"

"Like a necklace I purchased on my way here that day."

Edie pressed a palm against it. Still there, faceted and flawless.

Henry knelt down and made a cradle of his hands for Edie's glass-slippered foot. Not wanting to puncture his palm, she slipped off her shoes and tossed them through the window. He boosted her up so she could haul her body forward, funneling her enormous dress through the open window. As she leapt down and steadied herself, she took in her surroundings. From the outside, the church looked like a typical Mansfield building: formal, elegant, old but carefully preserved. On the inside, in the moonlight, empty, echoing, and vibrating with the thrill of the illicit, it was magical.

Twenty-foot-high stained-glass windows split the moonlight into kaleidoscopic shafts of red, green, and gold that speckled the floor and spilled onto the empty pews. An upright piano stood against a wall with a stack of hymnals on top. The air smelled of dust, wax, and incense. Every footstep reverberated against the polished but well-worn floorboards. This was a space that held stories, where people brought their hopes, their prayers, their sorrow and despair. Edie loved it. Henry was right, yet again. She bit back a smile. She wondered if she was ever going to prove him wrong about anything, though she didn't care much anymore if she didn't.

As Henry stepped up beside her, she whispered, "Come here often?"

"Never with such spectacular company."

"What are we supposed to do now?"

"We're supposed to climb."

Edie grabbed her shoes. Henry clasped her hand and led her across the church, through a door near the pulpit, up a long spiral staircase, and then up a service ladder. At the top, he drew open a little trapdoor in the ceiling. Edie followed him onto the top of the bell tower. The space was maybe forty feet square, with a waist-high stone wall, an A-frame timber roof held up by four corner posts, and an empty hook that awaited a bell. The tower was dingy and dirty, filled with old bits of rope, chain, and rusty hardware, but beyond the wall, the stars sparkled like fairy dust.

"It's the highest spot in Mansfield." Henry shut the trapdoor. "I thought you might enjoy the view." He stepped forward, leaned on the wall, and waved her over.

Edie left her shoes in the corner. Then she nestled into the curve of his arm and scanned the horizon for familiar landmarks. Henry pointed to a meandering residential street dotted with grand houses and orange-tinted streetlamps. The homes were largely indistinguishable from so far away, but Edie could tell by their orientation that she was looking at the Vernons' street.

"There's where I first saw Edie Price." Henry turned her to the left and pointed out a bookshop on the other side of the green. "There's where she let me buy her a tiny token of my affection." He pivoted her again and pointed out her school with the illuminated flagpole in the circular driveway. "There's where she reluctantly accepted a ride." He pointed to the hotel they'd just left. "And there's where I first kissed her. Can I kiss her again?" He laid a hand on either side of her face and looked into her eyes.

Edie nodded, already breathless just from a look.

"Say my favorite word," he implored her.

"Yes." The word came out easily, like it'd been waiting on her tongue, ready to spring into being and multiply itself a thousand times. *Yes*, she thought. *Good god, yes.*

Henry kissed her lightly on her cheek. He stayed there to murmur, "'Upon thy cheek I lay this zealous kiss, as seal to the indenture of my love.'"

Edie laughed, as much as a girl could laugh when hands and lips were slowly stealing her breath and making her heart ricochet against her ribs.

"I wondered when I was going to hear a little Shakespeare," she said.

"I could tell man-walks-into-a-bar jokes instead." His hands slid along her jaw line, strong fingers gliding beneath her ears, weaving through her hair, and pressing into the base of her skull.

"Shakespeare walks into a bar," she suggested.

"Shakespeare walks into a bard."

"Nice." She leaned in to his touch as she set her hands on his waist, steadying herself, slipping her thumbs over the edge of his tux pants and drawing him closer.

Henry tilted her head and placed a row of kisses along the side of her neck, ensuring each one was securely fastened to her skin before moving on to plant another.

"'A thousand kisses buys my heart from me.'"

"I'm not actually in the market for a heart." She inched up his shirt and slipped her hands around the base of his rib cage. His skin was warm, smooth, tightly stretched over muscles that twitched and tensed under her touch. "But you can have as many kisses as we can fit into one night."

"Only one night? Then let's make the most of it."

In the next moment, Henry's lips were on Edie's and the world blurred, fading into a haze of light and shadow, punctuated only by the feel of gloriously greedy hands and hungry lips that sought anything but words. His jacket came off. Her hair tumbled down around her shoulders. His cummerbund fell across his toes. Her balance wavered. Still he kissed her and she kissed him back, unable to draw away for more than a second.

When Edie's knees collapsed, she and Henry crumpled to the

floor, picking up where they left off, with her hands working their way across his back while his fingers tangled in her hair. Hairpins pinged against the floorboards as Maria's careful work unraveled, as everything unraveled. Hours, days, months of confusion unknotted themselves, making room for the overwhelming immediacy of lips, tongues, breath, hands, skin, heat, want.

Want. Yes. That was what felt so amazing. Wanting openly and being wanted back, without question or reservation. Not trying to read between the lines. Not trying to create any lines. Not defining things. Not analyzing how he felt and how she felt and what it all meant. Not trying to figure out the polite thing to do or say. Not trying to get things *right* all the time. Just being present, in the moment, in a way Edie had never felt before. There was no space for before, no room for later. There was only now.

Edie rolled onto her back as Henry settled his weight on top of her. The floor beneath her was cool, damp maybe, and rough, but all thoughts of the floor vanished as Henry peppered kisses across her bare skin from shoulder to shoulder, dipping down where her chest pressed against the bodice that seemed to tighten as each breath grew faster, shorter, harder to take. With a strange desperation to get closer to Henry's skin, to his body, Edie loosened his tie, slipped the tail out through the knot, and tossed it aside.

A smile stretched across his face, a little bit wicked and a lot dead-sexy.

"Two can play at that game." He unknotted the sash around her waist.

Edie pictured him toying with it when they'd first arrived at prom, the knowing look in his eyes, the way he'd teased a blush out of her as if he'd been deliberately planting ideas in her head.

"You knew you'd be taking that off me," she said.

"No, but I hoped. I like untying things." He kissed her neck. "Undoing things." He kissed her cheek, edging toward her ear, his voice low like thunder. "Returning things to a natural state of disorder."

"What are you, the Lord of Chaos?"

"Nah. I'm small-time."

"That's not what I heard."

He shifted above her, pressing down with his hips, his dark eyes boring into hers as she plucked open his collar button.

"I can't match that move," he said. "You don't have any buttons."

"Then I get to have all the fun." She opened his second button.

"Hardly." He traced a finger along the edge of her bodice, sending a shiver to her toes. "Nothing's more fun than the sound of a zipper coming undone."

"Nothing at all?"

"Well, now that you mention it." He slipped a hand into his pocket and pulled out a condom. "Only if you want to."

Edie paused, her hands on his chest, her eyes shifting back and forth between his face and the condom. She was a little unsettled that he'd planned for this possibility, but also a little grateful, since she hadn't planned for anything at all. She only thought she'd kiss him tonight, but what they were doing felt so good. Why stop now? She wanted this. She wanted him.

She nodded as she opened his third button.

"You sure?" he asked.

She met his gaze. She held it.

"Yes."

He traced the top of her bodice again, this time running his fingertips just inside the neckline, making her back arch toward him.

"They say a woman always looks perfect in white," he said.

"It's a nice dress." Fourth button. Fifth button. "But I don't know about perfect."

"You're right. It's terrible. We should probably take it off." He rolled onto his back, settling Edie astride his hips. He found the zipper at the back of her dress. He inched it down past her waist, drawing out the *clickety-whirr* of something coming undone.

Sixth button. Seventh button.

Edie opened Henry's shirt and pushed it off his shoulders. She ran her hands down his chest, tracing his bones and muscles, watching his body respond, fascinated with the relationship between her touch and his movement.

"Remember what you asked me the day we played poker?" she said.

"I remember a lot of things from that day."

"Well, this time, yes, the interest is mutual."

"Thank god." He shimmied her dress down around her hips.

Her bare back, damp with sweat, tingled in the warm night air as everything sped up. His hands circled her waist, rocking her forward and back, pushing and pulling, gently, and then not so gently. *Eyes. Skin. Heat. Want.* She dug through her skirts, shoving aside tulle until she felt him through her underwear. Sensing Henry's body react to her made her feel strangely powerful. It made her want him even more.

She leaned forward to kiss him. His hand groped her breast. Her thighs tightened around his hips. He ground against her. Her tongue pried open his lips. His pushed back. *Warm. Wet. Want. Yes.* She unbuttoned his pants. He found the hooks on her long-line bra and began to pop them open. Her hand slipped down his stomach, then inside his underwear, where smooth skin shifted to a tangle of hair. As her bra tilted away from her body, her locket trickled onto his chest.

Wait . . . her locket?

"Shit!" Edie gathered the chain, shuffled off of Henry, and backed against the wall. The locket popped open, revealing her mom's face, smiling as if to say, *If you let your heart drive, don't forget to bring your brain.* Her mom, who'd instructed Edie to focus on her education rather than her love life. Her mom, whose family had shunned her for her impulsive choices. Her mom, who'd gotten pregnant on her prom night.

"What's that?" Henry asked.

"Something I forgot." Edie shoved the locket back into place, pressing both the locket and the half-undone bra to her chest. "Something I shouldn't have forgotten."

Henry scooted up beside her and caressed her cheek.

"Did I go too fast?"

"No, *I* went too fast." Edie hiked up her dress to cover her bra.

"I can slow down."

"No. I'm sorry. I just . . . I need to stop. Okay?"

"Really stop? Or just take a break?"

"Really stop."

Henry let out a long, slow breath as he slumped against the wall and his eyes trailed to the far corner of the tower.

"Wow. Okay," he said. "If that's what you want."

"I want a lot of things, but I need to sort them out before I rush this."

He ran a hand over his face and held it against his chin as he shook his head, answering a question he'd only asked himself.

"This is about the swashbuckler, isn't it?"

"No. This is about the girl." And maybe a little bit about the swashbuckler. Dammit! Why was he still on her mind? He had no right to be there.

Henry nodded. Then he dragged his shirt onto his shoulders, tipped his head back, and watched Edie comb her fingers through her hair, picking out stray pins until her last remaining curl fell over her shoulders.

"Are you mad?" she asked.

"Mad? No." He laughed softly, a smile barely denting his cheeks. "Unless you're about to run away and leave me holding one of those shoes."

Edie nudged her glass slipper further into a corner. Then she assessed the abrasion on the side of her foot. It was red and swollen, curved like pursed lips.

"Looks like I'm not running anywhere tonight," she said.

"Then neither am I."

She adjusted the top of her dress and checked for both necklaces. They were still there, warm but hard and unforgiving, forcing their impressions into her skin. They'd both seemed so beautiful a few hours ago. Now they felt like brands. Her choices were becoming too big, too permanent. For the rest of her life, Henry would hold the title of First Boy She Kissed, ousting Sebastian now that Edie fully understood the difference between clumsily mimicking a statue at age ten and hungrily locking tongues at age seventeen. Did she want Henry to hold another first or did she want to save that spot for someone else, someone with whom it would really mean something? Given time to clear her head, could Henry become the guy with whom it would really mean something?

"Can we just sit here for a few minutes?" she asked.

"We can sit here for as many minutes as you want." Henry opened his arms and invited her in.

Edie leaned into his embrace and laid a cheek against his chest. She was torn about stopping something that felt so good but grateful she might've staved off a few potential regrets. Sure, she wanted minute seven (or whatever minute they were on now), and kissing Henry was as amazing as Maria had claimed, but once she paused to think about it, losing her virginity to him on their first real date didn't feel right. If she was going to have sex with Henry, she had to really want it, not just with her body, but with her mind and her heart, too. As her mom had said, that was where she kept the good stuff.

Henry hummed softly as Edie relaxed against his chest and closed her eyes, letting his voice drown out the anxiety and confusion that threatened to overtake the giddy little shivers flickering across her skin, the imprint of kisses and caresses, desire's tattoos. As Henry's arms wrapped tighter, and as Edie found the perfect nook on which to rest her head, a layer of loneliness shuffled itself off and scurried away.

Chapter Thirty-Three

THE MORNING SUN WAS STRETCHING ACROSS THE bell tower when Edie opened her eyes. She scooted upright, quickly shifting from dazed to panicked. Henry was breathing softly behind her, sound asleep, his shirt open and his trousers unbuttoned. As she checked for both necklaces, his eyes blinked open and his face broke into a wide smile.

"What are you so happy about?" she barked.

"I wake up to your beautiful face and you ask me what I'm happy about?" He ran the back of his fingers along her cheek, soft and tender.

"Don't be charming right now." Edie adjusted her half-unhooked bra and her unzipped dress, holding both against her chest with her forearm, feeling far more naked in the daylight than when her brain/copilot had been on hiatus a few hours earlier. "Do you realize we spent the whole night here? My aunt is going to murder me."

"I'll smooth things over for you." He caressed her other cheek. "I'm good with parents. The dads, not so much, but the moms . . ."

Edie ignored his smirk, still scrambling to reassemble herself.

"My cousins are never going to let me hear the end of this."

"I'm good with cousins, too."

She shot him the glare to end all glares.

"I changed my mind. I'll take Charming Henry. It's too early in the morning for Conceited Henry." She reached behind her back and struggled with her hooks, barely managing to get one fastened. She soon gave up and spun her back toward Henry. "Can you help me with this?"

"Absolutely." He popped open a hook.

"That's not what I meant."

"I know. I know." He hooked her bra and zipped up her dress, lingering to trace her shoulder blade with the side of his hand. His caress felt electric, like they all did, drawing the best kind of shivers across her skin, but she refused to be distracted.

"Come on. We should go." Edie quickly knotted her sash and retrieved her glass slippers. She clambered up, brushing the worst of the dirt off her no-longer white dress.

Henry remained seated with his head leaning idly against the wall. He looked like a marionette at rest, though Edie suspected very few marionettes were costumed in Henry's current state of undress.

"I'm serious!" She hauled open the trapdoor and motioned for Henry to get up. "I have to get home."

As the sound of choir voices floated upward, Henry checked his phone.

"You might want to wait a bit," he suggested. "It's Sunday. Service isn't over for another hour."

"Well, isn't that convenient?" Edie dropped the door, letting it thunk down and dampen the music.

"If you don't mind interrupting the priest, we could go give the congregation something to talk about." Henry lazily flicked a bit of grime off his knee. "I could even introduce you to my parents."

"Like this?!" Edie held out her filthy skirt. "It's hardly 'meet the parents' attire."

"We could clean up in the holy water."

"I thought holy water burned vampires."

Henry laughed but Edie glowered. She began to pace—three steps either direction—making the old boards tremble under her feet. Henry looked on, amused and unmoving, the picture of some-one content to remain precisely where he was.

"Want me to call Maria and explain what happened?" he offered.

"The less either of my cousins knows about our night together, the better."

Edie continued pacing, burning through her anxiety one step at a time until she realized she was only accomplishing one thing: mak-ing her feet sore. She didn't even know what she was so upset about: her own hasty choices, Henry's carelessness about the impending repercussions, or some complicated overlap between the two.

"Relax." He patted the floor next to him. "When the service lets out, we'll sneak downstairs and merge into the crowd. No one will even notice us."

"I guess another hour won't make much difference now." She sat down beside him, resigned to her fate. As she blinked into the sunlight, her eyelashes locked together. She peeled off the false bits and stuck them to the wall behind her.

"Anything else you want to take off?" Henry asked.

"Nice try, but no." She ripped away a dangling bit of tulle, appalled at her bedraggled appearance. "So, how should we pass the time?"

"You know what I want to do." He leaned toward her.

"Besides that." She leaned away and adjusted her sash, now torn and tassel-free.

He brushed her hair off her forehead, gently, sweetly, reversing the chaos he'd been so proud of only hours earlier.

"I do love you," he said.

Edie opened her mouth to say she couldn't possibly believe him, not after seeing him play Romeo for Julia, lure Maria away from Rupert, and talk about so many other girls like they were just a bit of meaningless fun. But something in Henry's eyes—and something in the story of a boy who'd been patient, persistent, and dedicated—made her give his words credence. Besides, her mixed motives for kissing him last night didn't land her on moral high ground, her present location notwithstanding.

When Edie failed to respond, Henry's smile dropped away for the first time since he'd opened his eyes.

"You really think I'm lying," he said.

Edie took his hand in hers. She felt awful for not being able to accept what he was offering, words and feelings that were so beautiful, and that she'd dreamt of hearing one day, but they didn't sit right for some reason. They were like glass slippers: nice to look at, hard to wear.

"Honestly?" she said. "I don't know what to think about anything anymore, especially about myself."

He raised her hand to his lips.

"Then I'll simply wait until you do."

She squeezed his hand and leaned her head on his shoulder as a V of birds flew past, high up in the blue-gray sky, silhouetted against a wispy streak of clouds. She didn't know how long Henry would wait for her to figure herself out—a month, a week, or maybe only an hour—but she liked the idea that to someone, for some amount of time, she was the one worth waiting for.

Chapter Thirty-Four

Persuasion

noun

1. Jane Austen's final novel.
2. Your prom date's cunning ability to convince you that a morning make-out session in a church tower would be a truly religious experience.
3. A clever orchestration of compliments and apologies that turns your aunt from pursed-lips-on-legs into a gushing, blushing that's-okay machine who thanks your date for taking such good care of you when he drops you off eight hours past your curfew.

To Edie's relief, Maria and Julia were still in bed when she crept upstairs to shower, change, and slather her hair with detangler. She could only imagine her cousins' faces if they'd seen her and Henry show up on the doorstep looking like they'd reenacted a sordid scene from *The Hunchback of Notre Dame*. Once Edie was back to her pre-makeover self, she carefully stowed Henry's necklace and slipped her locket on. Then she lay down on her bed and checked her phone, frustrated to discover that even her insinuation about spending the night with a guy hadn't garnered a response from Shonda.

As Edie remembered Ithaca High's prom was the previous weekend, she clicked on Shonda's Instagram page and flipped through the photos. Shonda was in several shots from the big event, looking fierce in a red strapless dress with her blond-streaked black braids piled high and a new pair of rectangular glasses that suited her heart-shaped face perfectly. James was nowhere to be seen, nor was any guy. Despite the fact that Shonda'd pretty much always had a boyfriend, she seemed to have spent the last couple months without one. Edie didn't even know Shonda had broken up with James. She didn't actually know anything about Shonda's life lately. Edie'd been so busy waiting and hoping for Shonda's forgiveness, she hadn't stopped to think about what Shonda needed. Maybe she was lonely too.

Racked with guilt for being such a selfish friend yet again, Edie began typing an apologetic text. She paused as she recalled her conversation with Sebastian in the sycamore tree. He'd suggested the friendship was likely repairable if she found the right way to reconnect. Not just any way. The right way. Edie'd been telling herself she'd tried everything but it wasn't actually true. She hadn't looked Shonda in the eye, in person, and said she was sorry. She'd been full of denial before she left Ithaca and she'd been hiding behind a screen ever since, too afraid to face the pain she'd inflicted and the fury that would likely emerge. If she truly valued her friendship, she needed to stop protecting herself from the consequences of her own actions.

Edie made herself a promise. No more lexicon posts. No more texts. No more emails. She was living in the Age of Yes now. As soon as school was over, she was taking the bus to Ithaca, even if she returned with a broken nose and no friend to show for it.

She was still looking through photos when a text came through. She jerked upright. The universe had heard her plea! Shonda was replying after all!

Sebastian: Can we talk?

Edie stared at her screen, feeling as if she'd been gut-punched. No. Not this. Not again. She'd *finally* moved on. He'd even encouraged her to do so in his own mangled, manipulated, moronic way. He had no place in her life right now. He'd only confuse matters. Someone loved her. She was happy. She wanted to stay that way.

Sebastian: Please?

The ache in Edie's gut moved up a few inches, settling itself somewhere inside her ribs, just left of center. Panicked, she wrenched open the bedside table and flung her phone into the drawer as if it were Kryptonite. While she was burying it under a pile of junk like a crazy person, Maria and Julia burst into her bedroom without warning, still dressed in their pajamas. They plopped down on the bed together. Julia hugged a pillow, biting down a smile. Maria folded her arms, sleepy-eyed and scowling. Edie braced herself against the headboard as the inquisition began.

"Tell us all about it," Julia practically squealed with excitement.

"Not *all* about it," Maria said with no excitement whatsoever. "Just, like, the family-friendly version."

"The two of you?" Julia gushed. "On the dance floor? Total movie kiss."

"It was just a kiss," Maria grumbled.

"Where did you guys go last night?" Julia barreled on. "And did you . . . you know? You totally did it, didn't you? Was it perfect and amazing? Tell me it was perfect and amazing. I want my first time to be perfect and amazing too."

"Slow down!" Edie waved her hands in front of her face. "We just hung out for a while and fell asleep—otherwise I would've been here hours ago." She spotted her pile of shed clothes on the floor. She scampered up to stash the evidence that "hanging out" had been far more athletic than she was implying.

"I was hoping you fell in love." Julia wilted against the footboard.

"Wow." Edie tossed her dress into the closet, ensuring it was out of view. "That's not how I thought you'd take things."

"Someone should get to be his girlfriend," Julia said.

"I'm not his girlfriend." The word sounded strange to Edie, incongruous and oversized. It was far too unwieldy to describe a relationship with a guy she'd spent one impulsive night with, especially a guy who'd always seemed averse to relationships.

"But that kiss!" Julia's sock-clad feet fluttered against the dust ruffle.

"It was *just* a kiss." Maria grabbed a stray hairpin and forced it to unbend.

"You swore you didn't mind that I asked him to prom," Edie reminded her.

"Yeah, but I didn't think you'd do a ten-minute face-dive in front of everyone."

"It wasn't ten minutes."

"Whatever. I didn't pull out a stopwatch." Maria began rolling her eyes, but she winced mid-effort. She tossed the hairpin onto the table and wrapped a hand over her forehead. "I'm just saying, you could've shown a little class. You're not in Podunk anymore where everyone knows who's banging who by which trailer's rocking."

Edie allowed herself to picture hairpins smothering Maria like a swarm of locusts descending on a field of crops. Then she shucked her glass slippers into the closet.

"Maria, I'll forgive you because I know you don't mean what you just said, but ease up a little, please? I didn't set out to hurt you but I had a good time with Henry and I'd like to see him again, with or without a trailer."

Maria sneered as she started torturing another hairpin.

"No more boy-next-door fantasies?" she goaded.

"No more of your business." Edie folded her sash into a sharp little square, surprised at her newfound assertiveness. It felt good. Better than good. With a concerted effort, maybe the Age of Yes could bring on the glorious downfall of the Empire of Polite.

"I don't know how you can be so calm about Henry," Julia said. "If he gave me an ounce of the attention he's given you, I'd be up to my eyeballs in love."

"Your eyeballs were floating with no attention at all," Maria said.

Julia swung her pillow at Maria's head. Maria swatted it away as her eyebrows plunged together. Before the bickering could escalate, Edie flew over to the bed and wedged herself between her cousins.

"I think we've all said enough about Henry." She took Julia's pillow and tucked it behind her. "Julia? How was your night with W.B.?"

Julia managed a halfhearted shrug.

"I had fun and he's an awesome dancer, but"—she paused, smoothing a wrinkle in the duvet—"once we left the hotel, we didn't really know what to do with each other."

"Because he couldn't find your boobs?" Maria chided.

"No! He didn't . . . I just . . . I didn't know he was gay."

Maria snorted with laughter.

"Classic," she said. "You finally ask a guy out and he's even less likely to kiss you than I am."

"Shut up." Julia quickly settled into full pout mode.

Edie drew her into an embrace.

"None of us knew he was gay," she said.

"I feel so stupid." Julia tipped her head onto Edie's shoulder. "He wasn't hiding it. I just never thought to ask. Then this song came on when we were driving away from the hotel. I said I liked it. He said it was his ex-boyfriend's band. I got really quiet. He said he thought I knew. I told him I didn't know how I was supposed to know."

Maria snorted again.

"Guess they didn't teach you how to deal with that one in *A Better You*."

Edie elbowed her. Maria grimaced and rubbed the point of

impact. Julia was too lost in disappointment to notice either of them. She straightened the hem of her camisole where it dipped over the waistband of her eyelet shorts, lining things up just so.

"Maybe I'll have a real date to next year's prom." She let out a plaintive sigh. "Someone who'll kiss me like Henry kissed you. God, I mean, that moment when he looked in your eyes and—"

"Seriously." Maria held up a hand. "Enough about the kissing."

"So, how was your night with Rupert?" Edie asked.

"Fine," Maria said. It was the only word she spoke on the subject.

For the rest of the day, Edie holed herself up in her room, resolutely avoiding her phone while manically editing her scholarship application. After eight weeks of debating who she wanted to be, she concluded that she was too full of contradictions to complete the task as assigned. She couldn't choose one role model any more than she could narrow the definition of *love* to one meaning as she applied it to Shonda, Sebastian, Henry, her mom, her cousins, or even her aunt and uncle. Life was far too complicated to reduce to singularities. Attempting to box, bind, and define everything only led to frustration and confusion. Edie was better off embracing the muddle.

At 11:56 p.m., four minutes before the deadline, Edie submitted all thirty-seven of her essays along with a short cover letter.

To Whom It May Concern:
    Please accept the attached submissions for the Imogene Stanwyck Memorial Scholarship Competition. While each

entry may be judged according to its own merit, I ask that the committee also consider my materials as a whole. The only person I'd really like to become is myself, but I can only do so with the support and influence of a vast network of other people. To reduce them all to a single name and 1,500 words would be like boiling me down to my nose. As someone who's never liked her nose, this strikes me as an ill-fated proposition.

I'd like to thank the committee in advance for considering my application(s) and for your patience in perusing the extensive enclosed materials. Best wishes for an efficient adjudication process.

Yours respectfully,

Edie Price

She had no idea what the committee would do with her application. They might read only one essay. They might read all thirty-seven. They might consider her cover letter impressive for its use of *adjudication* or impertinent for its reference to her nose. Either way, she'd tried her best. She'd been honest about herself. It was all she could do, really. The rest was out of her control.

Chapter Thirty-Five

EDIE SPENT THE NEXT FEW WEEKS STUDYING FOR finals, working at the tutoring center, and staunchly ignoring a growing text chain from Sebastian. She also reassured Julia her Romeo was out there somewhere and she did her best to blow off Maria's continued post-prom snarkiness. She passed any remaining time with Henry, who turned out to be as patient, persistent, and dedicated as he'd once claimed, gradually shifting from First Guy She Kissed to First Official Boyfriend. He took her to Cold Shoulder where they sampled flavors until Edie picked a new favorite. They attended the open mic night in Brockton, where they chatted with the organizer about getting Edie on the roster later that summer. They went midnight skinny-dipping at Fulton Pond, where Edie openly ogled Henry's extended benefits package and they *almost* used the condom he always had handy.

Henry was nothing like the guys Edie'd crushed on all through high school, the sort she'd always imagined dating. He wasn't bookish or artsy. He didn't have deep deliberations about the meaning of life. Instead he made her smile. He made her laugh. He distracted her from cyclical thoughts that weighed too heavily on her mind. She loved every minute they spent together, whether they were driving down the highway with the windows open and the music blasting, or sitting quietly in a park, draped around each other while he fed her contraband bread and cheese. With Henry, Edie learned the simple pleasure of holding someone's hand for more than a fleeting moment. She felt the effervescent thrill of unchecked anticipation. She shed the loneliness that'd haunted her since she boarded a bus in Ithaca back in early April.

When he dropped her off one night, she mentioned wishing she could tell Shonda all about him. Naturally, Henry asked why she couldn't. Edie evaded his question with generalities about a past miscommunication. Henry didn't need to know what happened with James. She didn't think he'd judge her, not after all the stories he'd told about his own indiscretions. He just wasn't the sort of guy she shared that stuff with. Henry was for laughter and joy, for music and moonlit kisses, for resounding yeses. Heartache and shame didn't belong in their particular us-ness.

As Henry got out of his car and met Edie on the curb, she took his hand and raised it to her lips.

"You know, you're pretty great," she said.

"I tried to tell you that weeks ago." He smiled at her, smoldering away with his bottomless eyes, his full lips, and the barely raised eyebrows that always made him look like he was awaiting the answer to a question he didn't need to bother asking.

"Your claim wasn't very convincing when you were bringing Julia to tears and mapping stars on Maria."

"Fair enough," he said with markedly little apology. Then he slipped his hands around Edie's waist and backed her against the side of his car. "Bet I can find a few constellations hiding in your skin." He pulled aside her collar, or rather, *his* collar since she was wearing his shirt.

"Guess I should give this back at some point," she said.

"Keep it," he murmured against her neck. "It looks better on you."

"Maybe you're not as vain as I thought."

"Yes, I am. But I'm not blind." He began kissing her freckles, one by one, gradually turning a few simple stars into a cluster of blazing meteors. Since Edie'd long since charted the one hundred and seventeen freckles between her hairline and her neckline, she suspected Henry's astronomical exploration could go on well past her curfew.

"I should head in," she said, making no move toward the house.

"I could come with you." He paused his exploration and cocked an eyebrow.

She raised both eyebrows, unsure how anyone did that single-eyebrow thing.

"My cousins . . ."

"Don't need to know." He popped open a few of her shirt buttons, ran a finger under her bra strap, and eased it off her shoulder, following its path with his lips.

Her heart strained against her rib cage, cramped in its too-close quarters, desperate for space.

"My aunt and uncle . . ."

"I'll be very, *very* quiet." He pressed against her, slipping a knee between hers and drawing her closer with a hand around her hip.

Her body began to tingle. Her resolve wavered. The tip of his tongue tickled her upper lip. His nose brushed hers. His dark eyes brimmed with suggestion. Feeling somewhat . . . suggestible, Edie leaned forward and kissed him. As Henry kissed her back, his hands wrapped her ribs. His thumbs skimmed under the edges of her bra. His hips shifted against hers. She gripped his hair and drew him closer, impatient for more, but when his hand slid down the front of her jeans, she pulled away.

"I just want to be close to you." He caressed her cheek, her neck, her collarbone.

"Another time." She glanced over her shoulder at Maria's lit windows. "And another place."

Henry protested, declaring her resistance to his advances cruel and unusual punishment. Edie caved temporarily, drawn in by his kisses while he somehow managed to unbutton her entire shirt. Before he could unfasten anything else, she rallied the willpower to send him on his way.

As Edie trailed Henry's retreating car, she wondered why she was so resistant to going all the way with him. She wanted to do it. She thought about it all the time. She liked him. He liked her. He knew what he was doing, which was a plus, since she didn't. He'd make her feel safe and cared for. He'd make her feel a lot of other things, too. She was ready to step past her last almost, to find out what all the fuss was about, to know if sex was even remotely as spectacular as everything that led up to it. Yet every time they got close, she found a reason to stop. What was she so afraid of? Where was the catch?

Edie cycled through these questions until she finally realized the problem: trust.

Shonda had been so happy the week after she had sex with James for the first time, but he hadn't been faithful. Edie's mom had fallen madly in love, but her husband left her with a baby and a napkin. Henry had openly professed to being a collector of hearts. The only thing he'd ever committed to was his car. He didn't even have academic or career goals. He just did what he wanted when he wanted with no forward planning, no looking back, no strings attached. While Edie didn't need a lifetime commitment in order to have sex, she wanted some reassurance that Henry would still be there afterward without instantly moving on to the next girl.

Still wrestling with that thought, Edie headed upstairs and peeked through Bert and Norah's open door. They were sitting upright in bed as if they'd sprouted there like cornstalks. Bert was reading an Audubon book and Norah was watching a food documentary while moisturizing her hands in a special pair of gloves.

"I'm back," Edie announced.

"How is that lovely young man?" Norah asked, all aflutter. "Why don't you bring him around for dinner one night?"

"Mm," Edie mumbled. She could just picture it: her cousins subtly competing for Henry's attention while he pushed his boundaries under the tablecloth and Norah wondered why no one was devouring her cucumber carrot kebobs.

"Maybe this week while Rupert's back in town," Bert suggested. "We could try out that new restaurant by the mall."

"The all-you-can-eat buffet?" Norah huffed with indignation.

"Really, Bert! After all I do to take care of you, are you trying to make me a widow?"

Edie left them to argue as she padded down the hallway toward her bedroom. She paused when she heard softly muffled sobbing behind Maria's door. She knocked but Maria didn't answer. Taking a cue from her cousins, Edie went ahead and peeked in.

Maria was lying facedown on her bed, still dressed from her date with Rupert, her feet dangling off the bedside, her fists gripping her pillow. Edie crept in. She sat down on the edge of the bed and rubbed Maria's back, unsure what else to do. She'd never seen Maria cry before, not once, even when they were kids and she fell off her bike or lost her favorite stuffed monkey.

After several minutes, Maria finally rolled over, revealing a face streaked with mascara-laden tears.

"What happened?" Edie asked.

Maria wiped her nose on the back of her hand.

"He broke up with me! Can you believe it? *He* broke up with *me*."

"I'm so sorry." Edie handed her a nearby box of tissues. "Did he say why?"

"Because he's an asshole, that's why." Rather than address the question at hand, Maria ransacked the tissue box while providing an extensive catalogue of Rupert's shortcomings. He was a total jerk, always showing up at the wrong times, lingering when he wasn't wanted, and embarrassing her in front of her friends. He was selfish. He was boring. He was a terrible dresser and an even worse dancer. He had the nerve to claim their breakup wasn't all his fault. He accused her of things that were totally untrue, or at least that he had no proof of, which was basically the same thing. He didn't appreciate the sacrifices she made for him. He wasn't even attractive. He didn't understand *anything*.

Edie listened patiently while wondering what, exactly, Rupert had accused Maria of, and what kind of proof she was referring to.

"I don't understand," Edie said. "At prom you guys were all excited you'd get to announce your engagement next month. Why did he suddenly change his mind?"

"How should I know?" Maria's eyes shot to Edie's for a fraction of a second before she buried her face in a tissue.

"He gave you no reason at all? That doesn't seem like Rupert. Why would—?"

"Okay, so he saw some texts on my phone." Maria hastily wiped her nose and tossed the tissue to the floor where it joined several others. "A bit of harmless flirting." She flung aside another barely used tissue. "Nothing a normal person would care about, but he blew it up into this big deal, lecturing me about trust and commitment, acting like he was so much smarter than me just because he goes to Harvard." A third tissue made its way to the floor. "I don't need to take that crap from him."

A knot of suspicion formed in Edie's gut, reinforcing her fears about Henry's trustworthiness.

"Maria?" she asked warily. "Who were the texts to?"

"It doesn't matter. Rupert had no right reading them."

"But the texts . . ." Edie pressed.

"Oh my god." Maria leapt off the bed and marched over to her full-length mirror. "I'm so over this inquisition. It's, like, practically medieval. You're supposed to be making me feel better, not attacking me. God!"

Edie spun toward her from the bed.

"I just want to know if—"

"I'm not sleeping with your boyfriend, Edie."

Edie reeled, stunned by Maria's leap of logic.

"I didn't say you were."

"You might as well have. Ever since you sucked his face off at prom you've been all paranoid about him." Maria snatched up the little bag on her dresser and began fixing her makeup. "I still can't believe I gave him to you."

Despite a jolt of annoyance and a prickling curiosity, Edie clamped her jaw and held her rebuttal inside. Maria had been there when Edie was at her lowest, even though it meant taking sides against a friend. Now it was Edie's turn to love without question.

While Maria dabbed away the last of her tears, Edie gathered the used tissues, tossing them away as though heartbreak could simply be shed and discarded rather than lingering long after a wound was inflicted.

"I should go tell Dear Mama the wedding's off. She was planning to mail the engagement party invites tomorrow morning." Maria repinned a curl over her ear, looking poised, polished, and perfect. Only her red eyes betrayed her pain. "She's going to be crushed. We'd finally agreed on a color scheme for the wedding." She crossed the room but she paused in the doorway. She stood there as if paralyzed, gripping the door frame. Then she turned around and extended a hand toward Edie. "Will you come with me?" Her voice was unusually timid, no longer tough as nails but small and afraid.

Without hesitation, Edie slipped her hand into Maria's.

"Of course," she said. "I'm right here beside you."

Chapter Thirty-Six

AT THE END OF THE THIRD WEEK IN JUNE, EDIE, Maria, and Claire graduated from Saint Penitent's. After the ceremony, the girls posed for awkward group photos in the auditorium while the Vernons and the Crawfords looked on proudly, unaware of the resentments and jealousies that simmered just below the girls' strained smiles. After a few wistful sighs, Julia seemed content to chat with her friends and ignore boys entirely. Maria put on a brave face whenever someone asked about Rupert, blithely claiming she'd let him go when the distance became tedious. Henry was perceptive enough to restrain his physical affection so he wouldn't escalate tensions. Claire doled out warm hugs to every girl who graduated.

Every girl but one.

As the auditorium began to clear, Edie slipped off her graduation robe and returned it to a beaky woman with a tight gray bun and a pinched smile. The woman checked off her name and turned her attention to the next girl in line. Edie was about to rejoin her family when she realized the next girl in line was Claire. The auditorium suddenly seemed smaller, brighter, and about twenty degrees warmer. Edie's instinct to bolt immediately kicked in but she forced herself to stay put. High school was over. If she expected college to provide her a fresh start, she had to own up to her actions, even if that meant facing down her darkest demons.

"Claire?" she asked tentatively. "Can I say something?"

Claire tensed but she didn't acknowledge Edie's question. Instead, she beamed at the woman collecting the robes, graciously complimenting her sweater set and remarking on Phoebe's inspiring valedictory speech. In her own good time, she turned toward Edie. Claire was far too well mannered to launch into a heated argument in public, but her eyes were stone cold as she folded her arms and waited.

"I, um, I just want to apologize," Edie stammered, stumbling over words that strained to emerge at all.

"For what, exactly?" Claire's lips pursed as the tendons in her neck twitched.

Edie shrank in on herself as she quickly cataloged almost three months' worth of bad choices about Sebastian: the thinly veiled flirting she convinced herself was only friendly conversation, the attention seeking, the unwarranted antagonism toward Claire, the little white lies that snowballed out of her control, the blundered declaration of her feelings at the world's least appropriate time.

"For a lot of things," she said. "Mostly I should've trusted how much Sebastian loves you. I should've left him alone. I'm sorry."

Claire narrowed her eyes, not like she was about to lash out but like she was trying to read something buried in Edie's expression. As

Edie shifted before her, profoundly uncomfortable with the scrutiny but unsure what else to say, the other girls started to gather. Catie and Katie ran over to take a selfie with Claire. Taylor introduced her older sister. Phoebe expressed relief for getting through her valedictory speech without hiccupping. Edie turned to walk away, assuming her conversation with Claire was over, but Claire's voice held her in place.

"Apology accepted. Now stop stringing my brother along." Her tone was light, her comment practically tossed away, but her words hit like daggers.

Edie spun on her heel, gripping the table to keep upright.

"Wait. What?" she asked.

The other girls went quiet, instantly rapt. As if the conversation wasn't excruciating enough, Edie was now the center of attention, her least favorite place to be.

"You can drop the innocent act." Claire smirked, a triumphant little glint in her eye. "We all know you're just using him."

"I'm not." Edie's whole body flushed. Why were they talking about Henry? Things were good with Henry. Practically perfect. That wasn't the problem.

Claire cast a glance across the faces around her as if ensuring everyone was listening. Then she took a few measured steps toward Edie, her heels tapping out a rhythm against the wooden floorboards.

"He showers you with time and attention. He drives you all over town. He pays for everything. He spent a fortune on that necklace." She folded her arms and settled her chin into its loftiest position. "So tell me, what does *he* get from *you?*"

Edie gaped, speechless, so stunned by the question she could barely stand let alone articulate a response.

"Exactly." Claire punctuated the word with a flash of her dark eyes and a flip of her thick black hair. Then she gathered the other girls and they marched away en masse, leaving Edie alone by the table, her knees weak, her hands shaking, her sense of self-worth completely obliterated.

Two hours later, after sitting through a class luncheon she was too polite to skip but too freaked out to eat at, Edie stood before Henry in front of the Vernons' house, holding out the black velvet box. She'd been stewing all afternoon, letting Claire's accusations fester, unable to parse truth from fiction. The moment Henry pulled over to drop her off, she ran upstairs to get the necklace, returning to hand it off to Henry.

"What are you doing?" He frowned as if wounded.

"I agreed to wear it," she said, "not keep it."

He shook his head and stepped away.

"It's yours," he assured her.

"It was mine for a night but it comes with a price."

"No, it comes *for* a Price." His smile crept upward but she didn't return it.

"Please take it." Edie waved the box at him. "I can't keep it without feeling like I owe you something in return."

"I don't expect you to buy me anything."

"Yeah. I know." Edie felt her face tighten, tugging at her hairline as though her skin had just shrunk a size.

Henry's smile dropped away. He knew what she meant. She didn't need to spell it out. She'd replayed Claire's question a hundred times. What else could Claire have been implying? Edie had nothing else to give Henry, and she'd given it willingly, last night, on the shores of Fulton Pond. They'd celebrated her graduation early, extinguishing her final almost and sharing another of her big firsts. Claire's assumptions about their sex life might've been off-base, but her insinuation still stung.

As Edie's palms began to itch, desperate to release the box, Henry stepped forward. He cradled her face between his hands and met her eyes, pleading with a quiet intensity that only increased her discomfort.

"I never said, never thought, anything like that."

"Maybe not, but other people did."

His expression hardened.

"You mean Claire?"

Edie shrugged, too embarrassed to fully admit she'd let Claire's comments rattle her, but too rattled to dismiss them. While her nerves reknotted themselves, Henry leaned back against his shiny white car. He tucked his thumbs into his pockets, chuckling to himself.

"You can't take anything Claire says seriously right now. You know she's only lashing out because of the breakup."

The word *breakup* hit Edie like an electric shock, zapping a hundred questions across her mind all at once. When? How? For good or just temporarily? Why didn't she know? Was that what Sebastian had been trying to tell her? Why did she think he should tell her? Because of what she'd said on the dance floor? Did he care? Was that why?

As soon as Edie's questions took shape, they were swept away by a massive wave of guilt. She felt sick at the realization that she was still holding on to some ridiculous notion that she was meant to be with Sebastian. She hated herself for allowing the thought to exist, even for a second. Henry wasn't the one who couldn't be trusted. *She* was. That was why she'd held back for so long. She didn't trust herself. And Claire had seen right through her, calling Edie out in front of everyone in her own clever way.

Edie glanced at the black velvet box, the car tires, the budding dandelions that pushed their way through the sidewalk cracks, anything but Henry's eyes.

"You didn't know?" he asked quietly.

Edie shook her head as tears stung her eyes and Claire's lilting voice echoed through her brain, asking that horrible question: *What does he get from you?* It wasn't about sex. It was about love. Henry had given Edie his heart. She'd kept part of hers for someone else, the bit with the unbreakable string knotted around it.

Through great force of will, she overcame her cowardice and looked up. She was so filled with shame she wanted to yank out her stupid brain and her selfish heart, throw them into the street, and let Henry run them over. Repeatedly. He passed a hand over his face as he watched her. He didn't accuse. He didn't push. He simply waited.

A car drove by. A dog barked. A breeze rustled the pear trees.

"Does it change things?" he asked at last. "Between us?"

Edie considered as her mind flew through a maze of emotions she needed years to navigate, not seconds, but she didn't look away. She stayed focused on Henry's dark eyes, so clear, strong, and sure, so different from the pale blue eyes that'd looked at her a hundred times but never actually seen her. She wanted this. *This.* What Henry offered her: joy, laughter, affection, anticipation. She loved the way he held her, the way he wanted her, openly, with no reservations, the way she wanted him, too. She craved his touch, his voice, his songs, softly lulling her overactive mind. Sebastian's breakup wasn't a catalyst for rekindling her crush, for wasting more time wallowing in doubt and confusion. It was an opportunity to turn an impulse into a choice. And yet it wasn't really a choice if she could only make it while she buried her phone. And her feelings.

"I wish it didn't," she said. "But it does."

Henry closed his eyes and took a slow, deep breath. Edie tried to read his expression but she couldn't see straight. Tears were welling up in her eyes and finding their way to her cheeks. She felt dizzy and untethered. All her little imagined futures were vanishing before her, all the smiles and laughter she'd come to count on, all the love she'd spent years longing for. She wanted to grab it back and hold on with both hands, locking her fingers around it with an unyielding vise grip. Instead, she let it recede. She knew she couldn't stay with Henry, not if she couldn't return his commitment. Letting him go was right. It was honest. It was brave. None of that made it any easier.

As Edie's tears turned to sobs, she collapsed onto the front stoop and let the emotion rush out of her, too overwhelmed by her impending loss to do anything else. Henry sat down beside her. He took the necklace from her shaky grip and set it aside. Then he wrapped his arms around her and held her close, gently shushing her until she caught her breath again. She didn't deserve his kindness. She didn't deserve anything. How did he not hate her right now?

"I'm so sorry," she blubbered. "I thought I could do this. You. Me. All of it."

"I always knew it was a gamble."

Edie forced herself to meet his eyes as she wiped away an endless flow of snot and tears. Henry plucked damp strands of hair off her face, somehow looking amused despite also looking a little heartbroken.

"You have a tell," he said. "You're in love with someone else."

"How long have you known?" she asked, barely.

"Ten seconds. Two minutes. Since the day I met you."

"But these past few weeks, and last night . . . ?" Edie pictured the two of them lying naked and entwined on the moonlit shore, his body sliding against hers while the firebugs danced and the unmown grass tickled her earlobes. Their night together was meant to be the start of a new chapter. Not the end of their story.

Henry took her hand in his and set the little knot in his lap. They looked nice, those hands: his strong and tan, hers freckled and callused, gently interlaced, fully aware of how close they were to each other.

"Remember when I told you about my high school girlfriend?" he asked. "The one who cheated on me?"

Edie nodded as another stream of tears began to flow.

"The lesson I learned, it wasn't about breaking hearts. It was about realizing good things sometimes end. I should enjoy them while I can."

Edie tipped her forehead onto his shoulder and sniveled away.

"Don't be charming right now," she begged.

"Want me to call for pizza?"

"It would make this easier."

He kissed her forehead and drew her into his embrace.

"Sorry. I'm not letting you off the hook on this one. If you're going to dump me for another guy, I'm going to let it hurt a little."

"Fair enough."

Edie cried in Henry's arms for what felt like hours, astonished at his patience and understanding. She couldn't believe she was letting him go. He wasn't just the first guy she'd kissed or had sex with. He was her first boyfriend, the first to hold her hand, open his car door for her, sing her a song, encourage her dreams, buy her a present, nibble her ear, hold her while she slept, make her feel beautiful. He was the first guy to say he loved her. In her own way, she loved him back, but she loved someone else, too, someone whose pull she could feel, even now.

"Take the necklace," she said. "I'll wash your shirt and bring it by tomorrow."

"Keep them. I like knowing you have things that make you think of me. I'm vain that way."

"I always suspected that about you." She smiled through her tears. God, she was going to miss him. "I'm really sorry."

"I know."

She breathed him in, taking advantage of his closeness while she still could.

"Will you stay in Mansfield?" she asked.

"Doubt it. Not much to keep me here. Boston'll be better for . . . distractions."

"I'm still planning to be there in the fall. Can I see you again sometime? As friends?"

"Maybe. In time." He circled a hand over his face. "This whole calm, cool, and collected thing? I'm totally bluffing. I've got a few wounds to nurse. Side effect of all that swashbuckling."

Edie drew away to wipe her nose on the hem of her T-shirt.

"I never did prove you wrong about anything," she said. "Not once."

"Maybe one day I'll give you another shot."

"Said the bartender to the man who walked into the bar."

"Said the guy sitting right here beside you."

Chapter Thirty-Seven

♥ ──────────────────────────────────

EDIE SAT ON A BENCH AT THE BUS STATION WITH her overnight gear packed beside her. The late-morning sun beat down, almost punishing as it soaked into the concrete and left the bench's scrolling ironwork too hot to touch. A few other passengers waited in the nearby shade, but Edie preferred a perch where she had some space to herself. Her eyes were puffy. Her nose was red. Her heart was sore. But after a long night of sobbing and an even longer morning of evading her relatives' questions about her well-being, she was finally ready to check her messages. *All* of her messages.

Sebastian: You busy?

Sebastian: How about now?

Sebastian: I'll wait by the fence until 6:00

Sebastian: Wait and hope, just like you said

Sebastian: Tuesday?

Sebastian: What about Wednesday?

Sebastian: Please stop avoiding me

Sebastian: I made a mistake

Sebastian: I made a lot of mistakes

Sebastian: I'm sorry

Sebastian: I was scared

Sebastian: I was stupid

Sebastian: Give me a chance

Sebastian: One conversation

Sebastian: I can't do this by text

Sebastian: Have you blocked me?

Sebastian: Are you even getting these?

Sebastian: I'll wait in our tree until 4:00

Sebastian: I wish we still had a wardrobe

Sebastian: Maybe Monday?

Sebastian: Your light's on

Sebastian: I'm waiting for you to look my way

Sebastian: Just like in The Age of Innocence

Sebastian: If you look . . .

Sebastian: But if you don't look . . .

Sebastian: Okay. Bad plan. Goodnight

Sebastian: I miss you

Sebastian: Our fence misses you

Sebastian: Have I said I'm sorry?

Sebastian: I'm really sorry

The texts went on and on, well over a hundred of them. Edie felt awful. No matter how badly Sebastian bungled their conversation at prom, he'd never stopped being her friend. She shouldn't have shut him out. How could she expect Shonda to forgive her if she wasn't capable of offering forgiveness herself? Then again, she hadn't shut him out because she was angry. She'd shut him out because she was afraid. Even now, when he no longer posed a threat to her relationship with Henry, the thought of seeing him sent little tremors of anxiety rippling through her. She wanted to reconnect but she was hesitant to open old wounds, especially while she was nursing such new ones.

She closed her eyes, wrapped a hand around her locket, and pictured her mom sitting beside her. She could almost feel fingertips brushing her hair off her forehead as a pair of lips planted a tender kiss on the exposed skin. *Be brave and be kind,* her mom would whisper. *Everything else is just a job.*

Edie: Just read your texts. Wow

As she started typing a follow-up, her phone pinged with a response.

Sebastian: Where are you?

Edie: Bus station

Sebastian: You're leaving?

Edie: Just visiting Ithaca for a couple days

Sebastian: When's the bus?

Edie checked the time.

Edie: Departs in 20 minutes

Sebastian: Can I come see you off?

Edie considered. She wasn't ready. She might never be ready. Still, a friendly goodbye wasn't much to ask, not by someone she'd known for so long and shared so much with. It might even be the perfect way to begin rebuilding.

Edie: OK

Sebastian: Be there in ten

Edie spent the next ten minutes playing out imaginary conversations in her head. What would he say? What would she say? How would being around him feel now that neither of them was in a relationship? Would new possibilities open up or would they both dance around their feelings, like always? The knot in Edie's gut suggested the latter but she clung to the hope that it would quickly unravel itself. She'd been honest with Henry. She could be honest with Sebastian. After all, she had nothing to lose at this point. Only something to gain.

When the bus pulled in to the station, Sebastian still hadn't arrived. The other passengers boarded while Edie watched the streets, craning her neck, searching for signs of Sebastian's little blue car, finding none. Eventually the driver called over to let her know he was about to depart. Edie slung her messenger bag over her shoulder and scanned the empty streets, still hopeful. She pulled out her ticket, gripping it so tightly that it buckled. The driver turned and boarded the bus. He settled himself behind the wheel. Pistons hissed as the tires filled. Edie took one last glance down the road. Then she jogged toward the bus, shouting for the driver to wait.

As Edie stepped onto the bus and handed off her ticket, car tires screeched behind her. She spun around to see Sebastian parking his car against the curb and flinging open the door. She shot a panicked look at the driver.

"Two minutes," he said. "Then I'm pulling out."

She stepped off as Sebastian ran over to meet her.

"Road construction." He pointed all directions, breathless, frantic. "Stop lights. Train. Squirrel. Fuck!"

Edie sputtered out a laugh. She'd never heard Sebastian swear before.

"I have to go," she said. "We can talk when I get back."

"Let me drive you," he offered, still winded. "Then we don't have to rush."

Edie peered over at his car. It struck her as uncomfortably compact. She was only prepared for a friendly goodbye, not several hours packed into tight quarters.

"Not a good plan," she said. "Really, we can just—"

"How much?" Sebastian asked the driver, wrenching his wallet from his pocket and thrusting out a few twenties. "Sixty bucks enough?"

"Get on." The driver took the cash and tipped his chin toward the back of the bus. "Buy your return fare at the station. It's cheaper than bribery."

Before Edie could process what was happening, let alone intervene, Sebastian leapt on board. He stumbled down the aisle and collapsed into a seat halfway toward the back. She exchanged a look with the driver. He shrugged and suggested she take a seat. Uncertain what else to do with the bus pulling out of the station and the rest of the passengers staring at her, Edie headed down the aisle.

She stowed her bag and sat down next to Sebastian. While Mansfield sped past outside, she watched him catch his breath, still startled he was sitting there beside her. Despite his manic arrival, he seemed tired and worn out, thinner than when she'd last seen him. His clothes were badly wrinkled. His usually tidy wedge cut had grown shaggy. His eyes were underscored with subtle shadows. Edie's guilt about ignoring his texts welled up again, reminding her how she'd been so wrapped up in her own wants and needs she'd neglected those of someone she truly cared about.

"So, um, hi," he stammered out at last.

"Hi." She fluttered a small wave, much like she had when she'd first seen him on his driveway back in April, doing yardwork while she tried not to blush.

He nodded at her T-shirt. It said MARY SHELLEY'S BARBECUE and depicted a cartoon of the author holding a hot dog and a mug of beer.

"That's funny," he said. "I can guess why she liked a good frank and stein."

"Most people don't get it." Edie eyed his plain gray oxford. "Yours is funny, too."

He laughed softly, just enough to coax his dimples out of hiding.

"How are you?" she asked.

Sebastian shrugged.

"Rough month. I registered for fall writing classes. My stepdad's furious. He's still pushing me about the law degree, trying to make sure my future looks just like his." He shook his head, sighing as if annoyed. "And you must've heard about . . . ?"

"You and Claire?"

He nodded while tracing the geometric print on the seat cushion.

"I'm sorry," Edie said. "I know you tried really hard to make it work."

"Too hard, apparently."

"Is that possible?" She considered the question. "I mean, if we knew precisely how hard trying something would be, we wouldn't really be trying. We'd just be doing, which might be easier, but a lot less interesting."

Sebastian's dimples reappeared.

"I've lost score," he said.

"Doesn't matter. It's not a quote."

"It is now."

They swapped a sweet but complicated smile, one that awakened a tiny butterfly in Edie's belly. It tickled the base of her ribs and began working its way up toward the places where she kept the good stuff. As she let it flutter freely, doubtful she could ground it if she tried, Sebastian gripped the armrests and inched his shoulders toward his ears, all unhinged, awkward, and adorable.

"Edie," he said, her name gentle on his lips, his eyes sad and serious, "I'm so sorry. I didn't know."

"Of course you didn't. How could you? I didn't say it."

"Yes, you did. I just didn't hear it." He smoothed out his hair, not like he knew it was messy, but like he still couldn't figure out what to do with his hands. "You've always been the smart one."

"Guess that makes you the nice one."

They both laughed, sort of.

"I'm not *that* nice. I just hijacked your trip," Sebastian joked. "But I needed to apologize. In person. About being an idiot. I also . . . um, can I say something else?"

Edie nodded, bracing herself. Sebastian settled his restless hands on his thighs, ticking and twitching until his eyes found their way to hers and stayed there.

"What you said to me at prom, well, I feel the same. I always have. I wanted to tell you a hundred times but I kept chickening out. I'm not proud of myself for that. I didn't think I had a chance. You were always running away from me." He paused as Edie grimaced, conceding the point. "And of course there was Claire. I care about her. She deserves a guy who treats her well. I wanted to be that guy. Reliable. Committed. I thought that if I didn't say or do anything, then I wasn't really cheating. But maybe I was, and maybe she knew it all along." He rubbed the back of his neck, further rumpling his already twisted collar. "I kept telling myself you were just a friend, but when I saw Henry kiss you at prom, all I could think was, *That should've been me.*" He shifted toward the window. The sunlight caught his eyes, making them almost translucent, as though it were conspiring to lay bare every last secret. "I know I've made a total mess of things so I don't expect you to say anything back. I just needed you to know."

Edie nodded as she let his confession settle, shoving aside a few of her less interesting quotes to make room in her collection. What good was a Velcro memory if it couldn't hold on to a moment like this? Shakespeare, Brontë, Dumas, Eliot. Their words were so clever and insightful but none of them mattered as much as the ones being said between two ordinary people, sitting on a bus, face-to-face, perfectly imperfect.

Edie loved that Sebastian loved her. She'd hoped for so long, but she was too raw from her breakup to leap into something new. Losing Henry hurt far more than she'd ever expected, leaving her uncertain what she felt for anyone. She had nothing to offer Sebastian right now. She needed some time on her own. Fortunately she'd have a few days to sort through everything, or at least to embrace the unsortable.

She tipped her head onto Sebastian's shoulder.

"We can both take credit for the mess," she said. "Guess that's why I love music so much. It's the only place the mess fits."

"Oh, I don't know." He linked his hand through hers and settled both on the armrest between them. "I think the mess fits pretty well right here too."

"Yeah." She felt a smile build. "I guess it does."

With a full but conflicted heart, Edie held Sebastian's hand all the way to Providence. Somewhere en route she told him about Henry, how she'd come to care about him, deeply, but how she'd hurt him, too. Sebastian listened, in turns sympathetic, apologetic, and curious to know what might happen next. He didn't push, though. He'd always been good that way, giving her space to feel what she had to feel. As he'd once said to her, that was all she could do, really. There was no way around it.

When the two of them settled into their most complicated silence yet, Edie realized she wasn't living in the Age of Yes anymore.

She wasn't living in the age of anything. She was just living day by day, as full of uncertainties as ever. The only thing she knew for sure was that her old motto — *Think it. Don't say it* — was a load of crap. It worked okay when dealing with annoying customers and persnickety aunts, but not when applied to close personal relationships. What would've happened if Edie'd told Sebastian how she felt weeks ago? What if he'd told her? It all seemed like such a waste of time. And yet, not.

Falling in love was easy. Learning how to love required some bumps and bruises along the way. If love just happened, like Wednesday, then it wasn't really love. It was a bit of giddiness she felt while watching cat videos and hiding behind other people's words. It was the flutter of fantasy, the dizzy anticipation of steamy almosts and endless what-ifs. Real love took effort. It embraced the what-thens. It overcame a few not-so-great choices. It let a girl be awkward, bashful, sulky, and temperamental. It allowed for both laughter and tears. It even let a girl change her mind. And then change it back again.

At the station in Providence, Sebastian bought a return ticket to Mansfield. Then he walked Edie to the dock for the bus to New York. She checked that she had everything she needed: phone, bag, brain, heart. She looked up at Sebastian, wondering if she should hug him, attempt to articulate something meaningful, or keep it simple and say goodbye. He was watching her in that way he had, like he was hanging on what she'd do or say next, like her words and actions were important, like *she* was important. It felt nice. It was also a big responsibility. Hearts were fragile things, prone to fractures, though they were surprisingly strong, too.

"Thank you," she said. "For telling me."

"Sorry it took me so long."

"Better at last than not at all."

He nodded as his features flickered and a dozen emotions passed through his eyes, reminding her of their ridiculous poker game and how terribly he'd played, how everything he thought or felt invariably showed up on his face. She'd always loved that about him, whether he was grinning giddily about an ice cream cone or weeping softly in a wardrobe. He felt things deeply and he shared those feelings with her, leaving himself raw and vulnerable, trusting in her care. All those little connections added up over time, weaving themselves into a string, one that would remain around her heart forever, no matter how hard she tried to break it, unknot it, or pretend it wasn't there.

"Are you going to be okay?" he asked.

"I think so. Eventually. You?"

His shoulders rose as his chin shifted, halfway between a nod and a head shake.

"Yeah," he said. "Once I figure out what I'm aiming for. I got so used to being what other people wanted me to be. You're the only one who ever liked me as I am."

Edie set a hand to her chest where his words hit home, nestled beneath a locket where she could shut them away until she needed them. *You're the only one.*

The driver announced last call for boarding. Sebastian shifted as though he was about to step forward but he changed his mind. He rooted himself in place, or at least he tried to, unable as always to stand still. Edie gripped her messenger bag with both hands. One hand alone couldn't manage the weight, not when two hands were desperate to straighten a collar, brush a cheek, or lace themselves slowly into another hand and stay there forever. Maybe one day she could do just that. One day. Not this day.

"See you soon?" she asked.

"I like the sound of that."

They swapped a semi-smile, subtle but sincere.

"You'll be all right," Edie said. "Just keep writing. If that fails to bring you joy, look for green Pixy Stix in the trees."

She placed a tiny kiss on his cheek. Then she boarded the bus and left.

Chapter Thirty-Eight

♥

THE BURGER BARN WAS EXACTLY LIKE EDIE REMEM-
bered it, with its bright red roof, white trim, and plastic hay bales, as
though a herd of cows were just hanging out inside, waiting to be
turned into lunch. Edie found the manager on duty, who informed
her that Shonda was cleaning the restrooms. She pushed open the
door to see her friend bent over the counter, scrubbing away the
congealed runoff from the soap dispenser. Her two-tone braids were
twisted in a loop at the nape of her neck. Her blue polyester pants
were rolled up at the hems to accommodate her short stature.

"Restroom's closed for cleaning," she said without looking up.

"Then let me help," Edie offered.

Shonda spun around, flashing Edie the look she'd been dread-
ing: pure hatred.

"What are you doing here?" she demanded.

"I came to apologize. And to ask if there was anything I could
do to—"

"To clean up the shit you left behind? Sure. Grab a plunger.
Middle stall." Shonda returned her attention to the counter, jabbing
away like she was trying to sand off the laminate coating.

Edie set down her bag and headed into the stall, plunger in hand, the task all too familiar.

"So, how are you?" She grimaced as she worked the plunger like a butter churner.

"Broke, bored, and picking hair out of a drain in Hell-burbia. Meanwhile, my ex–best friend is in the land of croquet and caviar trying to figure out which hot guy she wants to give her V-card to." She cut Edie a sharp glance. "How do you think I am?"

Edie braced herself against the stall divider and shoved downward with all her strength.

"I'm sorry," she said again. The words felt painfully insufficient, eroded by overuse, but she didn't know what else to say. "I was just trying to make you laugh. It's what I do. It's what *we* do. I don't know how to be me without you."

"You should've thought of that before you kissed my boyfriend."

"You're right. I should have." Edie yanked upward until the pressure gave way and the clog released with a nauseating slurping noise. "So you guys split?"

Shonda unzipped a large sac of bright pink soap powder.

"Turns out you weren't the only other girl he kissed that week." She began filling the dispenser. "I feel pretty stupid about all of it."

"I'm the stupid one. I hurt the person I cared about most, just so I could feel liked by a guy I didn't care about at all." Edie stashed the plunger under the counter. She gathered a few strewn paper towels and tossed them out. Then she waited while Shonda set down the soap and finally turned to face her. "Is there anything I can do, anything at all, to earn your trust again? I just . . . I can't picture my life without you in it."

"So you have someone to crow to when you finally go all the way?"

"No." Heat crept up Edie's neck and burned the tips of her ears. "I wouldn't, I mean I already . . ." She trailed off as she caught a glimpse of her beet-red face in the mirror, every last freckle blazing.

Shonda's eyes widened behind her funky new glasses.

"You dirty slut." She shook her head as if appalled.

"Not *that* dirty," Edie argued.

"Dirty. Adjective. One, defiled. Two, needs cleaning." Without warning, Shonda reached into the bag of soap powder and flung a handful at Edie.

Edie stood there, stunned, as the pink powder trickled off her forehead and down her chest. When she caught the laughter in Shonda's eyes and realized she was only teasing, Edie grabbed the sponge and pitched it at Shonda's head. Shonda dodged as the sponge spun past her, spraying her face with soapy water and sticking to the wall for a second before splatting to the floor.

"You did *not* just—" Shonda started.

"Oh, yes, I did," Edie boasted, already reaching toward the sink.

Within seconds, a full-scale war erupted. Soap powder flew everywhere. The garbage bin toppled onto its side, spilling wadded paper towels across the floor. Shonda poured an entire bottle of glass cleaner over Edie's head. Edie drenched Shonda with a well-directed spray from the faucet. As the girls faced off, one with a plunger, the other with the toilet brush, both of them soaked, someone started pushing open the door. Shonda backed against it and held it shut.

"Closed for cleaning!" the girls shouted in unison. They waited for a few seconds, frozen in place, until footsteps retreated. Then they burst into hysterics.

When they finally stopped laughing, Edie threw her arms around Shonda's soaked and sudsy shoulders. She hugged her so hard, bubbles formed between their chests.

"Shonda West, you're the smartest, bravest, funniest, most awesome person I know," she said. "I love you."

"You're a disaster." Shonda plucked bits of soggy paper towel from Edie's hair. "And you owe me some serious payback, but I love you, too."

There it was, like a pair of ruby-red slippers. What Edie'd been looking for all along: the kind of love that was big enough to leave space not just for fun, but for failure and forgiveness, too.

Edie spent the night at Shonda's house. They rolled out sleeping bags in the den but they didn't sleep. They stayed up all night talking. After a fair share of teasing about Edie's romantic misadventures as narrated through almost three months of lexicography, Shonda related her most essential news. On the upside, she'd graduated with honors, third in her class. She'd ditched James and vowed to only date boys with bicycles or bus passes. She'd kept up her drum lessons and begun playing with a local band on weekends. On the downside, Shonda's mom had lost her job, forcing her to dig into Shonda's college fund to support the family.

"Guess that means you can't come to Boston with me in the fall," Edie said, trying not to sound totally crushed.

"Not unless you have a load of cash to spare, but I can visit. I'll also take a closer look at that scholarship list. Maybe I can join you next year."

"Fingers crossed?" Edie held up a pinky.

Shonda linked her finger with Edie's.

"Everything crossed." She pushed her glasses up the bridge of her nose and settled back against the sofa. "Now, about this boy next door . . ."

Edie's cousins picked her up from the station on Monday. Julia was in the shotgun seat, scrolling through her phone. Maria was fixing her lipstick in the rearview mirror. Edie clambered into the back, much like the last time she'd been picked up after a bus ride, though this time she hadn't arrived with a stringless guitar and a friendless heart.

"Thanks for coming to get me," Edie said.

"We were shopping anyway." Maria nodded at a cluster of bags on the back seat. "Though I don't understand why Henry couldn't get you. I thought you guys would be all over each other after three whole days apart. For two people who can't keep their hands to themselves, that's, like, practically puritanical."

Edie avoided Maria's eyes while she fastened her seatbelt. She didn't want to get into the whole Henry mess with her cousins, but as she looked up and realized they were both waiting for a response, she decided there was no point delaying the inevitable.

"We broke up." Her voice caught on the words. They were too new, too unreal.

Julia gasped, all shock and awe. Maria went still.

"You saw the texts?" She eyed Edie sideways.

Julia spun on her, prodding her arm with a pointed finger.

"I knew it!" she crowed. "You were totally sexting him! Even after you swore you were 'so committed' to Rupert!"

For once, Maria didn't snap back. Instead she started chewing a fingernail. Edie stared, rapt. Maria never chewed on her nails. They were sacred territory.

"We didn't *do* anything," Maria barked. "Henry didn't even text back. I mean, he did, but not, like, in a sexy way." Her eyes darted around the car as her lips pursed and she got all jittery. Her anxious energy was so out of character, Edie and Julia could only watch and wait as though something was about to blow. "Okay, fine. You need me to say it? I'll say it. He liked you, okay? Like"—she cringed and set a hand to her gut—"better than me."

Edie almost laughed as she exchanged a look with Julia, one in which they silently acknowledged that Maria's hard-wrought admission was the closest thing Edie'd get to an apology. Edie didn't push the matter. Maria had been punished enough already. She'd lost Rupert's steady adoration, her dream wedding, her beloved spaniels, and the illusion that a perfect life would simply fall into her lap while she was out pursuing passionate kisses. Edie didn't need to heap guilt on top of all that. After all, Henry was just a guy. Maria was family.

"I'll forgive you," Edie said. "On one condition."

Maria folded her arms and scowled, awaiting her sentence with full indignation.

"I need to raise some money," Edie told her. "You are going to help."

The following morning, Edie asked Sebastian to meet her by the fence. He was peeling away paint when she spotted him. His hair was damp from showering. He was wearing rumpled linen shorts and an NYU T-shirt. She wore a pale blue cotton sundress Maria had offloaded to her a couple weeks ago. It wasn't her usual style, but she liked the way it made her think of laundry lines, summer breezes, and tidal pool eyes. Her style was a work in progress anyway, just like the rest of her.

"Hi," he said, shifting and shuffling.

"Hi," she said, surprisingly steady.

They exchanged a nervous smile. Before an uncomfortable silence could set in, Edie took a deep breath and began.

"I thought about what you said on the bus. And about what I said on the dance floor." She paused, steeling herself. "I still feel that way."

Sebastian stepped forward, his lips parting, but she halted him with an outstretched hand. She'd rehearsed her speech all night. She was determined to get through it.

"I'm also pretty confused right now," she continued. "A lot's happened really fast. I've hurt people I care about. I've made a lot of bad assumptions. I've focused on the wrong things. I need some time to let it all settle. I think you do too."

Sebastian nodded. He slipped his hands into his pockets, inching his bony shoulders up as his toe nudged the edge of his driveway and his eyes trailed downward.

Edie exhaled slowly, gathering resolve.

"Here's what I propose. We give ourselves a month to see who we are with each other for real. No more lies. No more hiding, withholding, or running away. Then, if we still like each other, we try again. Blank slate. Blank page. Fresh start."

He studied her, his face twitching away with the unmasked awkwardness Edie had always loved about him, namely because it was so much like her own.

"Thirty days of truth, huh?" he asked.

"Something like that."

"It's not going to be easy."

"I know."

He stepped up to the fence, squared his shoulders, and planted his feet.

"I have absolutely no interest whatsoever in becoming a lawyer," he announced.

Edie scooted forward on the gravel path, mirroring his stance.

"I cry over pet rescue videos. A lot."

"I hate my bedroom. It feels like a rented office space."

"Eating Norah's kale salad is like chewing on used Band-Aids."

"My forehead's too big."

"My chin's too small."

"I really want to kiss you right now."

Edie skipped a breath, caught completely off-guard. She hadn't realized how close Sebastian was, just inches away, on the other side of a picket fence, a painted-over memory, and slightly fewer unspoken feelings than once stood between them.

"Full honesty," he reminded her, a glimmer in his eye, a dimple in his cheek.

"One month?"

"Deal."

He held out his hand to shake. Edie took it. And there began the Age of Truth.

Chapter Thirty-Nine

Month

noun

1. A clergyman with a lisp.
2. A sound made when attempting to speak through a mouthful of peanut butter.
3. A span of thirty-one days you pack with as much activity as possible so you stop obsessing about the fact that you could've kissed him already!!!!!!

Throughout the month of July, Shonda renewed her correspondence with Edie, gradually building up the lexicon with entries of her own. She made a few digs at Edie's supposed taste for unavailable guys, but she softened as the weeks passed, sharing stories about band practice, a cute guy she met at the movie theater, and the rich bitches who were still sticking gum under tables at the Burger Barn.

Henry moved back to Boston. Despite Edie's best efforts to simply let him go, she found herself peeking at his social media pages. Within a matter of days, he was posting pics out partying with a group of friends and a string of beautiful girls. He looked like he was having the time of his life, though Edie knew from experience that looking happy and feeling happy were two different things. Henry lived in the moment. His wounds healed quickly but he carried as many scars as the next person, as evidenced by the fact that he seemed to have developed a new taste for vodka-cranberry drinks.

Julia left Mansfield to take an intensive language course in Paris. She departed in a plum-colored blouse, her first attempt to wear purple despite not being a winter. She'd required considerable persuading to dress outside her season, but Edie hoped the blouse would be a step toward a more confident Julia, one who read beauty blogs for entertainment, not as if they were textbooks for a test she thought she was failing.

The day after Julia left, Edie sat Bert and Norah down to ask for their help covering her academic expenses. Norah was hesitant. She didn't want to just "throw away money," but her interest was piqued when Edie revealed that she got into Yale. Bert took the opportunity to praise Norah's careful guidance and its instrumental impact on their once-unfortunate niece. The neighbors would be sure to remark on it in months to come. Edie humbly confessed that she'd declined her admission. Before she could explain why or what she actually planned for the fall, Norah and Bert began brainstorming ways of helping Edie reverse her decision, rattling off names of people who knew people. Uncertain her relatives understood the extent of the loans she'd require for Yale, or that they'd be equally as enthusiastic about UMB, Edie agreed to ask Sebastian's stepdad for help with a chicken sacrifice (a.k.a. a conversation with his golf buddies). After a lengthy negotiation, Bert and Norah agreed to contribute ten thousand a year to Edie's education, even if she couldn't reverse her Yale decision.

As penance for attempting to seduce Edie's boyfriend, Maria rallied to help fundraise the rest of Edie's targeted amount. Together the girls sorted through the barely worn designer clothes, shoes, and accessories Maria had no intention of wearing again. Maria modeled each item. Edie listed them on eBay. While Maria initially approached the task begrudgingly, she eventually got so into the whole listing process she started researching a degree in fashion merchandising, a career she hoped would eventually help her buy her own summer house.

When they'd finally listed the last item for sale, Edie opened the drawer of the dressing table and took out her prom necklace. Maria shoved her laptop aside and leapt up from the bed.

"You can't," she commanded.

"It could bring in a lot of money." Edie ran a hand over the stones, making the facets twinkle in the lamplight.

Without warning Maria snatched up the box and slammed it shut.

"Some things are more important than money," she said.

Edie gaped, barely holding back a laugh. *This* from the girl who needed separate houses for each season. Maria was right, though. The necklace was a token from a beautiful night with a beautiful boy, full of fairytale fantasy and amazing kisses. That was a good memory. That was a hold-on-to-it-forever memory.

She slipped the necklace into the drawer, nestling it next to her songbook, her dad's napkin note, her Yale acceptance letter, and her carefully folded blue silk sash.

While everything else was going on, Edie and Sebastian rebuilt their friendship. They shared ice cream, went swimming, practiced guitar, exchanged books, and tried with no success whatsoever not to flirt. In mid-July, he drove her to the open mic night in Brockton, where she performed a short set that included a sweetly sincere love song called "Too Many Fences Between Us." She didn't hide who it was about.

With Edie's encouragement, Sebastian started submitting his work to literary magazines. Eventually one of his short stories found a home in a small online publication. His parents were so proud, they even backed off about the law degree, though they continued instructing him to "make a fall-back plan."

At the end of the month, Edie finally received notification about her scholarship application. As it turned out, Alexandre Dumas had it wrong. "Wait and Hope" wasn't the epitome of human wisdom. It was the dumbest philosophy ever.

She collapsed on her bed and took out her phone.

Bureaucracy
noun

1. A method of policy-making dictated by strict adherence to fixed rules.

2. A system of government in which people are ruled by their furniture.
3. When you submit thirty-seven essays for a scholarship competition and all you get in return is a stupid form letter.

Edie was disappointed but she wasn't totally surprised. She was a songwriter, not an essayist, and she couldn't expect everything she did in life to pan out perfectly. She'd tried. She'd failed. It wasn't the first time and it wouldn't be the last. While all the work she'd poured into the competition might've seemed like a waste of time, she knew now that failure was a midpoint, not an endpoint. She'd use it to propel her onward. With her prior savings, her continuing wages from the tutoring center and online guitar lessons, Bert and Norah's generous contribution, and the anticipated income from the eBay sales, Edie was confident she'd be exactly where she wanted in the fall.

As she glared at her form letter, willing it to disintegrate before her eyes, her phone pinged, filling the screen with a photo of a bright green tongue, followed by a text.

Sebastian: Frog kisser?

Edie laughed as she propped herself higher on the bed.

Edie: How did you find them?

Sebastian: How do you think?

Edie: Hunting for birds' nests?

Sebastian: Fulfilling a promise

Edie stared at her screen, confused, until her phone pinged again.

Sebastian: There's a thing in the thing

Edie thought back to the last promise she remembered Sebastian making: a story in exchange for a song. As the memory sharpened and as Edie realized there was only one way Sebastian could've found the Pixy Stix, she threw on her sneakers and ran into the garden. Within minutes she was straddling the branch with the Mylar ribbons, the rusty compass, and a dozen other mementos of her childhood. Nailed to the trunk was a large zip-top bag containing a thick stack of printed pages. Edie tore open the bag and pulled out a two-hundred-page manuscript. Too excited to waste a single second, she settled herself against the trunk and began to read.

Sebastian's story was about two kids trying to save their kidnapped parents from evil pixies who'd developed a machine for turning fathers into money and mothers into blueberry-banana pancakes. The book was funny. It was sad. It was beautiful. It laid bare the loneliness Sebastian had felt since his dad died, and his struggle to find happiness without blindly succumbing to the expectations of others. It also depicted a close friendship between a boy and girl who could read each other's minds whenever the world around them went silent. Every word was honest, thoughtful, and packed with meaning.

Four hours after finding the book, when the sun had all but set, Edie read the final page and slipped the manuscript into the bag. For several minutes, she let the words sink into her brain, where they joined her collection. Then she left her perch to go knock on the Summerses' door. She waited, anxious and impatient, pressing the manuscript against her pounding chest, squishing her locket between Sebastian's words and her heart.

Mr. Hayes answered and called for Sebastian. Then he turned toward Edie, his arms folded, his expression stern, and his posture ramrod straight, making him look like he was guarding the house from intruders.

"Your aunt said you wanted to talk about Yale. Med school or law school?"

"I'm planning to study music, actually."

"Hmm." His brow furrowed further, etching his scowl into his face.

Sebastian came to the door before they could discuss the matter further. Mr. Hayes excused himself while Sebastian stepped onto the front stoop. As he shut the door behind him, his eyes darted to the manuscript in Edie's arms.

"I read it," she said. "Every word."

He cringed as though preparing for the worst.

"It's amazing," she gushed. "Can I keep it? So I can brag about knowing you before you were famous?"

He laughed softly as his cheeks reddened.

"I don't know about 'famous,' but of course you can keep it. It's yours." He scratched at his neck, shifting backwards on the small brick doorstep that just managed to fit two people, a fairytale, and one final almost. "I wasn't sure about the pancake idea. My mom used to make them and I thought a few silly details might balance the anticapitalist themes, which are probably way too heavy for kids so I should just—"

"I love you." The words leapt from Edie's throat as if they couldn't possibly stay inside any longer. "I'm in love with you."

Sebastian froze, his mouth ajar, his hand still cupping the back of his neck.

"I know it's not the thirty-first yet," she continued. "And we made a deal, but I thought you should know, in case there was any question about the matter." She paused, unsure where to go from there. "So, there it is." She rose up on her toes as her voice grew unnaturally high-pitched. "'The whole delightful and astonishing truth.'"

When Sebastian didn't say anything, Edie started to panic. She shouldn't have told him. She should've waited. Waiting was her idea, after all. As she scrambled for something else to say, he stepped forward and slipped a hand behind her waist, drawing her against him. He took the manuscript from her hands and flung it into the yard.

"Thank god," he said. And then he kissed her.

Edie threw her arms around his neck and kissed him back. She kissed him for being nice and being smart, for words written, spoken, and sung, for complicated silences, painful earnestness, unsettled smiles, and hard choices, for not knowing who was supporting whom, for the heart hanging from her neck and the one bursting from her chest, and for all the contradictory feelings that didn't fit into tiny tokens. She kissed him for forgiveness. She kissed him for longing. She kissed him for love. It wasn't her first kiss but it was her best kiss, complicated and beautiful in ways she couldn't possibly define, though she knew better than to try.

"Jane Austen," she said between kisses. "'The whole delightful and astonishing truth.' I was quoting Jane Austen."

"Stop knowing stuff and kiss me again."

Epilogue

EDIE GRUNTED AS SHE FLUNG HER DUFFEL BAG onto the bare mattress. The dorm room was small, just big enough for a bunk bed, two desks, and two dressers. The cheap, laminated furniture was chipped, the cinderblock walls were dingy, the linoleum floor was scuffed, and the overhead fluorescent light fixture was missing its plastic cover. But it was home. Her home. Hers and—

"It smells like three-day-old pizza in here." Shonda wrinkled her nose as she rolled her suitcase through the door. "Did someone hide a salami in our ceiling?"

"We'll pick up some incense when we go buy sheets and things." Edie set her guitar in the corner as she peered out the window. In the courtyard below, dozens of other freshmen were unloading cars, hugging parents, and making new friends. "The RA also said the bookstore carries those plug-in air fresheners."

Shonda joined Edie by the window, slipping an arm around her waist.

"I'll pay you back, you know."

"I know."

"You're really sure about all this?"

"Absolutely."

The eBay sales had brought in more than Edie could've hoped for, and although Mr. Hayes had assured her Yale would still be open to her admission, she had other plans. With some help from the UMB financial aid office, Shonda and Edie carefully worked out a way to afford their first year with a few small loans and their combined contributions. At first Shonda had refused to accept the money, but Edie argued against every denial, wearing her friend down with sheer persistence until she agreed to come. Despite the dreams Edie'd once harbored about Yale, she no longer cared that much where she spent her time. She did care who she spent it with.

As she set her dog-eared copy of *Auguste Rodin: Sculptures and Drawings* on one of the desks, her phone pinged.

Sebastian: I need to move the car

Edie: be right down

"Want to grab lunch before unpacking?" she asked.

Shonda waved her toward the door.

"You guys should go enjoy your last hour alone."

"It's not our last hour," Edie said. "We'll see each other in a couple weeks."

Shonda eyed the bunk beds as a wry smile rounded her cheeks.

"Are we going to have to work out some ridiculous scarf-on-the-doorknob code for when I'm allowed to enter on weekends?"

"No way. You're allowed in anytime you like."

Edie wasn't about to shut her friend out. She was a college student now. She didn't have time for boys. She was focusing on her education.

Mostly.

Acknowledgments

A few essential thank-yous:

To Jennifer Gadda, without whom this book never would've been written. For all the hours spent discussing Jane Austen, love, life, and art. For being one of those rare souls you know will always be there for you, no matter what.

To the friends and family who allow me to go through life with the certainty of a safety net. It's a gift and a privilege. I love you.

To my agent, Laura Bradford, for believing in my work, getting it into the right hands, and answering a zillion questions.

To my editor, Emilia Rhodes, and the entire team at HMH for seeing the story within the words, for providing patient insight, and for taking an idea and making it into a book.

To Maggie de Vries, Annabel Lyon, and Maureen Bayless for talking me off ledges, helping me bridge plot holes, and guiding me through the roughest patches of self-doubt.

To my beta readers and critique partners, who provided the perfect balance of critical input, warm-hearted support, and good, old-fashioned tough love: Arlene Avila, Meagan Black, Michael Goertzen, Dechen Khangkar, Mica Lemiski, Lauren Maguire, Anita Miettunen, Gillian Murschell, Emily Pohl-Weary, Kailash Srinivasan, Shannon Walsh, and Yilin Wang. It takes a village. A really, *really* awesome village.

To all the girls who don't walk through life wielding swords with the strength of a natural-born warrior. The girls who struggle sometimes. The girls who don't feel good enough. Be you, the one only you can be, made of all your triumphs, mistakes, and heartbreaks. You are your sword. Wield it well.